The Blood-Cursed Dragon

DC Sumner

To the love of my life, Sarah, the one who drives me onward.

Author's Note

Many readers love stories where the villain falls victim to the heroism of the protagonist, where lovers finally end up together. Stories where good prevails over evil. Stories where all is well and happiness abounds.

I must warn you then, for this is not one of those stories.

The Great Serpent

A TIME BEFORE KINGS *and queens. Dark days filled with savagery and bloodshed.*

"No... no," Pon grunted as his body writhed, collapsed, expanded. "Wha—" he began, but his human voice fled him. His friend smiled at him as Pon's flesh became scale and his legs melded together, forming a long tail.

He said something strange, but I didn't understand it, he thought. *This sorcerer has... done something to me.*

Agnus Yoshikai spoke a foreign utterance, and then Pon's body shifted. Now, he stood—or rather sat—coiled in the cramped confines of the Yoshikai temple. Before Pon shifted from a human, he'd been perfectly comfortable in the chamber.

Pon glared down at the man, firelight casting a glow onto his shimmering green robes. Agnus' hood was pulled up and there were chains wrapped around each wrist, glowing a soft orange. Pon could just barely see through them. There was a powerful force tethering the two together as he tried lunging for the hooded figure, but his progress was halted before he'd moved so much as an inch.

"Careful now, Pon," the man drawled. "I wouldn't want to damage this horrifying body I worked so hard to create."

A low hiss emitted from Pon. He'd tried to curse the man, but again, human words would no longer come out.

"Come," the man ordered as he walked toward the small opening to the chamber. The chains flashed once.

Pon felt his body sliding over rock though he hadn't decided to move. It became clear to him then, that his actions—his choices—were no longer his own.

How long? HE WONDERED. *How long have I been forced to kill as this cursed snake?*

Pon's tail flicked violently, sending a troupe of soldiers flying, smashing into a grouping of boulders. Their bodies crushed and split upon impact, blood and gore running down the boulder's faces. Horse riders dashed at him from the side, but Pon struck at them with powerful jaws. His movements were quick, decimating the riders with fangs sharper than the blades they carried.

They call me Bhishma, he thought idly. The taste of innocent blood was always the same: iron and terror. His wife's face flashed through his mind. *I'll never hear her voice, feel her touch, again.*

Pon often thought about her since his transformation. He often wished—prayed—that someone or something would come along and end his reign. For he knew he was nearly unstoppable in his current form. Though, if volition were given back to him, he'd lie down and allow someone to slay him.

If only someone could kill Agnus for me. Pon stole a glance at the sorcerer who always lingered in the nearby shadows when commanding Pon to commit atrocities.

There was a great commotion atop a hill in front of Pon. Soldiers parted for a newcomer. As a man took shape, Pon felt a shift in the atmosphere. *Is this the one I've heard speak of?* he wondered. *The young man who is meant to lead nations?*

A man with golden hair stood atop the hill. A gleaming sword dangled from his hand. Soldiers all around cheered as he walked down the hill and, behind him, came a horde of warriors larger than any Pon had yet faced. If a snake could smile, Pon was doing so.

Finally, he thought. *Perhaps, this is where my story ends.*

Part 1

Of Kings and Commoners

Chapter 1

ARA'S EXHAUSTED GRUNTS SOUNDED inhuman as she hacked away at the fleshy, segmented, creature before her. It was the size of a wild dog, only longer, fat as a pig with a body like that of a worm. Narrow eyes glared at Ara as if she was cruel for defending her home.

"Don't look at me like that," she chastised between gulps of air, pointing her hatchet at the creature while circling. "You try taking what's mine, you filthy *thing*. You get what you deserve."

A screech escaped the beast and its large, black, mandibles snapped. Her hatchet fell again. "2,000 years since Bhishma's execution and you worms *still* plague us!"

Sweat dripped down the side of her face despite the sun not yet bearing down on her; the wood of the hatchet was beginning to blister her palms. The hide of the nyssavir was just too thick for her to break through.

"Back up, Ara," her father shouted, running from the confines of their home. The sun creeped up and the sky was aglow with morning light. It was dim, but just bright enough to see the little monster. Gaius—Ara's father—stumbled sleepily up to the tangling duo and snatched the hatchet from Ara's hands. Just as she handed the weapon off, the nyssavir lunged for Ara's leg. Gaius, however, shoved her aside, causing the creature's mandibles to sink into his calf.

Gaius yelped, swinging the hatchet down onto the nyssavir's head. Again, he let the hatchet drop. A third time and the blade finally sank into the animal's brain. Gaius dropped the hatchet, falling back to his rear, breathing heavily. He looked down at his calf and chuckled.

"What's funny, Pa?" Ara asked, her brows pulled together tightly.

The nyssavir ate nearly half the crop, she thought sourly.

He chuckled again and said, "Of all the creatures in this world to destroy our crops it just *had* to be Bhisma's progeny. It's just ironic is all."

Ara shook her head, her hands going to her hips. "Pa, we won't be able to recover what we've lost before winter comes."

Surviving is hard enough as it is...

"Bah," he said with a wave of his hand. "We'll be just fine, dear. Now, help your old man up." Ara reached down, pulled him to his feet, then helped him back inside. The time to leave for work would come quickly.

Inside their home Ara cleaned and bandaged Gaius' wound. "Keep a close eye on that so infection doesn't set in."

The old man sighed. "What would I do without you, Ara? Always taking care of me."

She merely rolled her eyes, but the comment made her smile nonetheless.

You'd be doomed, she thought. That made her giggle and the look Gaius gave her—probably trying to figure out what was humorous—shifted the giggle into a fit of laughter. She sighed, looking into his glassy eyes.

How can one look so sad, she wondered, *yet so happy?*

Despite all the heartache Ara endured, she remained in the world, a beacon of light amongst the shadow. She tried, anyway. Ara couldn't remember her mother that well, and her father rarely spoke of her. She did, however, remember many of the boys she'd known and befriended who'd been taken by the age of sixteen, hauled away to die in the war.

Where are you, Gorenos? she prayed, thinking about the Lowborn like her she'd watched be stripped from all they knew over the years.

She'd called every god's name she could think of a thousand times over, but none would answer her prayers. She didn't need riches, didn't need to be named queen. Ara longed for a happy life; one without worrying about when her father would be taken from her, or which friend would be the next to leave.

And they always leave.

I want to be more, Ara though idly. *Why can't I change my status? Why am I doomed to being Lowborn, when I'm worth ten of the nobles? They don't deserve to live so lavishly; they do naught to help the world.*

Gaius wobbled to his room as Ara lost herself in thought. The motion shook her from the trance. Standing, she blew out the candle on the table as sunlight pierced through the one window in their home.

Shaking her head, she thought, *Happiness is a choice.*

As Ara moved to her room, turning to squeeze past her clothes chest, and plopped onto her bed, she thought of her life. The aches, the pains.

For as long as she could remember, Ara had desired to rise above being a Lowborn; then again, there wasn't a Lowborn alive who wouldn't want the same.

When Ara was younger she'd asked her father, "Pa, why is our last name 'Lowborn'?"

To which he sighed and said, "Those born without noble blood are not dignified with a surname other than 'Lowborn', my dear."

Ara tried not to think about it, but there was a constant reminder that she would forever be inferior to the Highborn. Ara promised herself as a child that she'd one day be worth more.

Of course, she'd never tell her father of those thoughts. It would break him and, he too, had endured enough pain.

Just then, Gaius limped into her room—squeezing through the cramped space—and sat down next to her, patting her leg. He gazed into her eyes for a moment.

He said, "I couldn't be prouder of the woman you've grown into. Your mother would be proud too."

As always—when speaking of her—there was a sad twinkle about his eyes.

Ara was finally woman as far as society in Gosatha was concerned. She didn't feel like a woman, however, and was not yet prepared to do the things that come with womanhood. There was an immaturity about her that she would be expected to give up, but she didn't want to. It was the childlike innocence, the lighthearted air she carried, that made Ara who she was. It may be a facade, but no one else needed to know that.

Ara smiled back and said, "Have I ever told you, Pa, of the admiration I have for you? I know you loved Mother; that's always been clear to me. You never let her death stop you from taking care of me." She covered his hand with one of hers.

It looked as if he fought back tears when he said, "You'll learn someday, when you have children of your own, that no matter what you do, you always feel like you could have done more. I just hope..." his voice cracked and Ara squeezed his hand. "I hope your 17 years haven't been too dreadful." He released a tearless sob, smiling sadly.

"Of course not, Pa," she said, wrapping her arms around him, feeling the stubble on his face against her cheek. The oil lamp in her room flickered, reminding her that the sun was up. They pulled away from each other and she said, "I best get ready for work."

He moved to the doorway, saying, "My dear, today you will do nothing. You've earned your keep this day, I must say. I want you to take a day for yourself."

She hated it when he insisted on her lying about while he breaks his back to earn a little silver down at the butchery. "Pa, you've worked for the butcher all my life and then some to provide for us. The least I can do is help put food on the table."

"That is my duty as your father," he argued, smiling haughtily. "You take this day off, Ara. I insist."

"Pa, I am perfectly capable of putting in work, no matter the circumstances," she protested.

He nodded. "Yes, I know you are. You're more capable than most, in fact. However, it's my wish that you would take a break. You've always been a tenacious girl, especially when it comes to helping your old man. It's been nigh on a year since you've taken a day for yourself. And you defended the rest of our crop from that *worm*. So, go see your friends. Enjoy the weather. Please?"

"Fine," she gave in with a groan. "Just this once, though."

"Excellent." He clapped his hands together. "I'll be back in time for dinner. I love you, Ara."

"I love you, Pa." She watched him go with a faint annoyance.

I hope he makes it there with ease, Ara thought, concerned over his leg. They'd never been able to afford a horse or even a mule and, with their home being just a league away from Osta, her father's trek was bound to take longer than usual.

Now, what to do with myself?

Chapter 2

ARA CHANGED FROM HER sweaty sleeping gown into a pair of tan pants and a white shirt with strings threaded through the chest. She tightened the strings to ensure none of the scoundrels in Osta got a peek at what was underneath. Then, she brushed her thick, red hair out; it flowed halfway down her back like a sluicing river of fire. Ara cauhgt the sight of dried blood from the nyssavir under her nail beds. After scrubbing her hands in the water basin and washing her face, Ara examined herself in the mirror. Fair skin kissed by the gods—or so her Pa would say—shone back at her. Tiny brown dots riddled the bridged of her nose, across cheeks that sat under violet eyes.

The few times Ara strolled through the village at night, men would call out to her, speaking of her beauty. Many Lowborn women were considered to be, well, less than beautiful. Ara disagreed with that notion.

"Calder's house it is," Ara decided once she'd finished getting ready.

They'd been friends since early childhood. Of the Lowborn in Osta, he was as close to being a noble as one could be without actually having the title.

A memory flashed through Ara's mind. "My family are tax collectors for King Torril Jardanis," Calder told her with gusto, as if it was something to be proud of. She'd laughed back then, but didn't realize how tough a childhood he would have. Nearly everyone in Osta hated his family; however, she had a soft spot for Calder. He despised being part of the tax collectors and would flee the village if not for Ara holding him back. She'd promised him when they were young that they'd one day set off on a journey of their own together, but it had yet to happen.

There were other things for her to consider, such as who would take care of her Pa if he were to become ill?

It's not like the king cares for his sick and dying subjects, she thought. *And how will I ever escape being Lowborn?* Ara figured she'd marry into a noble family one day, but that could just be wishful thinking.

She remembered reading about King Torril and his royal family—the Jardanises who ruled Gosatha for as long as anyone knew. Ara recalled what her father had told her when she was small.

"It is said they are blessed by Gorenos, God of all creation. The legend says the Jardanis family was the first brought into existence, that they exceed the limitations of man." Ara liked the way her father always got this look of reverence about him when speaking of the royal family.

Ara never met any of the Jardanis family, but the fables of their exploits stretched across the world. The history books she'd perused said the same thing, that Illiar—God of the night and all things dark—created a great evil shortly after thee world was formed. He released his beast into their world where it brought destruction upon the other creatures. The tomes all said the creature was a serpent of some sort. That it was large enough to swallow a thousand men at once. Bhishma, they called him. His children—the nyssavir—multiplied in his absence, as Ara saw earlier that morning. It wasn't her first time seeing the nyssavir, but it was her first time fighting one.

"I met them once, you know," Gaius told Ara when she was younger. She remembered the way he marveled when speaking of royalty and how that annoyed her. "The Jardanis men must stay in power, Ara, for if the world finds itself without the Sword of Gorenos strapped to a Jardanis man's waist, Bhishma shall return."

Ara wasn't sure if she believed in the great serpent or the superstition of ensuring one family be in rule until the end of time to stop a monster from rising from the dead. It was more likely they created the tale to ensure no one challenged them. And she would certainly like to see a queen take the throne. Either way, it was a wonderfully terrifying story, and Ara enjoyed stories.

Making her way outside, Ara took a deep breath and began walking the path towards Osta. A crow called as it flew over her head.

Ara looked up, smiling at the large bird and thought, *Another crow accompanying me to town?*

THE VILLAGE BUILDINGS SOON came into view; the way many of them listed lazily to one side showed just how poor Osta was. Most of them were made of wood, but some—the structures housing Highborn mostly—were made of stone. When Ara made it into the heart of the village, she smiled and offered good mornings to those she passed along the way. The few Highborn Ara saw, she avoided.

They were not kind people; they didn't care about the well-being of the villagers. They only cared about what they could fit in their pockets and mouths. Orphans lay on the streets while the nobility parade by as if they were kings.

I hate that more than anything... the children who suffer, she thought. *I'd rescue them all if only I had the means. Just another reason to raise my status.*

Calder's home seemed like a mountain compared to hers, made of gray stone and oak, and was filled with windows. She rapped her knuckles on the wooden door.

It opened to reveal her best friend. "Morning, Cal," she offered, her thoughts melting away as their eyes met.

Dimples appeared in his cheeks as he smiled. He replied, "Fancy that; I was *just* about to come see you."

"Oh?" she asked. "Whatever for? Feeling lonely, are we?" She enjoyed teasing him from time to time.

"Of course not," he said. "Bored would be a better term. What say we take a trek through the Wraithwood like old times?"

She nodded. "I've nothing better to do today." The two would often run around the Wraithwood as youths, not believing the rumors of wolves running rampant. They'd never even spotted a pup, much less an adult wolf.

"It's just as dark and creepy as I remember," Ara told him as they entered the forest. It had been a couple of years since they'd trapsed through the dark woods.

Calder draped his arm over her shoulder. "Fear not, young lady. I'll protect you."

Ara returned his smile with a glare, shrugging his arm off her.

A short hike through the woods brought them to a creek that imparted such peace within Ara that she could stay there for hours. Drinking from the creek was a stag with antlers jutting in all directions. The animal burst away at the sound of their boots crunching leaves.

The two plopped their feet into the water and Ara closed her eyes, inclining her face to the sky where meager rays of sun broke through the foliage. She felt Calder's hand caress hers, and she looked over at him incredulously. She pulled her hand back and he chuckled, clutching his heart as if in pain.

"I'll have none of that, Cal," she admonished. "You've yet to ask my father for permission. You know how important that is to me."

When Ara was honest with herself, she'd admit she loved Calder; however, nothing could change her loathing of being Lowborn. Her eyes found her feet in guilt. *How long can I keep lying to him?*

Calder sighed. "Yes, but you know he doesn't care for me."

"That isn't true!" They both knew she lied though she wouldn't admit it.

"We're tax collectors, Ara. He'll never like me; not that I blame him. But your father will never give me his blessing."

"We won't know that until you try." Part of her wanted him to try so that Gaius would deny his blessing, and maybe Calder would stop pursuing her.

"Come on," she said, tugging her boots back on. "It's getting late. We'd better leave these woods before nightfall or we'll never make it out." The Wraithwood was known for getting people lost, especially after the sun has gone down. Ara always heard that nyssavir are more active at night and she was loathe to cross paths with one unarmed.

The cry of a crow echoed around, bouncing off the bark of trees. They went on their way and a twig snapping in the distance startled them. They looked at each other and laughed at one another's fatuity.

Another twig snapped, closer this time, and Ara found herself dashing away before she even knew what was happening. Leaves crunched and panting issued from behind as Calder lumbered after her.

He wouldn't be able to keep up, she knew. Strength wasn't a virtue she possessed, but Ara could outrun nearly anyone. Calder called after her, but her sense of foreboding overpowered all sense, not allowing Ara to slow down. She could almost see the break of the tree line up ahead. Then she tripped. Ara hit her head on something hard, the trees swirled, and her vision went black.

Chapter 3

THE SORCERESS HEARD THE words of her father as she pulled the strings of her inferior's fates from the shadows.

"You're the last of us, Lyreath," he'd told her. "It's up to you to bring Bhishma back. You must do this; promise me!"

"I promise, Papa," she replied. Even as she crouched amongst the thickets of the Wraithwood, she heard the words echo from the tiny voice of her young self.

She remembered watching her clan fade; her parents were no exception.

"Lyreath," she whispered, watching her bandits-for-hire pick the slumped girl up from the leaves. No one would ever know her by that name, and so she said it to remember who she was. "Lyreath Yoshikai... step one complete."

Look at me, she thought, raising her hands slowly. *Talking to myself and pretending I'm not crazy. As if the last hundred years haven't driven me mad.*

She whispered in the arcane tongue, "Abragis," and a wind called forth by the hands of the sorceress swept across the forest, sending a swirl of leaves into the vision of the trailing young man. Ara's friend wouldn't be needed for what comes next. "Watch him, Lyreath," she whispered.

Disappointment flashed across her face as he turned away, running in the opposite direction as he called out Ara's name. She whispered to herself once more, "I suppose I can wait to redden my hands."

ARA HEARD A CRACKLING fire, the shuffling of feet in leaves, before her eyes dared open. There was a faint conversation being had. When she opened her eyes, her heart dropped into her stomach. Three men sat around a flame a stone's throw away, joking and laughing with each other. They said something incomprehensible about a strange woman. Ara's hands were tied behind her as she leaned on a tree. A pounding throbbed through her head, reminding her of the fall she'd taken.

Ara glanced around as the chill of the night assaulted her skin, calling little goose pimples to rise along her arms. She could only assume she was still in the Wraithwood. *Where is Calder?* She didn't see him anywhere. He had been right behind her, hadn't he? Her legs trembled as she began to fear the worst had happened to him. Maybe these men killed him and took her.

"Oi, look. She's awake." One of the men observed her as she looked around the forest. He rose to his feet and the other two followed suit, stalking toward her as if they were predators, and she the weakest prey.

"What do you want with me?" she asked, attempting to keep the fear from seeping into her voice.

They continued stalking through the shadows; Ara could see their teeth through the dark as they grinned wickedly. The foremost man said, "We haven't decided what we'll do with you, yet."

"You could just let me go," she offered with a warm, deceptive smile.

The men chuckled. "A funny one, you are." This man had a jagged scar running from his temple to his chin, apparently induced by a serrated blade. "Don't think we'll be letting you go anytime soon. Not 'til we've had our fun at least."

Ara's chest tightened and her eyes felt warm. One of the men cut her hands free and hauled her to her feet. "Move," he ordered, ushering her toward the fire. He sat her on a log, and she rubbed the cold from her arms.

"A frail thing you are, eh?" one of them asked. Ara didn't answer.

The man with the scar said, "See now, silence is unbecoming of a pretty girl such as yourself. Not long ago my brothers and I had just got done robbing some old coot with a wagon, when we decided to divert into the woods. That's when we found you just lying around in the leaves. A bit suspicious—a young girl alone in the Wraithwood. We thought you a nyssavir at first."

Another jumped in, "Of course, us being upstanding fellows and all, we couldn't just leave you there for the cold and the wolves to take you."

"You should thank us," the last one said. They all waited for her to respond. Their eyes glared hungrily.

She twirled her fingers in her lap, subtly biting the inside of her lip like she always did when nervous. "Th-thank you for not leaving me to die. Perhaps I have some coin I could offer you back at my home." Her voice cracked slightly at the last word. There was no spare coin for her to impart, but they didn't need to know that. The men appeared to be waiting for more, as if what she offered wasn't enough.

One of them said to his brothers, "I don't feel very thanked. Do yous two?" The others shook their heads and smiled devilishly. Then the three of them pounced.

Ara tried to fight them off. Her speed helped her slip from their fingertips once, but when she wrenched out of the grasp of one man, another took his place. Her arms were viciously pinned down, rendering her immobile. She grunted under the weight. Two of the men held her arms and legs while the other began unbuckling his belt.

"Don't worry, sweetheart," he said in between Ara's cries for help. "Just lie back and enjoy it." Her heart thumped with such ferocity it thundered in her ears. Heat pierced her skin as if a fire would burst from her, but as luck would have it, Ara remained the same.

Ara saw the man's face turn horrified just before he was yanked off the ground with a grunt, disappearing into the darkness above. Ara stared up into the shadows with wide, uncertain eyes.

What happened to him? Her chest heaved with labored breaths.

The others let go of her, ignoring Ara as she scrambled to her feet. They peered into the darkness above. "Klaus? What happened? You alright?" one of them asked nervously. There was a rustling above, and then two vines came down, snatching them off their feet and into the abyss.

Ara trembled, looking around frantically with her back to the fire. Shadows coalesced as a shape formed in the near distance. Squinting, she could see someone wearing a cloak. Reaching down, Ara grabbed a stone large enough to bludgeon with, or that was her plan, anyway.

"Stay back!" she cried out, hoping her voice didn't sound as weak and frail as she felt. *This can't possibly be a nyssavir. It's too... human.*

The stranger reached up and pulled the hood off her head, revealing a cascade of brown hair splashed with gray. She had emerald eyes and high cheekbones. Ara found her to be beautiful in a motherly sort of way.

"No need to be afraid, child," the woman said. Her voice was soothing. "Those men will never harm you again."

Ara's heartbeat slowed a little, but her nerves were still biting at her. She took a deep breath. "Who are you? What have you done with them?" The assault left her rattled; she didn't know if this woman could be trusted.

She gave a small curtsy before answering, "My name is Cassandra Morteum and I have sent those vile cretins to an eternal slumber." She said it matter-of-factly.

Morteum. Not Lowborn? That means she is a noble of some sort, Ara thought. *This woman killed those men.* Ara didn't know if she should fear the woman or not. This wasn't the first time she'd witnessed men die, but it was the *strangest.*

Shakily, she said, "Well, I believe thanks are in order, Lady Cassandra. Although, I can't help but wonder as to how you got rid of those men." She stole a glance upward but saw nothing.

Cassandra waved her hands. "Please, I am no *Lady.*" She said "Lady" as if it were an insult. "I simply do not conform to the decrees that Gosathan rulers have declared. I've been alive far too long to allow *men* to control my name. Our names are sacred, Ara. You mustn't allow those who consider themselves 'noble' to control your name."

Ara, she thought as the fear crept back in.

Ara took a tentative step back, gripping the stone tightly. "How did you know my name?" She didn't hide the suspicion in her tone.

Cassandra sighed, sitting in front of the fire. Ara could see then that the cloak was dark green with flecks of silver threading inlaid on its surface. The dress she wore beneath was a deep magenta with a silver bodice. Gold stitching held it all together.

"Perhaps you should sit down, my dear."

Ara remained standing.

Cassandra sighed. "Very well. I was once a friend of your mothers'. She and I met shortly before you were born."

Ara plopped forcefully onto a log, suddenly intrigued to learn more.

Cassandra continued, "Before she passed, your mother asked me if something were to ever happen to her, that I look after you. And so that's what I've done."

"But I've never even met you," Ara protested. "My Pa has never mentioned your name. Although, he doesn't speak much of Mother, so it makes sense that he wouldn't bring up her friends."

"Your father has endured many hardships in this life. I would never hold it against him that he finds it hard to speak of her. I watched you grow from a distance, Ara. I didn't want to put your life in danger."

A chill ran across her arms. "Why would you being near bring danger to me?"

"Because of what I am."

"And what are you?" Their eyes stayed on each other, unblinking.

"I am a sorceress."

Ara inhaled sharply. *That's how she got rid of the men; those vines that seemed to come from nowhere were conjured by her hands.* Magic was thought to be a lost art in Gosatha; Ara had never known someone to even *meet* a sorcerer before.

"I thought all the sorcerers were dead," Ara said.

"Not *all* of us..." she replied, trailing off.

"And what do you want with me now?" Ara asked, wondering what sort of sly trickery the witch could have up her sleeve. History records did not show mages to be in an honorable light.

"I only wish to spend time with you, Ara. Now that you are a woman, I want to teach you things that your mother would want you to know."

"Like what?" Ara leaned forward as she asked.

Cassandra smiled. "Well... you need to learn how to protect yourself, clearly." Ara frowned. "There is but one thing in this world that can set you apart from any man, Ara." She paused for a moment, then said, "Magic."

Chapter 4

PRINCE OLIVER JARDANIS KNEW he would one day take the throne; the ring with the king's seal and the Sword of Gorenos would be bestowed upon him, and he would inherit the armies of Gosatha. The notion of him ruling the greatest kingdom to ever exist made Oliver feel sick. However, being the oldest boy amongst three siblings—all girls—he was the one and only heir to the throne. For generations, the Jardanis family produced fine men to wear the crown, and the weight of it crushed Oliver in his young adulthood.

I've grown tired of this palace, he thought idly, picking at his nails. His mind was being consumed—yet again—by the ramblings of his father and the Royal Council.

Despite knowing his duty, his responsibility to the throne, Oliver disliked the politics of it all. He had a great sense of disdain for the separation of his people—the Lowborn and Nobility. Oliver was unsure what kind of ruler he would turn out to be, but he wanted to be fair to all.

One day I'll rid Gosatha of our societal divide. Listening to the council grumble about trivial matters always left Oliver in a petulant mood.

20 years in Gosatha, he thought, a swell of hope rising within him. *If only I can bring life to my ideas before my time is up.*

The prince sat to the right of his father, King Torril; the Royal Council sat further down the long table. The ten men dressed in dark blue robes with tall hats inlaid with white diamonds were said to be the most devout to the integrity of the crown. They were meant to be unwavering, unbiased, in their support for their sovereign. Oliver looked at those diamonds with derision. To him, they were but another symbol of the disparity of his people.

"Your Majesty," Lord Tobias began. "It has come to our attention the volunteer soldiers collected from many of our villages have been lower than normal. We suggest sending a party to hold these cities accountable. As you know, the Abithians will not miss their chance to pounce if a gap in the kingdom's armor is displayed. The queen and her ilk are all but savages, just a step above the Feral Ones. Without adequate numbers, I—as do the other councilors—believe our forces will soon face insurmountable odds."

King Torril had his fingers crossed in front of his face, staring down at the world map. To the North, Abithia lay leagues away from Gosatha with the Tamagau Sea separating them. What were they even fighting for? Because of a rivalry that began long ago.

Oliver thought humorously, *The Thousand Years War is a fitting title.*

Tobias continued, "As you're aware, Majesty, we can't give up the islands that lie between our countries. In past battles, the Abithians have always run us off the islands, and after a time we win them back. The Council believes if we double our usual number of troops before the cold season, we may be able to surge through their ships and breach their shores."

These discussions happened far too often, Oliver believed, and grew weary of it. Talk of politics, money, and war was all he'd ever known.

"I will go—" Oliver began, but his father held up a hand, cutting him off; Oliver stifled a groan. He whispered to the king. "Father, send me to the villages. Let me speak with our village leaders; I'll bring our recruitment numbers up to par."

King Torril's dark eyes found Oliver's. The two couldn't be any less alike. Oliver knew if the king were to go on his own, innocent villagers would be killed as an example for the villages' failure. Oliver would not do as much; he preferred a gentler approach when it came to interacting with subjects of the kingdom.

"You abhor war and all that goes with it," King Torril said, waving a dismissive hand, then paused. Oliver held his father's gaze. "Very well. The boy will go in my stead. Send two of the wolves with him. They leave tomorrow at first light."

The Gilded Wolves, Oliver thought, annoyed. *The finest guards in all Gosatha.*

He remembered when he was young, marveling at the Gilded Wolves in their guard's uniforms. They were fraught with intrigue, it would seem; boots made from black leather and gold buckles. Dark gray pants and shirt, gold embellishments along the sleeves, black pauldrons with the golden symbol of a wolf on their left shoulders.

"They are of the most elite warriors," his father had told him. He hadn't been old enough to be annoyed by them at that time. "Our wolves are guardians of the throne, keepers of the crown."

Prince Oliver's lip twitched—almost smiling—before he was pulled from the reverie.

"Are you sure only two is enough, Majesty?" Lord Leander asked with a slight smirk. By his tone, one would think he only cared of the prince's well-being; however, Oliver knew differently. Many of the Royal Council disliked Oliver; they thought him weak, that he would not rule with an iron fist as his father did. As had every Jardanis before them. There was truth to that, though.

I'm more caring about these people than any one of my predecessors, he thought. *They're wrong about me. Caring doesn't make me weak; rather, it makes me strong.*

"Do you wish to find out if I need more guards, Leander?" Oliver asked, rising to his feet. He felt the king's hand atop his own.

"Enough. Meeting is adjourned; you're all dismissed. Oliver, a word." The prince fumed as the others floated from the room with fading sniggers.

"What is it this time?" Oliver asked indignantly.

The king's eyes were cold, boring into the prince like daggers of ice. "Mind your tone, boy. I may be your father, but I am the king first. You *will* show me respect. Is that clear?"

"Yes, Majesty." It took a great deal of effort to keep the spite from his tone.

"Good. Now, do not allow the old councilmen to get under your skin, son. When you are king, they will see that you are just as capable as I. Until then, let them have their fun."

Exasperatedly, Oliver asked, "Why am I the one who must take the insults? Why is it my job to be perfect?"

Torril rose slowly. "Because you are to be king one day. It is your *duty* to be perfect. You are a Jardanis. Not them, you."

"I know that," Oliver snapped.

"Then act like it. I will not repeat myself on this issue. Do you understand?"

He nodded. "Yes, Father." He hid his contempt, squeezing his fists.

"You may leave. Prepare your things for the journey. You have a long trip ahead of you. Don't let me down, Oliver." The king held out his hand and Oliver kissed the ring on his pinky. It had the royal seal on it—a slithering snake with a sword plunged through its head to represent their ancestor who slew the abomination.

If only I could rid the world of Bhishma's ilk, he thought as he walked through the palace corridors.

The creatures weren't nearly the nuisance that Bhishma likely was, however, Lowborn farmers still had to deal with the destruction of their livestock and crops at times. He'd caught wind of lonely travelers being torn to shreds, or ships in the sea being ravaged by Bhishma's descendants. And yet, it seemed his father couldn't care less.

Oliver was only slightly nervous to make the rounds in the struggling villages. Most people he'd interacted with outside of the royal city of Valendra were kind to him; however, he often suspected they looked down on him just as the council did. Despite all of that though, he was excited to speak with the citizens of his realm. Oliver wanted to create a good impression of himself before he claimed the throne, though he assumed that day wouldn't happen for years to come.

The young prince was royalty but wasn't of the same thinking as even the lowest Highborn Lord when it came to his clothing. He preferred to dress down when outside his city. Instead of packing his finest garments, he only stuffed mute-colored garb into his bags, ensuring that he wouldn't appear pompous.

AFTER SAYING GOODBYE TO his mother, Queen Amelda, and his sisters, Oliver set off on horseback across the land. He and his two wolves left Valendra and began making their way to the first village on their trip—Khuress. Prince Oliver had never been there and hadn't heard much about it. He suddenly felt underprepared.

Khuress was nearly 20 leagues from Valendra; it took several days to reach by horseback. The journey took them over green, rolling hills, pastures of wildflowers, and through forests filled with myriad beasts. Once the village came into view, Prince Oliver realized it wasn't much in the ways of beauty. It was nothing like Valendra; there were no towers of stone that stretched to the clouds. The streets were dirty and filled with vagrants. Oliver wanted to rush through the village as quickly as possible, then was struck with guilt for feeling so.

These are my *people,* he thought.

Outlines of buildings popped up in Oliver's vision, growing into an expansive city. There were few tall structures; most were rather low to the ground and made of wood and thatch. It seemed to be quicker to build things that way.

When Oliver and the Gilded Wolves accompanying him made it to the village, the prince immediately met with the village lord—Goddard. He was a squat, little man with a bald patch atop his head. The hair from his head seemed to have fled down onto his face. Oliver didn't care for the man. He'd had the great displeasure of the toad's presence at royal parties in the past. When he relayed his message, he sugarcoated nothing.

"You're saying the soldiers I give from this stinkpot aren't up to snuff?" Goddard asked, the scent of ale wafting up from his breath. Oliver had already explained it to him three times and was growing impatient.

"Don't get it twisted, Goddard. The men you send are fine; however, the number is too few. We need more. Our war against the Abithians continues, and without increasing troop output, we will lose this fight. Do you want to be responsible for that?"

The lord went white at the notion. "Of course not, Sire."

Oliver gave the man his sternest look. "Good. Then I suggest you get your village in order. I'll give you three days."

Lord Goddard gulped audibly. "What happens after three days?"

Prince Oliver leaned in. His nostrils began to protest and his eyes watered. "We shall see if your nobility remains intact if this isn't rectified, Goddard." And then he left with a smile on his face. Generally, Oliver wasn't so brazen or threatening, but Goddard was a swine, undeserving of his status.

Oliver spent the rest of the day meandering about Khuress, saying hello to the citizens. The vagrants on the streets were suddenly less threatening in his eyes. His favorite part about leaving Valendra and visiting other places in Gosatha was mingling with the Lowborn. He even tossed a few coins out to those who seemed to have none. There were some very interesting people that would make excellent nobility. When Prince Oliver thought about it enough, he would begin to question if the kingdom would be better off if the hierarchy were to be reversed. Oliver put that thought aside, storing it away in the place where he kept dangerous ideas, the ones he was too afraid to utter aloud.

Chapter 5

Magic? Ara thought. This woman will turn me into a sorceress. Do I even want such a thing?

Laughter tickled her throat, but she was still apprehensive with the woman; after all, she didn't know her.

"You want to teach me magic?" she asked incredulously. "This is unheard of, Cassandra. I don't think I can get involved with that sort of thing, despite you saving my life this night."

The woman shrugged. "What's not to be desired, my dear? With magic, you'd be formidable against anyone who tried to harm you. If not for me and my sorcery, those men would have had their way with you, then left you to die in these woods."

"It's not that I'm ungrateful," she said softly. "But everyone knows that magic comes from dark places; it's users are nothing but villains." She kept her voice low, worried about upsetting Cassandra.

The woman raised her eyebrows as if surprised, then laughed. "I fear the lies of this world have deceived you, Ara. Do I seem like a murderous fiend?"

Ara tilted her head. "Well, you did just kill three men."

"Yes, but that was in defense of you. I would never harm someone without good reason."

Makes sense, Ara thought.

"Why are you so eager to make me into a sorceress?" Ara asked, becoming more curious, questions about her mother burning on the tip of her tongue.

"I want to change the world with magic," she said, as if it were a simple answer. "Mages have been looked down upon for eons; you confirmed this yourself. I want that to change. Any man or woman could change their status if only they knew how to wield this gift from the gods."

Ara perked up, her interest further piqued. *Perhaps this is how...* "How would one change their status with magic?"

"Just imagine it, my dear," she continued. Cassandra's eyes were wide as she leaned forward with excitement. Flames danced like a jester in their reflection. "With magic, one could overthrow their oppressors. The *Highborn* have nothing against a practiced mage!"

Ara let out a deflated breath. "It sounds as though you mean to change the world by force. Even if you are a strong sorceress, what makes you think you're any sort of match for the king's army?"

Cassandra waved her hand. "You misunderstand me. By our magic, we can show them we are strong, yet merciful. That we could be great allies to the king's armies, or their greatest foes."

"It still sounds like you want to instill fear into them."

"A little fear never hurt anyone," the woman said with a smile.

Ara almost laughed, but a flash of guilt went through her. She'd been so caught up in everything that she forgot about Calder. Questions of her mother may have to wait. "Oh, Cassandra, I came in these woods with a friend. Tell me you've seen him."

She frowned, her eyes glancing down then back up. "I'm afraid I haven't seen any others in the forest besides you and the three demons who meant to harm you. They would be sons of Bhishma if I didn't know any better." Ara shivered at that.

"We must find him." Ara rose to her feet, meaning to flee off into the darkness.

Cassandra grabbed her wrist gently. "I promise, when first light shows we will search for your friend. Until then, let us attempt to steal a few hours of sleep, yes?"

Ara nodded, realizing then how tired she was. She took a roll from one of the bags belonging to the men and laid down. Her nose curled away from the musty smell, but she grew accustomed to it and shut her eyes. The sounds of the night mixed with the melodious crackle of the fire lulled her mind to sleep.

THE EARLY RAYS OF sunlight bursting through the trees woke Ara. She knuckled the sleep from her eyes, sitting up and gazing upon the smoldering embers of the previous night's fire. She rubbed a chill from her arms, replaying the events in her mind. Ara noticed her savior looking at her.

"Have you been awake long?" Ara asked.

"Oh, I don't sleep much." The silver threads in her verdant cloak shimmered beneath the sunlight.

Ara glanced up, regretting it as she saw the dangling feet of her assailants. Bile ceased in her throat and she choked it back down. It wasn't the first death she'd witnessed, but the first she'd been directly involved in. Cassandra must have noticed; she followed the girl's gaze.

A pitying look washed over her. "Don't worry yourself over them, child," she said. "They would have killed you when they were done. Men like that don't deserve the mercy of living in this world, nor even of a proper burial."

Ara nodded, standing and stretching her arms. "I must search for my friend now. Calder must be worried terribly over me. If something horrible..." She trailed off, unable to finish the sentence. If something happened to him, she would never forgive herself.

"Then I shall assist you," Cassandra said with a smile. Her upbeat attitude helped alleviate some of the guilt in Ara's gut.

They began searching, retracing Ara's steps as best they could. It seemed like half the day had gone by when Ara finally decided to give up. Calder was nowhere to be found in the Wraithwood.

As if reading her thoughts, Cassandra said, "Perhaps, he wandered home. You should look for him in Osta, I think."

Ara nodded. "Maybe you're right, though I can't imagine he'd leave me." There was a slight bitterness to her tone at that notion. "Besides, I'm certain my father is worried sick as well. Can you help me find my way?"

Cassandra smiled. "Of course, my dear."

The two drank deeply of a crystalline creek and then marched back through the Wraithwood. When they made it to the road, Ara didn't see any sign of a robbing such as the men had told her. There was no disturbed earth in the road, no debris from dropped supplies. She found it odd, but waved it from her mind, thinking that it must have been a lie. Or perhaps the robbery had happened further down the path.

"I must leave you here, Ara," Cassandra told her, stopping.

Surprising to herself, Ara didn't want the woman to leave her side yet. "Why?" *I haven't had the chance to ask about Mother.*

Cassandra sighed. "The Wraithwood is my home. The world isn't friendly to those of us who practice magic as of yet, and I'd like to be able to conjure freely without facing executioners."

"I see," replied Ara. "But do you not fear the nyssavir?"

Cassandra looked at the girl like she was disappointed in her. She spun in a circle with her arms stretched wide. A wind swept in, leaves and grass sucking in toward her. When the debris converged at her hands in a swirling mass, she thrust her arms to the side, scattering the refuse. "My dear girl, they should fear *me*," she said wryly.

If not for her worry for Calder, Ara would have laughed at that. Instead, she asked, "Will I see you again?"

"That depends on you."

"Me?"

Cassandra nodded. "You have a decision to make. Whether or not you will take up my offer to teach you what I know. Take some time to think it over; I don't want to pressure you, for this is *your choice* to make. I'll meet you at this very spot in three days. You shall give me your answer then."

They wished each other farewell, and Ara departed, heading towards her home. Flat plains with scattered plots of trees surrounded her as she pushed down the dirt road; she strolled with invigorated purpose, eager to see her father. When she came upon her quaint home, Ara noticed a small gathering outside. She recognized many of them as friends to her father.

"There she is!" she heard someone shout.

The rest of the group turned into a raucous uproar. Ara's father came running out from the group, wrapping the girl in the firmest hug she'd ever known. "Pa, what in Gorenos' name is going on?"

"I should be asking you that," he shouted. The relief she'd seen on his face shifted, turning to anger mixed with deep worry. "Where have you been? That *friend* of yours came back, raving about you disappearing in the Wraithwood! And then you don't come home all night! We were mounting a search party to come find you. Explain yourself, Ara."

Her eyes drifted to the ground, relief and anger swelling up, mixing. *He came back without me?*

She didn't know where to begin. "Can we talk about this without all these people?" Her teeth chewed the inside of her lip.

Gaius sighed deeply, rubbing the back of his neck. Then he turned, thanking the search party for coming, and dismissing them to take their leave. He turned back to Ara once the grumbling Ostans had disappeared. "Now, tell me what happened." His tone had calmed slightly.

She took a calming breath. "Cal and I were in the Wraithwood—"

"*Alone?*" her father interrupted.

"Yes, alone," she huffed. "You may not trust Cal, but I do. He has never been anything but good to me." Gaius snorted at that, mumbling under his breath something about Calder abandoning her.

She continued, "As we were heading back out of the woods, something spooked the both of us. I panicked and ran. Cal tried to stop me, but I kept running. I tripped and hit my head. I guess he couldn't find me."

"He says you disappeared from sight and never came from the woods," he said. "Fool of a boy; you could have been eaten by any number of—"

"Please, Pa," she interrupted. "Stop this. As you can see I'm perfectly fine."

Gaius crossed his arms. "Why didn't you come back until now?"

"I woke up in the night," she recalled, remembering how frightened she'd been at the sight of the three men. She shuddered. "There were three men. They tied me to a tree. Then someone else showed up and chased them away." Heat rose to her cheeks.

She thought, *If I tell him Cassandra killed the men, he may very well report her.*

He nearly wilted at hearing of the men. "Who was it that saved you?"

"She said she was a friend of my mothers'," she replied, noting the raising of his eyebrows. "Her name is Cassandra Morteum."

What followed was a sharp inhale, and the color flushed from Gaius' face.

Chapter 6

AFTER LEAVING KHURESS, PRINCE Oliver and his wolves began the journey to Osta. There was a small forest with tall, scattered trees they could either cut through or go around. Oliver headed for the woods at the plight of the guards. Places with dense trees were more likely to host the nyssavir. The prince wasn't keen on dirtying his blade, but it had been a while since he'd killed something. He didn't mind tangling with the cursed spawn.

In the woods, the horses became restless; their whinnies echoed around the trees. A sound like a distorted whisper reached the prince's ears. "Careful, Sire," one of the guards said. "I hear them."

"Aye. I hear them as well." Oliver felt his adrenaline spike. He dismounted from his horse, scanning the trees for them. "There," he whispered. The wolves followed him as he made his way toward the slithering beast.

It was segmented like a worm and as fat as a young pig. There were ten spindly legs jutting out from its body, barbed and venomous if one were to break a man's skin. The nyssavir's face was a mesh of horror. Black, beady eyes glared at Oliver; mandibles on either side of a black hole of a mouth. Two slits on either side of its thick head provided excellent hearing.

Oliver called to his men, "Even without working legs, these nyssavir are speedy; don't be careless with them." A twig crunched as Oliver prepared to strike with his sword. The creature lunged at him, mandibles flashing and snapping with ferocity. The prince's blade cleaved the beast in two, splitting it lengthwise. Sticky sludge the color of swamp water dripped from the sword.

"Whoa," the prince pinched his nose. *I'll never get used to that smell.* His accompanying knights chuckled. He was glad they didn't jump in to defend him; it showed trust.

"Best move on, wouldn't you say, Sire?" one of them asked, a tone of humor in his voice.

Unlike the one in Khuress, the Lord of Osta wasn't a squat man with a drinking problem, nor was he incompetent. Prince Oliver felt for them, as the city was one that normally came up short on all its requirements: taxes, soldiers, crop production. Still, the prince needed to meet with the village lord.

"Lord Simeon, pleasure to see you," Oliver said as the man offered a respectful bow. The prince and his guards had gone to the local tavern and sent for the lord.

"Likewise, Sire. What brings you to Osta?"

Oliver sighed. "I'm afraid Osta is lacking in its contribution of soldiers. Though, I know Osta is quaint, it is still prudent that we boost the numbers of our forces. The king has sent me to all the lacking villages in Gosatha to... inspire village leaders. I wish things were different, but something has to be done."

Simeon nodded as if he already knew. "Aye, I was afraid of that. As you know, Osta has always struggled; however, I will make some changes to get the numbers up. Please, don't worry yourself, Sire." He paused, sipping his ale. "Say, how long will you be here? I'd like to have you for dinner."

"Very kind of you, Simeon," Oliver replied. "I think we have a few days before we need to move on. Let us get settled at the inn and I will send Beric here to arrange a dinner with you." Oliver gestured his head toward the man to his right.

Simeon clapped his hands. "Excellent! Have a good day, Sire. Let me know if you need anything at all." He bowed again, dismissing himself.

Prince Oliver departed the tavern shortly after, and went to the inn. The innkeeper gave him the finest room, and the two Gilded Wolves shared a room across the hall. They stayed in tower roughly thirty meters high with a room overlooking all of Osta. It had been many years since Oliver had visited Osta; the last time, he'd been with his father. How many times had his father dragged him around the kingdom to witness things no young boy should bear witness to?

I've lost count, he thought. *Seeing boys my age taken to fight in the war. Seeing the heads of their father's roll when trying to protect their children. And Father says it's all necessary to win the war against the Abithians.*

Oliver shuddered at the memories flooding him.

"What they lack in war strategy and weaponry, the Abithians make up for in sheer numbers," his father had told him. Oliver always heard tales of their savagery. Poliander—one of the Gilded Wolves escorting him—spoke of the things he'd seen in battle. He said he once saw a boy no older than sixteen wielding a hatchet in each hand. The boy fell ten of the king's men before he was finally struck down. And those were just the comrades that Poliander saw die; he could only assume more had fallen before that.

Poliander always got a far-away look in his eyes when recalling tales from battle. Those stories made Oliver woeful. He just wanted a peaceful world where the two nations could get along. How much better would it be if the two could trade commerce and share the world without bloodshed? Perhaps they could deal with the Feral Ones together.

Oliver recalled what he'd heard of them, seeing as he'd never laid eyes on them. Once—when Oliver was young and gullible—one of the generals had told him a story. The young prince had thought it a myth, but he kept hearing the same thing over the years. General Gerrity told him, "There is a land beholden to a people we call 'Feral

Ones'. Each time our ships come close, there they are, with spears and arrows. Crudely made, of course, but they've killed our men more than once. Their land is too high above the sea to reach by any means beside grappling hook, but the Feral Ones bar our passage. We've even gone at night; it's as if they have eyes all around their land. Their garbled shouts that reach us are incoherent, to say the least. When it is your time to lead, Sire, I suggest forgetting they even exist."

The man had been three pints into ale, and promptly slumped in his chair, passing out in the great hall at the palace. Oliver smiled as he remembered it; Gerrity was one of his favorites before the old man was called to Volharis. A cold, wet night had left him ill; he never recovered.

Prince Oliver tore away from the windows of the tower, slipping past his guards as he went. The prince had been trained by the kingdom's finest swordsmen, and yet, his father always insisted that he be guarded when leaving the palace. Oliver wondered if that was part of the reason the Royal Council always thought so poorly of him.

"I need no man's protection," Oliver mumbled to himself.

Oliver's sword was strapped to his waist as he made his way out of the inn. His journey through the city began, and he offered greetings to his people as he went. He strolled through the rolling hills of the countryside, taking in its beauty. Blue sky and sparse clouds were above him. The natural charm of their lands often left the prince in awe.

Oliver found himself thinking—once again—of the changes he would like to make when he is crowned as king of Gosatha. He wanted to do something that he'd not heard of his predecessors doing in centuries, which was to meet with Queen Gadiel Lotus—ruler of Abithia.

Father certainly hasn't the gall to do so, he thought.

The last king who'd tried never returned, but it wasn't Gadiel who'd been in rule then. If Oliver could be different from his forebearers, then so could she. Oliver was aware of assassins within Abithia, and didn't care if they tried killing him; he wanted the fighting to end. If there was a way to ensure peace by trading his life, he'd gladly do so.

The prince looked around at the grassy hills. His mind flashed back to when he was a boy; his father had told him to be mindful of himself, lest he become lost. He then found himself, indeed, lost.

Amongst the tall grass, he found a lonely shed of sorts. It was near enough for him to see a fire whipping in the wind near it. He walked towards it, realizing that it wasn't fire at all, but rather the hair of a girl. She was sitting on a log with her knees pulled into her chest, and the soft breeze tossed her locks. With her being drawn into herself, her frame made her appear as a child.

"Hello there," he called out from a distance, causing her to start. She jumped to her feet and spun toward him. Her face struck him. She was beautiful. *I've never seen such eyes,* he thought, then realized he was staring. The prince held his hands up to show he meant no harm. "Apologies if I startled you, madam."

The girl relaxed, scoffing at him, then folded her arms across her chest. "May I help you with something?"

"Yes," he said, smiling brightly. "I'm Prince Oliver Jardanis. I seem to have gotten a bit lost."

Her eyes widened slightly at the mention of his name. She curtsied, dropping her gaze to the ground. "What brings you to Osta, Sire?"

"Please, rise. You needn't be so formal at your home." He just realized the "shed" was a house. The girl straightened, her gaze locking with his. *Those eyes,* he thought. *Violet, just like the flower.*

The girl looked at him, smiling awkwardly as if waiting for him to say more. "Forgive my staring. You're just... very beautiful." Where did that come from? He was always so careful about offering such compliments to women. Many of them would kill to be royalty.

The girl's cheeks blushed. "I don't mean to make you uneasy," he said.

She smiled. "No, that's alright, Sire."

Oliver realized a fault in his decorum. "Please forgive my manners. I should have asked sooner but, may I have your name?" His cheeks became warm.

"My name is Ara."

Ara, he thought. He felt the name roll off the tongue of his mind's voice, and decidedly, liked it.

Ara asked, "What brings you to Osta, Prince Oliver?"

Rubbing the back of his neck, he said, "Unfortunately, Osta has fallen short of the men we need for the war. Many villages have done the same, so I've been sent by my father to see what we can do to fix this."

"I see," she said.

Oliver opened his mouth to speak but found himself short of words. *Why is this girl inciting a panic in me?*

"It's not the most ideal situation," he finally blurted. "I'd rather be traveling under better circumstances, and I simply care about you people too much to allow my father to make this journey."

Her brows pinched and she crossed her arms. "What do you mean by that?"

It seemed he was making matters worse. He shouldn't judge the king's actions publicly, but still said, "Well, had my father been doing this, I fear there would be many innocent lives taken by his hand. Most likely those who were already unfit to serve in battle. With me being here... well, I can spare you all from his rage." The last thing he needed was their lives on his conscience.

Ara looked at him for a moment longer, then shrugged. "I suppose you're some great hero then, hm?"

He chuckled, "I don't know about that."

"Oh, don't be so modest, Sire. Now, I must step inside a moment. You can wait here, or you could come in and meet my father. I know he wouldn't mind having royalty in our home. Fair warning though; he's in a rather cross mood."

"Noted," Oliver said with a grin, gesturing to the door.

Oliver could see nearly the entirety of the home from just inside the door. An oil lamp sat on the table two arm lengths away.

"Pa, there's someone here you should meet," Ara offered to a closed door.

It slowly cracked open, and Oliver put on a friendly smile. A man with lines around his eyes and across his forehead stepped out looking grim. "And who might you be?"

"I am Prince Oliver Jardanis, sir."

The grim look shifted into awe. "In my home? Please forgive me, Sire." He bowed quickly. "I would have tidied up if I'd known you were coming." He glanced around nervously.

Oliver smiled broadly. "Think nothing of it. It's a lovely home you have, sir. I wanted to appear inconspicuously, and it would seem as if I succeeded."

"Please, call me, Gaius," the man said. "What brings you here, Prince Oliver?"

"Fate, it would seem," he said with a chuckle. There was a silence, and he went on, "I'm travelling to various villages in Gosatha to carry a message from the king. It's our armies, sir, that are hurting for soldiers. Without more fighters this war will be lost, or so the Royal Council thinks. It's a difficult time to be a soldier, what with the feeling that your brothers are dwindling." Oliver was only assuming, of course; he'd never been in battle, lost men he called "friend".

"Yes, it is difficult for many," Gaius said, almost sounding incredulous. "Why, we just fought off one of the nyssavir recently. Bastard got into our crops."

"Pa," Ara warned.

Oliver tried not to notice the derision from Gaius and continued. "It's my hope to eradicate the vermin some day." There was no answer so he continued, "I was clearing my mind with a stroll when I happened upon your home. It appears I've wandered too far from the village."

"Allow me to show you the way back, Sire," Ara offered, her hand motioning for the door. Oliver got the sense she was trying to usher him away from the older man.

"That will be most appreciated. But call me Oliver." *What would Father think of that?*

"Of course," she said with a smile. "I'll be right back, Pa."

"If you aren't back by the sun's dying light, I'll be coming for you," Gaius told her sternly.

She huffed, rolled her eyes, and led the prince out of their home. "Don't take his sour attitude to heart; he's a great man and all, it's just been a difficult couple of days for us. He's normally not so grumpy."

"I understand," Oliver said. "He hasn't offended me in the slightest. I know Osta generally struggles with sending war fighters. A lot of Lowborn here are underfed and poor." He said it as a fact, not an insult.

Ara shot him a look, seeming to want to say something, but thinking better of it. Oliver tried to recover his words. "I didn't mean anything by that. Just that I understand his consternation."

She scoffed. "How could you understand? You've never had to struggle with surviving the taxes that are leeched from those of us who barely make enough to feed ourselves. Never had to watch your friends get dragged away before reaching adulthood." As the last word left her mouth, her cheeks reddened, and she clasped a hand over her mouth. "I shouldn't have spoken to you like that. Please, f—"

Oliver held up a hand despite the burning in his cheeks. "Don't apologize. You're free to speak your mind with me." *Though, Father wouldn't tolerate such an outburst.*

Frustration made his palms sweat, his brows pinch. The conversation was not going in a direction that Oliver wanted it to. His temper was rising but he kept his voice calm and level. "Perhaps I can't understand those toils, but I've struggled with things in my life too; let's suffice it to say that neither of us can fully understand the other's experience."

She nodded but didn't argue. "Despite what you've said, I must beg my forgiveness." She offered a curtsy. "My manners could use some work, Sire."

Oliver shook his head. "I know how it seems, Ara. My father has ruled the kingdom free of mercy for his people for many years, but I am not him. I don't aim to be anything like him. I want to be a greater leader than he; I want to lead with compassion and mercy. You must believe what I say."

Her smile reached her eyes. It seemed they were both cooling down. She looked down, then back up. "I can tell you're a good man, Prince Oliver. I do believe you." She paused for a moment, then pointed and said, "Continue that way. The village isn't far. It's been a pleasure meeting you."

She turned to walk away. Oliver didn't know what came over him, but he found himself grabbing her arm. "Wait," he pleaded. "I must see you again before I leave. Please."

Ara looked momentarily angry when he grabbed her, but her eyes softened as she looked at him. His hand slid from her arm to her fingers. He looked down at them, small in his larger hands, then released them. What would his father think of his ogling a Lowborn? He didn't know, didn't care at that moment, either. Something about her just drew him in.

She looked down at her feet. "I don't think that's such a good idea."

His heart seemed to fall. Was she rejecting him? "Just think about it, okay? I'll come back tomorrow in search of your answer."

"I'll be working tomorrow," she shot back.

"And what is it a young lady such as yourself does for work?" he asked.

She grinned. "I assist the butcher with cleaning and such."

Oliver recoiled slightly. "Surely not! I would have taken you to be a seamstress or something of the sort. No, working in a meat shop simply won't do." He exaggerated his words, facetiously making a big deal out of it.

Ara laughed. "It's an easy enough job, helps to feed Pa and I, and the butcher is a very nice employer as well."

Oliver shook his head. "Allow me to cover your wages for the day. I'd like to take you on a lunch picnic."

Her hard visage began to dissolve then, becoming a softer version of itself. Her creased brows straightened, and her pursed lips loosened.

She giggled to herself like a young girl would. "I won't let you pay me a thing, but I'll go with you on one condition."

"Name your price." The prince gazed into her eyes with butterflies swarming inside him.

"You must first ask my father's permission."

"Of course," he said, bowing to her. That was an easy request. Even if the older man was cantankerous, Oliver had dealt with crabby old men since his youth.

"Good. I'll see you then." She trotted off back toward her home, giving him a tantalizing smile, and a simple wave of the hand.

Oliver watched her go until she faded from sight, then spun on his heel and trekked on. Prince Oliver was not accustomed to asking for permission for anything. Asking for a man's blessing to court a girl was foreign to him, as was courting a girl at all.

He knew his father wouldn't approve of this. Jardanis men were to marry women of noble blood, not commoners such as Ara. Maybe that was part of his reason behind chasing after her so fervently. However, this seemed like an issue for a later day; he'd be remiss if he passed up the chance of gaining the girl's hand, if only for a short time. Perhaps that was foolish, or perhaps he was just foolishly wishful in his desire for a simpler life.

Chapter 7

ARA COULDN'T RECALL A time when her father had been so vexed, especially towards her. His lighthearted attitude was altered, poisoned, by what Ara told him of Cassandra. When she'd told him the woman had saved her from the men who wished to harm her, he'd gone white as if he'd gazed upon an apparition. Ara tried to get him to say more, but he simply forbade her from going into those woods ever again.

Then Prince Oliver showed up and the droll man put her worries at ease for a moment. The prince was a pretty man; blonde hair and dark green eyes with a youthful light about them. His face covered in a thin layer of stubble. He wasn't like many of the men she'd ever conversed with; he was charming, giving her compliments in such a way that they remained respectful. Ara was used to the men in Osta calling after her with obscene words, commenting on her figure in inappropriate ways.

Not Cal, though, she thought idly.

After the prince had gone, Ara saw Calder jogging up to her home. He must have heard that she'd returned, but then she wondered why he wasn't with the original search party.

"Ara," he yelled, "I'm so glad you're okay!"

"It'll take more than the Wraithwood to kill me," she said coolly.

"I was terrified that a nyssavir or something had gotten its fangs in you," he told her, wrapping her up into a sweaty hug. She didn't return it, but rather pushed him away gently. "What's the matter?"

"There was a search party preparing to hunt me down this morning," she noted. "Where were you?"

He sighed. "It isn't my fault, Ara. My father wouldn't allow me to leave my home. I had to finish filling out some ledgers before I could do anything else. I'm the one who told your father about what happened, though."

"You mean that you left me in there alone?" Ara could see the words hit him like an arrow to the heart. She was being unfair to him. Perhaps it was because of Prince Oliver's interest in her. It was as if something in her wanted to push Cal away, because knowing that he wanted to be with her, was too much for Ara to bear. He'd always been there for her, and if she were to be with another man, it felt like a betrayal. A betrayal that she was prepared to commit.

His voice lowered. "I didn't know what to do. I looked for you, I swear it. But I couldn't find you. It was as if you had vanished into thin air."

"Well, I hadn't," she said, folding her arms. "I awoke with three bandits about to have their way with me."

His face flushed, rife with guilt. He began to move toward her as if to embrace her, but Ara took a slight step back and he stopped. "Are you alright? Did they hurt you?"

"I'm fine enough," she stated dryly.

"Ara, I never would want harm to befall you. You know that, right?"

She nodded, softening a bit. Despite the confusing feelings she was developing for the prince, she couldn't stay mad at Cal over something so trivial. "I know. I shouldn't have been so hard on you. It wasn't your fault. The important thing is that I'm alright."

Cal nodded. "Is there anything I can do to make it up to you?"

Ara shook her head. "No, I'm okay, really. I had better get inside and start on dinner for Pa. You should go home; it'll be getting dark soon."

"Right. Listen, I wanted to ask for your father's blessing. I think I'm ready." He smiled a wide, toothy smile.

Of course, she thought. *He picks* now *to go to my father.* Ara sighed. She'd already agreed to a rendezvous with the prince. "Listen, Cal, I don't think it's a very good idea."

Calder's face fell. Ara could see the hurt in his eyes. "Is it because of what happened last night?"

"It's not *just* that," she replied. "Pa isn't in the best mood right now. I don't think the conversation would go over well, and I don't want to see you get hurt." It was only a half truth.

"I understand," he said, nodding. "I guess I'll see you tomorrow?"

"Sure."

Calder left and Ara went inside her home to begin making dinner for the two of them. When they broke bread, the only interruption in silence was the clink of their forks on plates. The tension between them had never been so palpable. The small flame of a candle made dark shadows dance across Gaius' downcast face. Ara drizzled honey onto her buttered bread.

"Pa," Ara said, "please tell me why my being near Cassandra troubles you so."

His fork slammed onto his plate, causing Ara to jump. When he spoke, his voice was an octave lower than normal. "Ara, there is something awful about that woman. I can feel it, deep in my bones." She relaxed. His animosity was with the mage, not her.

"But she said she was a friend of mother's."

"Yes, she and your mother met a long time ago. The two of them became very close, nearly like sisters. Adina was always trapsing off with her. I never knew where they went. Then one day, your mother disappeared and never returned."

"I thought you told me she died," Ara said, her heart quickening.

"Ara, your mother *always* came back. Until she didn't. She would not have simply *abandoned* you or I. It can only mean that she died, and *that woman* had something to do with it! I can feel it. She always made me uneasy." His eyes became as if he were looking at something far away.

Ara's cheeks warmed, she gritted her teeth. "I can't believe this. Mother could be alive, she could have gotten lost, like me. You never even searched for her, did you?"

"I did search for her!" His eyes were wide and filled with tears. "I searched all over Osta. I looked for days and never found a trace of her. I even found Cassandra and asked if she'd seen her, but she couldn't be bothered by me. She waved it off, saying she was certain Adina would show up eventually."

"I'm sorry, Pa," Ara said, taking one of his strong hands in hers. There was still a notion in Ara's mind saying her mother could still be alive, but she pushed it away. She willed the heat that had risen to her cheeks to be gone. "I must figure this out, though. I promise I'll be careful. If Cassandra did have something to do with her disappearance, I'll make sure she suffers." Truth ebbed from the words.

"I don't want you going anywhere near that woman, Ara," Gaius said, getting to his feet. "She is nothing but trouble, and I *will not* lose you too. I can't even bear the thought." His voice cracked with the last word.

Ara rushed into his chest, wrapping her arms around him. "Okay, Pa. I'll stay away from her." The guilt assaulted her gut instantly. She knew she had lied to him. Ara would go to Cassandra. She had to. Knowing she could have been the cause of her mother's death and doing nothing to find out for sure, was something Ara refused to do.

THE FOLLOWING DAY, ARA awoke to hushed voices. She stood from her bedroll, cracking her door open slightly. Her eyes widened at the sight of Prince Oliver. She ran to her mirror, finding her hair disheveled. As quickly as she could, Ara brushed out her hair and changed into something a little less dingy. The gown she'd thrown on was simple with nothing more than square patterns of white and brown. She hated wearing anything other than her pants and blouses, but to be going on a picnic with the prince was like a dream, and Ara didn't want to seem too uncivilized.

"Ah, good morning, Ara," Gaius said as she crept from her room. The unpleasantries of the previous night no longer apparent on his face. "Prince Oliver here was just asking for my blessing in courting you."

"And?" she asked hopefully.

"I gave it, of course. I must be heading off to work now. You two enjoy yourselves." The candlelight danced in his eyes.

"You're sure I'm not needed, Pa?" Ara asked.

"No, no. We will manage just fine." He gave the prince a respectful bow of his head.

"Thank you, sir," Oliver said, walking out of the home with Gaius. Ara was trailing them. "I'll take care of her. You have my word." Ara found herself impressed with the prince. He didn't have to ask for blessings; he could demand that she go with him, and they'd be powerless to stop it. Yet, he'd still asked.

Outside, there were two disgruntled-looking men with crossed arms awaiting the prince. Gaius nodded to them respectfully and waved goodbye to the four of them before heading off.

"What's with the audience?" Ara asked curiously.

"Two of the Gilded Wolves were sent to protect me from rambunctious women," he said with a wink, conjuring a chuckle from Ara. She heard the two men sigh in unison. "In honesty, I gave them the slip yesterday, hence their poor attitudes." He turned to the men. "Come on gents, there's a picnic to be had!"

"You know how we feel about this, Sire," one of them grumbled.

The other said, "King Torril would never approve of your courtship with a Lowborn, though she may be a fine young l—"

"Enough," Oliver snapped, glaring at the knights. "My father's opinion doesn't matter. I won't hear of it again." They nodded and the prince turned his attention back to Ara, who was biting the inside of her lip. "Shall we?"

Ara had adorned a bashful look because of the guard's apprehension toward her but perked up a little when Oliver gestured to the beautiful steeds before them.

It seemed the prince had borrowed a horse for Ara to ride on, and after helping her up, the four of them trotted away. There was one lake in all of Osta, and it seemed Prince Oliver thought it to be a beautiful sight.

When they stopped their horses near it, he asked, "This will do just fine, don't you think so, Ara?"

She smiled as she climbed off the animal. "Yes, Sire."

"Enough with the formalities," he replied. "Let me escape the politics just this once." He seemed sincere, not at all angry.

"Very well. But only this once." She chuckled at the annoyed look on his face.

For a while they sat there with the guards atop their horses several meters away. They ate bread with butter and honey and drank red wine. She wasn't new to the fruity tang of wine, but it wasn't a regular drink she could partake of. During their meal, they told each other stories from their childhood. According to Oliver, he'd grown up with both parents, but rarely felt the love of his parents. Ara never would have guessed that based on how kind he was. Assumption told her he got that from his mother—a woman who was kind as well, albeit distant when it came to affection. She couldn't help but feel herself being more and more drawn to him the more they shared. He gave her such attention, revealing deep feelings that Calder had never shared.

Why must I compare the two?

"Want to know a secret?" he asked low enough for only her ears. She nodded, her eyes glinting with excitement. Ara was always thirsty for knowledge. Oliver's gaze went down, his face looking more solemn. "I've thought of many changes I want to make to the kingdom once I'm on the throne."

"What do you mean?"

He sighed. "My father rules mercilessly, never giving a second thought to his actions. I don't want to be like that; however, I am constantly ridiculed by those in the council for my kindness. They think me soft. I only want what's best for my people. The Lowborn, the Highborn; I want the distinction to end."

"I don't see anything wrong with that," she said, her head buzzing with the thought of *finally* having a surname. She would finally feel like a *person*. "There is more to being a king than just waging war on your enemies, I would think. But then again, what does a Lowborn like me know?" She smirked so he'd know she wasn't being too serious.

He chuckled. "It's not just the war, either. Have you heard of the Feral Ones?"

Her brows pinched in thought. "No, I can't say that I have."

"There is a group of people—savages—who live in a land we cannot reach. Their land sits atop cliffs high above the Tamagau. Whenever our men have attempted to approach, they're always there, waiting with their primitive weapons."

"Primitive?" she asked.

He nodded. "Nothing but sharpened stone tied to wooden shafts. Deadly, nonetheless. It's like a whole other world apart from our own, unattainable. We've sent priests there as well. They tried to communicate from boats, but the result was the same. Any sound uttered from the Feral One's lips is incomprehensible."

Ara could relate to that; speaking with royalty was similar. It wasn't as bad as what the prince described, but she could tell they live in two different worlds all the same. "This place sounds terrifying."

"Aye," he said. "This is what I must think about. How to end this war. How to deal with the Feral Ones."

"Surely you could just leave them be," she pondered.

He scoffed. "We don't know what sort of weapons they possess, resources they hold. Every king of Gosatha has tried to find a way into their land. If only I could figure it out..."

"Then everyone would love you more?" Her voice was far more sarcastic than she intended. His eyes snapped to her as if he were angry. "I'm sorry. I shouldn't have said that. It must be difficult to be in your position."

His visage softened. "Thank you. It's alright. Ridicule and questioning are things I'll need to get accustomed to."

"What's this?" a voice interrupted them. The wolves rushed forward without hesitation. Ara looked up to find Calder slowly stalking up from behind.

Chapter 8

"Ⅿᴀʏ ᴡᴇ ʜᴇʟᴘ ʏᴏᴜ?" Oliver asked the striking young man who'd interrupted the picnic. The guards trotted over, putting themselves in between them. Oliver thought it an overreaction; the man wasn't armed in the slightest, nor did he have a particularly threatening build about him. Sure, he was tall, but there wasn't much as far as muscle mass went.

The man ignored Oliver, addressing Ara instead. "What's going on, Ara? Who are these men?" Oliver saw the stranger look the knights up and down before settling his eyes back on Ara.

She rose to her feet, followed quickly by the prince, and let out a weary sigh. There was an awkward silence, save for the sound of a crow somewhere nearby. "This is Prince Oliver Jardanis, and two of the king's Gilded Wolves. Prince Oliver, this is my oldest friend—Calder." The young man's eye twitched at the word "friend". The prince suspected there may be some history between them. Calder's feet shifted nervously.

"Pleasure," Oliver remarked, not at all enthusiastic about meeting a possible old flame of Ara's.

"I see," Calder said to Ara, taking a half step back. "Apologies for the interruption, Sire. Allow me to be on my way. Good day."

"Good day," the prince replied.

"Cal," Ara called out, but her friend continued to walk without turning back. She looked at Oliver. "I feel I should go after him. He seems upset."

That was the last thing the prince wanted to hear, but he didn't want to appear insensitive or jealous. "Very well. I should be going, anyway. Lord Simeon and I have dinner plans, plus I have a few more villages to visit. I shall come back to see you, Ara. You have my word as a man, if you wish to have me back, that is."

She smiled at him wryly. "I'm sure that's what you tell all the girls."

"There are no others. Much to my father's displeasure, I've yet to find a woman I can stand to be around longer than an eve. Although now I'd rather not be leaving your side. You've allowed me to...forget about things for a bit."

The girl's smile brightened, and her eyes twinkled. "I would enjoy another visit, if you so decide to return."

"Excellent," Oliver said, planting a soft kiss on Ara's cheek. He had to crouch down slightly to reach it. Her mouth hung open, and he worried he'd overstepped, but then she grinned and rubbed where his lips touched. "I shall be back, my lady. Until then, may Gorenos be with you."

"And same to you, Prince Oliver," she replied with a deep curtsy. "But what of this horse? Shall I return him for you?" She gestured to the chestnut-hued steed.

"Of course not," Oliver replied, feigning offense. "My gift to you!"

"I cannot accept this!" She almost looked worried.

"Nonsense," Oliver waved it away, climbing atop his horse as the two Gilded Wolves did the same. "I purchased him for you. You'll find a day's wages in the saddlebag." And then he turned his horse, storming away before she could protest further.

After all, what's the point in being royalty if I can't pamper the people I care about?

As he rode in between his guards, Poliander shouted over the clamorous hooves, "Very smooth, Sire." Oliver laughed deeply, knowing the man's qualms with Oliver courting the Lowborn, but appreciating the jest all the same.

He knew it may be temporary; however, Oliver believed for the first time in... well, he didn't know how long, that his life was headed in the right direction.

Chapter 9

ARA STROKED THE NECK of the horse, taking in the magnificence of the powerful animal. His chestnut fur and mane, the tail swishing back and forth. Then she climbed atop his back and ushered him forward. *Well, I'll have to call him something.*

"How about Oswin," she said to the horse, patting his neck. The horse whinnied softly, and she took that as approval. She smiled.

Ara kicked the horse, urging him to move faster. She caught up with Calder, bringing the horse around in front of him before climbing down.

"Cal, please wait," she begged. "Talk to me."

Calder shook his head, trying to move around Ara. "No, it's okay, Ara. You can run off with Prince Charming and become queen one day. I won't stop you."

"You don't even know if that's what I want!" He couldn't have known what she wanted; *she* didn't even know. Her temper was rising; Ara felt heat coursing through her. The darkness inside her body was replaced by the rays of the sun.

Cal shook his head, laughing sarcastically. "I saw the look on your face when you were ogling him. I've known you all our lives, Ara. You promised we would leave this place someday. Together. But that's alright, I know people change. It's probably my fault for being so hopeful. You're allowed to be with whoever you choose. Even if he is a royal milksop."

"At least he had the gall to ask my father if he could court me," Ara snapped. Her fists were clenched, a flash of guilt striking through her as he stopped his progress.

Her friend looked at her for a moment before storming away. He had a pained look in his eyes, but he held back, marching off through the grass.

Ara's eyes became warm, filled with tears. She wiped them away before they could spill. Climbing back onto Oswin, Ara spurred the horse away, heading for the rendezvous point with Cassandra. She spurred the horse several times, urging the beast to run faster. She would run its legs off if it meant her anger was vanquished.

When she made it to the spot where they'd previously departed, a crow flew past her and into the woods. She wondered if it was always the same bird that had watched over her throughout her life. Moments later Cassandra exited the Wraithwood.

Something came over Ara; she wasn't sure what it was, but she had the desire to throw her arms around the woman's neck. Her breathing became heavy as she attempted to hold in tears. The recent few days put calamity to her emotions like a thunderstorm.

"What's the matter, my dear?" Cassandra asked. Her voice sounded concerned, but her eyes told a different story, as if they already knew what the girl would say.

Ara couldn't withstand it. With a whimper she flung herself onto the older woman. Cassandra cried out in surprise, chuckled, and then returned the embrace. "I don't mean to be so intrusive," Ara said, words muffled against Cassandra's chest. "The past few days have been dreadful."

Cassandra pulled her away by the shoulders. "Tell me all about it. Let's get you some tea, hm?"

They tied the horse to one of the trees, and then Cassandra led Ara into the woods. "Where are we going?"

"My home, of course," Cassandra laughed.

The trip to the hut didn't take long. Ara stood in the center of a sitting room larger than the whole of her home. From the outside, the house looked nothing more than a quaint hovel. "It's not much," Cassandra commented, "but it's enough for me." With a wave of her hand, the tea kettle filled itself with water, then hooked onto the frame suspended over the flames of the hearth. Ara's mouth was agape with awe before the show of magic; seeing flames conceived from the woman's hands was brilliant.

"Not much?" Ara scoffed with a shake of her head. "Why, it's just *marvelous,* Cassandra. How is this possible? From the outside, I would have thought it more like my meager home."

Cassandra laughed. "It's simply magic, my dear. This home of mine has been enchanted; took me a time to get it right, though." She glanced around dazedly.

While they sat there, Ara recalled the recent events of the days they were apart. Cassandra did nothing but nod every now and then, listening intently to what Ara was saying. She seemed to be very understanding of Ara's ill feelings.

"I didn't expect your father to come around to the idea of you and I spending time together," Cassandra said. "He has always believed I am in some way responsible for your mother's death."

"I didn't know you knew about that," Ara replied, her eyes shooting down to her feet. She felt guilty that she'd already forgotten about her father's accusation of Cassandra. This only compounded with her guilt of lying about her Pa's approval to visit the woman.

She dismissed it. "Don't worry, dear. Gaius accused me years ago when Adina first passed. Another reason I never came around you. I was never sure what he thought I'd done to her. She was my only friend." Cassandra's head dropped sadly.

"From how kind you've been to me, I can't imagine you harming my mother."

Cassandra looked back up, a smile growing on her face. "That's splendid to hear." She clapped her hands together, rising to her feet as the tea kettle began to whistle. "Now then, shall we have some tea before we begin?"

"Begin what?" Ara asked, confused.

"Why, your first lesson in the world of magic, of course," she said, hands going to her hips.

THE SORCERESS HELD UP a medallion with a circular emerald in the center. It was opaque, almost cloudy. The gold around the stone had points all around, like the tines of spears. She wore an identical one, except the stone was brighter, more translucent. A soft breeze flitted through the treetops above their heads.

"This medallion is necessary for our magic to work," Cassandra said. They'd gone outside to begin practicing. "Magic is born from the energy found in life; it's all around us, gifted to us by the gods." She draped the golden chain of the medallion over Ara's neck.

"So, how does it work?" Ara asked, rotating the stone in her fingers.

"It's very simple. Let's start with something small." Cassandra bent down, plucking a weed from the dirt, then gestured for Ara to do the same. "The secret to making this work is to imagine the plant's lifeforce melting away and becoming your own. Close your eyes, focus on the energy coming from the weed."

Ara did as Cassandra instructed. "Yes, very good," Cassandra said. "Now, pull the energy into yourself."

Ara felt a faint pulsing coming from the plant. By focusing, it was as if she could feel a heartbeat. She did as instructed and felt the plant she was holding fade and wilt. When she opened her eyes, the weed was a duller version, closer to death. There was a small part of it that felt wrong, unnatural, to be taking life from something. There was another part that gave Ara a great sense of power and accomplishment. Cassandra beamed at her. The medallion pulsed softly one time, and then stopped. It looked a little less cloudy.

"Excellent!" Cassandra picked a flower for Ara. "Again."

"What happens if we take too much?" She studied the little thing curiously.

"Well, do it and you shall see."

Ara did it again, keeping her eyes open the second time. She watched the life flee from the plant, and once again saw the emerald stone pulse. Ara wondered if it was possible to do this with something larger. "Cassandra, what does this do? Collecting the life of plants, I mean. Wouldn't it be more efficient to use something larger?"

She nodded, walking circles around Ara as she spoke. "As you take the energy of life from living beings, it gets stored in this medallion. When you've garnered enough energy, you'll be able to conjure magic. It's figuring out the proper way to *use* magic that's hard. It took me years to decipher it all—and I seriously doubt I know all there is to know about it—but luckily for you, you have me. But yes, using larger beings would make collecting faster; however, it will take a toll on you as well. You don't notice it because the plants are so small, but if you were to say, take the life of a cow, well... you would likely die along with it. Through time and practice you will grow stronger, and the size of beings you can drain will increase."

Ara chuckled with a shiver. "I'd say it's best if we stick to the plants." She abhorred the thought of taking life from animals so brazenly.

I could use this on the nyssavir, though, she thought.

This process went on and on until a pile of crumbled plants lay at Ara's feet, and the emerald was far clearer than it had been. "Now for the fun part," Cassandra said, her eyes wide and a grin splayed on her face.

The woman demonstrated what she wanted Ara to do, first by gathering up the lifeforce of several plants. When she was satisfied with the glow coming from her stone, she turned Ara's attention to her palm. Cassandra whispered something and, before Ara's eyes, orange flames began dancing across her hand, flickering across her fingers. The ball of fire grew to the size of a small boulder, and then Cassandra hurled it at a small patch of dried dirt. The flames flickered for a moment then waned, suffocated by the lack of kindling.

"That was... amazing," Ara said, her eyes wide with excitement to try her hand at the magic. "What else can you do, Cassandra?"

The woman smirked. "The limit of magic is only our imagination, Ara. It would be easier for me to name the things I *can't* do."

"Don't worry, you'll get it eventually," Cassandra told Ara. Ara had uttered the word, "helsha", which meant fire in the arcane tongue. She'd done everything the sorceress told her but was still unable to create so much as a spark in her palm, much less cast a flame. Ara looked at her, feeling dejected; she didn't want to disappoint the woman after all that work. It had been nearly half a day; Ara was drenched to the bone with sweat, and her head ached from the mental exhaustion of trying to magically produce a flame. She'd repeated the steps countless times, taken breaks to drink water and rest her mind, and still... nothing.

"Maybe magic isn't for me," Ara said.

"Oh, nonsense, dear child." Cassandra stared into her eyes intensely. "Allow me to look within you, see if I can find that which blocks your magic from rising to the surface." Ara stepped forward and Cassandra placed a hand on her head, closing her eyes.

The woman's face was tight with concentration for several seconds before her eyes opened and she stepped back, breathing hard. "What is it? What did you see?" Ara looked at her, fear widening her eyes.

What's wrong with me?

"There is something blocking your magic, as if the magic were a river being stopped by a beaver's dam. Worry not, Ara; I know of a way to remove the blockage. Let us end this lesson. Go home and rest. I will send a message to you soon. I must first take a trip to gather some materials. There is a ritual I know of that will help remove this blockage. Are you up for a grand adventure, Ara?"

"An adventure?" Ara perked up. "I've never traveled more than a league away from Osta." It sounded daunting.

"Sounds like you're due an adventure or two anyway!" She seemed excited for the trip, but Ara worried it would be too much trouble.

"I hate to be such a bother," she said. Despite the accusations her Pa had made against Cassandra, the woman was nothing but kind to Ara. *She couldn't* possibly *be responsible for Mother's disappearance.*

Cassandra pulled her into a hug. "Don't speak like that, my dear. This is not your fault. Sometimes things just don't happen the way we want them to." They broke apart and smiled at one another. Ara turned on her heel, waving goodbye to the mage.

Ara made her way home, trying not to feel defeated by her failure to produce even the slightest bit of magic. When she arrived, her father was washing his hands in the water basin. The door banged shut behind her, and he turned with a smile on his face. Ara saw his eyes drop to the medallion. The smile fled from his face; the towel he'd been using to dry his hands fell to the floor. The blood in his face fled, a ghostly pallor taking root on him.

Chapter 10

SANDIN RAVOC'S STEP WAS light as he leapt across stones just big enough to catch the ball of his feet. He'd spent many a day navigating the slippery terrain in the mountains of Abithia. Many of his countrymen were burly and rugged due to the nature of living in the mountains, but Sandin was not like most. Not in any sense of the word. He crept down from the rocks like a predatory cat.

His mark was nearby, drinking from a stream in the Maranthol Pass. Ice covered the pass nearly year-round, melting during the day and refreezing as the moon emerged.

A man by the name of Therndil had wronged the queen. She did not take lightly to treason, and to her, making a pass at her in her throne room—even in a drunken stupor—was considered treason.

Perhaps, Sandin thought, *we would have been friends in a another life, Therndil. However, this is not another life, and you have been marked.*

In the night, Sandin became one with the shadows. How many times had he done this? Too many for him to remember.

Shadowspire taught him well.

Sandin liked to watch his marks from time to time, especially when he was not pressed for another mission. It was interesting to watch a man live out his last moments. Therndil's breath created plumes of white against the chill of night. It was the way they all seemed oblivious to their mortality that intrigued Sandin.

But first, Sandin thought. *Let's have a little fun.*

A pebble—flicked from Sandin's hand—skittered across the ground. Therndil spun toward the sound, a dagger gliding from his belt. "Somebody there?" he asked. He looked directly at Sandin, but the assassin was too skilled at hiding within the shadows. He'd put his head down, allowing his cloak to conceal his face from the dim moon; he was stalk still. The silver clasp on his cloak was expertly covered by a piece of fabric, disallowing the moonlight to reflect off it.

He waited for Therndil to turn back to filling his waterskin, then looked back up. Sandin crept up on the man. A blown breath on the man's ear, and he was gone before Therndil could turn around. Sandin tapped the man on the shoulder, behind him again. Therndil started and turned slowly, breath coming from him rapidly. His eyes went down to the clasp—now visible—holding the assassin's cloak shut.

His eyes went wide. He stuttered, "Y-you're him. The…" Therndil's voice trailed away. Sandin tried to stick to the edges of their society; easier to move about undetected without people recognizing his face. However, there were things about him that he just couldn't keep hidden from everyone. His fame had risen substantially over the last couple of years, much to his displeasure. Stories of the Royal Dagger wafted through pubs; some of them were true, others were not.

Sandin nodded. "I would allow you to say a prayer before entering the afterlife, but you're already dead."

Therndil opened his mouth to speak, perhaps to try bartering his way out of the situation. It wouldn't work. The only person who could stop Sandin's hands was the queen. There was a flash of metal, a squelch as pink mist peppered the air, and then gurgling. Therndil clutched at his throat, blood spilling over his fingers as he dropped to his knees. Within seconds, he'd fallen face down into the mud.

Curious work, being an assassin. Therndil had probably thought he was safe; maybe even thought he would escape Stoneforge Keep and hide out in the mountains until his name was just a memory to people. He should have known better. He was no different than any other whose name was passed from the queen's lips to Sandin's ears. Sandin liked to refer to his marks as the living dead, because once a target was given to him, their life was forfeit.

Chapter 11

OLIVER FINISHED HIS ROUNDS through the kingdom after having his dinner with Lord Simeon and was back in Valendra before long. When he marched back into the palace, he saw many people wearing charcoal gray robes. *Gray robes of mourning; someone has died.* Dread slowly enveloped him, a cloak of shadow creeping up his back.

"Prince Oliver," Fatilda—one of the royal cooks—exclaimed at the sight of him, "thank Gorenos you're here." He looked at the woman who'd always been like a beloved aunt to him. She had tears rolling down her cheeks; her eyes were red.

"What has happened, Fatilda?"

She sobbed, taking a deep breath to try to regain her composure. "It's your father. King Torril is dead."

Prince Oliver's heart dropped into his stomach. "Where is he?" The words came out like a growl.

"I believe he's in the morgue now, Sire."

Oliver touched her gently on the arm. He didn't want her to think he was angry with her. "I must go." He raced through the corridor toward the stairs that led down into the morgue. The smell of death was in the air—likely from those who'd been long dead.

Shoving open the wooden doors, he first saw his father's feet sticking out from under a sheet. The prince shuddered slightly as his eyes moved over the king's body.

It's true. He's really gone, he thought.

Oliver thought he would be angry, sad; however, it was more like a numbing ice had spread over him. He didn't know what to feel.

The royal physician was examining the body, attempting to glean the cause of death. The old man's voice croaked out, "Terribly sorry for your loss, Sire. Your mother and sisters are in the king's chambers if you'd like to see them. They've been mostly inconsolable since it happened."

"What *did* happen here, Philip?" Oliver asked.

"As far as I can tell, Sire, it was likely a poison of some sort; ingested through the wine, though I'll need to test the bottle he drank from to know for certain."

"Poisoned wine?" Oliver shook his head. *He wasn't supposed to die like this. It's too easy.*

"Well, the day started like any other," Philip began. "King Torril was having breakfast with the rest of your family. They opened a bottle of wine from the pantry, and the king was the only one to drink from it—thank Gorenos. Within the next few minutes, he began breathing rather haggardly, and then ultimately keeled over. I tried to revive him, but it was no use."

"I see," Oliver replied, nodding. "This wine, where did it come from?"

"The stewards who brought the wine from the pantry have all been questioned, and none claim to have any knowledge of its origin. To top it off, the bottle bore no label."

"Thank you, Philip. I'll leave you to it." Oliver dragged himself from the room, feeling bile working up his throat. Puking on the stairs, he stood there a moment and could smell his sick. He walked up the stairs at a snail's pace.

The prince gently pushed the door, opening the king's bed-chamber. His mother and sisters were sitting on the extravagant bed, talking quietly. His youngest sibling, Ruelle, ran to him. She flung her arms around his waist, crying into his stomach. Reaching beneath her arms, Oliver lifted the small child up, holding her in his arms like he used to. She was far too big for it now. That's when his tears broke free. Seeing his father's dead body brought no tears from his eyes; however, seeing his family in such a state broke his heart. His soft spot for them shone brightly at that moment.

Prince Oliver carried Ruelle back to the bed, sitting down next to the others. Queen Amelda, Camille, and Layla all wrapped their arms around him and Ruelle. They sat that way for a while, so long that

Oliver didn't realize how much time had passed until the darkness of the sky through the windows dimmed the light of the room.

TENSIONS IN THE PALACE were at an all-time high; Philip had declared that King Torril was murdered, resulting in a full-scale investigation to be launched by the High Inquisitor—Lord Tiberius Theron. The word of King Torril's poisoning spread quickly. Thinking of that made Oliver tremble. Attempts had been made on the lives of past kings, but he couldn't recall any that had been successful. He knew of an ancestor who'd lost use of his legs after a failed attempt on his life. The man who'd made the attempt was a saddle maker who'd rigged the king's horse with a torn saddle. His death was prolonged.

The prince found himself eternally grateful to Gorenos that his mother hadn't also drank from it. Oliver felt he was in no position to be raising children. He also didn't think he was ready for the throne, but knew there was no stopping his ascension.

A fortnight had passed, and Oliver was preparing for his official coronation to become king of Gosatha. His mother would be the one to perform the ceremony as she was acting as regent. He wished Ara could be there to see it; perhaps her presence would loan him some courage.

After departing her village, Oliver found that his thoughts would constantly wander back to the girl he met there—Ara. She had a grip on his heart. Thinking of her—of her beauty and fiery spirit—made all other things seem to melt away. It was like having a reprieve from the troubles of life plaguing him.

Coronation day left the prince with jittery nerves threatening to explode from his body at any moment. He rocked back and forth on the balls of his feet. "Calm your mind, child," his mother told him in that soothing voice of hers. "You're ready."

"How can you be so sure?" Oliver was still rife with doubt that he could lead his people. "Father never believed in me."

"Never mind what he would think, boy," she snapped. "You *must* be ready, and so you will be. Gosatha is doomed without a Jardanis on the throne."

He didn't respond, save for a simple nod.

Oliver didn't think himself ready for the responsibility he would inherit when the crown was placed on his head. There was so much more for him to learn, he felt. Regret built in him. Regret for not focusing more on politicking, for not listening to the wisdom his father had tried to impart to him so often. And though he wasn't ready to take his rightful place upon the throne, he already knew what his first act as king would be: find his father's murderer.

And to Icuzar I shall send them, he thought.

Inquisitor Tiberius had been as exhaustive as he possibly could. He'd interrogated every member of the king's retinue, every person who was seen entering or exiting the palace on that *dreadful* day. The investigation was fruitless; the killer still roamed free, and they were no closer to knowing who it was. Oliver was almost certain that meant it had been someone sneaky, someone who might have even come in the dark of night.

Despite the lack of care—or love—that King Torril had shown Oliver, he hadn't wished for his father's death. He still loved him as a son should. He didn't know how he was going to do what the High Inquisitor couldn't, but was determined, nonetheless. Oliver shook his head to rid himself of those thoughts as he trudged down the corridor.

The colossal oak doors to the throne room opened, and murmurs reached Oliver's ears as he strode across the threshold. He set a steely look upon his face; if he couldn't gather the confidence needed for such a high duty, he'd fake it. The chatter ceased. They marched toward the empty throne with Amelda slightly behind him. To the left and right of the throne stood the royal councilmen. Lord Tobias held a small pillow with the crown atop it, his face twisted into a scowl. That perked Oliver up some, to see the councilmen being forced to watch the prince they so deeply despise become their king.

Lord Ozin on the other side of the throne held the sword in one hand, the ring in the other. He didn't appear to be quite as unhappy about the occasion.

Oliver stopped, spinning around to face the crowd of witnesses—lords and ladies from all over Valendra. Queen Amelda walked around behind him. He heard the clinking of the sword. His nerves were alight with jitters.

In a voice louder than he thought his mother capable of, she said, "This ceremony is one that brings me both great joy and deep pain.

The death of King Torril Jardanis was unexpected, though we must surge forward. You, Valendrans, bear witness to this coronation of Oliver Jardanis." She paused, letting her words melt with the crowd, then addressed the prince. "Do you, Prince Oliver Jardanis, swear to bear the Sword of Gorenos, to protect this kingdom from the forces of darkness until the day you draw your last breath?"

"I do," Oliver said loudly enough for all to hear. The sword was strapped around his waist.

"Do you, Prince Oliver Jardanis, swear to make decisions that are in the best interest of the Gosathan Kingdom?"

"I do." She slipped the ring onto his pinky. He wanted to glance down at it, but kept his eyes forward, begging his hands not to shake as he knew they wanted to.

His mother stood directly in front of him, her gaze unyielding. "Do you, Prince Oliver Jardanis, swear to do your duties as protector of our realm, to crush your enemies without mercy?"

Without hesitation, Oliver replied, "I do."

"Then I, Amelda Jardanis, with the citizens of Valendra as witness, crown you with great confidence." She placed the glittering crown atop his head. "*King* Oliver Jardanis—sovereign of Gosatha!"

The people rose to their feet, cheers of delight roaring around the throne room. All those things he wanted to change about his kingdom came rushing to him. He made two vows to himself that day. First, he would lead with more love than anger, more mercy than judgement. Second, he would become the greatest king the world had ever known. Even if it killed him.

Chapter 12

NEVER IN HER LIFE had Ara's father not spoken to her for such a long time. She worried the magic of the medallion had suddenly released without her knowing, that it struck him, causing him to lose his wits. When he'd laid eyes on it, Gaius became pale and fainted. Beside herself, Ara worked at the butcher shop for days, awaiting her Pa's recovery.

She would come home, check on him, trying to rouse him from the comatose state. He would mutter incoherent ramblings, roll around, and then become still again. She was at a loss as to how to help him. She feared he would starve or die of thirst before waking up.

Ara tracked down the Ostan physician and asked him to see her Pa. When he'd finished examining him, the man told her he couldn't figure out why Gaius would not wake. He couldn't be helped. He would either snap out of whatever it was, or he would stay sleeping forever. Ara cried herself to sleep most nights, the guilt eating away at her. She couldn't help but feel that he would still be okay had she not gone to see Cassandra in the first place.

Despite knowing the medallion was most likely what set Gaius off, Ara went back to Cassandra's home out in the Wraithwood. She found the shack empty, wondering if perhaps this was Cassandra's plan all along. First, she'd done something to Ara's mother, and then tricked her into taking that devilry into her Pa's midst. *No, I'm just pushing off the blame,* she thought. A fortnight had gone by and there'd still been no word from Cassandra. Ara was becoming increasingly antsy.

"Please, Pa," she whispered, stroking her father's head softly after returning home. "Wake up. Whatever I did... I... please come back to me." A single tear raced down her cheek.

Gaius didn't stir. Ara left the confines of their home, unable to look at her incapacitated father any longer. A crow landed on the eve of the hut, making no sound aside from the bird's feet on wood. Ara glanced up at it.

"Just me and you, I guess," she said to the bird. Then a thought struck her. What if this was a sign from Cassandra? When they met, Cassandra told her that she'd been watching from a distance. *Can she communicate with this creature?*

Ara wasted no time, rising to her feet and jumping on the back of her horse. Being on top of the magnificent beast brought back thoughts of Prince Oliver. The skin of her cheek felt prickly at the memory of his lips, but there was no time to reminisce on that. She spurred the horse forward as the crow took flight, soaring high in the sky over Ara's head.

"Faster, Oswin," she commanded. Then to herself, "She *has* to be there this time."

Fawning over Oliver made her feel silly. She was acting as if the prince was going to wed her or something. She'd only just met the man; thinking he was serious about courting her was nothing but a fantasy.

Finally, Ara reached the Wraithwood.

Cassandra stood in wait at the edge of the trees, her teeth shining from the smile on her face. Ara jumped off the horse, pulling the medallion from a pocket. She looked at the faint emerald in the center as the dying sun glinted off it. She tossed it to Cassandra.

"I can't do this anymore," Ara told her.

"What do you mean?"

"Being a sorceress; this magic... I can't do it. Something h-horrible has happened to my Pa." She began to choke up as she said the words aloud. "He took one look at that necklace and fainted. I don't know if he will ever recover."

"Oh, dear," Cassandra said, looking at the medallion. "I hate to hear that, Ara. Gaius is a good man." She sighed, then looked back at Ara, holding a finger up. "There may be something I can do."

Ara brightened. "There is?"

"I don't want to get your hopes up too much, but it's possible. I'd like to try; it's the least I can do." She moved toward Oswin. "Take me to Gaius, girl."

ARA RODE LIKE HER life depended on it with Cassandra jostling around behind her. Her arms were like a snake tightening around Ara's waist. They made it back to her home as the dark of night engulfed them. Ara rushed into her home with the sorceress trailing.

She lit an oil lamp so they could see and brought Cassandra to her father. Ara watched eagerly as she took Gaius' head in her hands, closing her eyes. Enough time passed that Ara began to worry that Cassandra would be unable to fix him. She bit her lip before rambling.

"I have something to ask you," Ara said, then waited to see if Cassandra would reply.

"Go on," she finally said, keeping her eyes closed.

"When we met, you told me that you'd watched me from afar," she recalled. "Do you control the crow?"

"The crows are many. You'll need to elaborate, Ara."

She sighed, hoping Cassandra wouldn't think she'd gone mad. "For as long as I can remember, there's always been a crow following me around. Just this night I spotted one atop the roof of my home, and that's when I found you waiting for me."

"I do not control the crow," Cassandra said, a faint humor in her tone. "I am the crow."

Ara almost laughed. She probably would have if not for Gaius choosing that exact moment to awaken.

"Pa!" Ara couldn't resist throwing her arms around his neck. He coughed slightly as she helped him sit up. Cassandra moved toward the door.

"What in the world has happened?" Gaius spluttered.

"You don't remember anything?" Ara stroked his bearded cheek.

"I remember seeing something... something horrible," he said.

"It was the green medallion."

His eyes went wide. "Yes. That was it. That *dreaded* medallion. Your mother had one just like it. Right before she disappeared." He looked like he was remembering it all again. "I was trapped in my mind, nothing but darkness and despair. Oh, damn it all. How did you pull me from that wicked place, Ara?"

Ara looked over her shoulder. Cassandra had slipped out silently while they reunited. "It wasn't me, Pa. I couldn't rouse you from your sleep. It was Cassandra. She brought you back somehow. I gave that medallion back to her. You won't be seeing it again."

Gaius nodded. "Good, good. Give her my thanks and be done with her. I'm serious, Ara. Now, I know this may be hard to believe, but I need to rest. My head feels... heavy." He kissed her forehead and laid his head back down. She watched him for a while, listening to the soft sound of his exhales.

Ara checked outside for Cassandra, but didn't find her; she laid down on her bedroll, wondering about the mage and her secrets yet again. What did the sorceress mean when she'd told her she was the crow that watched over her all those years? How could that be possible? There was something strange revolving around Cassandra and her mother. If she'd had a necklace identical to the one Cassandra gave to Ara, does that mean she'd also tried teaching her magic back then? Does that have something to do with her mysterious disappearance? Ara wasn't sure she would sleep that night as her mind pondered all the implications.

She closed her eyes and thought, *I must find the truth... for Mother. If it's the last thing I do.*

Chapter 13

KING OLIVER SAT ON his throne—a throne white like the ivory of a bull horn—with one hand in his lap, the other folded into a fist with his chin resting on top. His elbow was propped up on the armrest. He tuned out the men standing before him, gathering battle plans as the war with Abithia raged on. There were days when Gosatha was winning, and others they saw defeat. The bloodied bodies of Gosathan soldiers—*his* soldiers—no longer made his stomach twist. It was far too often he watched them be carried into the morgue to be prepped for warrior funerals.

King Oliver couldn't dial in to focus on the words flying at him. His thoughts were stuck on the woman who visited him in his chamber the night of his coronation. It was impossible to sleep that night;

Oliver tossed and turned in what was once his fathers' bed. King Torril had been given a king's funeral, laid atop the finest wood they could find, and his body burned. They'd decided to keep the affair small; only family, councilmen, and aides found themselves there.

Oliver had returned to the king's chamber, and as he struggled to sleep, a woman appeared at his bedside. He'd nearly had a stroke as she materialized from the shadows.

"Apologies, young king," she'd drawled. Her voice was mesmerizing. The ends of dark hair spilled out from beneath the hood of her cloak. He'd thought it was his mother at first, but she hid her face from him which he found odd.

"Who are you?" He'd demanded, slowly reaching for the sword beside his bed. "And how did you get past my guards?" He was only a moment from calling out to them.

Her voice sounded almost panicky. "Please, your Majesty, I mean you no harm. I was sorry to hear about the passing of King Torril, but I am privy to some information about his death; that which I'm sure you'd want to hear."

It was all very strange, but he had leaned forward, curiosity taking hold of him. "Tell me."

He thought he saw the hint of a smirk on her lips but told himself it was a trick of the dark playing with his eyes. "The poisoned wine... I know where it came from. I know *who* it came from."

"Yes?" King Oliver's heart was slamming with anticipation to learn who'd killed his father.

"Gaius Lowborn of Osta." In a blink the woman vanished. Oliver was left with a slackened jaw, unable to question her further.

Oliver's hands shook with vehemence. How could this be possible? *How could Gaius do such a thing after being so kind to me,* he thought. No, Oliver told himself it was just an illusion born of his sleep depravity. Gaius would never commit such a crime. Unless, of course, he wanted his daughter to be queen. Afterall, he didn't know the man—or Ara for that matter. They could be conspiring together.

Gaius would have had plenty of time to get the bottle here before I returned.

Several days had gone by, and he still couldn't pull his thoughts from that night. As he sat there thinking about it, the king made a decision—one which the Royal Council would not approve of. He needed to travel to Osta to find out for himself. He would interrogate Gaius—perhaps with the help of the High Inquisitor—and if he found the man guilty... well, his head would roll. His feelings for Ara be damned; justice held mercy for no one.

"Did you hear what I said, Majesty?" Lord Leander asked, yanking Oliver from his rumination.

Oliver's eyes snapped up. "Hm? Forgive me, Leander. My mind was elsewhere. What did you say?"

The lord sighed impatiently but held his tone level. "There is an island that our forces have been fighting the Abithians over for many moons. The soldiers have begun to call it the Isle of Death. The surrounding waters are filled with blood and bodies, destroyed ships. Our numbers are dwindling, Majesty, and if we don't do something, we will be overtaken. The queen's men will push us back to our shores."

Oliver nodded, closed his eyes, and pinched the bridge of his nose between thumb and forefinger. "Do you know what drives Queen Gadiel? What makes her continue this onslaught? Do you know why *we* have continued this fight for so long?" Nothing but silence was his answer.

"No, of course you don't," Oliver continued. "I will meet with Queen Gadiel." He turned to Tobias, ignoring the sharp inhalations of surprise. "Tobias, send a messenger to the shores of Abithia. Carry the message of peace. I want to meet somewhere neutral, somewhere free of bloodshed."

"Majesty, I must warn against—" Leander interjected, but the king cut him off with a raised hand. His father would have never allowed someone to question his orders.

"Enough," King Oliver said. He put on the sternest face he could muster. "You will do this. Now." With that, the king dismissed them and made his way to High Inquisitor Tiberius' chambers. Three of the Gilded Wolves moved through the corridors with him.

"Wait out here," he ordered them once they'd reached the inquisitor's chamber. He knocked lightly and then pushed his way in.

"Good thing I'm decent, Majesty," Tiberius grumbled.

King Oliver smirked. "You needn't worry. I'll not tell a maiden of anything I see." The two chuckled and he continued, "Your help is needed, Tiberius." He lowered his voice. "I'm not sure of who all I can trust, but I know I can count on you."

"My King, I am yours to command," he replied dutifully.

"Yes, I know, but this is of the utmost importance. You were always very loyal to my father, and I hope you will share that loyalty with me now. I have a lead on my father's death." Tiberius perked up; half of his face was illuminated by a flickering candle. "I can't tell you how I've come to know this information, and you mustn't tell anyone else about this. I don't want to incite a panic."

Tiberius nodded. "Where will we be going?"

Oliver was glad the older man didn't protest. "Osta."

"And when will we leave?"

"This night. Meet me at the stables after nightfall."

"Understood, Your Majesty."

KING OLIVER SPOKE WITH his mother about what he was planning to do; she was the only one who could know. The Royal Councilmen would not approve of the king riding off to a village that was nearly a hundred leagues away to investigate the death of his father. Not that they could stop him even if they wanted to, but the old coots held a lot of favor with the citizens of the kingdom, especially the Highborn. They could turn them against him if he wasn't careful, and the last thing he needed was a revolt.

"Come back to me," the Queen Mother had told him. She kissed his cheek as a silent tear ran down her face. Oliver said nothing to her, but gave a stern look as if to say, "Of course I will."

A guard was left at his door and was ordered not to enter, nor allow anyone but the Queen Mother passage until told otherwise. Amelda would act as regent until Oliver's return in case of emergencies. He just hoped none would arise.

King Oliver and High Inquisitor Tiberius fled through the night on horses so black they would be lost in the darkness. Nothing but the light of the moon, and the memory of the roads led them across the land. He made sure to dress in his mute garb, rather than the lavish robes of a king, and left the crown sitting atop his pillow.

The closer they drew to Osta, the more Oliver's excitement grew—as did his dread. As the horses' hooves crashed along the ground, the sounds echoing around the hills, King Oliver pictured Ara. When he thought about making her his queen, it made his heart sing with joy. The image of her blazing red hair was burned into his mind.

Let me be wrong.

That also came with knowing what he was going to do in Osta. If he and Tiberius found Gaius to be guilty, he would execute him on the spot, and Ara would never forgive him. He could tell that she was a kind and forgiving person, but even if she knew that her father killed the king, she wouldn't want him to die. That was the power of a daughters' love.

Riding through the night—and only stopping a couple of times for the horses to quench their thirst—the two men arrived in Osta the following day. As the structures of the village came into view, they slowed their horses so as not to scare any of the villagers. Those who recognized his face bowed as he passed, showing that word of his ascension to the throne had made it there.

Oliver's mind began playing out different scenarios as they trotted out of the village. Gaius' home laid just another league away. He wondered if the man would attack them. Would he beg and plead for mercy? Would he threaten the life of his daughter to aid his escape? That thought made Oliver's blood boil. *Surely Gaius isn't that foolish.*

"It's just there," Oliver said, pointing at the small house. Two figures materialized outside.

"I'll follow your lead, Majesty," Tiberius told him, falling back just a little.

As he got close enough to see their faces, Ara's lips spread into a wide smile; he couldn't contain it and allowed a smile on his face as well. Oliver's eyes darted to Gaius; the man wore a simple smirk, and Oliver's anger threatened to burst out with great vigor. It killed the smile.

"I didn't expect you to return so soon," Ara said as she rushed forward. Oliver climbed down and heard Tiberius grunt with the effort of doing the same. The inquisitor was an excellent fighter, but he was getting far in age, and it had been some time since his combat skills were used.

Gorenos, guide my words.

"It wasn't originally part of my plan," he said solemnly. He was fatigued from the long ride which only enflamed his dour mood. His lips pressed into a hard line.

Ara's eyes glanced to his waist. She pointed at the golden sword. Even the lowly people of Osta would know the sacred Sword of Gorenos. It was the one item of his kingship he couldn't leave behind. By her surprise, Oliver assumed she hadn't heard the news like the rest of Osta. "Does this mean—"

"That I've been made King of Gosatha?" Oliver interjected, then nodded. "Indeed, it does."

"I had no idea," she replied, taking a knee. Her father followed suit with a bewildered look on his face. Oliver eyed him.

"Please, rise," he said flatly.

"I suppose congratulations are in order," Gaius said, coming forward with his hand outstretched. The sound of a sword unsheathing cut through the air, and Tiberius was at the king's side instantly. A sword tip beckoned for the man to try something nefarious.

"That's close enough," Tiberius growled.

Ara and Gaius both recoiled, fear written on their faces. Ara said, "Oliver, what is going on?"

"*King* Oliver," Tiberius corrected harshly. Oliver didn't speak.

Ara recoiled further, glaring at the king.

Instead of looking at the girl, Oliver held eye contact with Gaius. "King Torril Jardanis died while I was on my rounds through the kingdom. Murdered." He didn't stop at their gasps. "It was learned that he drank from a bottle of wine containing poison. For a time, we didn't know who or where the wine came from; however, I have come across new information. The poison came from Osta. It came from you, Gaius Lowborn." Oliver wasn't certain if it *was* Gaius, of course, but he wanted to see the raw reaction those words induced. And what he saw did naught to sway his mind.

Chapter 14

"HAVE YOU LOST YOUR wits?" Ara stepped in between King Oliver and her father. "He would never do such a thing!"

King Oliver's companion pointed at Ara. "Watch your tongue, *Lowborn.*" He spat the last word like it had a bad taste.

Oliver didn't react to the man's words, didn't react to the hurt on Ara's face. She turned to find her Pa just staring back at the king with his mouth hanging open, stuttering as if he was having trouble speaking. "Tell him, Pa."

Gaius shook his head. "I don't understand why this accusation is being thrown at me, Majesty. I would never harm another person unjustly, especially not the king. What evidence do you have against me?"

Oliver sighed. "Thus far, I have only the word of one person. We are here to gather any evidence we can. I hope to not find anything, Gaius, but we must find the truth at all costs. I hope you understand."

Tensions seemed to die down a bit. Ara cocked her head to the side. "Wait, who accused my father of this crime?"

"I'm not at liberty to say," he said, his eyes darting away. He looked over his shoulder at the man behind him. "This is High Inquisitor Tiberius Theron. Tiberius, search the home."

Ara moved like she was going to protest but thought better of it. The man was tall and thick, built like a woodland bear. Small scars riddled his cheeks. His eyes were a golden brown—matching his hair—and held wisdom that came with the experience of age. Tiberius moved around them cautiously, eyeing Gaius as if he posed some sort of danger. Ara moved next to him, grabbing his hand in hers. He was trembling. "It's going to be okay, Pa." He smiled sadly at her.

"This *is* rather unfortunate; I would have preferred to be here under different circumstances," Oliver told them. "This was not what I envisioned for my return to your home."

"Nor I," Ara noted. She didn't see how a relationship could blossom from that point. How could she go on humoring Oliver's advancements after he'd levied such a horrible accusation at her Pa? She found her infatuation that she'd felt for him begin to slip away, and it was replaced with aversion.

I was foolish to think anything between us could happen, she thought. *Blinded by my desire to leave my Lowborn status behind.*

A silence came between them, only interrupted minutes later, when Tiberius came from the small house. His hands were not empty; in each hand was a bottle of wine with no label. Ara looked at them. Was this the proof they'd use against her Pa? She'd never even laid eyes on those bottles before.

"My King," Tiberius said. "I found these in a cupboard." He held up the bottles of wine.

"What do you have to say for yourself?" King Oliver asked, glaring at Gaius as he turned one of the bottles over in his hands, the fire in his eyes alight again.

Gaius' eyes widened at the sight of the bottles. "I don't under-st—", he began but was cut off.

"An identical bottle was given as a gift to my father. That very bottle killed him." His words came out low, almost as a growl. "If these are so different, then prove it by drinking from one, and our business here can be finished."

Heat ignited in Ara's cheeks. "Now, wait just a second. I've never seen such a bottle in our home; if someone planted that bottle and it is poisoned, Pa would die too!"

"Be that as it may," Oliver continued, "Gaius has yet to defend himself."

"Pa?" Ara said, turning to him. He looked mortified.

Gaius shook his head slowly. "I'm innocent, Majesty. These are not ours; we don't even drink wine in our home," he said quietly. "There must be another way."

A sigh left Oliver's lips. "I suppose we could find something else to test this wine on."

The group looked around for a moment before Ara caught sight of a small toad sitting nearby. It was hidden by the shadow of a large rock, but she was able to catch it easily. She held out a hand. "Shall I make it drink?" Her lips were pressed into a thin line.

She saw Oliver's eyes linger on her for a moment; just long enough to make her squirm beneath his stare. There was something in his gaze—a sense of apprehension? Eventually, he handed the wine bottle to her. Carefully, Ara pried the toad's mouth open, dribbled a couple drops of purplish liquid into its gullet, and placed the creature back down.

So barbaric, she thought. *Please live. Please live.*

For several moments, the toad was fine; it merely sat in the grass. Then—as if struck down by a deadly force—the toad started writhing. It swiped at its face, squeaked a cry that made Ara recoil, then ceased movement. She took a step away from it as if she would catch a disease from standing too closely. Oliver nudged the thing with his foot.

No. This can't be.

The creature didn't stir. Ara could see the anger building within the king. His eyes slowly drifted up to her Pa, becoming like daggers the closer to his face they became. She jumped in front of him, drawing herself up in defiance.

"This is a mistake, Oliver," she said, her tone strong. "Someone has *framed* us. You must believe me."

His gaze flickered to her, softening. "Oh, Ara," he muttered. "You don't understand." He shook his head. "It isn't just I that demands resolution for the murder of my father. The law demands it, the *kingdom* demands it. The evidence is against you, Gaius." He turned back to the older man.

"Is there any other explanation you can think of?" Tiberius asked them.

Ara looked at Gaius. His mouth opened, closed, then he shook his head in defeat. Tears rimmed his eyes. "I can't explain any of this."

"Very well," King Oliver said. He ripped his sword free of its sheath. The magnificent sword gleamed in the sunlight. "On your knees." He pointed the tip of the blade at Gaius.

"No!" Ara wailed, jumping in between them. "You can't do this!"

Oliver's eyes darted toward her and then back to Gaius. She could see him struggling with what he was doing; she just needed to change his mind. He turned to the inquisitor. "Tiberius." The man grabbed Ara by her arms and dragged her out of the way. "On your knees, Gaius." The man did as ordered, tears coming down his face.

"No, stop this!" Ara continued to protest, struggling against the grips that Tiberius had. His fingers bruised her arms, but she didn't care. Her skin was searing with rage. Oliver stalked closer to Gaius, no longer listening to her words. He stood in front of him, looking down into the man's eyes. "I will *never* forgive you for this, Oliver!"

The king looked at her, hesitation in his eyes. His voice came out low. "I know. I don't blame you, Ara. If anyone can understand, it's me. Your father's actions have brought this upon himself. I wish things had turned out differently for us."

"Then leave," she begged. "Don't do this. You *know* he didn't do this. Put your sword down and walk away. It's not too late!"

His eyes turned back to a silently weeping Gaius. "Gaius Lowborn, as King of Gosatha, I find you guilty of the crime of treason by way of murdering your king. I hereby sentence you to execution to be carried out by my hand immediately. Have you any last words?"

Gaius looked up at Ara who'd gone still and silent. "I love you, Ara." Then he looked forward. Ara saw his face set in stone—a man prepared to die.

Everyone leaves me, she thought.

The king said, "May Gorenos have mercy on your soul and allow you safe passage to Volharis."

Ara wanted to believe that Oliver meant the words. Her mind flashed back to one of the religious texts she'd read.

A book titled, *The Path to Eternal Jubilance* read: Only those who find favor with Gorenos will be given entry to the joyous world of Volharis—a realm flowing with bread, cheese, and wine. Those who were found to be unworthy would spend eternity in Icuzar—the realm of shadow. A place where no light touches the ground, where nothing but the cries of mad souls can be heard.

The wingbeat of a hummingbird echoed in the silence following Oliver's words. With nothing else left to be done, Oliver laid the blade's edge on Gaius' shoulder, inches away from his neck. Ara dared not breathe, dared not look away. She watched Oliver's arm pull back, the sword level. The blade was said to be sharper than any other in creation. The king let his blade fly. Ara heard the sickening sound of metal gliding through flesh, muscle and bone.

More silence for a moment. Then Ara began to scream as her Pa's head fell from his shoulders, rolling across the ground. Tiberius let her go and her knees buckled. They hit the hard ground, sending a jolt of pain up her legs, nothing compared to the pain in her chest. Tears were streaming down her face. Sobs racked her body, and her breathing quickened. She felt lightheaded.

She saw Oliver move to help her up, but she swatted his hands away. "Leave," she screeched, slinging spittle from her mouth. He looked at her, his eyes bearing pity, before climbing back atop his steed.

Without another word, the king and his inquisitor fled on horseback. She peered toward the sky and, through sobs, said, "As the gods as my witness, Oliver Jardanis will pay for what he has done. I will make him suffer as he has made me suffer." She didn't care if that made her a monster. The one man who'd always been a constant, who had always given her unconditional love, was dead. Murdered by the king of Gosatha. Killed by a man who'd intended on courting her not that long ago. The dirt in front of Ara turned to mud before she found the strength to gather her feet beneath her.

The rest of that day was filled with the sounds of Ara burying her Pa beneath a pile of stones. When it was done, Ara lit the house on fire. She wouldn't return to that place; she *couldn't* return. The memory of watching her father's head falling would haunt her forever. Picking it up to bury with the rest of his body would leave unfathomable wounds; however, not all wounds can be seen.

AFTER NOTHING BUT ASH was left, Ara saddled up her horse, hating the way it made her feel to ride something that Oliver had given her. Part of her wanted to kill it out of spite for him. She spurred the animal away from the rising flames, heading for Cassandra's house.

"He's gone, Oswin," she said to the horse, not caring if it made her seem crazy. "You understand me well enough."

Ara tied Oswin up at the tree line, not wanting to spook him in the woods. Storming through the Wraithwood, Ara came upon the house quickly. Not bothering to knock, the girl burst through the door, causing the sorceress to jump.

"Dear gods, Ara, what in..." she trailed off, probably seeing the tear tracks on Ara's soot-stained face, the sweat on her brow.

"He killed him," she growled. "Oliver killed my Pa."

"What are you talking about, girl?"

"While Prince Oliver was away, King Torril was murdered by a poisoned bottle of wine. When Oliver returned and learned of this, someone told him that my Pa gave him that wine. He killed Pa." Ara's voice rose with each sentence. Tears scratched at her eyes to be released. A knot formed in her throat, but she choked it back down. She would not let them fall again; Ara was done with crying. She wanted revenge. Blood for blood.

"I am so terribly sorry, my dear. Come here." Cassandra pulled Ara into a hug. She didn't return the embrace.

When the woman let her go, Ara said, "Make me into a sorceress, Cassandra. I'm ready now. I'll do whatever it takes." She paused, looked down, and back up. "Oliver Jardanis will die."

Chapter 15

KING OLIVER AND HIS companion stopped for the night on their way back to Valendra; flames danced between the two men. Heat made Oliver's eyes swelter, but he wasn't sure if it was from the flames or remorse. He held his face in his hands and pulled back to find his palms wet. When he glanced over at Tiberius, the man was staring at him with a look on his face that the heat in Oliver's cheeks intensify. He was a king; he should not be crying.

"Don't pity me, Tiberius," he said quietly.

Gently, Tiberius replied, "It's not that, Majesty. I don't feel pity often, though at the moment, I feel that I can empathize with how you feel."

"Really?" he asked. He wanted someone to make him feel better about everything, to tell him there was nothing to worry about. Admitting that—even to himself—wasn't so easy, though. Doing the right thing had always seemed easy until being face-to-face with decisions that could affect his people.

"Aye," Tiberius said with a nod. "I've killed many men in my time, Majesty. Some of them were rotten, guilty, deserving of a slow death. Others I only thought guilty at that time. There have been moments when my work has led me to find men innocent only after I'd slain them. Taking a life is not an easy task for a kind man. You, Majesty, are one of the kindest men I've ever had the pleasure of knowing."

The tears flowed freely then, silent torrents rushing down his face. He still did not believe Gaius to be innocent, but he couldn't help but wonder why the man didn't fight for himself more. And if Oliver *was* so confident in his decision, why did it plague him so?

His mind wandered to the woman who visited him in his chamber that night. Who was she? Would she return to guide him to another execution?

"Please don't speak of this to anyone, Tiberius." He released a sigh. "Not until I'm ready."

"You have my word, Majesty" the inquisitor replied.

"You're a good friend," Oliver noted. "You're not like the councilmen."

Tiberius smiled. "Did I ever tell you about my time in the king's army, Majesty?"

"I don't believe so, no." Oliver leaned forward as Tiberius launched into a story.

"When I was a young man like yourself, I served in your father's army. For ten years I fought for Gosatha, killing the men of Abithia. I was deadly in the ways of the sword. When holding a blade, it's as if the weapon is as much a part of me as my arm."

Tiberius paused, the flames casting shadows over his face. Then he continued, "As I'm sure you know, you're Uncle Garmon died in battle, but I doubt you know the story behind it."

"Father said he was struck down in the Battle of Ten Nights," Oliver remembered. It was almost akin to a bedtime story his father would tell. The battle was so devastating that when it was over, the two forces had peace for sixty days. Oliver recalled there being an island so large it could be its own kingdom if not for the constant fighting. *Perhaps at one point there were people who lived there in peace,* he pondered.

"It happened on the island of Pertaman," Oliver said.

Tiberius nodded. "As you know, Pertaman was one of the main battlefronts in the war—and still is. The Abithians attacked in the dark of night; flaming arrows and boulders from stone casters rained down on our troops. The warriors held off the surge until daybreak, when the enemy relinquished. Gosathan generals returned the favor that following night. The battle continued every night for ten nights, only breaking to recover and strategize during the day. It was a bloody ten nights. The stink of dead men filled the air for many weeks after."

The inquisitor paused, looking down, the haunting of that time written plainly on his face.

He looked back up at Oliver. "It's true that Garmon was killed during that fight," Tiberius said, "but it was not an enemy that felled him. It was me."

"You? I don't understand."

"Despite the fires that burned, the flaming arrows that dropped from the sky, it was impossible to see through the pitch. We could only see those within a few feet of us. Someone ran into me from behind, and when I turned to defend myself, I only saw a blade in my face. I parried what I thought was an enemy sword and skewered the man behind it. It was only when I'd wetted my blade with Garmon's blood that I noticed he was a friend. My tears assaulted me instantly, just as yours do now."

Oliver nodded, completely in awe of the revelation. Tiberius went on, "I fled from the battlefield, feeling a coward for running from the pain I felt at killing my friend. I went to your father, turned myself in for the crimes I'd committed. He was so forgiving, so understanding of what I felt.

"King Torril didn't have me punished for what I'd done but rather lifted me up. He told me to let my tears flow proudly. To let the pain out, and then recover from it. The following day he named me an inquisitor. I'll never forget that.

"I know our stories are very different, but the point remains the same. Let your tears fall with pride, do not be ashamed for crying. Shame is only for the cowardly, and you Majesty, are no coward."

"Thank you for the kind words, Tiberius. The story as well." King Oliver wiped his face dry. The doubt in his decision to execute Gaius grew slightly then. What if he got the wrong man? What if he ruined his relationship with Ara for nothing?

Oh, Ara, he thought. *How I wish things could have been different.* She'd confirmed his fear that he'd live on as the man she hated most. He probably would never see her again, and he'd be a fool to try visiting the girl at her home after what he'd done. Oliver laid back and closed his eyes, deciding to accept that he'd gotten the right man. Afterall, a king needed to be unwavering in his decisions.

OLIVER SLIPPED INTO HIS mother's chamber to let her know that he was back, and she ordered the guards away from his room for a bit. No one ever knew that he'd left. The councilmen were waiting in the war room impatiently when he entered.

King Oliver felt... different, changed. The young boy who'd left his home had fled the moment he decided to end Gaius' life. As he took his seat, Oliver had but one thought.

Perhaps father and I aren't so different.

"Where were you, Majesty?" Lord Tobias asked.

He answered frankly, "You needn't worry over my whereabouts." Then, "Tell me, what of the messenger that has been sent to Abithia? Has he returned?"

Tobias chuckled. "About that, King Oliver, the rest of the council and I have agreed this is not a good idea. Queen Gadiel—" the king slammed his hands down as he rose from his seat.

"You have openly defied me for the last time, Tobias," he growled. The pain and anger of the past couple days rushed through him, mingling with the memories of all the snide remarks that issued from the Royal Council, especially Tobias, and rippled through him. Grabbing him by the front of his collar, Oliver nearly towered over the lord. He began pushing him away from the table, his hand flying to the hilt of his sword, ignoring the cries of surprise.

Words from his late father echoed in his mind from the many days he'd spent learning how to rule. *Gain the council's respect and your job will be ever easier,* he'd said. *If their respect eludes you, then capture them with fear. Fear is an excellent motivator.*

"What is the meaning of this?" Tobias screeched, batting at the king's grip futilely. His mousy voice just fueled Oliver's frustration.

"Let this be a warning to the rest of you," Oliver growled. "I *will not* have my word challenged." He shoved Tobias to the ground, pulling his sword free. He could see the fear in the man's eyes. Just a day ago, Oliver had been deeply saddened by the life he'd ended. He killed a man who seemed kind at first, though foolish for what he'd done.

Tobias, however, was a snake; he deserved to die, just as Gaius had. Oliver plunged his blade toward the wide-eyed face of Tobias. The gleaming tip stopped a hair's breadth short of Tobias' right eye.

The man blinked and his lashes grazed the steel; he gulped audibly. Oliver's teeth were clenched, his lips pressed into a hard line.

He seethed, "Defy my orders again and I will rip out your eyes and feed them to the nyssavir myself. Is that understood?"

The smell of piss unexpectedly filled Oliver's nostrils as piss darkened the stone beneath Tobias. "Y-yes, Your Majesty," he whimpered.

"Go clean yourself." The king pulled his blade away, tucking it back into its sheath. He turned back to the other councilmen as Lord Tobias gathered himself and scurried away, leaving tiny droplets in his wake.

Eyes moving over each of them, Oliver thought they seemed shocked, looking down at their hands, averting from his gaze. His father never had to shed blood in such a way, but he wouldn't have thought twice about it; he never had to buy anyone's respect with the price of blood.

And I am not him, he reminded himself.

Oliver took a deep breath. "Lord Leander, send a messenger to Abithia. Have twenty men go with him to the port city of Rambil. The ship is to be outfitted with the flag of messengers. They are to strike only in retaliation. Can I trust that you will make this happen?"

"Of course, My Liege," Leander said, his eyes darting up nervously. "I will see to it immediately." Leander rose and shuffled from the room.

Oliver sat back down in the king's seat. He looked around at each of the men, lingering on their eyes for a moment. He could see it there now. Fear. Respect. At that moment, he didn't care which it was. He solidified in their hearts that his word was law, that they were not above being killed for their impertinence.

Chapter 16

Taffy Raolin had only been a royal messenger for a couple of years when he received the order to sail to Abithia. The edict came as a world-shattering shock to the boy. To his knowledge, no Gosathan had ventured to the shores of Abithia without the intent to fight since before the war began. He wondered why he'd been chosen for that task. Was this a curse from the gods? A test from Gorenos himself?

Taffy prayed that he'd be allowed into Volharis if he were to fall during his quest. As a messenger, he was required to show up unarmed. The only thing he could find solace in was knowing he'd have the standard of a messenger flying above him. Then again, that may not mean much to the Abithians. To his understanding, mountain men were not known to be level-headed.

The twenty men that King Oliver sent on the ship did little to comfort the boy. If the Abithians decided to slaughter them, it would be all too easy in their territory.

Doesn't help that I'm scrawny and can't fight, he thought simply. It didn't fill him with dread, though; he'd grown used to the way he was made.

The waters of the Tamagau Sea churned against the hull of the ship, the *Dispatch.* Taffy stood at the prow, looking over the dark blue water, wishing to be anywhere but on that ship. *The nyssavir lurk in these waters,* he thought, shuddering.

"Are you ready, boy?" Captain Barnum asked him. The man was as large as Taffy's father, but his skin was darker. He had a couple of missing fingers and scars along both arms.

They were closing in on their destination and would reach Rambil before nightfall. Sea birds flew overhead, calling down with their loud cries. How badly Taffy wished he could be a bird, to fly away from everything and the impending sense of dread gnawing at him.

"I don't think nothing could make me any more ready, sir," he replied. "Although, I have never regretted being a messenger more than now, I think." He smirked at the amused look on the captain's face. Taffy enjoyed letting his natural dialect—that of the poorer Valendran Highborn—shine through at times.

"Chin up, son. We'll make it through this."

"How can you be sure?" Taffy shifted on his feet.

"I believe Gorenos rewards those who do good," the old captain said. "We're bein' sent straight into enemy lands to try gainin' a little peace between our two nations. If that ain't doin' something good, I don't know what is."

"Then maybe Gorenos will protect us," Taffy said, a little bit of hope rising in him.

"Well, I sure hope so, because Abithia is just there." He pointed as the faintest shape of land became visible. What made Taffy uneasy, though, was the ships carrying the Abithian standard closing in on them, separating them from their shores.

GRAPPLING HOOKS FOUND PURCHASE on the railings of the *Dispatch;* the Abithians trapped their ship on both sides and clambered over the railings. The captain stood next to Taffy, as calm as if he'd been boarded by the enemy more than once in his life. The crew of the ship all stood in a line, each of them unarmed. They weren't warriors in any sense.

The man who spoke sounded funny to Taffy. His voice was deep and gravelly, like he'd spent too many years smoking from a pipe. "The name's Temark Fai-hon, captain of the fourth defense fleet of Abithia. Her Majesty, Queen Gadiel Lotus, sent me to find out why you approach our shores so brazenly. It's clear you are Gosathan warfighters. Do you deny this?"

Captain Barnum nudged the messenger forward. The young boy was shaking in his boots. He cleared his throat before saying, "Pardon our intrusion, Captain Temark, but we come only with a message." He forced the eloquence back into his words. His speech training from the school of messengers paid off. "We are not warfighters but come bearing a gift in the hopes of having your queen's ear."

The giant moved quicker than a viper. Taffy's tunic was raptly furled inside his hairy fist. His breath smelled of tobacco and meat. "What gift could you *possibly* offer, boy?"

Captain Barnum snapped his fingers, and a few of his men retreated into the ships' cabins. The Abithians' hands went to their weapons, clearly expecting a trap of some sort. The men returned to the deck with a large basket of cakes and other pastries. It was a rumor—Taffy hoped to prove true—that the Abithians had a rather particular sweet tooth. The king wanted to make a good first impression, so hopefully this would do the trick.

Captain Temark dropped him and began pilfering through the basket for a moment before turning back to Taffy. The boy couldn't make out anything on the older man's expressionless face. Then he threw his head back and burst into laughter. All his comrades followed suit, and then the Gosathans joined the chorus.

Taffy wanted to cry from the relief he felt. His heart was apprehensive to slowing, though.

"Very well," the captain said. "If you come with a message like you say, then you'll have no argument against the searching of this vessel." He waited a moment, probably to see if they'd resist. When they didn't, the captain ordered a couple of his men to scour the *Dispatch*, and when they returned with no findings of weaponry, he said, "We will escort you to the port." The Abithians retreated into their ships, escorting the foreign members toward the nearest port.

"Welcome to Rambil," Captain Temark told them as they unloaded from the ship. "Ah, ah, ah," he said, wagging his finger left and right at the rest of the crew. "Only the boy may have an audience with Queen Gadiel."

Taffy's chest puffed out slightly, his confidence increasing. This was what he was made to do. Captain Barnum was about to protest, but the boy stopped him. "It's alright. I'm the messenger. This is my duty."

"Smart boy," Temark replied with a smirk. Taffy studied the man's face then, finding the dullness of his left eye to be most unsettling. He had short hair that was turning from black to gray, bushy eyebrows, and eyes so dark they were almost black. The left one, though, looked like it was going blind. There were a few shallow scars on his face and neck.

They marched along the pier as the *Dispatch* crew climbed back into their ship. Taffy looked around, taking in the sights of the port city.

There were many ships in the port, most of them being outfitted with soldiers and instruments of war. Swords and spears, bows and arrows, shields being hauled aboard in large barrels. Some even had stonecasters. Men were walking on some of them, and others had men being carried off with bloody rags drooping from their bodies.

To be so close to these evil doers, Taffy thought with a shudder.

Temark seemed to notice the boy watching. "Lovely sight, isn't it? What your people have done to mine?" One brow was raised as he waited on a response.

"There has been much death on both sides, sir," Taffy said simply. The man scoffed and continued in silence. In the distance stood the largest mountain the boy had ever laid eyes on.

The buildings in the city were different from what he was used to, Taffy noticed. In Valendra, most of the structures were tall and built of gray stone. Everything in Rambil was squatted and made from brown stone and wood. Taffy took it all in as they rode down the street in a carriage. He sat quietly with the captain while one of the other Abithians led the horses in front.

The keep came as a great surprise to Taffy. It was nestled within the mountain itself. Barnum told him the Maranthol Mountains spanned much of their nation.

The stone edifice was built into the face of the looming mountain; it was so tall that Taffy couldn't see its peak for the clouds. Large shadows stretched away from it like world-crushing giants as the sun dropped behind the mountains. Taffy felt his mouth dry out from being open so long.

"Wow," he whispered to himself, although, Temark chuckled so Taffy knew he'd heard him.

"Never seen anything quite like it, eh?"

"No. We have nothing like this in Gosatha."

"Good to know," the captain said. Taffy wanted to slap himself for offering that tidbit of information to the enemy. But then again, perhaps they would not be enemies soon and they could travel between the two kingdoms freely.

A portcullis was raised as their carriage rolled over a bridge. Taffy stole a glance outside the carriage to find they were suspended over a trench so deep they'd be dead on impact if they fell. They clearly took protecting their queen *very* seriously. They rolled to stop inside a courtyard where they climbed out; Taffy noticed the ground was mostly cobbled there. People milled about, mostly men dressed in furs or thin tunics, carrying small axes, swords, or spears.

"Right this way, messenger," Captain Temark said as he gestured for Taffy to follow him.

The man led Taffy through winding corridors deeper into the mountain fortress. Flaming torches lined the walls providing the only means of light. After what felt like forever, the corridors finally expanded, opening into a grand throne room. Up on a regal throne of dark blue stone sat the queen.

Taffy gazed at her, taken aback by how normal she looked. Her hair wasn't extravagantly done or terribly long. She didn't have jewels glittering all over her fingers, or the crown that sat upon her head. She looked like any of her subjects might. The fur of a weasel draped over her shoulders. What was different about her—the thing that let Taffy know she was queen—was the radiant air she gave off. Even with his young mind, he could sense it.

The captain stopped walking just a few paces away from the queen's throne which sat up on a dais. Two men stood just behind her throne, outfitted with a sword and shield. The circular shields had a spot of red painted in the center. They wore no armor or furs, but rather a tunic with the emblem of Abithia on the chest. An owl of silver with its wings spread wide sewn into the brown fabric.

Captain Temark dropped to a knee, and Taffy offered a bow. It was customary to show respect to other members of authority, but it would have been inappropriate for Taffy to bend his knee to her. He was not one of her subjects, after all.

"Rise," Queen Gadiel ordered, and they did. Her voice was like honey mixed with snake venom.

"My Queen, this is Taffy Raolin of Gosatha," Temark began. "He is a messenger of their king, harboring a message for you. I believe him to be of no harm to you or the queendom."

She smirked at Taffy. "No, I can't see him being a threat either." Those in the throne room chuckled except for him. "Go on, boy. Tell me your message."

"From the mouth of King Oliver Jardanis," he began. Before he could continue, the queen interjected.

"Not King Torril? What has happened to the old bastard?"

Taffy did not like hearing her speak ill of the late king. He closed his eyes and took a calming breath so as not to get himself into trouble. "He died not long ago, Excellency. His son, Oliver Jardanis, has taken the throne."

"Very curious. Please, continue." Her face remained stoic the entire time.

"This message is one of peace and friendship," Taffy recited. He'd committed the message to memory. "I would like to meet with you. This war has gone on far too long, and why? Do you even know?" The queen smirked when he said that, but he ignored it. "I know I don't. My father never passed that information along if he knew, and to be honest, I don't care. I want it to end. Pick a time and place, give them to the messenger, and let us discuss a way to come to an agreement of peace. To show good faith, I will be pulling my forces away from Pertaman and other islands near your shores."

Queen Gadiel's brows lifted. "Well, I can't say I'm not surprised." She let out a small laugh. "None of you really know why this fight exists, boy?"

"No, Your Highness," he answered with candor.

She laughed. "That family is nothing but *fools*. The first of them may have stopped a wicked beast from devouring mankind, but in doing so, created an even worse monster. If they'd had their way, the entire world would have bowed at Jardanis feet. *We* stopped this tyranny. The Abithians are the last hope against a family of liars, a family who has swindled its own people into believing they must maintain the throne to protect the world.

"That snake will never rear its ugly head again; that threat is no more. No, Oliver Jardanis has become this realm's greatest threat." She stopped speaking, breathing harder as anger seeped out. Taffy glanced at the captain to see a grin on his face.

Taffy's heart beat like a mad drummer on his ribcage.

Taffy shook his head slightly. He wasn't sure what to say. He didn't want to believe her, but also didn't want to upset her further. "Your Highness, I'm not sure what to believe; however, I can assure you that King Oliver is not like the others. He was always kind to me when I was younger, while other men bullied me because of my size. King Oliver admonished those men for their attacks on me. Look at what he's already done in favor of you. He's pulled soldiers away from Pertaman just for a chance to sit down with you."

The queen nodded as Taffy spoke. "You make a good point, messenger. No other king in your nation's history has ever made such an offer, that I know of. If he is planning to cross me, that would mean he has some sort of secret weapon up his sleeve, but I doubt that's the case."

Taffy was silent, awaiting her decision, hoping she agreed so that his older brother could come back home. *If he's still alive.*

"I will meet with him," the queen said, causing Taffy's eyes to light up. She held up her forefinger. "However, there will be conditions."

Taffy raised a brow. "Such as?"

Chapter 17

"YOU ARE TO MAKE no threat to the life of the king unless *absolutely* necessary. Do you understand, Sandin?" Queen Gadiel gave Sandin his parting words.

"Yes, Your Grace," Sandin replied.

"Defend yourself if harm should befall you. Slaughter your way back to me if that's what it takes. You *must* return alive."

"I understand." Sandin left the throne room and headed for the port. Rambil wasn't far from Stoneforge Keep. He double-checked his gear as always, ensuring his two blades were tucked discreetly into the waistband of his trousers. The black cloak would cover the handles, concealing them from passersby.

As Sandin prepared to leave his home, he remembered the day his attendance at Shadowspire began.

Ordinarily, boys were around ten years old when entering the school; however, Sandin was a bit younger, making him smaller and weaker than those around him. He made up for it with primal instinct, that which was bestowed upon him whilst living on the streets after his parents died.

Sandin left his chambers, heading for a carriage that would bring him to the port. Grandmaster Helfi waited there for him.

"And so, the Dagger leaves us," Helfi said with a smirk.

Sandin was given the moniker of the Royal Dagger—a title only earned by the best of killers. He was above the law, above reproach, but never above the word of his queen. The assassin had killed many men for Queen Gadiel, most of them foe, but some not. He never questioned her commands, never thought twice about taking the life of those she'd marked. All of this he'd done for the safety of Abithia.

"No better way to serve my queen," Sandin began, "than by travelling into the enemy's walls with a messenger boy." Sandin was only mildly annoyed by the task. "Though I'm going only to learn what I can; killing at my leisure is forbidden."

"Perhaps that is for the best," Helfi argued. "You're dangerous, boy. But you're still only one man."

Haven't I received enough of his lectures? he thought.

Sandin pondered, "What good is the Royal Dagger if he can't slit the throats of his queen's enemies upon his discretion?"

Helfi shot back, "What good is a Royal Dagger who argues with his queen's commands?"

Air shot from Sandin's nose—his version of a laugh. He reached out and Helfi grasped his forearm in embrace. "Be careful," the grandmaster told him. Sandin nodded, climbed into the carriage, and sat back as the horses pulled away.

The trip down to the port was slow, and Sandin closed his eyes, shoving away thoughts of nervousness that bit at him. He'd faced giants, crawled through tunnels and swamps to get at his targets, but he'd always been protected by the shadows. Now, he would be out in the open air of day, unhidden.

The carriage came to a stop. Sandin climbed out, offering a nod to the man commanding the horses as the carriage spun back around.

No turning back, he thought, stepping onto the docks.

Sandin found the boat named the *Dispatch* and hopped nimbly atop the edge, grabbing hold of one of its many ropes.

"I assume you'll be Sandin, then?" asked an older man with an air of authority about him.

"That I am. You must be the captain." Sandin dropped to the deck.

"Aye. Call me Captain Barnum. Or Captain. Or just Barnum, it's up to you." The man grinned.

"Very well. When do we leave?" Being on the boat made him shift excitedly.

"Not afraid at all?" Captain Barnum asked. Sandin didn't respond right away, and the man added, "Goin' into the enemy kingdom and all? I was nervous enough comin' here."

Sandin almost laughed. "What do you know of Shadowspire, Captain?"

He thought for a moment. "Can't say I've heard of it."

"I was raised by the Abithian guild of assassins—killers loyal only to the ruler of Abithia. It's a school known as Shadowspire. At Shadowspire, young boys are taught how to kill in every way imaginable." The color rushed from the captain's face, making Sandin grin. "It's there I learned to kill before learning proper dining manners. And while I was there, I went through many trials—as did all of us. During these trials I received no marks against me.

"The other children would often have marks against them for things like showing emotions when they should not or failing to keep up with the physical requirements. Some of them were even removed by our teacher for their constant failure. I decided early on in my attendance that I would not fail." He paused again, turning his back to the captain.

"While the other kids were playing in the creek with one another or napping in their free time, I was studying my craft. I honed my skills; my specialty was small blade manipulation." The two tucked in his waistband had become his favorite; the blades were only a few inches long, but they were curved like the claw of a mountain cat. The handles crafted from black stone, a circular hoop at the end where a finger could enter, spinning the blades around for various purposes. They'd taken many lives.

He turned fully around, stopping a few inches from the captain's confused face. "I say all this, Captain Barnum, to answer your question. No, I'm not afraid to be in the presence of your king. And if I were afraid or nervous or excited, you'd never know."

Captain Burnum scratched his beard as he looked around, checking on the progress of the crew. He chuckled nervously. "Well, it'd be rude if I left your question unanswered, eh? Now that you're here, we'll be leaving soon." The older man turned, waddling away, but Sandin noticed a wary glance shot over the captain's shoulder.

"Excellent," Sandin replied as Barnum strode away. He sat down on a pile of bags that had been used to house potatoes. That's when he noticed a boy peering around the mainmast. Sandin gazed at him curiously, lowering his hood to appear less menacing. His hair fell almost to his shoulders, black and wavy. He kept his facial hair cut closely to his face, never getting too long; it would get in the way if not maintained. Sandin's jawline was almost as strong and sharp as his knives.

The boy inched out from behind the mast. "My name is Taffy. You're Sandin, right?"

"That's right," he answered. He knew the boy had probably heard most of the conversation with the captain, but it didn't seem like an issue... yet. "Taffy sure is an odd name, isn't it?"

"My parents were odd people." Sandin stifled a chuckle, finding his honesty humorous. Something about children made Sandin forget himself at times.

"I appreciate the candor, Taffy." Sandin looked at him for a moment. In just a few short years, this boy would be the same age as Sandin, if he lived that long. War is a fickle thing, and Sandin didn't foresee it ending anytime soon. He wasn't sure he wanted it to end either.

Sandin didn't care about the lives of others; it wasn't a luxury he could afford. Caring about such things was a liability to an assassin. He'd killed many generals for his queen, always darting into the enemy camp to cut the throat of sleeping adversaries and escaping back to Abithia before the bodies could be found. Without war, what would he be? Certainly not the Royal Dagger.

"What can you tell me of Gosatha?" Sandin asked, making room on his pile. He patted next to him, gesturing for Taffy to sit. The ship lurched from the port.

"I'm not sure I'm allowed to say much, sir," Taffy said, looking sideways at Sandin.

Sandin laughed. His training didn't only require the absence of emotion, but also knowing when and how to use it; many a man had been manipulated by such skills. "Loyalty to your kingdom. I respect that. I just wondered what you could tell me of the land. I've heard it's beautiful, and that the women are everywhere, ready to be wed by strapping young men such as yourself." He nudged the boy's arm with his elbow.

Taffy giggled. "I don't know about that. I don't think I'm old enough for a betrothal yet. I am a Highborn, of course, so when the time comes, I'm sure it will be rather easy for me."

"Oh, you're a Highborn, are you?" Sandin asked, not entirely sure what Taffy meant.

"I am, indeed," he beamed. "Usually, the job of messenger is left for the Lowborn, but I was always tiny, not a good fit for a soldier, so the Messenger Corps allowed me to join. I don't mind it. I mean, it's not every day that we get to see Abithia. The queen was terrifying, but I wouldn't trade this experience for anything. My friends aren't going to believe it."

Sandin chuckled. "Well, I'm glad to know you enjoyed your visit. We wouldn't be doing our duty if a guest thought ill of us."

There must be a social construct separating two classes of people, Sandin thought. *He mentioned both Highborn and Lowborn. I still don't know exactly what it means, though.*

"Taffy, why are there Highborn and Lowborn? You'll have to forgive me; we don't have such disparities in Abithia."

Taffy tilted his head slightly. "All I know is there are those born superior—the nobles, or Highborn. Then, there are others who are born inferior—the Lowborn. If we didn't sort ourselves into these two classes, there would be chaos. That's what we were told in school, anyway."

"And do you believe all that?"

He shrugged. "I guess. It's worked this long; I don't see no point in changing things now."

"Very curious," Sandin muttered. The change in dialect wasn't smooth, and Sandin wondered if it was purposeful. *This boy isn't stupid.* Taffy gave an odd look, as if he noticed Sandin caught the slip up.

Even with as much evil as he'd committed in his time, having a system that automatically lofted certain people over others because of their blood did not sit right with Sandin. Abithia was a cutthroat empire if there ever was one, but at least his people had a fair chance to make a name for themselves.

Chapter 18

Dark rings rimmed Ara's eyes; she hadn't slept in days. Each time the girl attempted to do so, she only saw the images of her father dying over and over. She wondered what she'd done to deserve such eternal punishment. Had she already passed from life and been cast into Icuzar? Ara pleaded for the gods to have mercy on her soul and allow her to move forward. However, the anger that burned within would not allow her to move away from the thoughts of revenge running rampant in her mind.

"Please," she begged Cassandra, "do what you must to awaken the magic within me. I must kill the king. I will never truly be free of my anger until then." Tears cast from her rage balanced on her lower eyelid.

Cassandra sighed. Thus far, she hadn't agreed to teach Ara magic since the declaration that she would stop at nothing to kill King Oliver. "Ara, do you really think killing him will bring you joy?"

Ara smiled at her. "Not just Oliver, no. His entire family must fall first. He will know the pain, the anguish that I feel every day. I will make him endure the torture of watching each of them die. Only then, when I've taken everything from him, will I allow Oliver to join them in the afterlife."

"I don't believe this is the right path for you, my dear," Cassandra said. "I don't believe revenge is what you truly want, and you must be *certain* if you are to venture down this path of vengeance. You haven't taken the time to properly grieve. I'll make you a deal."

"What kind of deal?" Ara leaned forward in the wooden chair. They were sitting in Cassandra's home, drinking tea that tasted like leaves, dirt, and honey.

"Take a few days to visit your home, visit whatever friends you have left in Osta. Mourn your father's death in a healthy manner, and when you return, if you are still determined to carry out this task, I will do what I can to unlock the magic inside you."

Ara sighed. "Is this *really* how you want to proceed? I mean, what's the point?"

"Yes, it is. And the *point* is regret; I'd be remiss if you regret your actions because I let you go through with your rash actions. An angry mind thinks brashly. You need to return with clear thoughts, and then we will know your true feelings." It seemed Cassandra could not be swayed. "I need your mind to be clear and steady before anything else happens. If you truly want to go down this path of darkness, then maybe I can be the light beside you."

"Fine," Ara said indignantly. "I'll go. But when I get back, you will not attempt to change my mind, yes?"

"That is correct," she replied with a nod.

"I'll be back in a few days then." Ara exited the lady's home, trudged through the woods, and grabbed her horse. She rode Oswin slowly out of the Wraithwood, urging him to move more quickly as a pack of coyotes began to cry behind them.

She knew she'd be unable to go back to her home and felt there was no need in it. Nothing was left. There was only one person from Osta that she thought could make her feel better, but she wasn't sure he would even want to see her. She also wasn't sure she *wanted* to feel better.

"Cal," she whispered to herself as he exited his family's home. Watching him brought back a flood of their memories together. Playing in the creek as children, holding hands as they walked through the Wraithwood, the nights they'd spent having dinner together. In that moment, Ara almost forgot about her vow, but remembered the promise she'd made years ago to leave Osta with him. Leaving may just fix that which was broken within her.

And what use am I if I don't keep my word to someone? she thought sadly, her self-worth declining slightly.

His eyes were fixed on her, but Ara couldn't tell what was in them. Anger? Pity? A mixture of things, probably. He started toward her with long strides. She wondered if he would yell, if he would tell her to leave his sight. She didn't know how angry he would still be over Oliver. When he reached her, Calder wrapped his strong arms around her. Ara's head landed on his chest as he pulled her in.

At first, she just stood there with her hands at her sides, unable to do anything. Then, after a moment, her arms wrapped around him too. Her eyes closed as tears began to spill out. She cried silently against him for a time, not knowing how long they'd been standing in an embrace. Tension seemed to melt from her body. Only when Calder pulled away and tilted her head up, did she open her eyes. Their gazes met and it was like an intense pressure had lifted from her chest.

"Gaius didn't deserve to die," he said gently.

"So, you know," she replied. Words weren't coming to her easily.

"All of Osta knows. We saw the smoke from the house; people went to check and found his grave. A letter came from the palace messengers saying that your father was punished for murdering King Torril. I can't imagine what evidence they had. I know—as surely does everyone else—that he was innocent." Ara just nodded her head. "Are you alright?"

"How could I be? Would you be if it was your father?"

He looked at her incredulously. "You know how I feel about him."

She almost laughed. Ara had forgotten her friend's animosity toward his father. "Surely there's a part of you that would be saddened if he was murdered unjustly."

"I'm not so sure. I'd like to get out of this village before it happens, though. I could never leave Mother here alone."

"Then let's leave," Ara said. It just slipped out, but it was genuine all the same. "Let's leave Osta like we used to talk about."

His eyes lit up. "Don't play games with me, Ara."

"No games," she replied. "We'll leave in two days. I have no other reason for staying here. I have no home to go back to, and even if I did, I wouldn't."

"Two days it is," Cal said with a nod. His eyes were alight with excitement. "I'll meet you at the old tree. Do you remember?"

"Of course I do." The tree he referred to was where Calder had first told Ara of his feelings for her. It was a dogwood that bloomed beautiful pink flowers in the early spring.

Ara left with her mind feeling much clearer; however, there was still a bitter feeling eating away at her. Oliver put a hole in her heart that may never fill. Had she really considered killing his family? It wasn't like her to feel such vitriol toward someone, least of all someone she'd never met. Oliver had spoken very lovingly of his mother, sisters, and father. Ara galloped her steed back toward Cassandra's home to tell her the news, ensuring her knife was tucked into her boot in case the coyotes dared test her.

Chapter 19

So, THIS IS WHAT one of them looks like, King Oliver thought. His father told him a long time ago of the Abithian assassins, taught him to recognize them. Oliver never thought he'd find himself in the presence of one, though. The man was tall, carried himself as if he could kill everyone in the room if need be. He couldn't be more than 24 years old. Dark, moss green eyes gazed at the king from beneath black, wavy hair. The man wore a black, hooded cloak fastened at the front with a clasp shaped like a dagger piercing a silver loop. Taffy, the messenger boy, walked just ahead of him through the throne room. Oliver found himself very amused—though annoyed—and wondered why Abithia would try to have him killed before hearing him out.

Taffy kneeled before Oliver while the other man offered a simple bow. "My King," Taffy began, "this is Sandin. Queen Gadiel Lotus sends him as an emissary of her court. The message she sends is one of gratitude. She said she will meet with you, but there are a few things she desires. Sandin is here to discuss terms with you."

He smiled. "Of course. I will hear them, but first, let me welcome our guest. Sandin, was it?"

"Yes, Your Majesty," Sandin replied. His voice carried the accent of an Abithian—one that would be difficult to replicate. "I am honored to be here."

"I appreciate the courage it took to honor your queen's request. Coming to the enemy land alone must be a rather nerve-racking quest, especially without bearing the standard of a messenger. Do you realize there is nothing that can stop me from having my men take your life?"

Sandin did not flinch in the slightest, however, he did look around at the guards in the chamber. "I believe your men would find that undertaking a bit difficult, Majesty. But I know you won't do it."

"Oh?" Oliver smirked.

Sandin's voice remained calm, steady. "You want peace. I could tell by your messenger's words that you're sincere in this endeavor. Killing me would do nothing to aid your peace negotiations with my queen."

King Oliver nodded. "Yes, that is true; however, it is highly impudent to send an *assassin* into the kingdom of a future friend." At the word 'assassin', guards shifted around. Oliver saw the faintest twitch of Sandin's mouth.

"I fear my reputation holds true," Sandin said. "You have my word as a man that I will cause no trouble while here. I am loyal to the death to Queen Gadiel, and she has forbade me from harming a single hair on the heads of any of you. As long as no harm comes to me, of course."

The king began to laugh, diffusing the tension in the room. Even Sandin smiled. "Very well. We certainly have plenty of guest rooms that you will find accommodating." He turned his gaze back to the stalk-still Taffy. "Taffy will show you to your chambers once we've come to agreement. Now, what conditions does your queen require?"

Sandin nodded once. "She says the meeting will happen in a fortnight, that each of you will bring only one other person along, and that no weapon is to be present."

"Well, that's absurd," King Oliver said. "The Sword of Gorenos mustn't leave my side. She must know this."

"Then you refuse these terms?" Sandin asked, almost sounding eager.

"No, no," Oliver muttered. "I will think on it. There must be something I can do to change her mind. What say you, Sandin? You know the queen better than any others here."

Sandin took a breath. He spoke slowly, calculated. "Queen Gadiel is cautious of you, Oliver Jardanis. She knows very little about you, unlike your father. The queen doesn't trust you, but she is open-minded. It may not come as a surprise to you, but I must side with my queen in that caution is necessary here. I've worked under her rule for several years, and in that time, I have come to know her quite well. If you refuse this bargain, or try to change the rules in the slightest, she will not agree to meet with you. Peace will be taken off the table for another few decades, at least until the both of you have gone to the afterlife."

King Oliver nodded slowly. "I see. She drives a hard bargain." There was silence for a moment. Then Oliver said, "I suppose there is nothing left for me to do than accept. I want peace more than anything. If Bhishma returns while the sword is not with me, though, Queen Gadiel will have to answer for it."

Sandin chuckled. "I'm sure it will be fine, Majesty."

The king clapped his hands together. "Now then, it is getting rather late. I feel a feast is in order." His smile was infectious.

THE BANQUET HALL WAS filled with uproarious laughter and conversation, as well as the clattering of silver plates as people dined. King Oliver wanted to host a night of celebration as talks of peace were finally becoming real. He'd never heard his father speak of peace in a way that made it seem plausible, and now, they were on the brink. It was perhaps wishful thinking to believe the assassin would take back a good word of confidence to his queen.

Sandin sat across from the king, tearing into the roasted chicken on his plate. "Sandin, tell me how you came to be such a notable assassin. I must admit, I find myself most intrigued by you."

Sandin looked like he didn't want to reveal much. "My parents died when I was very young; I hardly remember them. I lived on the streets until a man found me and took me to the assassins' guild."

He paused for a moment. Oliver said, "That's horrible, Sandin. It couldn't have been easy, them leaving you at such a young age. I only just lost my father and still struggle with him being gone, despite the distance between us."

Sandin nodded. "Yes, it was difficult, to say the least. Although, I'd imagine having more time with them would have made it worse. If not for the man who trained me, I'd be dead. He taught me everything I know, took the stone that was my body, soul, and mind, hammered and chiseled until it was perfect."

He's very confident, Oliver thought.

"So, if I were to order my men to take you right now, you'd be able to stop them?" He asked with an amused grin splitting his lips.

Sandin looked around the room. "There would be much bloodshed, but with the number of guards you have here, I'd probably break a sweat, at the least."

Oliver laughed, "You needn't worry. I'll honor the promises I've made to you."

"I know, Majesty. That's the only reason I didn't run when you called me out. I know an honorable man when I've seen one; perhaps you've not been in war long enough for your honor to be taken."

Oliver's smiled faded. He said, "Honor isn't something that should come and go with a whim. My honor will stand the test of time." He paused, watching Sandin's expression which gave away nothing. "And what do you think of peace between our nations? Do you think it has a chance at working? I can't even remember why we began fighting in the first place. Candor, if you please, Sandin."

Sandin looked down at his plate. Was that hesitation? "I believe it could work, King Oliver. I think it will take much effort from both sides, but as long as everyone holds true to their word, nothing should go awry."

Oliver nodded, ripping a piece of bread off and shoving it in his mouth. Through a mouthful he said, "Ever since I was young, I've dreamt of uniting the world." His eyes shone brightly as he thought about it. "I will do whatever it takes to ensure our world has peace."

Sandin smiled. "A peaceful world would be... something."

Chapter 20

As darkness deepened in Valendra, Sandin snuck around the palace to glean all he could. Sandin found the place in all its gawdy glory to be guarded poorly, but still, he skulked around in the shadows, making no sound as he did so. He'd been thinking back on that night as the *Dispatch* carried him back toward Rambil. When the blue waters of the Tamagau transmuted into a deep green, an eerie sense came over Sandin. He began looking around at the waters. He thought he saw movement under the surface, but it must have been his eyes playing tricks on him.

He shook his head clear and went back to recalling all that he could from Valendra. The city was vast with tall buildings; the palace was heavily guarded on the exterior, but bare on the inside. There was a barrack on the outskirts where he watched soldiers practice their weapons skills in a courtyard.

I should have figured out how to spend more time there, he thought. *The information I have won't be invaluable, I fear.*

What he saw of the enemy's land was more plains and forestry than that of his home country. It was a beautiful place, but the mountainous regions of Abithia would always feel like his home. Sandin's memory flashed back to his childhood, to the village in which his first memories were created. He was born in Serethim; his parents had been smiths from what he could remember. While training to become an assassin, Sandin was encouraged to let go of his past, to purge his old self away, to become something else entirely. 'Sandin' wasn't even his birth name. When he closed his eyes, he could almost hear his mother calling out to him. *Luca. Luca.* He twisted the silver ring that belonged to his father. It was always on his right hand, wrapped around his fourth finger. It bore an inscription that he was told comes from a dead language, one his people once spoke: *seratu il venocte.* Strength through adversity. A philosophy he clung to.

The ship was slammed by something, listing hard to port. Sandin fell onto the deck of the boat, nearly smacking his head on the mainmast. The crew of the *Dispatch* scrambled around as barrels rolled and sails threatened to fall from where they were tied.

Sandin jumped to his feet and ran to peer over the edge of the ship. A finned spine crested the surface of the water, appearing to slither beneath the boat. Captain Barnum was shouting orders. Sandin turned to him and yelled across the ship, "Something surrounds us, Captain!"

"Aye," he called back. "Nyssavir in the water, lads; to arms!" The crewmen began grabbing swords and spears that were hidden beneath planks of wood or stuffed into barrels. Sandin had been under the impression that the ship harbored no weaponry and felt a twitch at the corner of his mouth. He was impressed. Two smaller men grabbed crossbows and stood next to Captain Barnum.

Water churned onto the boat. "To port!" the captain ordered. As men flooded that side, a monstrous head exploded skyward, sending seawater splashing over the boat and its' passengers. Shouts of "nyssavir," rang out from the crew.

Sandin had killed many men, but never had he seen a beast such as that. Its eyes were like pits of black, scales a pale green that almost matched the water. Spikey fins flared out on either side of its head like ears and ran down the length of its back. The creature hissed a horrible sound causing Sandin to cover his ears and grimace. Its head was diamond-shaped, snakelike. The serpent had two rows of sharp teeth on the top and bottom of its mouth. A stench wafted from it and assaulted Sandin's nose, like death mixed with horse dung.

He'd seen nyssavir before, but none as large or powerful as this.

Then the snake struck. Where there had been a sword-clad man shaking in his boots the moment before, there was nothing but a crack in the wood of the deck, the sword he'd been holding, and a puddle of water. Some of the crew began to panic, running around wailing. Sandin watched the creature gulp down the sailor and then look around for the next meal.

"Fight back!" The captain gave the order, trying to rally his men to show some sort of fight. The command snapped Sandin out of the trance he'd been stuck in. He dashed forward, leaping over some spilled cabbages.

He found an extra spear lying on the deck; he hefted the slick shaft, gripping it in his fist. Taking aim, he waited for the serpent to turn its massive head. When it did, he let the spear fly. The spear struck just beneath the eye where he'd been aiming. The tip of the spear stuck for a moment but fell when the beast shook its head. Its eyes were locked on Sandin. The assassin felt something he'd not known in a long time: fear.

The snake lunged; fanged mouth wide-open, ready to take Sandin from the boat. Sandin's survival instinct kicked in. He dived to the side just in time, narrowly avoiding the jagged teeth which plunged deep into the ship. The *Dispatch* rocked from side to side as the beast tried to wriggle its teeth from the hull.

"Attack!" Sandin shouted. Spears and swords stabbed into the head and neck of the nyssavir, but it wasn't enough to bring it down. Scooping up the sharp end of a broken spear, Sandin sprang over the edge of the boat as the nyssavir pulled free. With a cry of desperation, he plunged the spearhead into the creature's head. It cried out in pain, a terrible sound. Spears flew, sticking into the softer flesh of the serpent's underbelly. Bolts from the crossbows landed in its gaping mouth.

The serpent's movement began to slow, which was lucky, because Sandin's grip was beginning to give out. His strength was rapidly fading, and he was breathing rather hard. Gathering his feet beneath him, Sandin rose to his full height, ripping the spear tip free. It steadied beneath his feet, black eyes swiveling to him. He couldn't waste the opportunity.

The assassin stabbed into its eyes, once, twice. With one final jab, the behemoth nearly shook him off; he dangled by a single hand with the broken spear still lodged in an eye. He had to pull his knees up to keep his feet from finding their way into the snake's mouth. Just as Sandin was about to lose hope, another spear landed right next to him. The serpent screeched again, now with two spears in its eye. Sandin stole a glance back. *Thank you, Captain,* he thought.

Barnum was hunched over after having thrown the spear.

Sandin was able to use it to climb back atop the nyssavir. Pulling the full spear free, he jammed it into the beast's head. Finally, it flicked its head backward, sending the assassin falling, flipping. The sky and water melded as one; he couldn't orient himself before landing.

Sandin hit the green water, kicking away from the snake as it submerged. Fear coursed through him like poison; he didn't know if the snake was alive or dead. Luckily, he was accustomed to poisons, and quashed the fear before it could destroy him.

Sandin went under, eyes searching for the serpent, but it was gone; either swam away or sank to the bottom of the sea floor. He gasped as his head felt the cool air, sucking in wind aggressively. He was disoriented, looking around for the boat. The adrenaline was riveting. Then a length of rope found him and he was pulled back onto the ship.

Hands laid him on the deck where he gazed at the sky, breathing harder than he ever had. *What a fight,* he thought.

That night, there was nothing but laughs to be had between the men aboard the *Dispatch*. They drank ale in honor of their fallen shipmates. Sandin couldn't stop himself from joining in the festivities. He'd almost died earlier, and didn't feel like being his usual broody self; however, he wouldn't act jovial. Many of the men on that boat had great stories. Who knew defeating a nyssavir was all it took to gain their trust? It was the first time Sandin had ever worked with others to kill something.

"I can only imagine how horrifying the great snake was, seeing how strong that one was," one of the crew noted. Sandin found it humorous that they all believed the same story of a god-chosen man who slayed a giant serpent. How foolish mankind could be, especially when they have been lied to for eons.

This blind faith in the Jardanis family, the belief that they must stay in power to keep Bhishma from reawakening, was nothing but wool pulled over their eyes. The Abithians knew the truth. The undying faith these people had, however, made Sandin question whether any of it was real.

He found himself pondering what would happen when all was revealed to King Oliver. Would he become mad, outraged by the falsehood of his belief system? Would he try to kill them because of perceived blasphemy? Only time would tell.

Sandin didn't know what the future would hold, nor if peace would ever be had. However, he did know this meeting between his queen and King Oliver would be most intriguing. Something told him that Gadiel would choose him as her one, the man who would be by her side. The King Consort—Orion Lotus III—would not be going as that would put Abithia in even more danger if Oliver were to show up with ill intent.

Sandin sighed, sending a thin layer of fog into the air around him.

Rambil was finally coming into view; the flames of the port city burned brightly against the darkness of the night. The moon bounced off the waters.

"We're going to miss ya' on the way back, Lord Sandin," one of the men said. "Won't have nobody to kill any of the wicked beasts we startle." The men chuckled, but there was an air of tensity about them, as if they were worried they'd run into something else.

Sandin slapped the man on the shoulder and squeezed. "It was an honor to have fought at your side, my friends. Something tells me we will see each other again one day." And he meant that. Sandin could picture each of them as a friend, in another life, of course. Whether they would meet again as friend or foe, Sandin couldn't be sure.

Part 2

Atop Mountains, Through Tunnels... Despair

Chapter 21

C ASSANDRA'S EYES FLASHED ANGRILY as Ara spilled out with her plan to leave with Calder. It only lasted a moment before it was gone. She smiled, but it didn't seem genuine, and said, "But what about the magic, Ara? I was going to teach you, remember? You may not *really* want your revenge, but surely you still want to be a sorceress."

Ara looked down, feeling guilty. "I don't mean to hurt you, Cassandra, but I need to do this. I need to get as far from Osta as possible. Being here isn't good for me; you saw how angry I was." Her anger had only subsided slightly, and she knew if she stayed that anger would resurface with a vengeance.

Cassandra crossed her arms, releasing a long breath through her nose. "Aye. You were *ferocious.*" She almost sounded reverent. Then,

"Fine. Go on and leave. Just know that I will not be here if you are ever to return. Watching over you was my *one* responsibility; with you gone, my life here is pointless."

"Are you angry with me?" Ara asked.

"Of course!" Cassandra stomped over to her door, wrenching it open. "You're abandoning me, just like everyone else has. I suppose I'm just an unwanted, old woman. Now leave."

"Cassandra, I—"

"Leave. Now." The sorceress glared daggers into Ara, and it made her stomach hurt.

Ara stepped outside. Cassandra muttered something about "what am I going to do now...", but the crunch of leaves drowned most of it out. Without bothering to argue further, Ara choked down her guilt and strolled away. What had she meant by being abandoned?

I can't worry about that, she thought. *Calder's waiting.*

When Ara found him at his home, she hugged him and asked, "Are we doing the right thing?"

He nodded. "I've never been more certain of anything." He smiled in that way that always made Ara feel safe. Together, they packed their horses and left Osta with the early morning light shining down on them.

Ara looked down at Oswin. Her nerves were still slightly on edge, a feeling that only distance from the tragedy of her home could remove. "Cal..." she didn't know the right words to say. Her peripherals caught him glance over at her and she met his gaze. "About Oliver, I—"

"It's okay," he interrupted with a laugh. "You owe me nothing, Ara. I would have been proud to see you as queen. Devastated that you ran off with the prince, yes, but proud, nonetheless."

Her eyes smiled. "Thank you," was all she could manage.

When the sun began to drop that day, the two of them halted their steeds by a small creek. Calder started a fire as Ara let the horses moisten their dry mouths. Calder pulled a rabbit from a bag that he'd killed earlier that morning, stripped the meat, and began roasting it over the flames. Ara watched him, the first inkling of peace trickling into her since her father's death.

Thinking of it brought a pang of sadness, but it wasn't as strong as before. Perhaps she was beginning to move on.

"So, where do we go from here?" Ara asked. They always talked about leaving Osta, but never discussed where they'd like to go.

"I've heard talk of a village that lies in the Gorgaw Mountains called Eskasin. I think I'd like to go there, if it's alright with you. I hear it's beautiful."

She thought about it, shrugged. "I don't see why not."

"I heard in the winter it snows, but not so much that everything is buried, and in the springtime, everything melts. Rivers of snow water run down into the valley below the village. There's a river there where the villagers fish, and next to it is a field of wildflowers that stretches as far as the eye can see."

Ara closed her eyes as he spoke, imagining it. She smiled. "That sounds lovely."

"Wonderful," he replied. "We should get there in a few days."

That night they ate some bread and salted ham, talking softly with each other. Calder scooted next to Ara and draped his arm over her shoulders. She laid her head against him, and he kissed the top of her head. The butterflies he gave her then made Ara regret always spurning him in the past. Longing shot through Ara as she remembered Oliver's kiss he'd left on her cheek, which then brought another wave of guilt.

"Are you alright?" he asked. "Your skin is burning."

Her skin became hot at the thought of that man; pain and anger swirled inside. Ara figured it would take time for those feelings to go away completely—if they ever did.

Her hand found his and their fingers intertwined. She looked up at him and he down at her. Ara leaned into him as he craned his neck down. They shared a kiss—Ara's first—and she took note of the softness of his lips, and the gentle—but passionate—embrace he offered. A tear leaked out of her burning eyes as they parted.

"What's wrong?" he asked, concern evident in his eyes as he cupped her cheek with a warm hand. He brushed the tear with his thumb.

She shook her head. "I'm just a mess, Cal. I've hurt you with my foolish words, my actions. You've only ever been kind to me. I should never have entertained Oliver. That was wrong of me. It was always you."

He smiled and pulled her closer to him. "Forget about all of that. I'm happy here in this moment with you. Our past choices became null the moment we left Osta. What matters is the present, the future. I pray this moment never ends."

Ara wanted it to be everlasting as well, but there was a small part of her that knew nothing this good could ever last. Her mending heart would break again, but maybe that was just her skepticism running rampant in her mind.

Who was she kidding? She almost laughed. Happiness never lasted. Not in their world. Their world was one where children live without parents, without a roof to shelter them from the weather. A world where those children would starve or be taken by the cold, their bodies destroyed by scavenging birds. She knew happiness never lasted a lifetime, not for a Lowborn. She only hoped Calder couldn't see that written on her face.

ARA SAW ESKASIN FROM the dirt road she and Calder traveled on. The hooves of their horses padded softly along the ground as the sound of birds and insects filled Ara's ears. There was a path that wound up the side of the mountain leading to the village. Ara couldn't believe something like it existed. Had they come in the winter, snow may have blocked their journey.

The trail leading up the side of the Gorgaw was narrow, making Ara feel as if she would slip each time her horse stumbled in the slightest.

"We're almost there," Calder assured her.

After what felt like forever, the trail finally opened, and they'd made it to the village. People were milling about, attending to their chores unbothered. There was a fence built onto the edge of the mountain to keep people from falling to their deaths. Small structures made of stone and mud and thatch littered the village, chickens and pigs in their pens chattering loudly.

The people didn't seem to pay the newcomers much attention; they simply carried on with whatever task they'd been doing. Ara saw a woman with greying hair washing undergarments in a bucket of water as two small children—a boy and a girl—played nearby, chasing one another, laughing all the while.

"Hello, I was wondering if there was an inn here?" Calder asked an older man who sat in a wooden chair with his closed eyes upturned toward the sun.

The man cracked open one eye and chuckled. "First time in Eskasin, eh?"

Calder smiled. "What gave us away?"

"Well, there's no inn around here. No taverns or shops either. Only hard-working people. Go around the bend up there and find Elenor. Tell her Thorpe sent you. She'll give you a place to stay."

"Thank you, sir," Ara said, offering a nod to him as they pushed on. Around the bend, the village curved into the face of the mountain. "How do you think they carved out so much rock?" she asked Calder.

"I haven't the slightest idea. Maybe magic." He wiggled his fingers at her jokingly. She didn't laugh; jokes of magic were too raw still.

There was a woman with white hair—although, she didn't appear to be elderly—throwing scraps to a pen of pigs. "Are you Elenor?" Calder asked.

"Aye, what of it?" She faced them with her hands on her hips. Her face looked hard, withered by years of back-breaking work.

Ara smiled, though she didn't feel much like it. "Thorpe said you would have a place to stay?"

"Tie up your beasts and follow me," the woman told them, gesturing to a couple of hitching posts near a water trough. They did as she said, following her into one of the larger structures.

"There's a room just there," Elenor said, pointing. "No funny business while you're under my roof. I don't need to hear anything I don't want to hear. Got it?"

"Got it," Calder said with an awkward laugh, rubbing the back of his neck. Ara felt her cheeks get hot and was thankful it was dark in the room.

They entered the room Elenor pointed out. They had to shuffle around each other to fit at the same time. They looked at each other, shrugging. "I guess we shall make the best of it," Ara told him with a faint smile. Calder nodded in agreement. "How much will we owe you for the room, ma'am?"

Elenor waved it away. "I couldn't be bothered by charging you, girl. And don't call me ma'am; makes me feel like an old lady." A hint of a smile tugged at her lips and Ara giggled.

They gathered their bags and brought them back into the room where they collapsed onto the warm bed. The sun wouldn't be down for several more hours, but Ara heard the soft snores of Calder beside her and, she too, drifted off to sleep.

Chapter 22

GRIBAN WASN'T AT ALL what King Oliver thought it would be, although, he hadn't quite known what to expect. There wasn't much talk of the island; so small that it wasn't fit to have a decent battle on. In fact, as Oliver walked onto the land with Tiberius Theron at his back, the king could see clearly across to the opposite shoreline. The sand transitioned into soft ground with ankle-high grass. A tuft of dirt and rock tripped the inquisitor; he stumbled but found his balance as the two men glanced back at the ground.

Oddly soft, Oliver thought. Something about the ground seemed... unnatural. Still, he tossed the thought aside as he strode forward.

Royal ships sat moored on opposite sides of the island. The Abithian queen was waltzing up with Sandin trailing. Oliver watched her intently, noticed the regal posture of a queen who was practiced in the art of politics. Her shoulders were pulled back, fingers crossed in front of her. The rulers stopped a few arm lengths away from one another, gazes unwavering.

King Oliver wasn't entirely sure how to begin, so he offered a friendly smile as he said, "It's a pleasure to finally meet you, Queen Gadiel. This is High Inquisitor Tiberius Theron." He waited for her response, but none came, and he continued. "I want to thank you for agreeing to meet with me. Peace has never been this real between us. I feel the end to our war is on the horizon."

Finally, she said, "Sandin here tells me that you appear to be sincere in this endeavor of yours. I was surprised—to say the least—to hear of this. Your father *certainly* would have never attempted such a thing. I—admittedly—probably wouldn't either. Of course, I'm told you don't know why we fight. Is this true?"

Oliver gave a nod, feeling a bit embarrassed. "It is. My father never told me before he passed." A wind swept through them, rustling the short blades of grass at their feet. "Why do you ask?"

A slight smirk teased at the corners of her lips. "It's just that when a soldier doesn't understand the reason in which he fights, he lacks motivation. Many changes are to be made if peace is to be reached between us, Oliver Jardanis."

"I agree," he replied. "I've already pulled my men away from the islands as a gesture of good faith, but you already know that. What terms do you require of me? What holds you back from choosing to end the war right here, right now? To call away your forces and ending this bloodshed?" Oliver hoped she cared enough about her people's lives to not argue much.

She sighed. "My nation is not like yours, Oliver. My ancestors did not believe there to be a single family capable of protecting the world. Only *yours* believed that and because of them, the free men and women of the world have become slaves."

He narrowed his eyes. "I beg your pardon; we do *not* have slaves in Gosatha. If that is what you were implying—"

"It's not," she cut him off. There was anger in her eyes. "If not for Abithia, the entire world would find themselves under Jardanis rule. My ancestors didn't stand for that, and neither will I. History is written by the victorious; however, your history differs from mine."

Oliver pursed his lips, trying not to get too heated. Then said, "I'm not sure I understand what you're referring to."

Queen Gadiel turned so that Oliver was kept on her left side; she gazed over the waters with her hands behind her back as she spoke. "The story that has been told by generations of your family to instill fear into the hearts of man. You claim that a great serpent, created by Iliar, once stalked the world, obliterating the ancient wonders that once roamed freely. That Gorenos created your ancestor to defeat this beast with the god-forged sword, and a Jardanis man must remain in power to protect the world from the snake's return. Do you deny this?"

"Are you saying this is a lie? I believe the beast not returning is proof enough of our history."

"That is a folly, *boy*," she replied, cutting her eyes at him, and then returning her gaze to the sea. "The lack of that wicked creature does not mean your story is true. There's so little you know. It's quite sad."

Oliver shifted around, unappreciative of her condescending tone.

"I don't see what this has to do with peace negotiations," he muttered. "I came to talk about laying down our weapons for good, to discuss trading opportunities, maybe even work out a plan to make landfall in the Feral One's territory. Not to be questioned on my faith in the gods."

She looked at him again, turning her head slowly. "I need to know that you and your people are capable of *real* change. I do not have room for error in this matter. If I give the order to stand down and you betray me, my council will have me removed from the throne. Allow me to make myself clear." Gadiel waited.

Oliver waved his hand welcomingly.

Gadiel nodded, turning her body back toward the king. "Long ago, there were mages who lived among us, masters of the arcane. They could call on the energies that flow through every living thing. Their power was *truly* something to marvel, a gift bestowed by the gods.

Oliver interjected, "I thought you didn't believe in the gods."

She smiled wryly. "I never said I didn't believe in them. Only that your history of them is false." Oliver didn't reply and the queen continued, "These sorcerers were the most powerful of mankind. They were honorable, but even they fell. Before they fell, their lust for power and control intensified; they began to fight with the Jardanis family, creating a rivalry between them.

"The Jardanis family in that time were known to be quite gifted with weaponry, creating products of destruction such as the stonecaster. In response to this, the mages began experimenting with new weapons themselves; however, their experiments were more focused on magic, rather than weaponry. They created a monster who you know as Bhishma. The sorcerers controlled the snake with their dark magic, making it kill, eviscerate.

The king nearly scoffed but held it in so as not to seem rude. "You're saying these mages created the serpent, rather than Iliar?" Oliver asked, trying not to laugh at the absurdity. *How could one believe that mere men birthed something so monstrous?*

"Aye," she replied, no hint of deception detectable on her face. "Bhishma killed many of our ancestors. There were other nations with their own leaders back then; Bhishma killed thousands. Then Atreus Jardanis came along. He wasn't the king, nor appointed by Gorenos; he was a boy around your age. Atreus led many soldiers bravely, admittedly, but with a sword crafted by his family. He *did* kill the snake, but Bhishma is no more, and his spirit will not return. So, you see, there are half-truths in your kingdom's history."

"And I'm supposed to just take your word on this?" Oliver asked indignantly. "What's the point? Why can we not believe what we want, and you believe what you want, and still have peace? There is a beauty to that, I think."

"Because your beliefs have led to thousands of years of fear. Thousands of years with your family being put on a pedestal due to false claims. It's an evil thing, to secure power by way of instilling fear in one's people. Without your change of heart, what's to stop you from tricking me, casting your influence on my people?"

Oliver bobbed on the balls of his feet. He didn't understand why this was such an issue with the stubborn woman. His eyes darted to Sandin—who'd been quiet this whole time—and could not read the assassin's expression. "What say you, Sandin?" There was something trustworthy about him.

He didn't answer for a second. "My queen has spoken," he offered.

"I cannot," Oliver began, then corrected himself, "I *will not* renounce the beliefs of my people. There must be something else I can do to broker peace with you. Anything other than strip away everything we have held dear for so long. Perhaps we are wrong about it, but there is no harm in keeping things as they are!"

The queen shook her head. "Unfortunately, King Oliver, that is where you are wrong. We will not have peace now, not in your or my lifetime. It is *clear* that you will not be swayed; I must say I'm not surprised by this. Your unwavering naivety was expected. I must commend you on your loyalty to your religion, but you've only one option now." She stepped closer with Sandin following. Oliver heard Tiberius shuffle behind him.

"And what is that?" Oliver asked, nearly growling at her.

Her eyes smiled with triumph. "When you pulled your forces from the battlefield, I did as well, sending them to your southern border. They should be making landfall as we speak." She spoke the next sentence slowly. "Surrender, or watch your kingdom be razed."

Chapter 23

Surrender? Sandin thought.

Queen Gadiel hadn't prepared Sandin much for this trip, only telling him to stay close. Something told him she feared King Oliver, or at least feared that he would make an attempt on her life. The more he listened to the king speak, the more he could see why the man wanted peace so badly. Sandin thought about his life and how he'd grown up without parents; the only fatherly figure he'd had was Grandmaster Helfi, and that man was nothing short of a cold-blooded killer. Well, he used to be.

What if Sandin were to give up murder, fall in love, and settle down with a wife and children? He thought about how he'd feel if his sons were pulled from his home and thrust into a pointless war with no end in sight. When first hearing of these peace talks, he thought only of himself and how ending the war would mean a shortage of work for him. Without a nation of enemies, targets would be scarce. In that moment, however, he began to think of others; something very out of character for him.

Oliver's talk of a better world must have gotten to me. And yet, he still felt loyalty to his queen. Was she the motherly figure he'd always been missing?

And when she mentioned sending her warriors to the southern border of Gosatha, a different thought struck through Sandin.

She planned this all along and my queen doesn't trust me. My title... means nothing.

King Oliver's face contorted in rage, turned red as a beet. "I will *not* surrender," Oliver snarled.

Queen Gadiel smirked. "So be it." She turned away, stepping toward their royal ship where the captain of the *Swift* awaited with the crew to take them back to Abithia.

"Where are you going?" Oliver shouted after her, stepping forward as if he may rush the queen. His cohort followed suit and Sandin put himself between them, his knees bent slightly and head lowered.

Gadiel paused, looking back at Oliver with a murderous gleam in her eyes. Sandin would recognize that look anywhere. She'd done something wicked. Her eyes found Sandin's as she whispered to him, "I could see it in your eyes when you returned from Gosatha, you know? A spark of doubt in your mind, a parasite that will destroy everything you've become. You've been loyal to me all these years,

Sandin. Don't taint that now just because you believed in this man's sincerity."

Behind King Oliver the ground began to shift. Sections of earth fell away as twenty men rose from the ground like the dead ascending from their graves. But these men were very much alive; Abithian warriors clad with leather armor under furs, and small axes and short swords in hands.

The queen prepared for this in advance; she didn't tell him because she didn't trust him after what he'd told her of the king. A part of him felt hurt, or maybe that was guilt at how easily Oliver got in his head. He shoved those feelings into a box; the same box where he put all the things he didn't want to think about. There was little time for him to make a decision that could alter his life forever. Either help Oliver and betray his queen and Abithia, or turn his back on the heinous crime that was about to unfold and leave with his queen.

He glanced down at his ring.

"My King," Tiberius said, grabbing Oliver by the shoulder. Oliver turned quickly.

Sandin looked over his shoulder at Queen Gadiel as she walked on toward her ship without being bothered by the events unfolding behind her. He looked back at the Abithian fighters. His hands crept up beneath the tail of his black cloak, finding the familiar leather-wrapped, stone hilts of his curved knives.

Fools should have come armed, he thought of Oliver and his guard. *Luckily, I brought these.*

Being an assassin meant killing so many people that one's soul could not be retrieved from the dark pits they lurk in. Sandin was no exception. But he was not a coward either and would not abide by cowardice from his master. This betrayal set forth by his queen was nothing more than cowardice. With the speed of a man who'd spent life running from himself, the power of an ox in his legs, Sandin dashed in front of King Oliver and his guard.

Sandin set his sight on one man, the nearest of them. He didn't know any of their names, but it was clear they'd heard of him. The man's scowl turned into fear as the curved blades erupted from behind Sandin's back. In a flash, the warrior's throat was slashed; he slumped to the ground, dropping his axe as blood gurgled from his neck. "Grab the axe!" Sandin called over his shoulder as Oliver and Tiberius looked on in shock.

Not waiting to see if they were going to jump into action, Sandin blazed on to the next Abithian. The shock of seeing the assassin fighting them wore off, and the remaining warriors began closing in. Blades clashed against one another; Sandin could hear the echoing clang of metal behind him, the shouts of the men rising.

The edge of a sword ripped across Sandin's forearm, red blossoming around the tear in his dark tunic. The pain was hardly felt; he lashed out, narrowly missing the man in front of him. The Abithian growled as he hacked at him again. Sandin rolled out of the way just in time, but heard a sickening crunch, and worried the blade had struck King Oliver. Sandin popped back up to his feet, turning back to where he'd been standing. The blade was lodged in the skull of an Abithian who'd been sneaking up on him. A faint choking sound emanated from the man's mouth as he slowly fell.

The one who'd dealt the killing blow let go of the hilt of his weapon as his comrade fell to the ground, the life fleeing from him with a few jerking twitches. Sandin dispatched him swiftly in his horror-stricken stupor.

He saw the crew of King Oliver's ship shuffling down a rope ladder to come to their aid. They were too slow, but that's probably for the better as they didn't appear to be experienced fighters.

Within minutes, the Abithian fighters were dispatched, leaving Sandin, King Oliver, and the High Inquisitor breathing laboriously. None of them escaped the battle unscathed, each of the men bleeding from small cuts. Oliver and Tiberius held axes, looking around to ensure there were no others. A golden crown sat lopsided on Oliver's golden head of hair. The boat crew climbed back aboard at the order of their captain.

"That wench!" Tiberius yelled. His eyes settled on Sandin as if he just noticed him. He pointed the axe at him as he moved to close the distance between them. He shouted, "Did you know about this?"

King Oliver caught the man's weapon hand. "Stand down, Tiberius."

"I didn't know," Sandin said, his voice coming out quietly. "She didn't tell me any of her plans. I'm sorry."

"No need to apologize, Sandin," Oliver said, moving in between them. He stuck his arm out for Sandin to grip. "I thank you for fighting for us. Tiberius and I owe a life debt to you." Sandin took his arm, squeezing once, then let go.

"It's safe to say that I will no longer be welcome in Abithia," Sandin noted. "I must request safe passage into Gosatha, King Oliver."

He nodded. "Of course. I fear we'd both be dead now if not for you, Sandin. It would be criminal to leave you here stranded. My home is yours."

"Thank you. Your generosity does not go unnoticed," he said, bowing.

The three men ran to the king's ship, *Gale*, scrawled on its hull. Up the ladder they went; Sandin peered in the direction of where the *Swift* had been. The ship was nothing more than a small, blurry object in the distance.

"What now?" The captain asked, eyeing Sandin warily.

Oliver didn't answer right away, so Sandin offered, "A messenger falcon will have been released by now telling the queen's army to attack. I'm assuming, had the two of you come to terms, the message would have been to stand down."

The king nodded. "Set course for Valendra. The fight is coming to our lands, and I must prepare for battle."

Chapter 24

Eskasin had no village lord or lady that was in charge, Ara learned. She was determined to learn their ways, which differed from what she was used to in Osta, and become like one of them. According to Elenor, their village didn't get bothered too much by the king's men, but they did have the occasional wanderer pass through. The biggest threat they faced was the eagles.

"Our greatest competitors for survival are the eagles," Elenor told her. "The younglings don't like competition."

Ara had shivered at the thought of being carried off by an overgrown bird.

In the little time they'd lived with Elenor, Ara and Cal had defended the older woman's livestock against the giant birds several times.

Feathers of gold, talons black as night and sharp as a blade. The eagles lived higher up on the same mountain, and mostly left Eskasin alone, but there were times when the younger birds would venture down and try to steal from the villagers. Elenor said that a fully grown eagle was larger than Ara. Thus far, they'd only seen adolescents, the ones that were the size of a newborn calf.

Ara sat on a cliff's edge with Cal beside her, his hand caressing the small of her back. The previous night was one she would remember forever; despite Elenor's rule, the two couldn't seem to keep their hands to themselves. They'd been caught in a sea of blankets, their bodies becoming like a single ship tossed amongst tumultuous waves. The look in Calder's eyes and the smile on his face told Ara he was happy—something Ara wished she could be.

I may never feel true happiness again, she thought. *But this will have to do.*

"Care for a walk?" he asked. She nodded and they arose, their hands locked tight.

They approached the entrance to several smaller trails leading through the mountains; some of them wrapped around to the opposite side of the Gorgaw peaks. They followed a young man near their age, Hesperus, through one of them.

"Have to be careful on these goat trails," Hesperus told them. Mountain walls stretched toward the sky on either side of them, the path only wide enough to fit one or two people at a time walking side-by-side. "The adult eagles like to hunt the goats through here.

While they generally leave us be, you never know when they may change their minds. I just hope I'm not around when it happens."

"Surely you could fight them off," she offered.

"Well, I *am* the strongest boy in the village," he noted, not at all sarcastically. "Best to keep our heads on a swivel, though." He ended that with a chuckle. Calder laughed as Ara snorted, rolling her eyes.

"It's so peaceful here," Calder noted.

"Certainly more than the rest of the world," Hesperus replied. "It's nice to be left alone; it's almost like we have our own little kingdom up here."

After hiking for a while, the trail finally widened. The sun was coming close to the horizon, turning a dark shade of orange. "We'll need to head back soon," Hesperus said.

"I want to explore this entire mountain," Ara said, marveling at the beauty before her—hills and valleys as far as she could see in one direction. Forests of lush green and brown hues, small lakes and creeks that cut through the countryside.

"Hold on." Calder moved past Ara, blocking the view of whatever he was looking at. "What is that?" She could tell he was gazing toward the Tamagau, but she still had to move to see around him.

"Oh no," Hesperus muttered, his voice breaking slightly.

Then Ara saw them. Hundreds of ships carrying the standard of Abithia moored along the southern border; she could just barely make them out. Villages in the distance were already aglow with the flames of war, long pillaged and beyond rescue. No one in Eskasin saw it happening because of the mountain blocking the line of sight.

The side of the mountain angled down from where the three stood; nearing the base were thousands of Abithian soldiers. Ara didn't know how much they knew of Gosatha; if they didn't know of the village, they should all be safe.

Her heart pounded rapidly. *If those soldiers storm the mountain, all will die,* she thought.

There was nowhere to go but down or through the trails. "We have to warn them," she said, her voice coming out weaker than she'd intended. It didn't seem loud enough to shake the men from their daze. "Hey!" They turned, both with fearful eyes. "We have to warn them!"

They began sprinting, Ara in the front. Her mind flashed back to the Wraithwood, pangs of homesickness and guilt running through her all at once as she remembered outrunning Calder, knocking herself out. She thought about her father and his death. After all she'd done to put distance between her and that place, the memories still brought a sting to her eyes.

When the goat trail opened back up into the village, Ara found Elenor sitting in a wooden chair outside of her pig pen. "Elenor," Ara said breathlessly. Calder caught up with her, but she didn't see Hesperus. "They're... coming."

"What are you talking about? Slow your breathing, girl." Elenor stood to her feet as Hesperus finally caught up. Ara glanced at him. The young man's face was red and slickened with sweat. His breath came out like a wheeze, as if he was going to faint.

Ara closed her eyes for a moment, gathering herself as best she could. "There are Abithian soldiers storming around the base of the mountains. Right now."

The woman looked at her as if in disbelief. "No, that can't be. Abithians haven't set foot on these lands in ages."

"It's... true," Hesperus managed in between coughs.

Her skin went pale. "Come. Quickly now!"

Elenor ran through the village as quickly as her old legs could carry with the other three behind. She was shouting, "Put out the fires! Douse the flames! Abithians are coming!" There were seldom arguments hurled at her; it was clear that Elenor was a trusted member of Eskasin, sort of like a village elder. "Arm yourselves!"

With the flames of all the fires extinguished, the villagers searched for anything that could wound or maim. Many wielded short swords or daggers, but some opted to carry pitchforks. Ara looked around at them. Their numbers were far too meager to win a fight against the forces she'd seen.

"Hesperus, I want you to scout further down the path of the mountain," Elenor said. "At the first sign of trouble you come back and let us know how close and how many there are."

"Aye, ma'am," he replied, jogging away. Ara was surprised he could still carry on after the way he'd looked moments earlier.

She gave him a nod of thanks, turning to the crowd of people who'd gathered upon the commotion. "The rest of you, hunker down and wait. Pray that Gorenos sees us favorably and allows the Abithians to flow around our home."

"The people listen to you," Ara observed. "It would seem that *you* are the Lady of Eskasin, no?"

Elenor smiled. "I just happen to have a good head on my shoulders. People tend to notice things like that."

Ara cleared her throat. "Despite what happens here, I'm glad Cal and I came. We'll do all we can to defend Eskasin."

"I'm glad as well," she said.

Ara went on, "I've been through several... dark events as of late, and if my life is to end here, I'll be happy that I've met all of you." She offered a smile, breaking the forlorn expression she'd been wearing. Ara had grown tired of seeing people she cared about get hurt.

Elenor smiled sadly, but then her gaze went past the girl. Her visage shifted to one of concern. Ara turned and saw a figure stumbling up the path in an awkward shuffle. "Hesperus," she whispered.

The young man looked dazed; his tunic was slick with sweat. *No, that's blood,* Ara thought. As he got closer, Ara noticed a deep gash pumping crimson from his ribs. He came to a stop, looking around at the villagers who were too stunned to react. He'd only just left; they couldn't be that close, could they? "Run," he whispered.

As his body hit the ground, a face materialized along the path behind him. Then another. More and more, the Abithians surged up the path in a storm of leather-armored, fur-clad, bodies. Their breeches and tunics were nothing but brown, helping them blend in slightly with the wall of rock. They were so quiet. How could they have gotten so close without any of the villagers hearing? Even then, as Ara looked at them fearfully, their footsteps were silent, and their mouths uttered nothing. She heard no clink of metal.

Only when they noticed they'd been spotted did the Abithians let loose thunderous cries of rage and death. The front of the horde dashed forward; the younger men of Eskasin stepped up to fight as the elders retreated into the goat paths. Ara didn't know what to do.

"Come on," Calder ordered, grabbing her wrist. The dagger she'd been holding fell to the ground. She was in too much shock to stop Calder from dragging her along, and her weapon was left behind. They disappeared into a goat trail they hadn't explored, but there were other villagers going that way, so Ara figured it was safer than staying behind. She looked over her shoulder as the cries of men and women being slaughtered filled the air. She saw them fall, saw their blood spill on the ground in crimson puddles.

And then, she couldn't see or hear them any longer. They were far enough away that the sounds of battle faded completely. "Where are we going?" she asked. There were a few people in front of them.

Merilda—one of the women ahead of them—answered back, "This path leads to the other side and connects with other trails. If we get far enough away and wait them out, the Abithians may leave, and we can return. Let's just hope they don't search these trails too well."

Ara felt somewhat like a coward. But she was no warrior. *I should have learned magic from Cassandra first.* She hated feeling helpless. Had she taken Cassandra up on learning magic, she may have been able to protect the entire village. That guilt was already gnawing at her, finding the fresh wounds of everything else she'd endured recently.

They found a small area on the outermost part of the Gorgaw Mountain; it was on the eastern side of the rock face. Ara nearly laughed at her luck. A younger girl named Frida sat in Ara's lap while Ara stroked the girl's hair gently. Frida's mother hadn't made it into the trail with them.

As the sun rose, Ara sat up groggily; she leaned with her back against the rock face of the mountains. She'd not slept a wink, though Calder had been snoring lightly for most of the night. They'd survived one full night without being discovered.

How can he sleep with so much going on? she thought idly. She froze.

Something inhuman was a breath away. Unnatural wind from above, the sound of wings beating. Ara's fear doubled when she glanced up. Two Gorgaw eagles descended upon the group but went only for one of them. The eagles landed on Frida, tearing at her legs with their talons, trying to lift her. She flailed and kicked, screaming as blood trickled from gashes in her flesh. Calder woke with a start, his eyes not quite focusing on what was happening for a second too long.

"Get off her, you bastards!" Calder shouted as he jumped up. He brandished the sword he'd been carrying, slicing at one of the massive creatures. He clipped one of their wings just as they lifted Frida into the air. "No!" The eagles carried her higher. Her screams vanished among the clouds.

Merilda began crying quietly. "I can't believe this is happening. What have we done that the gods would leave us to this fate? That poor child..."

"Hush," Ara said, turning her head toward the goat trail to her right.

"Ara, that seems a little insensitive," Calder scolded.

"No," she whispered harshly. "I heard something." As the words left her mouth, a form took shape from around the corner, growling. More followed, swarming them.

Calder swung with his sword, but he was not well-practiced. The Abithian disarmed him, and as he did, Ara heard a sickening crunch come from his wrist. He cried out in agony.

"Calder!" Ara shouted as her arms were pulled behind her. *Not again.* "Get off him! Let go of me!"

Merilda was yanked to her feet by her hair. The man held her graying locks in a tight fist; she whimpered, begging him softly to let go, that she would obey his every command. The man had short, black hair, and dark eyes. His face was chubby, his nose narrow, and his body muscular.

"A bit old, don't you think?" he asked the other men. He had the deep accent of an Abithian, one Ara had heard about, but was only hearing it with her ears for the first time. There were grunts of agreement. "May you grow wings." He walked ten paces to the edge of the mountain and shoved her over without another word. Ara only heard her scream for a second.

"What have you done?" Calder shouted as he struggled to wrench himself free, garnering him a punch from the man who'd shoved Merilda.

"I'd keep better guard over my tongue if I were you," the man warned. Ara looked at Calder; his right cheek was red and swollen, blood trickling from his bottom lip. His hand and wrist hung limply at his side. A fire ignited within her, just itching, clawing to be set free.

The man who struck Calder roughly gripped his cheeks, turning his face as if inspecting. "This one looks workable," he said. "What do you think? Should we discard the rabble?" He glanced at the man holding Ara.

"Let's get them back to the captain," the other man said. More agreements and then they were being hauled back through the goat trails.

Chapter 25

KING OLIVER PRAYED THAT the winds would be on their side; a strong gust caught in their sails, pushing them through the green waters with fervor. He noticed Sandin watching the waters apprehensively. He twisted a silver ring around his finger, almost nervously.

"Have a fear of water, Sandin?" The assassin almost looked startled as he turned to the king. Almost.

"There are things in this sea that haunts me, I'm afraid," he replied, rubbing the back of his neck.

Oliver offered, "Fear can be healthy if it keeps one alive." Sandin nodded grimly. "What's with the ring? If you don't mind my asking, of course."

Sandin glanced down at it. "Oh, not at all. It was my fathers'. All I have left of him. He never took it off, and after he and my mother died, this was all they were able to leave for me."

"I'm sorry to hear that." Sandin didn't reply but looked back at the waters.

The wind whipped through their hair, the sea-salty breeze bringing a sensation of elation to Oliver as he inhaled deeply. "I love the sea. When I was younger, I begged my father to let me go out on the water daily. Of course, he usually declined; a life at sea isn't fit for a future king." Oliver chuckled but Sandin offered no response. He continued looking over the waves. *He must be struggling with his decision to leave Abithia,* Oliver thought.

"Why did you protect us? Kill your own people for me?" Oliver asked.

Sandin's expression gave nothing away, but he eventually said, "I thought about a world where children wouldn't be plucked from their homes to be raised as fodder for an endless war. A world where I may be able to get rid of the darkness of death that plagues my soul. And I found it to be beautiful in my mind's eye." He looked down, twisting the ring idly. "It became clear to me that Queen Gadiel is a coward, someone who doesn't want peace unless her every demand is met. I no longer care to serve a master like that."

Oliver nodded. "Well, I thank you for joining us, my friend. You will have a place in my retinue."

"Majesty—", Tiberius began.

Oliver cut him off. "No, Tiberius. I know what you will say. You still don't trust this man, nor do you believe that I should, but he has proven himself. Look." Oliver pointed to one of the cuts on Sandin's arm. "He has bled for us. Sandin has my every confidence."

Tiberius nodded once. "Very well, Your Majesty. What of the southern border? What is our plan from here?"

Oliver turned to Sandin and asked, "Do you have any insight as to how the Abithians will attack?"

The assassin folded his arms over his chest. "How fortified is your southern border?"

"Not well," Oliver said with a sigh. "It's mostly fishing villages on that side of Gosatha. Usually, naval ships would be there in defense, but... well, I've shifted them. I was so sure this would work." He paused, silently admonishing himself. "There are guard towers and barracks with a handful of soldiers in every village but they're not equipped to handle a large opposing force. It was never needed."

Sandin nodded. "It's probably safe to assume these villages will be overrun. Queen Gadiel would not have sent a small number of men to achieve this undertaking. I'm afraid you should prepare for the worst. I don't know much of your land, but if the Abithians attacked as the queen said, they'll be many leagues into your kingdom by the time we make landfall." The ship rocked, smashing against a large wave; Sandin's arms shot out to the side to balance himself as he looked around frantically for a moment before standing straight again.

Several small villages inhabited the southern region; Oliver could only hope that word was spread before the enemy made it too far inland. If warnings were to reach Silvesca before the Abithians make it to the city, Gosatha stood a good chance of defending. The king and those on board the *Gale* would reach Valendra by nightfall. He would need to rally the council immediately in the war room. The king felt his cheeks flush the more he thought about enemies flooding his home, attacking his people.

Oliver moved a step closer to Sandin. "Will you fight at my side again? Help me stop your people?"

Sandin didn't break his gaze from the king's eyes. "They are no longer my people. Aye, I will help you, King Oliver."

THEY'D COVERED THE DISTANCE across the sea, taking to the palace almost immediately to iron out the details of their next move.

"Silence!" The Royal Councilmen were arguing, shouting over one another, hurling accusations at Sandin. Oliver corralled their raucous conversation. "You are to send the bulk of our men to the south. They are to take up arms south of Silvesca. If the city's troops can mobilize in time, they should be able to hold the enemy at bay until reinforcements arrive."

"Reinforcements, Majesty?" Lord Bevil asked. "Who will our men be reinforcing?"

"I'll be going with Sandin and five of the Gilden Wolves to fight alongside the men of Silvesca. The Queen Mother will take control of political matters in my stead."

More cries of disagreement arose, dying as the king slammed his fist down. A jolt of pain shot up to his elbow. He growled, "Enough. I must leave before our people are wiped out."

"Your Majesty," Lord Leander said softly, leaning toward the king. "Why are you so trusting of that man?" He gestured to Sandin who remained in a corner of the war room, standing silently with his hands folded in front of him.

"I don't have time for the smaller details," Oliver began to explain, "but peace is off the table, probably indefinitely. Sandin has bled for me, and I owe him my life. This matter will not be questioned again. Dismissed." The men flowed from the war room to carry out King Oliver's orders.

"Tiberius," Oliver waved the man over to him. "Ensure that my mother's word is followed as law while I am away. You have every authority to do what is needed."

"But, Majesty," he said. "I don't mean to show disrespect, but I think it a bad idea for you to join this battle. Send me; allow me to fight for you. If you fall before an heir is in line... well, I don't have to tell you the implications."

Oliver placed a hand on the man's shoulder. "I promised myself that I'd be different from my father; he never put his neck on the line for his people. I'm going to fight alongside my men, and that's all there is to it. Now, can I trust you to help my mother take care of our city while I'm away?"

Tiberius gave a single nod, his face stern. "You have my word. It has been an honor to serve you." He knelt before the king.

King Oliver laughed softly, pulling Tiberius to his feet. "You speak as though I am about to die, my friend." He grabbed the inquisitor, pulling him to his feet. "If I am to die, they'd better prepare to walk into the afterlife with me." Tiberius laughed at that.

They grasped forearms, squeezing firmly one time. They released and Oliver turned to Sandin. He asked him, "Are you ready to face death, assassin?"

Sandin smiled. "I thought you'd never ask, Your Majesty."

Chapter 26

"YOU ARE... BREATHTAKING," SAID the man introduced to them as Captain Vel Azaius. He caressed Ara's cheek with the back of a dirty finger. Ara had to crane her neck to look up at him. His thick arms were ever thickened by the blanket of hair growing from them. A small axe hung from a loop in his belt. His touch sent a chill up Ara's spine. "Good catch, gentlemen," he said to the men who brought her and Calder back.

Ara flinched when Captain Vel tried touching her face again. The color of grime under his fingernails could be dirt, but she suspected it could also be the blood of her people. There were bodies being dragged all over the place; many were dead, and those who weren't would likely become slaves of some sort back in Abithia.

"Don't touch her, *you filth*!" Calder admonished the man.

"Cal, don't," Ara said weakly, but it was too late. One of the men thrust his fist into his stomach. He doubled over, retching bile.

"Your lover doesn't know how to keep his mouth shut," Captain Vel said. "You two should be grateful that breath remains in your body. Go on, show your gratitude." He crossed his arms, waiting for them to respond with a smirk on his face. Ara could feel her limbs shaking.

She glanced over at Calder; he was still breathing hard from the blow to his gut. It took all of this for her to realize how much she loved him. She would do anything to keep harm from befalling him. To lose Calder... she just couldn't bear that.

"Thank you," she said, her voice hardly audible even to her. Looking at the monster before her was like staring into the face of a woodland bear. It reminded her of that time in the Wraithwood, and she silently begged for Cassandra to arrive and save them all.

Vel laughed. "What was that?"

"Thank you for not killing us," she said a little louder.

"Your turn, boy," Vel said to Calder.

"Piss off." Another blow to his stomach sent Calder to his knees, coughing. Ara's eyes were burning. Why wouldn't he just do what they want?

"Listen up!" the captain yelled. His men stopped rifling through the dead villagers' belongings. "Head back down the mountain. Regroup with the others." A resounding growl of agreement echoed off the walls of the mountain.

"What of these two, captain?" the man holding Calder asked.

"Bring the girl. She'll fetch a good price at any number of pleasure houses back home. Get rid of the bull."

Ara's blood churned and her skin was burning. Calder grimaced as he was yanked to his feet. The captain marched away. One of his soldiers pushed Ara from behind. She winced from the pain of the ropes binding her wrists digging into the raw skin. "No! Don't hurt him!" she yelled.

"Don't worry. I'll make it quick." The man holding Calder spun him around as he pulled a small blade from a pouch attached to his belt. He thrust the knife in between Calder's ribs. A sharp inhale escaped his lips.

For a moment their eyes met, and they were the only two people to exist. It was like time had come to a stop, and all Ara could see was that look in his eyes. He was afraid. The fear she saw only compounded with hers. The world came rushing back; her heart pounded rapidly.

"What have you done!" Ara saw the light leave his eyes. In the time it took to release a breath, her oldest friend had been taken from the world. Tears balanced on her bottom eyelid. *No, I refuse to let this happen.* She'd watched her Pa die, weak and helpless as it happened. These men would have to kill her too.

All the anger, the rage, the madness burst from her soul. Remembering how she took life from that plant all those days ago, Ara could suddenly feel the lifeforce of the man holding onto her. Touching her skin was his undoing. She closed her eyes, ripping his essence from him, compiling it within herself as she didn't have the medallion to store it. She hadn't realized this was even possible until that moment.

The man crumpled to the ground. The energy of magic flowed through her; it was unlike anything she'd ever known. A liquid fire ignited in her veins, spreading to her fingertips, to her toes. Ara's chest pumped wildly as she breathed hard, a growl emanating from deep within.

"I'll kill you all," she snarled. The man who killed Calder looked at her with bemusement on his face, then changed to confusion at the sight of his dead friend.

With a scream—like a primal beast erupting from her chest—the bindings on Ara's wrists burned away. A blaze of fire ignited from every pore on her body, covering every inch of her. Calder's killer stood stalk-still, his eyes wide and reflecting the flames reaching out from her body.

"What—" he was able to get out before Ara reached him.

She stretched out an arm, her hand touching his face delicately. The flames that covered her skin spread to him; he began running around Eskasin, body aflame. An arrow flew at her, but it became ashes before it could penetrate her body. Ara ran from person to person, scorching the Abithians until bodies littered the mountainside. She was faster than them and they could not escape. She ran through the village and then started down the narrower path that wound down the mountain.

There.

Her eyes found Captain Vel; though he was surrounded by sol-diers, his escape wouldn't come to pass. "You," she growled. The man turned, his eyes wide, unmoving. That brought a wicked smile to her face. He moved to run as Ara dashed forward. Her arms thrashed as she chased him, hair flowing behind her like the flamed tail of a shooting star. The man's legs were like trees—thick and strong but failing to carry him away quickly. She dispatched the soldiers; villagers ran up the path as the Abithians released them to fight Ara. Livestock ran around in a panic. Then she reached Captain Vel who continued his feeble attempt at escape.

Ara thrust a fist at the center of his body. The flaming appendage exited Vel's front, burning him from the inside. The Abithian wailed, choked, and then died as his body burned from the inside out.

Looking around her, Ara found no other Abithians. Her surviving countrymen had fled back up the village. Glancing over the steep edge of the mountain, Ara saw the horde of Abithians moving away. She'd never reach them. Orange flames danced across her skin a mo-ment longer before dissipating. She shivered then, naked, as the fire had burned away her clothes. Heading back toward the village, Ara let the rage keep her warm. She didn't want it to fade, didn't want it to transform into sadness. The girl's mind swam with confounded thoughts, wondering of the possibilities of what she'd done. Cassan-dra had told her the medallion was the storer of magic. Perhaps she just didn't know of this. Ara hiked back up to the village, her eyes glancing around at the villagers as she came upon Calder's body.

The villagers watched her, their eyes red with fatigue and pain for lost loved ones. A mother shielded her little boy's eyes from Ara's naked form. There was something in their eyes that was more pronounced than weariness, though. Terror shone through them, bearing down on Ara like an accusation.

Let them think me a monster, she thought. *Maybe I am.*

Not far away, Elenor's body lay dead—another stab of pain hit Ara like a thrown stone. Unlike Calder, Elenor hadn't been stabbed through the heart, but a deep wound seeped red ichor from her weathered throat. Their eyes remained open, devoid of life. She closed their lids with a hand. The bodies of children were strewn about the rocks—the ones who had fought back. The surviving little ones still cried in earnest. Ara raged at the gods for allowing such atrocities to occur. And then, with nothing but questions, Ara clothed herself with garments found in what remained of Eskasin and turned, heading back down the Gorgaw Mountain without a word to anyone.

She didn't bother with burying the dead; the Eskasins would have to deal with that. She was only vaguely aware of it, but something deep inside her had shattered. The part of Ara that made her the girl people once loved had been taken. 'Taken' was too mild a word for it, though. It was *ripped* from her. Just as all she'd known and loved was ripped from her.

THE ONLY ANSWER WAS to find Cassandra; the witch was the one person Ara knew of who had even the slightest knowledge of magic. Ara peered down the mountain to find the Abithians marching past. She hoped they didn't send any others up the Gorgaw, fearful that she'd be unable to bring the flames forth from her body a second time. The first had been accidental. She didn't understand how she'd done it.

As she neared the bottom, darkness descended from the sky. Ara crouched behind a bush, watching the flames of torches bob up and down in the distance. *What I did to them,* she thought, then shuddered.

Her stomach churned and she let loose her sick, covering the ground in front of her. She still smelled the burning flesh, heard it sizzle beneath the heat of her flames. Ara thought of how strong she'd felt when her fist rammed through the captain, and she... smirked.

Wiping her mouth, Ara pressed onward down the mountain trail. She didn't know how she would find Cassandra, didn't even know where to begin. The southern region of Gosatha was a mystery to her. Without Calder, Ara would never have heard of Eskasin.

Oh, Cal, she thought. *I should have never sought you out.*

The truth was that Ara blamed herself; she was at fault for his death. Had she just left him alone to continue his family's tax work, he'd still be alive. There was a silver lining to everything that had happened, though. Just one upside to Calder's death and the destruction of Eskasin. Ara had been able to exact revenge on the Abithians, and now that she'd tasted of it, she found that revenge was indeed sweet.

Her life had spiraled out of control over the last several months; she realized that she could let things go, move on, but where was the justice in that? Oliver still needed to pay for what he'd done to her father. She hardened her mind then, as her boots crunched over the dry dirt at the base of the mountain, to make them all pay. Ara knew that she was powerful, knew that all she needed to do was learn to control the magic, figure out how to call upon it. The king and his army stood no chance against her, and after Oliver felt her pain, she would deal with the Abithians. They would all suffer for the crimes of their kinsmen.

Chapter 27

Broad gates and walls of gray stone surrounded Silvesca, hence its moniker, the "silver city". Sandin itched to fight, not caring that his next battle would be with his prior countrymen. The gates were open when the king, Sandin, and the five Gilded Wolves arrived by horseback, but Oliver ordered them shut. "Send scouts to the south. Have them return at the first sight of enemy invaders," he ordered the knights standing sentry at the main gate. They fled down the cobbled street to meet with the village lord.

"Your Majesty," the man said as he bowed deeply. "What brings you to Silvesca?" It was early morning, and they had been riding through the night. A scowl crinkled Sandin's forehead for a moment—the irritation at having no sleep getting to him—but he quickly recovered his composure.

King Oliver spoke matter-of-factly. "First, my men and I will need a room to sleep off our fatigue. Then, we must gather all the forces we can muster and take them south. A horde of Abithians come this way; they've already destroyed several villages in their path."

The lord recoiled slightly. "How in the gods' names did they make it so far inland?"

"That isn't important. For now, let's worry about stopping them, and pray to Gorenos that we can hold them off long enough for reinforcement."

"Aye, Your Majesty. Consider it done."

The lord led them to an inn where they were given rooms. Sandin washed his hands and face, dunking his dark hair into the water basin that sat below a windowsill. After drying off, he plopped down onto the bed, sinking into it with a sigh. It felt like he hadn't slept in ages. Shortly after, his breathing slowed as his thoughts quietened, and he drifted to sleep.

The sun was still up when Sandin awoke from his slumber. He felt as though he couldn't recall where he'd been, but upon sitting up, he remembered arriving at Silvesca. The sun shone brightly through the window and he wondered how long he'd been asleep. Climbing down the stairs of the inn, he found the king sipping from a mug of tea.

"Welcome back to the land of the living," King Oliver said. "I thought you'd sleep forever."

Sandin asked, "And you? How did you sleep, Majesty?"

Oliver sighed. "I hardly did."

Sandin took his seat, noticing the bags beneath the king's eyes. He asked, "Any word from the scouts?"

"None yet, however, we need to gather the troops we have here. We must press forward with readying ourselves for attack, lest we be caught with our pants down, so to speak."

"Aye," Sandin agreed with a nod. "Best we don't waste time." The assassin swiped some breakfast ham from the innkeeper before heading to the door.

They left the inn, stepping onto the cobbled road with the wolves trailing them. Oliver ordered two of them to find Lord Peton and bring him to the village square. They went there and waited. Silvescans milled about, opening their markets, preparing produce and goods to be sold or traded. The king's entourage collected many stares as they stood there patiently.

Sandin tried to feel less awkward, but their penetrating gazes left him feeling like they knew he was an outsider. It didn't help that the citizens were probably wondering why the king was in their midst. He'd left his crown back in Valendra, mentioning how it would only get in the way during battle. Sandin figured his subjects would still recognize him, though.

King Oliver asked, "What do you make of what Queen Gadiel said? About the history of the world. Do you believe her?" Their was something hidden in his expression.

Sandin wasn't sure what to believe anymore. "I have never known her to be one for lying; however, her recent actions would permit otherwise. I've killed allies by her command, Abithians who she believed would foment discourse in her queendom. When she spoke of the past, I saw no tell in her behavior that would indicate dishonesty. I'm only now realizing that I never put much thought into our world's history; I merely believed as I was told. All of Abithia is raised to believe what the queen told you, that the Jardanis family wants to rule the world under the guise of protection."

King Oliver shook his head, leaning against a wooden post that held a shade cloth, blocking the sun from spoiling crates of tomatoes. "To be completely honest with you, she now has me doubting what I've always known as well."

Rather bluntly, Sandin said, "I don't think any of it matters." Oliver shot him a questioning look, and he continued, "What I mean, is that no matter which of you is correct, the great serpent will not return. If you and your family maintain rule, and Bhishma doesn't return, then all is well. If Gadiel is right and it was a sorcerer who created the monster, then we'll still be safe. I should think this 'clan' has been dead for a time. I've not heard of any sorcery happening in my lifetime. Either way, the serpent is long dead, the world is safe."

"I supposed you're right. It's like me to overthink these things," Oliver said, looking around at the growing crowd of buyers and sellers. His expression appeared to sour, and he grumbled, "Where is Peton?"

"Ah, there you are, Your Majesty!" A man came through the bustle of people along with the knights King Oliver had sent away. He was shorter than Sandin and the king, a thick beard on his face. Bushy brows laid over the top of gray eyes. He wore a smile that was inappropriate for the situation. Perhaps he didn't understand how dire things were.

Oliver looked relieved. He gently grabbed the man by the collar, leading him away as he spoke. "Lord Peton, there you are. This is Sandin." He gestured to the assassin; Sandin offered a curt nod as they pushed through a sea of people.

"Ah, and from which part of the king's royal body do you issue?" Lord Peton asked. Sandin didn't know how to answer him and found himself becoming embarrassed by his silence. Luckily, the king answered for him.

"He is my Dagger."

Walking behind the two men, Sandin saw Peton glance at the king with a confused look. "I'm not sure I follow, Majesty."

"This man," Oliver went on, "has been trained for the sole purpose of taking life. I am now indebted to him until my final breath. Sandin has joined us, and will fight at my side, no doubt keeping me alive when I make a mistake on the battlefield." It didn't last long, the words the king spoke, but it felt like forever.

When King Oliver stopped speaking, it was then that he noticed his fists were clenched. The fingernails were digging into his palms. The life of learning to be an assassin—as well as the multitude of lives he'd taken—would haunt him for an eternity. Many of the things he'd suffered, the iniquities he'd committed, had left scars on his mind. Scars that would most likely never fade and would always be with him until the day he ceased to live.

"Peton, we must move out at once to meet this spawn of Illiar," Oliver said as the crowd thinned. "Gather all able-bodied men. I fear the enemy will be here soon; send your men to the main gate by midday. Outfit them with whatever weaponry there is. Understand?"

"Aye. It will be done." Lord Peton marched away, leaving Sandin, Oliver, and his wolves in the square.

"Now what?" Sandin asked. The itch of battle pricked his fingertips once again. That's when a bell began to ring. Sandin looked up to find a high tower with a large, black bell sounding off. He noticed the people of Silvesca freeze in their tracks. "What does that mean?"

No one answered for a moment, then one of the Gilded Wolves uttered, "Enemies are nigh."

Chapter 28

"Let's go," Oliver shouted at Sandin. They ran through Silvesca, grabbing the first pair of horses they saw. The village people swarmed around them like a mad mob in a fit of panic. The gate came into view and on the other side were Silvescans readying themselves for battle.

This won't be enough, Oliver thought.

Lord Peton moved the word quickly through the village. Silvesca sat atop a hill. In the distance, Oliver could see thousands of Abithians converging toward them. The horror of how many Gosathan villages they'd already pillaged to be this far inland struck the king, causing his face to scrunch.

His people were suffering, and it was up to him to put an end to it. The land between Silvesca and the encroaching horde sloped downward before leveling. Oliver's eyes landed on the small forest that began where the decrescendo ended. Horses would not be ideal in the dense foliage, but it would be the perfect place to set up an ambush.

"We can't wait any longer," Oliver muttered to himself. He glanced around, noticing Sandin watching him idly. "This will have to do for now."

With a vast number of Silvescans gathered, the king led a surge of men, their swords, spears, and shields at the ready. He glanced back at Sandin; the man's face had transformed from its usual unreadable expression to something different, something darker. Written on his face was murderous intent.

To give his men courage, Oliver began shouting, "Look onward, men; for today, you shall earn your place in Volharis. Today you will cull the enemy, end bloodlines. Give back to the dry soil, quench its thirst. Water the ground with the blood of Abithians." He paused, looking around at his soldiers. Many of them were young, too young to be doing such a thing; however, he needed them. When he spoke again his voice was slightly lower. "And if you are to die today, then drag from this world as many Abithian stains as possible."

And the cries of several hundred warriors was his answer as the army surged toward the trees.

Oliver's thoughts meant to admonish him as he hid amongst the trees. *I'll never live up to him,* he thought. The king glanced up to where Sandin sat, higher up in the same tree Oliver used as cover. The limb he was on was thick and wide enough that he could sit on it comfortably.

The enemy approached, only a stone's throw away from the woods; some on horseback, others on foot. The king regarded them with respect for how quiet they were despite their number. Oliver and his soldiers waited a few paces into the forest, concealed by the trunks of trees. He'd ordered any gold and silver be removed, leaving many of them with sparse armor—most of it leather. Surprise was their greatest advantage, and he endeavored to play that card prudently.

Gorenos, see me and my men. Show favor on us this day. Help us to crush our enemy—that which is yours as well, the nonbelievers—beneath our heels, he prayed silently.

Moments later a rumble issued overhead. The dark sky fell then, raindrops pattering leaves, dripping down onto Oliver's hair, running down his face. He smiled as the first Abithian stepped into the trees.

"Now!" Oliver gave the command, alerting his forces to attack.

Bolts were released from crossbows. The twang of strings, dull thuds and sharp screams filled his ears as the arrows found their marks. When the first volley of arrows ceased, the remaining soldiers stormed forward. King Oliver sprang from behind a tree, rainwater running down his body. The Sword of Gorenos flew from its scabbard; clashing metal reverberated up the king's arm.

He parried, knocking the man's blade away. Pulling back and then thrusting, the tip of his sword glided easily through the leather armor of an Abithian. The man died almost instantly. Another Abithian immediately took his place, not giving Oliver even the time to consider the life he'd ended.

Battle raged all around him; flashes of metal, screams of rage and agony was all that Oliver could hear. A motion of black to his right and then Sandin was there, cutting into an Abithian who was trying to flank the king.

Reinforcements will come, he thought. *They have to.*

He'd ordered the council to send aid before departing Valendra, though he knew it would take a bit longer for help to arrive. Gathering and moving troops was no light task, but the king had faith they would arrive in time. Perhaps not in time to keep Oliver himself from being killed, but in time enough to save Silvesca.

"Push forward!" he cried out, the force tearing at his throat. Shouts of agreement returned to him.

Oliver noticed Sandin slashing throat after throat in a flurry, the black of his cloak and dark silver of his blades converging as he whipped about. It was a sight to behold, to marvel at how easily he moved through them. Seldom could the Abithians block his attacks before it was too late.

"Move as one," Oliver ordered. "Stay together! Push them back!"

As if they were of one mind, his soldiers stepped into a line together, pushing the enemy back inch by miraculous inch.

"Archers!" The king called out. The front line ducked as bolts flew over them. They gathered their feet under them and pressed forward.

More Abithians surged into the forest, but looking like they were trying to run from something. The king's men in the trees pushed back harder, cutting down enemies, making the more cowardly recoil back out into the open. He smiled broadly, turning his face upward, breathing hard.

The reinforcements from Valendra had arrived.

His smile faded as he was rushed by two enemies. Oliver lunged for the closest, knocking his blade to the side as the other stabbed for his heart. The king twisted away, the blade catching and cutting into Oliver's arm, but missing its intended target. As Oliver turned back, a sword dropped toward his head. He blocked the strike, grabbed the attacking wrist with his free hand, then swiped upward with his blade. The arm severed brutally, spurting blood as the Abithian screamed.

Oliver focused on the other Abithian who still held a sword. He was already swinging; Oliver parried, kicking the man in his chest. The sword fell from his hand and the attacker ignored it, ripping free a small axe from his belt instead. His eyes were wide and his teeth ground together in an animalistic snarl. As he rushed forward with axe held high, Oliver leapt forward, meeting him. The king ran through his enemy, twisted, then ripped his sword free and watched the Abithian slump to the wet ground. He looked around, his chest heaving for air.

Gosathans swarmed the enemy from every angle, like ants on a morsel of bread, pinching the enemy between them. Men on horseback galloped through the field of battle. Swords were rolling heads, spears impaling chests, shields splintering. Bodies littered the ground, many of them his own soldiers. His heart sounded like a drum in his ears.

Blood mixed with rain and mud. Looking around, Oliver saw many injured trying to crawl away or begging for help, for mercy. He remembered Queen Gadiel's betrayal, her words of derision at his beliefs, the mockery of which she made his religion. He remembered the men she'd ordered to take his life.

Had the circumstances not been what they were, he probably would have taken prisoners. However, with all that had occurred, his mood was anything but forgiving.

Wet, gold locks of hair dangled in the king's eyes. "Leave none alive," he commanded to the men, making eye contact with Sandin. The order resonated. Spears were thrust into the hearts of Abithians on that blood-soaked soil—whether they showed signs of life or not—just for good measure.

Sandin's eyes suddenly became wide; he lunged forward, hands outstretched toward the king. A sharp pain, searing, exploded from the ribs on Oliver's back, making him wince. He whipped around to find an enemy thrusting a small knife into him. Sandin was there a moment later, finishing the man off. Oliver felt the blood running before he reached back. It was hot, plentiful. His head swam as he slumped to his knees in the mud.

Chapter 29

How long had she been walking? What she would give to have her horse back; Oswin wasn't one of the animals to survive the attack on Eskasin. Legs burning, mouth dry with thirst; clearly Ara hadn't thought ahead, had not considered how long it would take to find Cassandra. In her current state, Ara didn't care where she ended up, she just wanted to find some fresh water.

Tall grass brushed along her knees, the sound of sparrows calling to one another rang out in the distance. She remembered the crow. How she wished that crow would return because that would mean the return of Cassandra Morteum as well.

I should never have spurned her, Ara thought. *Please, Cassandra, show yourself to me.*

The sun bore down on Ara relentlessly. How her body could have been ablaze the day prior, and the sun still scorch her, she couldn't discern. The heat from her fire-lit body hadn't bothered her, but at that moment, the heat of the sun was all she could feel.

Dust floated upward, the particles dancing in front of Ara's eyes as the rays of sun caught them. Her feet dragged, she noticed. Not even able to pick them up and place them down in front of her any longer. Ara licked her lips, trying feebly to get any moisture on them. She tasted iron.

Her lips had gone so dry they'd begun to split. She suckled at the blood, almost relishing it. The relief it gave wasn't adequate, nor did it last. Soon, she found herself slinking to the ground, a stone prodding at her stomach. She thought that perhaps the magic she expelled the previous night had taken a harsher toll on her body than she first thought. Her eyes closed, and she hoped it would be for the last time as the flutter of wings sounded. The thought of vultures tearing at her flesh made her stomach swirl; fortunately, Ara felt her consciousness slip before it began.

Ara was awoken by the cool touch of a wet rag on her forehead. Her hands twitched at her sides, jostling dry leaves. The sun shone in broken pieces through the tops of trees, and a woman was smiling down at her. A sad smile.

"Cassandra?" she asked, her voice raspy. "Is that you?" It had to be a mirage, trickery of her mind or something.

"I'm here, Ara. And I am never going to leave your side again. Here," she helped the girl sit up and pulled a water skin out from a bag. "Drink."

Ara drank happily, draining the water skin. When she finished, she croaked, "I don't understand. Where are we? How did you find me?"

The woman shook her head sadly. "I felt terrible after you left. I should never have treated you the way I did. Shortly after you and the boy had gone from Osta, I began tracking you. You two were always a day ahead of me. I flew through the sky in my crow form. Then I found what was left of Eskasin." She paused, sighing. "At first, I feared I would find your body among them, but when I didn't, I began searching for you again. I found you not long ago and took you to these woods to get your body out of the sun. We're just a few leagues east of Wemdal."

Ara couldn't decide if she was more shocked or thankful. "I was... looking for you. After they came. They... killed him—Cal. They were going to sell me to a pleasure house." Her eyes were wide, unblinking. "I slaughtered them, Cassandra."

The lady looked taken aback. "I *did* sense powerful magic in Eskasin, but I assumed the Abithians had a mage under their sleeve. Are you saying this was you?"

Ara nodded her head. "It was like nothing I've ever felt before. My rage overtook me, my body was aflame. The Abithians melted as I lashed my fists at them. I didn't even have one of your medallions to siphon energy into." Ara thought she saw Cassandra's eyes flash with something, but it vanished before she could decipher it.

"All of that with no guidance," Cassandra noted, almost sounding impressed. "I have heard of mages being able to wield without the medallion, but that would make you extraordinarily gifted. Ara, with my help, I believe you will become even stronger than I."

"That's why I was seeking you. Too much has been taken from me. This world must pay for what it has done. I want to become as strong as my body will allow. For vengeance."

"You have said similar things in the past." The woman's eyes went down to her hands.

Ara felt guilty but her desire to rid the world of her enemies was greater. "I will *never* abandon you again, Cassandra. Whatever you need of me, I will be here. I will do *whatever* it takes. You and I will show them how strong we are. Think about it; together, we'll be unstoppable I swear it." Ara felt the apprehension in Cassandra and would say anything to coax her in the right direction.

"You swear it?" Cassandra asked, eyes darting up to Ara's face. "You swear this is what you want?"

Ara nodded. "I don't care if it kills me; we will show the Jardanis family what happens when they cross a mage."

Cassandra smiled brightly. "Well, we had better get you all mended up. We have *quite* the journey to make."

"Where will we go?"

Cassandra rose to her feet, reaching a hand down to help the girl up. Her smile never faded, and her eyes nearly twinkled with excitement. "The Temple of Yoshikai; a holy place unlike anything you've ever seen—or heard of. A place of great tragedy, but of also great fortune. There you will grow into a force to be reckoned with. There we will unlock your full potential. Are you prepared to become something else? Something more than a mere Lowborn?"

Ara took her hand, standing with wobbly legs like a newborn fawn. She could feel heat rising to the surface of her skin once again. It wasn't the same heat that had come from the sun, but rather that burning fire that lived within, the one that burst forth in Eskasin. This sounded like everything she'd always dreamed of. With finality, she said, "I am."

Chapter 30

THE WOULD-BE KING KILLER was already half dead when the assassin sent him into the afterlife. There was a bloody wound on his chest, but he somehow found the strength to rise for one more chance at victory. Luckily, the blade was no longer than the length of a finger; had it been any longer, the blow would have killed him swiftly based on its positioning.

Initially, panic set in for Sandin. *They'll blame me for this,* was his first thought. Then, resolved to saving the king. Sandin recalled being lectured, in that moment, of how life saving techniques were meant to be used on oneself; not others, and especially not Gosathans. He nearly chuckled.

As Oliver fell, Sandin began examining the wound. "Oh, this isn't so bad. I've seen far worse."

"Dealt by yourself, no doubt," the king laughed, then groaned as Sandin put a bit of pressure around it to soak up some of the blood.

"We can't remove the blade here," he said, dabbing at the blood. The rain made the crimson run down his side. "We must get you back to Silvesca. I learned a bit of wound care in my training, but you'll need a surgeon."

"Aye, I'd agree with that notion," Oliver said, his words beginning to slur. "Sandin, I—." His words cut off abruptly, and his body began to slump against Sandin. Turning his face so that he could see his eyes, he noticed the king was staring into the sky, as if he was looking at something far away. His lids fluttered, his eyes rolling back to reveal only the whites.

"I need a horse!" Sandin shouted as the rain slowed to a sprinkle, elevating the agonized screams of the wounded. "Someone bring me a damned horse!" Then Lord Peton was there to answer the request.

"What happened?" Peton asked.

Sandin nearly growled, "Stabbed. He needs a surgeon. Quickly!"

The lord helped Sandin heave King Oliver over the back of a horse. Had Oliver been conscious, the jolt of a horse's stride would probably pain him greatly. "I'll get him taken care of," Lord Peton said, trotting away.

Looking around, Sandin couldn't help but notice how worried he was for the king. He'd learned long ago to deal with emotions, to shove them away if they did not help him. Why was he finding it so difficult to not care for the man? King Oliver was just the kind of person that changed those around him, made them better people.

Sandin found a horse for himself, leaping onto its back and riding to catch up with Lord Peton and the king.

"WILL HE BE ALRIGHT?" Sandin asked the surgeon. They were in a humble building made of wood and thatch. King Oliver lay on a bed with thick, white bandages wrapped around his abdomen. A gray blanket covered his legs. Peton sat on a wooden stool in a corner of the room. There was a table in front of him with an oil lamp flickering atop it.

Sandin's garments were soaked with rainwater and blood. He glanced down at his hands; blood was embedded beneath his nails. The lines of his hands were stained with it.

My blades are such messy things, he thought.

"King Oliver should be fine," the surgeon said. Sandin learned his name to be Taven. He was an older man, probably forty summers strong. "The blade didn't hit any vital organs; however, he did lose a good amount of blood. A rib is slightly broken, but not severely enough to have punctured a lung."

"When will he wake?" Sandin asked.

"That, I am unsure of. All we can do is wait and hope he stirs soon."

"What shall we do next?" Lord Peton asked.

Sandin waited, listening for an answer from Taven. None came. When Sandin looked between the men, he found them both looking at him, awaiting his answer. The last thing Sandin expected was to be making any sort of big decision on behalf of the Gosathans.

He cleared his throat. "Ride out and gather any leaders that remain on the battlefield. Have them return to Valendra."

"Valendra, sir?" Peton replied. "What if Abithia sends another attacking force from the same direction?" There was fear in his eyes.

"That won't happen, not for a while at least. You can calm yourself."

"How do you know for sure?"

"I was once an Abithian," Sandin said, expecting them to be wary of him. He didn't expect the lord to jump to his feet, assuming a fighting stance. "I have the full confidence of King Oliver, my lord."

"How am I supposed to know you aren't spying for them?" The man's voice quavered; he was clearly on edge still.

"If that were the case," Taven cut in, "he would not be so concerned with the king's recovery. He would have let him die out there, I think." Sandin looked at the surgeon, surprised at his defense. The older man gave him a nod of acknowledgement.

Lord Peton nodded his head, taking a calming breath. "Very well. Forgive my wariness, Sandin. The emotions of the battle are still with me."

You don't say.

"I understand," Sandin said, calming his own nerves with an easy breath. "Now, this would have depleted the Abithian forces some. The queen will be overtaking the warring islands now, setting up defenses. Our best hope is to set up defense on Gosatha's shores.

Have the military leaders return to Valendra and carry that message to the council."

"I will see to it," the lord said, bowing out of the building.

SANDIN SAT ATOP THE thatched roof, watching the sun dip beneath the horizon when Taven exited the building, calling for him. He hopped down, passing by the line where his cloak hung to dry. A gentle breeze swept through, the air getting colder as winter pressed in. Down the street were a couple of children—no older than ten by Sandin's guess—sitting with their backs resting against each other. Their hands were outstretched, begging for food as Silvescan citizens walked by.

Sandin's brows pinched as he thought, *Here too? Why must this happen?*

"He's waking," Taven said, holding the door open for him.

Sandin followed the surgeon inside, seeing the king's head turning left and right. His feet were moving subtly under the blanket, and his eyelids fluttered open. He looked around slowly and Sandin found himself smiling at the king. He felt at odds with himself; previously an assassin for Abithia, and now what? A subject, a killer, a friend to the king of Gosatha? Oliver said he was his Dagger.

But can I be the Dagger for another ruler? he pondered.

"Welcome back from Middaras, Majesty," Taven said. Oliver looked confused, so he explained. "It's what Abithia refers to as the middle in reference to death. It's the place one goes before entering Volharis or Icuzar."

Oliver nodded. "Where is the bastard that stuck me?"

Sandin replied, "He's been dealt with, of course, King Oliver. If you are to exact revenge, you'll have to chase his soul down in the afterlife."

Oliver chuckled, grimacing as the effort caused him discomfort. He prodded the bandaged wound with a finger. "It would seem that you kept me alive," he said to Taven. "I owe you a debt."

"Think nothing of it," Taven replied with a dismissive wave. "It is my job—and my passion—to keep those of Gosatha alive. And to save the life of the king? Well, that's a dream come true. Not that I would wish for your life to be in danger; however, I am glad it was me who kept you kicking."

"When can he leave?" Sandin asked.

"That depends on how he feels. Are you ready to try sitting up, Majesty?"

"Aye," Oliver said, gathering his elbows under him. He winced as he did. "Anything for the pain?" The king was able to move into a full sitting position as Taven handed him a bottle of transparent, brown liquid.

"Only the finest for you," he said with a wink.

King Oliver took a deep draught of the liquid. His voice came out strained. "Aye, that burns nicely." He handed the liquor back to Taven and turned to Sandin. "What have I missed during my beauty sleep?"

Sandin told him what he'd passed on to Lord Peton. The king nodded as he listened. "Good idea. I'm glad I can trust you to make wise decisions, Sandin."

Sandin kept his expression hidden as he asked, "Why do you?"

"What?"

"Why do you trust me? I was an enemy not long ago. I was the Royal Dagger of Abithia. It would seem foolish to trust a man like me."

Oliver seemed to consider it. "You had a great sense of loyalty to Queen Gadiel, don't you agree?" Sandin nodded. "Even with that strong of loyalty you had for her, you were able to see her wicked actions and act against them. You killed your people to see that justice was upheld. Even though you've killed for her many times, when faced with a tough choice, you did the right thing. That's why I trust you."

Sandin beamed, feeling reassured in his place at the king's side. "What shall we do now?" Sandin asked as Oliver rose to his feet gingerly.

"We'll gather our dead, give them a proper burial. Then, we will go back to Valendra, gather the Council, and develop a plan of attack that will leave Abithia in ashes." A chill ran up Sandin's spine; the peace that Oliver had wanted so badly had fled him. He wanted—or so it seemed—to destroy Abithia entirely.

Chapter 31

THE PAIN OF MOVING around was intense, but it was nothing compared to the rage King Oliver felt, the motivation he had to crush Abithia beneath his heel like a bug. He and Sandin travelled back to Valendra; the five knights who'd come with them all fell in battle. All Gosathans were given a warrior's funeral. Pyres were erected around the battlefield; priests of Gorenos set them ablaze, saying a prayer to the gods for hope that his soldiers would be given passage into Volharis.

As for the Abithians, the dead were piled up and burned as well; however, no prayer was said over their souls. The battlefield was rife with fire, filling the air with the stink of burning flesh and hair. Flies swarmed, unable to break from the meal of a lifetime even as flames destroyed them.

Oliver passed through the battlefield prior to the burning, letting his eyes fall over the faces of his fallen. How those faces will be burned into his mind until he breathes his last...

I failed them, he thought, turning toward Valendra.

The horses carrying them home moved slowly; each step of their hooves jostled Oliver, causing a stinging pain to shoot through his ribs. The pain of the broken rib made each breath shallow. Sandin wore his cloak with the hood up; Oliver had a coat of fur on, and still had goose flesh on his arms, though sweat beaded on his forehead.

He cleared his throat. "I must ask you something, Sandin."

"Go on."

"How hard a blow do you think this was to Gadiel? Do we stand a chance at defeating her now?"

"This was only a fraction of her warriors," Sandin replied. "It won't be easy to bring her down, Majesty. I will do what I can to aid you; however, I must be forthcoming with something. I don't wish to see the queen die. She's the only motherly figure I had in my life after my parents were taken from me. If it comes down to it, I won't be able to end her life."

Oliver stared at the path in front of him. "I understand. There are people in my life that I've crossed that I wouldn't wish to see die as well." He remembered Ara, wondering what the girl had made of her life since he last saw her. He hoped she was well.

"Your Royal Council distrusts me," Sandin noted. "They won't heed my advice without struggle."

Oliver chuckled. "I don't much care what the Council thinks. I sat back and let them *prattle* on in the past, when my father ruled. He would entertain their pretentiousness, but I, however, will not."

KING OLIVER STARED AT his hands as he sat in his sunlit bed, remembering the way they'd been covered in blood at the end of the battle in Silvesca. Faces of the men he'd slain flashed through his mind, the screams echoed in his head. His hands reached up to rub at his face. A mug of ale sat on a desk near his bed, and he reached out, fumbling with the handle to bring it to his lips.

The wound in Oliver's side had become itchy; it would crack if he twisted too far one way. He and Sandin arrived at Valendra, notifying only Tiberius and the Queen Mother. Sandin snaked off into a bed chamber to rest as Oliver did the same. Oliver melted into the sheets, wanting to stay there forever.

He stretched, groaning as the stitches pulled taut. Rolling over, Oliver brought his feet over the edge of the bed. The stone floor was cold, but he welcomed it. He stood and dressed himself. His father had always used one of the royal body to aid in getting dressed, but Oliver felt it was unnecessary.

Oliver pulled on his tunic and breeches, followed by a surcoat with the emblem of Gosatha emblazoned on the chest. He drank deeply from his mug, emptying its contents, then propped the crown atop his head. After cleaning blood and grime from the Sword of Gorenos, Oliver strapped it to his waist. As Oliver left his chamber, he idly twisted the king's ring on his pinky.

"Tiberius." He found the inquisitor in one of the corridors. The guards who'd been outside the king's chamber followed closely behind. "I have a task for you to see to." Tiberius nodded his head once. "Send the heralds throughout Velendra; I want every available citizen gathered in the courtyard around midday."

"I will see it done, Your Majesty," the man replied, bowing at the waist before marching off.

Walking further, Oliver found his mother, hugging her gently. Her returned embraced made him wince. "My poor boy. How are you feeling?"

He smiled softly. "I feel okay. The mending rib is the worst of it, I think. Makes breathing rather bothersome."

"Your father had a similar injury once," she told him. "He acted as if it were nothing but a scratch; of course, when we were alone, he whined on and on about it." The two of them laughed.

"How are the girls?" he asked.

"Good, good. Ruelle says she misses you. The others do as well, but they won't say it. They're in the phase that makes them think they needn't show much emotion."

"I believe we all need a day out together," Oliver said with a smile. "Perhaps a picnic?"

She smiled at him. "That sounds lovely, dear. I'll let the girls know."

"Mother," he said, grasping her wrist as she turned away. "There is something else I need you to do first. Inform the council that I will be addressing the citizens at midday in the courtyard. I expect them to be there."

She nodded. "I will ensure their attendance."

"Thank you." He kissed her on the cheek, allowing her to leave.

KING OLIVER HAD COUNCILMEN to his left and right, Sandin directly behind him. He gazed out over his subjects, his eyes bouncing from face to face, taking in as much detail as possible. He felt a slight shake in his hands, his legs, as hundreds of eyes looked up at him. The two mugs of ale hadn't calmed his nerves much. The crowd was caught in clamorous chatter.

As loud as he could muster, he said, "People of Valendra, be silent." He waited for their voices to dissipate. "Much has happened as of late. Just a couple of days ago, the Abithians breached our shores to the south." More talking broke out until the king lifted his hands, silencing them. "I met with the queen of Abithia in an attempt to come to a peace agreement. She betrayed my good faith, tried to have me killed.

"Several of our villages burned to the south of Silvesca before we were able to stop them. All who attacked us are now dead. I mean to strike back at the Abithians now, while their forces are weakened. This will be a difficult time for us as we lost many in the battle at Silvesca. I will ask much of each of you, whether you are a smith, a surgeon, or a butcher. It is possible that many of you will be taken to fight this war. For that, I am truly sorry. It's not my wish to continue fighting, but justice must be had."

Raucous conversing rose up as people protested the notion of being drafted to fight in a war that he knew they didn't understand. Getting louder, King Oliver called out, "The queen has insulted our gods—our way of life. Her armies come for you, for your families. She means to destroy us entirely, so stand with me, stand up and fight for what is right!"

What was derision before, then turned to adulation. Fists pumped in the air as people cheered. Oliver turned on his heel, marching back into the palace with Sandin and the councilmen behind him.

"What is your plan, Majesty?" asked Lord Tobias.

Without looking, the king replied, "To the war room, all of you."

Oliver allowed the men to flow past him. Only Sandin remained behind. "You've developed a plan so soon?"

"Aye. Let's just hope the council doesn't bellyache much."

As if that's ever happened, Oliver thought.

The council waited silently when King Oliver and Sandin entered the room. Oliver walked over, glancing down at the large world map on the central table. The models of ships—both friendly and foe—remained scattered about.

Oliver leaned on the table, his eyes moving around the map before looking up at the councilmen. "Listen closely, lords; this is what we are going to do..."

Chapter 32

THE RIVER BALSKA EMPTIED into the Tamagua sea in the western region of Gosatha. Ara and Cassandra went down the river, passing through the port village of Kierith in the cover of night. The sorceress told Ara that the king's soldiers may try stopping them if they saw the two trying to leave the kingdom, as such an act in the dead of night could be considered suspicious. The muscles in her arms burned as she rowed the oars of the skiff. Water sloshed against the front of the small boat, splashing over the sides and wetting Ara's feet every now and then.

"How far is it?" Ara asked, glancing back at the shore of Kierith. The moon was bright, bouncing off the water around them.

"Do you see that star?" Cassandra pointed at the sky. Ara followed her finger, her eyes landing on a star that appeared to shine brighter than the others. She nodded. "If we follow this star's path, we should be there by morning."

"You've been to this temple before?" Ara asked.

"Aye," Cassandra replied, smiling softly. "Only once before."

"What was it like?" Ara leaned forward slightly. The mystery of the temple struck her with curiosity. There seemed to be so much about her world that she was ignorant to.

"That is a story best saved for a later time, my dear."

Ara frowned as she sat back. A seed of doubt blossomed in her mind as she asked, "Do you think this will work? Will it really make magic come easier to me? What if the flames I created were a fluke?"

Cassandra waved her hand. "Nonsense. It's in your blood, my dear. I know this to be true, and in time, you will realize that I am right."

Ara's brows pinched. "But I'm Lowborn," Ara argued. "My blood can't be so special."

The woman shook her head. She sounded slightly exasperated, saying, "Is your body erupting in flame not enough to show that you are special?" She sighed. "I didn't know how to tell you this, but your mother had similar abilities. Would you say her blood was ordinary too?"

Ara nearly dropped the oars at the mention of her mother. She ignored the question. "Why wouldn't you tell me this sooner?"

"I didn't wish to get your hopes up back when you struggled to produce even a spark, Ara. To be honest, I wasn't sure if magic was in your blood or not. But now that I know, I felt I should tell you."

Ara looked down. "Well, thank you for telling me now." There was silence, save for the crash of waves against the hull of the skiff. Then Ara asked, "Do you think I'll be able to change shape like you?" Ara had seen her change into a crow a handful of times since reuniting, and it seemed to amaze her unceasingly. The mage was always there, nearly her entire life, it would seem.

"It's difficult to say for sure," Cassandra answered. "History shows that mages always differ in ability and power. There are certain things we are adequate at, and others, not so much. For instance, my father was *quite* savvy at manipulating the mind. He could place images in one's head that would make them go insane. I have never been able to figure that out; however, I have always been gifted at changing my shape."

Her body began to warp, turning from a human to a small, black rabbit. Ara looked down at her, amusement on her face. A second later, Cassandra shifted back to her original form with a wide smile. The moon lit up her pale skin, making it almost glow.

"I've never seen you be anything other than the crow," Ara noted.

"I can replicate most living creatures, but the crow I relate to the most. I find flying to be rather exhilarating."

Ara could feel her arm strength beginning to fade. "This is tiresome work," she grunted. "It's too bad I can't summon a great wave to push us along."

"Allow me. Rest your eyes, dear. We shall be upon our destination soon enough."

Ara laid down in the bottom of the skiff, curling up in a ball. She laid her head on a pile of coiled ropes, closed her eyes, and let the gentle waves and Cassandra's soft humming send her into sleep.

"ARA, WAKE UP."

The girl stirred in the skiff. Early morning light was on the horizon. The moon had almost disappeared completely. Sitting up, Ara stretched her stiff arms and climbed back up to her seat. She knuckled the sleep from her eyes and began looking around. They approached a small island.

"That's it then?" she asked, becoming more nervous.

"That it is," Cassandra replied, rowing them closer. Her eyes were wide. "I have only dreamed of coming here again; I never thought it would be reality."

"Is this where your magic grew to what it is?" Ara asked.

"No," she replied. "I once tried to see my birthright fulfilled here but was left disappointed." Her voice was solemn. Ara tilted her head quizzically, but the lady didn't say more.

Ara jumped from the skiff as she grabbed the rope and pulled the boat ashore. Cassandra followed, helping her drag it further up into the sand, lest the tide carry it away and strand them.

Tall trees rose up around them, and a mountain peak could be seen in the distance. Ara pointed at it. "Is that where we go?"

"Aye," Cassandra answered. "The Temple of Yoshikai lies within the mountain. *In the heart of stone where shadows play, lies the holy temple in the mountain's face.*"

"Where did you learn all of this?" Ara asked as they began walking into the forest. She regretted not having a sword of some kind as thickets and brambles pulled at her clothes.

"My father taught me much of magic. Our bloodline goes back ages, all masters of the arcane." The green emerald on the chain fell out of Cassandra's dress, dangling and glinting in the low sun that was shining through the canopy.

"Will I be getting another of the medallions?" she asked, gesturing to Cassandras.

"I think not, my dear. Based on what you told me of the fire coming from you, I believe the medallion would be of little use to you. In fact, the last one could have been what was blocking the magic from rising to the surface in the first place."

"Confusing business, magic is," Ara said. "Cassandra, look." Just up ahead was the base of the mountain.

"Turn here," she said, pointing to Ara's right. "The entrance will be subtle, a small crevice in the base of the mountain."

"Are there any dangers here that you know of?" Ara turned to her right. The mountain was tall, but not as tall as the Gorgaw. A pang of hurt entered her heart just thinking about it. Her skin burned once more as she grinded her teeth.

I wish Cal was here, she thought.

"None greater than you would find in Osta. Here," Cassandra said, handing her a chunk of bread. "Eat before we get to the temple; it may take us some time."

Ara ripped a piece of bread with her teeth, wishing she had a stew to dip it in. After walking for a long time, they finally happened upon a narrow slit at the foot of the mountain. Ara peered inside, seeing nothing but pitch. She looked back at Cassandra who looked the utmost elated to have found the entrance.

"After you," Ara said. And then the sorceress stepped foot into the darkness with Ara on her heels.

THE COLD MET ARA'S face almost immediately, contradicting the heat that radiated from her skin. "I can't see a thing," she complained. The light that cut in from outside didn't make it far before being swallowed by shadows.

"Hold on." A small flame appeared and then Ara noticed it was floating above Cassandra's palm. "Let's go."

The sorceress led the way. There appeared to be only one direction for them to travel. They walked down a wide path. Ara looked up but couldn't see the ceiling. The cold of the cavern left chills crawling all over her; she shivered, wishing she could control the magic inside her already if only to warm the numbness in her fingertips.

The path was dirt-covered, directed toward the center of the mountain. Ara felt it decline, diving down below the surface. The squeak of a bat rang out, echoing off the rocky walls. The sound of crashing water issued from ahead of them, getting louder as they approached.

"This is going to be miserable for you," Cassandra shouted over the sound of a waterfall. The words confused Ara.

They were a few paces away and the light provided by the mages' flame allowed them to partially see the torrent of water ahead. They found themselves in a vast cavern; a pool of water lay ahead of them. The thought of stepping into water in such a dark place made Ara tremble. She could swim just fine, but not knowing what was in the water scared her.

"I don't know if I can do this," she said, taking a small step away from the pool.

"Nonsense. You are a strong, young woman, Ara. I will go first, and you will follow." Her piercing gaze left no room for argument.

Ara nodded. Cassandra took a tentative step into the water. Following her, Ara inhaled sharply as the icy water went over her boots, freezing her legs. Each step was harder than the previous, her limbs becoming heavy as rocks.

"How... are you... doing this so easily?" Ara asked in between rocky breaths. Her teeth were chattering as the water touched her belly.

"Physical ailments are not something that have plagued me for some time, Ara. With practice, you too will be able to block such things out."

Ara couldn't wait for that day.

"Don't fear the darkness, girl," Cassandra called back. Ara was waist-deep in the black waters. The waterfall was an arm's length away. "We must go through. Take my hand." She reached back and Ara grasped it.

The flame lighting their way winked out; Ara was dragged through the waterfall. It was like liquid ice raining down on her. She gasped, then regretted it; water spilled into her open mouth, and she gagged, spluttering. She tried pulling back, but Cassandra didn't let go, continued to drag Ara through. Finally, the torrent dissipated; Ara fell onto semi-dry ground, coughing. The flame in Cassandra's hand was reawakened and then she was in the girl's face.

"Ara, are you alright?"

Ara nodded and coughed one more time before gathering her feet beneath her. She rubbed her arms with cold hands. "Let's just get this over with. I want to be free of this place."

Cassandra smiled. "Very well." She turned and they went on. The water squelched from her boots as they continued. Ara's clothes felt heavy on her body, and she found herself hovering closer to the flame in Cassandra's hand, absorbing what little warmth it provided.

There was no telling how far they'd trekked, Ara just wanted the heat to return to her stiff limbs. The stabbing pain of frozen appendages was all she knew for a time. Then Cassandra said in an awed voice, "Ara, look." She looked around the sorceress. The glow of the flame cast upon a wall. Carved into the wall face were symbols that Ara could not read in the form of an arch.

"What is this?" she asked.

Cassandra moved closer, finding and lighting two torches on the wall. Their glow made it much easier to see, and the woman was able to release her magic. She read, "*Tor nain il pelim, fiet il geso pratium.*" Ara waited a moment and Cassandra translated, "To enter the temple, find the key that lies within. It's a riddle that was once a nuisance to me."

"What does it mean?" Ara asked, unsure of what to make of the riddle. A key that lies within? Within what?

Cassandra turned to face Ara, her eyes bright. "Do you trust me, Ara?"

Ara didn't answer her for a moment. Trust was a hard thing to come by, although, it hadn't always been that way. Finally, she nodded, despite the dread that filled her. She'd trusted Oliver and look where that got her.

Cassandra isn't at fault for that, she thought.

Cassandra pulled a small knife from a pouch in her dress, the blade reflecting the dancing flames. Ara's eyes widened as the woman dragged it across her palm. A line of red dribbled out, pooling in her hand. She slapped her hand against the wall. At first, nothing happened, but then the crimson liquid began crawling up the rock of its own volition.

The blood spread as if the mountain had veins, crawling up to the nearest symbol. The blood filled the symbol, taking on a faint glow. It continued up the arch of markings but stopped halfway. Cassandra looked at her hand to find it still dripping blood. She tore a piece of her dress, wrapping it tightly around the wound.

Then her eyes moved to Ara. "Your hand, dear." She didn't wait for Ara to respond but reached down and grabbed her wrist rather forcefully. The woman dragged her knife across Ara's palm. The stinging pain made her grimace. Blood leaked from her hand as Cassandra pulled her over to the wall, slapping her palm against the stone.

Just like before with Cassandra, Ara's blood began crawling up the wall, connecting with the symbols. When her blood filled up the strange markings, she stepped back and wrapped her hand as well. The blood warmed her hand a bit.

The ground beneath their feet began to rumble; Ara threw her arms out to keep her balance. Cassandra stepped back as well. Dust fell from the ceiling, and the sound of rock grinding on rock filled the air. In front of them the wall split just beneath the symbols. Ara's eyes found Cassandra's which were smiling, a spark of excitement lighting in them. The rock slid open, and they stepped inside. Cassandra's hands reached out as they crossed the threshold, flames spit away from them, igniting torches all along the walls.

"We've made it," Cassandra said reverently, her voice barely a whisper. "The Temple of Yoshikai."

Chapter 33

KING OLIVER'S PLAN WASN'T the worst one Sandin had ever heard; it was risky, but if executed properly, it would work. He thought about it as they walked through dark corridors to their chambers. Sandin would be instrumental in the undertaking. His knowledge of Abithia—of Stoneforge—was paramount. They would move around the smaller islands that Abithia currently held, probe the enemy shores with distracting assaults, and send a smaller force into Stoneforge to kill Queen Gadiel.

Sandin rarely got nervous, but thinking about taking the life of the woman he'd killed so many for, made his legs feel weak. The time to move on Abithia was closing in, and as it grew nearer, the more difficult falling asleep became. Once King Oliver was feeling well enough, they would set sail on the Tamagau.

Sandin dreaded being out on those waters almost as much as the thought of killing Gadiel. It needed to be Oliver, the one to make her draw her final breath.

Oliver will kill her, he thought. *And leave her lifeless body for all to see, claiming Abithia as an extension of his kingdom.*

A regent would be put in place—an Abithian—to carry out King Oliver's royal decrees, maybe even the King Consort. Sandin believed it would work; the Abithian citizens wanted the war to end as well. The nobles are the ones who will resist; they are the ones who profit from war, the men who gain coin from selling weapons and armor, and horses for the riding soldiers.

Sandin's time in Shadowspire came back to him, would always be with him no matter how many times he tried to forget the pain he endured there.

"Without pain, one cannot experience peace," he remembered Helfi telling them.

As they walked, King Oliver asked, "Would you tell me more of your time in Shadowspire?" Sandin glanced over and he explained, "So that I may understand your life better."

Sandin nodded, not seeing a point in hiding his life from Oliver. "There were twenty of us in number, all boys older than I. Even now, I can see their faces. Not only were they older, but larger; I'd been on the streets of Myrathis for a time, eating scraps and rats outside of taverns to survive. Helfi asked me if I'd like a place to sleep, to eat, to live in exchange for work. I remember not caring what sort of work the man would have me do; I just wanted some security." He paused, almost chuckling at the nostalgia of getting plucked from the streets.

"Sounds like you were strong from the start," Oliver said.

Sandin shrugged. "The other boys had been in Shadowspire longer and had better technique when it came to hand-to-hand combat. However, I was a survivor, and in the school that bred assassins, rules were scarce. I would often go for eyes, jamming my tiny fingers into sockets, or twisting single fingers to make opponents release me. In Shadowspire everything was a competition. In the end, only five of the original twenty I'd trained with graduated; the others either died during training or were expelled."

They reached King Oliver's chamber, bid each other a good night, and Sandin strolled to his chamber. It was stark within as Sandin lit a single candle to bash some of the shadows away. Sighing deeply, he took off his boots, letting them plop beside his bed.

The flame of the candle flickered. A movement so slight that Sandin could almost have imagined it. He glanced around, moving nothing but his eyes, and noticed an unnatural shifting to the shadows of his chamber. To the untrained eye, everything would have appeared normal; however, Sandin's eyes were trained for such things. He knew how to move about the shadows unnoticed, which meant he could also detect others with similar skills.

Sitting on his bed, Sandin swiftly choked the flame of the candle, breathing in its smoke as he laid his head back as if to go to sleep. The image of the candle flame was burned into Sandin's mind as he blinked against the dark. Moonlight broke through a small window, but it wasn't bright. The dark offered fairness in a fight; it leveled the playing field, for no man could see properly through it. Sandin had spent several days in the chamber and knew it well, or better than the stranger within, at least.

Almost complete silence as a blade cut through air. Even his ears were trained to recognize such a subtle change in sound. Sandin gave this killer his respect, admired him for being able to sneak into Valendra and into the king's palace without alerting guards. But what else would he expect of a trained assassin?

Sandin felt the wind of the blade move past his neck as he turned ever so slightly in the bed. He heard the dull thud of the knife tip plunging into the mattress. Sandin grabbed his attacker's arm, thwarting him from retracting the blade to make another attempt on his life. He held the assassin's arm with one hand, reaching up with his free one and grabbed the man's throat. A fist connected with Sandin's cheek. In the dim light, he faintly made out the assailant's outline.

Getting his legs in between them, Sandin kicked the man away and then clambered to his feet. The floor was like a shock of ice on his bare feet. His face was hot and throbbing, but he ignored the pain. It paled in comparison to what he'd endured during his training.

He stalked forward slowly as the other assassin circled toward the door. Sandin changed direction to make it harder for the attacker to escape if he tried. "Who are you? Tell me your name," Sandin demanded. The assassin was silent. They were in a dance of wits, a competition to see who would make the first mistake.

Dashing forward, Sandin struck out at the man. His fist was a breath away from connecting when the man arced his arm upward, deflecting the blow perfectly. He struck out with a kick that landed on Sandin's inner thigh. He could already feel a deep bruise forming beneath the surface. Sandin jumped at his would-be killer, feigning a strike with his left knee. Whilst in midair, he saw the man move to block and, just as he'd planned, Sandin switched knees at the last second. His right knee crashed into his opponent's chin. He heard the man grunt as he fell backward.

Sandin landed on top of him, straddling his body. He let punches fall, raining down onto the attacker's face. The man turned away, a feeble attempt at avoiding the strikes. This only gave up his back. Sandin wrapped his arms around the man's neck, squeezing slowly. The attacker reached back to gouge Sandin's eyes, to pull his hair, to do anything to make him release his hold. Sandin felt the man's body become limp; he held on for another couple of seconds before letting go.

Sandin breathed hard as he bound the man's wrists behind him with a short length of rope. Only when he was sure the attacker would be unable to wriggle free did he check for a pulse. After confirming he was still alive, Sandin patted his body down for more weapons. He removed a glass vial that was undoubtedly poison. Then he struck a match, lighting the candle once again, and bringing it close so he could see the man's face. Based on the skill of the assassin, Sandin had already sensed who this was, but still found himself surprised to see the face before him.

THE MEMORY FLASHING THROUGH Sandin's mind took him back many years. In this memory, he was around twelve years of age, still growing into his young body. His limbs weren't yet strong; however, he was far stronger than he'd been before entering Shadowspire.

Charcoal corridors ran throughout the school—a building that sat atop tall cliffs, and held passageways leading beneath the ground. It was dark and wet mostly. Sandin recalled being an outsider amidst outsiders, finding himself bullied by other students a lot of the time. Grandmaster Helfi had ensured his survival on many occasions, but there was one other who had a hand in making Sandin into an adept assassin.

Sandin found himself—not for the first time—a breath away from death. It had been a while since any of the other students had messed with him. Two larger boys stood to Sandin's left and right, barring his escape, as a sword was aimed for his heart. He'd been tricked into thinking they were his friends, lured from the confines of Shadowspire.

"Go on, jump, you *flea*," the sword-wielding boy said. His name was Agalo: the first boy Sandin had *truly* hated. "Jump or I skewer you first."

Sandin's mind had been reeling in effort to formulate a plan of escape; however, hope slowly drained from him. Trying to get past the larger boys was fruitless; they were too strong.

His heart thumped against his chest like a drum as they shoved him forward, ignoring his protests, and laughing. Then the hands vanished with the sounds of painful grunting. Agalo had gritted his teeth in anger, running toward Sandin. With the numbers more even—and rage abundant—Sandin decided to fight back, ignoring that which was occurring behind him.

He twisted as the sword tip was thrust at his sternum, catching just a hint of the blade. It cut him shallowly enough for him to ignore it. He grabbed Agalo's wrist and twisted it toward the ground. The blade fell when the wrist crunched. Sandin's assailant dropped to the ground with a cry of pain.

When Sandin turned to face the other two, he found them writhing on the ground. They bled lightly, clutching at their backs where they'd presumably been wounded. One lone boy stood there. Another boy who kept to himself like Sandin did. In that moment, a friendship was born, and the two grew closer for a time. Over the years, they made each other better fighters—better killers. It was when Sandin had been named Royal Dagger over him that any friendliness between them died.

"His name is Ysra," Sandin told King Oliver and High Inquisitor Tiberius. They had him tied to a wooden chair. Ysra had awoken, now sitting there looking straight ahead. He hadn't uttered a word. "I know him from Shadowspire."

"The school for assassins in Abithia?" Tiberius asked. Sandin nodded.

"And the two of you were friends?" Oliver asked.

"Aye. Or as close to friends as two could be in Shadowspire. You don't make *real* friends because of moments such as this. I'd say it's safe to assume Queen Gadiel is less than pleased with me." Ysra looked at Sandin then, smirking.

But why not go after Oliver, he wondered.

"How did you make your way into the palace?" Tiberius asked him.

Ysra turned his eyes to the inquisitor and smiled. "This palace's defenses are laughable. Your guards have become too comfortable; they do not expect the likes of me to make such an attempt. You have my admiration for having the king's chamber well defended, though. I cased it out before, just for future use."

Tiberius growled, "That didn't answer my question."

"I know." Tiberius struck him across the cheek, only making him laugh.

"He'll never tell you what you want to know," Sandin commented, taking his tunic off to reveal a series of scars on his chest, back, and arms. "We learned how to withstand pain even under the scrutiny of a blade. Not even an open flame upon his skin would loosen his lips."

Tiberius turned to the king. "What shall we do with him, Majesty?"

Oliver crossed his arms. "Sandin was this man's target; he should decide." Then he turned to Ysra. "Why *did* you go after Sandin? If you're near to Sandin's skill, my guards may not have proved much of a match for you. Why did Gadiel order you to pursue him?"

Ysra smirked. "As there's no point in me keeping it to myself now... The queen harbors grudges for a long time, Gosathan. Sandin is a *traitor*; he deserves death. As well, his knowledge of Abithia is great. He is, perhaps, our most dangerous foe, now that he has defected."

The king nodded, considering his words. "Well, Sandin. You're his mark; what shall we do with him?"

If the roles were reversed, Sandin had no doubt that Ysra would have him killed. Perhaps quickly, perhaps not. He'd probably do it himself. What kind of man did he want to be? He didn't want to show weakness, nor did he want to be perceived as a monster—although he knew he'd become a monster a long time ago.

Can a man who has gone to such dark places change? he wondered.

"We take him with us on the Tamagau," Sandin began. Ysra gave him a questioning look. "We release him into those waters, give him a chance at reaching Abithia. If he makes it there alive, then he deserves to live."

Oliver chuckled. "Very well. A bit ironic; I'd have killed him while tied to that chair." He turned to Ysra. "Ysra of Abithia, you shall accompany us aboard the *Gale* where we will surrender you to the beasts of the sea."

Ysra stared at Sandin. He only looked away when he was hauled to his feet. Shackles were slapped on his wrists and ankles before being pushed into a dirty cell.

Sandin released a deep breath. "You could have heard my side of all this, Ysra. The queen is not a goddess; she is but a coward."

"That may be," he answered quietly. "But she is still my queen, *Tyilnoir*."

"What did he say?" Oliver asked as they walked down the corridor away from the cell.

"*Tyilnoir*", he repeated. "It means traitor in the assassin's tongue."

Tiberius laughed, "You have an entire language just for killers?"

"*Hais*," he said with a smirk.

In truth, Sandin was sad for this to have happened. He would have wished for any other person to be his would-be killer, but Ysra was sent for a reason. The queen kept close tabs on Shadowspire students, and knew the two had been friends as boys. She knew the effect this would have on Sandin, and she wanted him to feel pain, to know her wrath. Sandin figured Queen Gadiel knew Ysra would fail unless Sandin was caught off guard. Sandin was *rarely* caught off guard.

The queen knew that Sandin would either kill an old friend or be forced to watch him die at the hands of others. She wanted to hurt Sandin's soul, knowing that hurting him physically was not likely. In a matter of moments, Sandin found himself not that bothered at the prospect of watching the Abithian Queen's breath leave her body.

THE WARSHIPS WERE ARMED to the tooth, outfitted with enough weapons, men, and supplies for a fortnight. The *Gale* carried the king and a small order of men setting out on a quest to take Abithia down in one fell swoop. The seas, however, seemed to be against their endeavor as the waves crested high and crashed hard on the hull of the ships. The fleet moved out together, each captain with their own specific orders to carry out. Before long, the boats began to spread and scatter through the Tamagau.

Rain and wind battered Sandin, leaving his cloak sopping wet yet again. Rain was becoming Sandin's least favorite of all the elements. Their captain shouted orders at the crew as they fought against the storm to get the sails stabilized.

Besides King Oliver and Sandin and the crew of the *Gale,* there was Inquisitor Tiberius and a couple of the most trusted and promising Gilded Wolves. Sandin learned their names to be Drago and Arlith. Each of them had seen combat and had taken a man's life more than once. When Sandin searched their faces for signs of weakness, he found they at least *looked* hardened on the outside. All who were not part of the ship's crew tried to stay out of the way but were jostled about the ship.

Then finally, as the sun peeked out from behind ominous clouds and descended beneath the horizon, the storm and waves faded. They'd become a bitter memory that Sandin would soon forget. He had done Ysra the courtesy of not releasing him amongst the ravenous water during the squall, but the time had arrived; they could carry the assassin no further.

Sandin dragged Ysra to his feet, holding him by the ropes binding his wrists. "I wish things had been different, truly," Sandin told him. "May the gods guide you."

"I thought you didn't believe in the gods," Ysra sneered.

"I'm not sure what to believe in anymore, but I know that you believe in them or used to." Sandin found himself hoping that Ysra lived, that they would see each other again one day, but as friends once more. "Do you have anything else you would like to say?"

Ysra said nothing but spat in Sandin's face. The saliva dripped down his chin. With a snarl, Sandin cut the ropes and took a step back. He and the others surrounded the Abithian, blades stretched out from every angle. "Go now, before I change my mind," King Oliver ordered. Ysra smirked, turned, and dived into the green water. Sandin kept an eye on his old friend until he was but a dot in the distance behind the *Gale.* Perhaps one of the nyssavir would find him, make quick work of devouring him, and his suffering would not be prolonged.

Chapter 34

THE TEMPLE OF YOSHIKAI was not all that large, no bigger than the tavern back in Osta. A set of stairs carved into the natural rock of the mountain led down into a square pit. There was a narrow bridge of stone that stretched across a shallow moat of water, connecting to a platform that held nothing but a stone table. Shackles and markings reminiscent of those outside the room adorned the table.

A shiver ran down Ara's spine. "This looks like a torture chamber."

"The process of unlocking one's magic can be... dangerous," Cassandra said. "This was put into place as a precaution, meant only to protect those who are in the temple."

"So, I am to be bound here then?" A ripple of fear tore through Ara. The atmosphere of the place made her uneasy. Then she noticed something in a corner of the chamber. "Is that..." she trailed off, eyes locked on a pile of bones. A bit of garments littering them and shreds of what appeared to be some sort of translucent paper.

"Look at me," Cassandra snapped. Ara's gaze ventured back to the sorceress. "I told you this is a place of great tragedy. I told you that magic is dangerous; it doesn't always go as planned. Don't you trust me, Ara?" She looked at Ara pleadingly.

Ara nodded, taking a deep breath. "I want to, I swear. It's just..." She didn't know. Trust was a difficult thing. Trust had done nothing but burn her as of late.

"Everything will be okay." Cassandra smiled. "Just get up on the table."

Ignoring everything that was screaming at her, telling her not to get on the table, Ara climbed atop it and laid down. She allowed Cassandra to snap the shackles closed, the iron like ice on her wrists and ankles. Her wet clothes stuck to the cold surface. When the last shackle was locked, Cassandra let loose a loud sigh. Then, she began to laugh.

The laugh grew into a cackle, her head thrown back as she cried out with glee into the air. "Finally," she said exuberantly. "I have *finally* got you here. After all this time, all this waiting. I have lied, manipulated, connived, all to get you on this table. Bhishma will rise again; the Great Snake will be once more and will devour the enemies of the Yoshikai Clan for good!"

Confounded, Ara asked, "What is this? What are you talking about, Cassandra?" It was nothing but drivel to her. She pulled on the shackles to no avail.

Cassandra had been facing away when Ara addressed her, but she turned back then. A disgusted look of derision on her face. "You *insolent* girl," she spat. Fingers went into Ara's hair, pinning her head back. "I have waited *years* to bring Bhishma back to this realm. You thought you could just run away from me? No, it is my birthright to call the Great Snake back from his slumber. And it is *your* destiny to be his vessel!"

Ara's chest began to ache with the pain of betrayal. Had her life not delved into the darkest of pits as it was? And now this? "Why? Why are you doing this? I don't understand. I... I trusted you!"

Cassandra leapt onto the stone table, straddled Ara, and crouched down close to her. She said, her voice a league lower than it was before, "You are a fool, Ara. But I can't blame you for that. The whole of your people—the Gosathans—are all fools. What this nation believes of the gods is nothing but fodder. We have magic because of them, yes, because of this world they have created for us; however, they don't care for us. They don't create heroes to slay giant beasts, nor do they forge weapons with their breath to fight battles."

"What are you trying to tell me?" Ara asked quietly.

Cassandra exhaled a sigh. "Everything you believed in this world has been a lie. The Jardanis family has hoodwinked the Gosathans for centuries; they sowed fear into the hearts of men to spread their influence in the early days. This ruse has been so substantial that not even a Jardanis in a few hundred years has known the truth. The Great Snake—Bhishma—was once alive, yes, but not created by a god. He was given life through the hands of the Yoshikai clan, *my* clan. My people would have ruled the world." She paused for a moment staring off as if thinking of something else, then climbed off the table, her face a mask of disdain. "If not for that *boy*—Atrius Jardanis. He ruined everything! Oh, and the nyssavir; creatures older than any other. Not even I know their true origins, but when people began calling them Bhishma's children, well... That was just comical."

Ara felt as if her chest would explode.

The woman stalked away, walking towards the human bones littering the floor. She picked up a piece of the translucent paper, rubbing it between her thumb and forefinger.

Ara squinted. *Is that a snakeskin?*

Cassandra continued, "You wondered if your blood held a special quality; it does, possibly the most important bloodline in our world. My ancestor used their magic to change shape—the same magic that I'm attuned to—and combined it with the blood of *your* ancestor. This man's bloodline continued on after, of course, otherwise you would not be here." She paused and smiled wickedly.

"My clansman commanded Bhishma, battled against the ancient rulers with the snake as their mightiest weapon. Now, it is my turn." She looked over at Ara with hopeful eyes. "You are my last chance to raise the Great Snake once more. His spirit still lingers, neither alive nor dead; I can feel it all around me. Just as I did last time." She looked down at the bones. "This time will be different; you are far stronger than your mother."

For a moment, Ara forgot to breathe, lost focus of all around her. Her mind went dark as her body went rigid. Only when Cassandra kicked the skeletal remains did Ara snap out of her reverie. "It was you," Ara whispered. "You tried turning her into that *monster*. But what... you failed? Is that it? Your little spell didn't work, and my mother has been here rotting since?"

Cassandra giggled. Her smile—which could be no bigger—dug into Ara like a knife. "Yes, my dear. Your mother was just too weak."

Ara glanced over at the bones. *Pa was right all along,* she thought.

Her skin began to burn; flames danced along her fingertips. She growled, "You will not get away with this!"

Cassandra looked at her and began laughing. A wave of her hands and the uttering of a word, and water began to crawl up from the moat, dousing the flames in Ara's hands. Ara's chest heaved as she panted, her rage making it difficult to breathe properly. Steam from the water and heat of her skin wafted. The iron shackles dug into her skin as she pulled her arms and legs with all her strength. They wouldn't budge. Cassandra continued to laugh.

"Look on the bright side," Cassandra said. "Your mother's spirit has moved on from this life—and once Bhishma's has replaced yours—your spirit will go on too. Perhaps, the two of you will be reunited soon." That was a silver lining if ever there was one. "Just relax, Ara. The transformation will be painful at first, but once it's complete, you will feel nothing." She came over, stroking Ara's hair.

"I told you your blood was special. I learned long ago that it was only your bloodline that can coalesce with Bhishma's spirit."

"Why?" Ara figured it was more likely that her family's blood was cursed.

"I don't know. Truly," she answered. "Enough chatter; it is time. Pray to the gods to see you to Volharis if you wish; once my incantation is complete, your soul will flee to be with your mother and father."

Oh, Pa, she thought. *I'm so sorry I didn't listen to you. I never should have trusted her. This witch has ruined my life.*

Something dawned on Ara. From the moment she met the sorceress, the events of her life were cursed. "It was you this whole time, wasn't it?"

"Elaborate, dear," Cassandra said, pulling various items from pockets and pouches on her person.

"Calder and I ventured into the Wraithwood countless times, and we never had any issue with getting lost, or running into bandits. The worst thing that happened was being chased up trees by coyotes. Then I find myself in trouble, and the next thing I know, you're there. That was you, wasn't it?"

Cassandra looked up from her rifling with a smirk. "Aye, it was me. I lured you away, caused you to trip. I hired those rubes to tie you up and scare you a bit. All so I would appear to be a savior in your eyes. They thought they were getting a fair payment; never knew I was going to kill them." She laughed then, seeming to think herself clever.

Ara continued putting the pieces together. "I met Oliver, and you knew I would leave Osta with him if you didn't intervene. *You* sent the poisoned wine to King Torril. *You* were the one who accused my father, knowing that Oliver's thirst for justice would not allow him to see reason. He said he couldn't tell me who accused Pa. It was you; that's what your trip was about."

Cassandra kept smiling, seemingly glad that Ara was figuring it all out. "All of this to get me here." Ara was baffled. What was wrong with this woman that she would go to such great lengths in pursuit of such an evil quest?

"It all could have been avoided," Cassandra said. "Things could have been much easier on the both of us." Ara's eyebrows knit together in confusion. Cassandra rolled her eyes, then grabbed the emerald pendant and smashed it on the floor. "These pendants are fake; they mean nothing, Ara. I fooled your mother with them as well, so don't feel too bad about that. That is why your father panicked upon seeing yours; he remembered your mother wearing one. The trick worked on her, but she wasn't so wrapped up in chasing *princes*."

Ara continued, "I see. So, had I just gone with you from the beginning, my Pa would still be alive. King Torril would be alive. Cal wouldn't have been killed."

"Well, none of them would have died by my hand," Cassandra said dismissively. "Unless, of course, they were to get in the way of Bhishma. Your friend's death wasn't my doing, though; his death was just a happy accident." She chuckled as if Calder's death was something to laugh about.

She knows nothing of love, Ara thought. *Cal was more than a friend. I can't let her get away with these sins.*

"You evil *witch*," Ara hurled the insult. "I will see to it that you rot in the pits of Icuzar!" This only made the sorceress laugh more.

"Ah, here we are," Cassandra said, holding a small, glass vile in the air. A dark liquid floated within. "Open wide, dear." Ara clamped her mouth shut as the woman removed the stopper. Cassandra grabbed her cheeks and squeezed, forcing her lips to part just slightly. Ara tasted nothing but iron and what she assumed rotten meat would taste like, as the dark, thick fluid touched her tongue.

She tried to resist, but the liquid seemed to almost *want* to slide down her throat. Cassandra released her and Ara coughed. "What was that?" she shouted, spitting the ichor.

"Blood of the first," she said slowly, articulating each word individually. "You should feel honored to have Bhishma's blood coursing through you."

"I hope you choke on your lies," Ara snarled. Cassandra laughed and began placing items on the stone table. Gemstones, bones of assorted creatures, powders that Ara didn't recognize.

She began to chant in that ancient language again. She walked a circle around the table. The white-hot pain of a blade being dragged across Ara's wrist made her cry out. "No, stop!" Cassandra ignored her. The other wrist was slit, then both ankles. The blood moved around the table, filling the symbols and casting them aglow just as before.

A wind swept through the temple, but from where it came, Ara didn't know. She felt her strength beginning to fade; dots bounced around her vision. Glancing at the witch, she noticed orange-hued chains glowing slightly around her wrists, could feel a strange connection forming between them. Then, just as she was about to give in to an encroaching sleep, her mindset shifted.

I don't have to do this. Fight back, Ara!

She would *not* be a victim any longer. The wrath that made her skin ablaze was replaced by something that caused her to burn hotter: willpower. Her will to fight back increased tenfold, and she screamed aloud. It wasn't a human cry, but something primal, something beyond her recognition. Before her eyes, Ara's skin began to shift. What was once the pallor of a freckled girl with red hair, was now becoming scale. Something about it was off, though; it didn't quite look like that of a snake. Ara roared again as her limbs expanded, the shackles popping away from her. Cassandra's chanting stopped, her eyes wide, as Ara's restraints clanged to the stone floor. A low growl escaped Ara as she looked down, readying to wipe the filthy mage from her world.

Chapter 35

CASSANDRA MORTEUM'S LIFE FLASHED before her eyes as the monstrosity that was Ara towered over her. *How has it come to this?* she thought. *How have I failed* again?

No... I'm Lyreath Yoshikai. The last of my clan. I can still have victory.

She looked down at her hands, whispering the words of subjugation fervently. "Espiritus vinoctem il magiri. Espiritus vinoctem il magiri." Cassandra repeated the intonement several times, staring at her hands until the chains appeared. Gleeful chuckles spilled from her as Ara thrashed against the binding.

The iridescent, orange chains flickered as Ara fought back, trying to break the tether.

Cassandra shouted, "No! You *will* be mine!" Her hands curled into fists; every part of her being tried to maintain control of Ara. She growled, "You may not look like Bhishma, but you will kill—*destroy*—just as he once did."

Ara's head shook again, her powerful jaws snapping, dagger-like teeth dripping saliva.

If only I could bludgeon her, she thought. *Maybe then I'd have some time to think up a solution.*

Cassandra glanced around as Ara's clawed feet dug into the floor of the temple, scraping to get closer. There was nothing loose in the chamber except the bones of Ara's mother. *She's going to break through any moment now.*

Sweat dribbled down Cassandra's cheek as the chains flickered once more. She groaned, "Damn this," and released her hold. "It is a fight you shall get!"

Chapter 36

IT WAS MIDDAY AND there was a gentle breeze blowing, causing waves to slosh against the hull of the skiff that Oliver occupied. Upon Sandin's suggestion when battle planning, they switched boats after getting rid of the Abithian assassin. This would provide them with a way to cut through the water more stealthily. Sandin was silently watching the horizon. Tiberius sat behind the king, taking a turn at staffing the oars of the small boat. Drago and Arlith—the wolves—were in the party as well. Each of the men in the skiff were battle-hardened, and out of them all, Oliver was the least experienced. He trusted them with his life; there was no other choice.

If everything was going according to plan, Oliver's naval forces would be distracting the Abithians with their warships by now. They would gather as much attention to themselves as possible, leading the Abithian warriors away from their land, while the king's skiff meandered about the vast Tamagau, waiting for the perfect time to strike.

Sandin had been mostly silent during their journey, either worried about facing his previous master, or fearful of the waters after what happened with the nyssavir before. Oliver thought it could be both.

He never worried much about the children of Bhishma, knowing that his ancestor had slain the beast. Whether it was god-created or manmade didn't matter; he was of the bloodline that slew the monster. Something about that knowledge gave Oliver the courage to know that he—as a Jardanis—was predestined to crush every snake beneath his heel.

"What is your plan, eh?" Drago asked, his gaze moving on Sandin. He was a squat man with a stalky build and bald head. A short beard sat on his face. "How will you get us to the queen unnoticed, *Abithian*?"

Sandin's details for how they would get to the queen had been explained to Oliver, but the Gilded Wolves with them were unaware.

King Oliver cut in. "There will be none of that, Drago. Sandin may have been born elsewhere, but I trust him as much as I trust any of you. Treat him with respect."

"Aye, Majesty. My apologies, Sandin."

Sandin eyed him with an amused look. Ignoring the man's jabs, he answered, "There is a small shore near the village of Kinesto. It lies beneath an overhanging cliff where people don't venture. That is where we will start as the sun falls."

"Why do people not go there?" Arlith asked. He was taller than Drago but shorter than Sandin. He wasn't particularly muscular, and not particularly impressive to look at. His hair was long and blonde, reaching halfway down his back. What he lacked in physical prowess, however, he made up for with intelligence.

Sandin answered without looking at the man, "The cliffs there are dangerous, very steep. Children used to play there, but after several died, the Warden of Kinesto ordered no entrance."

"No one would ever expect us there," Arlith noticed.

"Exactly," Sandin said, nodding.

"Your turn, young man," Tiberius said as he stopped rowing and stood, making the skiff teeter left and right. He gestured to Drago, letting him know that it was his time to row for a while.

Drago smirked. "Yes, I would hate for your heart to give out before the action begins, you old coot." Tiberius rolled his eyes in response as Oliver and the other two chuckled.

There was silence for a time, and then the high-pitched cry of a bird rang out. A small shape appeared nearby, flying low. Sandin started, leaning forward as the bird flew closer. It cried again. Sandin stuck an arm out.

What is he doing? Oliver thought. Then the bird landed on Sandin's wrist.

It was a falcon with a note of some sort tied to its ankle. "What's this?" Tiberius asked as Sandin unraveled the twine holding the paper in place.

Sandin said, "It's a message. This is how Abithians communicate over long distances. Our falcons are remarkable at locating people. It must be for me." The assassin unrolled the note, reading it to himself before turning to the others. He tossed the falcon in the air, and it soared away, screeching one more time, a farewell.

"Who's it from?" King Oliver inquired, his curiosity piqued.

"Grandmaster Helfi," Sandin replied in a whisper. His hand seemed to tremble slightly, which was terribly uncharacteristic for him.

"Who is Helfi?" Arlith asked.

Sandin looked up at him over the note. "He was the head teacher at Shadowspire—the school for Abithian assassins. I learned all that I know from him. Helfi was more than a teacher to me; he was a mentor. After my parents died, he pulled me from the streets, gave me my life in a way. After that, he watched out for me. I never knew why he took such a liking to me."

"What does the note say, Sandin?" Oliver asked gently.

"Helfi has been imprisoned," he said, followed by a sigh. "He says that Queen Gadiel jailed him because of me, accusing him of teaching treasonous behaviors in Shadowspire."

"I'm sorry," Oliver said. The other men voiced their agreement as well.

"Do you know what this means?" Sandin's eyes locked onto Oliver's. He waited, but the king didn't know what he was getting at. "I must rescue Helfi. He's locked up because of me. I won't allow him to rot in that dark, nasty place. Many say it's what they imagine Icuzar to be."

"How do you know this isn't some sort of trap?" Tiberius asked. "The queen could have written this and sent it herself. Or—more likely—she could have had him tortured until he agreed to write it."

Sandin shook his head. "I have seen both Gadiel and the Grandmaster's writing before. I learned the patterns, and I recognize this to be authentically Helfi's handwriting." He smirked. "And as far as torture goes, Helfi would *never* give in to torture. I saw firsthand my teacher remove a fingernail from his hand just to prove that suffering pain was possible. His face showed no sign that he'd felt it. It was brilliant."

Oliver nodded, trying to formulate a response. Nearly the entire undertaking required Sandin's help and expertise, his knowledge of the innerworkings of Abithia. "Sandin, it's troubling to hear about your friend, but I'm relying on you here." His eyes were pleading.

"There must be a way for me to do both. I will guide you to the queen, Majesty. But I must also liberate Helfi. I cannot leave him to rot in those cells."

Oliver nodded. "Very well. But if you die trying to save that man, I *will* kill you." Sandin's lips split into a smile, and their laughter made the water around the boat vibrate.

Chapter 37

ARA STARED DOWN AT Cassandra who had an enraged look on her face, eyes narrow and brows cinched tight. A white-hot rage burned, incinerating Ara from the inside. She felt an inhuman roar tearing from her throat. The anger boiled to the surface and Ara lashed out, but what she saw was not the fist of a human, but rather the clawed foot of something else. Dark gray talons attached to a scaly paw, raked across Cassandra's forearm as she attempted to shield herself from the blow, and simultaneously shifting into a crow. Ara felt a slight tear in the flesh of the woman's forearm just before her form changed completely.

In bird form, Cassandra flitted back where they'd entered. Ara glanced over at the pile of bones, walked over to them, and sniffed.

There was no scent left. *Mother,* she thought, but her inner voice sounded different. *Cassandra must die.*

Ara tried to follow the woman but found that while her head fit through the door, her shoulders became stuck. She backpedaled, realizing then that she walked on all fours; it was the strangest sensation. Despite the rage burning in her, Ara noticed her senses had been heightened beyond anything she could ever imagine. Closing her eyes, she could hear the fading flutters of Cassandra's wings as the distance between them increased.

Opening her eyes and looking down, Ara saw the legs of a scaled monster. Looking left and right, she found wings that would stretch out or fold against her sides. She noticed that her head and neck could twist and crane around to look over the length of her new body. Black scales with tines of orange-tinged bone ran the length of her spine. A long spined tail flicked about.

What am I? Ara wondered.

She would need to figure that out later. At that moment, fitting through the door was a more pressing issue. Ara tried to squeeze through the door in every way she could think, but nothing would work. The frustration was festering. Despite having a new body, the fire that came to the surface felt the same. She pushed to release the fire, and it escaped from her mouth. A spout of flame that was almost like liquid. The rock around the door sizzled and cracked, and then finally crumbled. Finally, she could fit through.

Shoving through the door, Ara found that she could see plainly, which was odd when she remembered how pitch black it had been.

She saw no fires or signs of natural light and then realized that her vision must have improved along with her hearing and smell.

Ara breathed deeply, taking in smells she hadn't noticed before. She recognized the scent of bats, though she didn't know *how* she knew what the smell belonged to.

Through the waterfall and the pool of water on the opposite side, and then up the path where they'd entered the mountain. The small crevice that led outside shone before her. There would be no way for Ara to fit, so she breathed fire on the surrounding rock again. More stone melted this time, and as Ara crashed through, a large portion of the mountain collapsed behind her, sealing the entrance to the Temple of Yoshikai.

Ara sniffed the air. She smelled the plants, the animals, the insects, in a way that was unknown to her before. On one of her claws, was the scent of blood. Cassandra's blood. She sniffed it deeply, lowered her foot, and then sniffed the air. Her mind rifled through all the different scents she picked up until finding what she was looking for. It was like a visible trail of faint red appeared before her eyes. The scent rose upward, curving left and right and then leveled out. She started forward at a trot.

The sand felt different under her feet. She could detect the individual particles of sand more clearly. She walked slowly, forgetting for a moment about the witch. There was a shallow pool of water that had gathered up on the shore, becoming stagnant. Carefully—as if she would become afraid of her appearance, Ara stood above the water and looked down.

As far as she could tell, she'd grown to the height of three average-sized men, and the length of five—including her tail.

A scaled face, black, and her strange eyes. They were still just as violet as before, but the pupils were narrow, inhuman. When she opened her jaws, large sharp teeth reflected back. They were made for tearing apart flesh. Orange-tinged horns sprouted from the top of her head, twisting. Two of them, each the length of a spear. She wasn't afraid of what she saw. Ara found herself to be beautiful, to be magnificent and fierce. In the most horrifying way, she'd received what she'd always wanted: to be more than Lowborn.

The smell of Cassandra's blood was beginning to fade; with one last look over herself, she decided it was time to test her wings.

Ara looked at both wings, rolling her shoulders. She closed her eyes then, feeling the weight of the new appendages, probing through her body for which muscles would activate them. It was a new sensation—odd—to feel the wings move as two independent limbs. Her eyes opened once more, confidence being born.

With a running start, she launched from the ground and flapped the wings. The thin layer of skin connecting the hollow bones caught the wind and lifted. She waivered, dropping right back to the ground, stumbling. Again, she ran, jumped, and spread her wings. The attempt at flying was steadier this time, and as the wind caught her, Ara lifted into the air and soared above the island. She found it to be much easier than she thought it would be. It was as if the knowledge was inside her all along.

The wind pulled at her frame like cool hands moving over her body. If not for the plundering rage Ara felt, the joy would have been enough to last for a lifetime. It was like riding a horse but amplified tenfold by the speed and power she felt.

Ara flapped several times, noticing that she climbed higher up with each pulse of the wings. Turning into such a creature didn't seem to have a downside. Then—when she tried to shout with glee—her human voice would not come out, but rather a deep screech. Nothing about her was human any longer. She would never feel the touch of her skin on someone else's, would never speak to another person again. This rekindled the flames of wrath, and she flew faster, following Cassandra's scent. The sea of Tamagau was beneath her, and Ara could hear the waves colliding with one another.

I will do this for them, she thought. *Pa. Cal. I will make them pay for what they did to you.*

The creature glanced around, trying to pick out as much detail as possible. By concentrating on her sight, Ara found that she could adjust the distance at which her vision would go. Suddenly, she was able to see *much* further than before. Her sight locked onto the shape of a small bird.

Cassandra, Ara growled in her mind, her voice darkening. Beyond Cassandra's flying shape, there was another object rising in the distance. Ara was able to make out a shoreline but couldn't perceive much else. Perhaps it was another island to which the sorceress would try to escape.

Before long, the adjusted vision caused Ara's head to swirl. Her wings seemed to get confused, and she began to plummet toward the sea. Her sight corrected itself, and just before she hit the water, her wings levelled out and she began to glide. Her claws skimmed the water, sending a small spray into the air.

She beat her wings, again rising into the air. In the water below, there was a small boat with several men aboard; however, Ara decided to ignore them. She focused instead on catching the witch. She was the main source of everything wrong in her life. The sun was beginning to falter, lowering across the horizon. With her new sight, the sunset had never looked more beautiful. If Cassandra hadn't ruined everything Ara possessed, taken from her all that she held dear, she may have thanked the woman for cursing her so.

Chapter 38

"THIS SEA IS WRETCHED, I'm telling you," Sandin complained. "I'm ready to be rid of it."

"The poor Abithian assassin is scared of a little sea snake?" Drago taunted him. The others chuckled.

Arlith looked up, squinting. "What's a crow doing all the way out here?" The others craned their necks to see the bird fly by.

"That's bizarre," Oliver said.

The crow had just flown past their skiff. They were edging closer to Abithia, just waiting for the sun to drop low enough that they wouldn't be spotted from a distance. As the crow passed, an unsettling presence came over Sandin. Something unnatural was happening; he just didn't know what it was yet.

My intuition has never let me down, he thought, glancing around.

"Don't worry," Drago began with a smirk, "I shall pro—," his voice dropped off. Sandin turned to see what the issue was.

"What in Gorenos' name is that?" Arlith asked, a tremor in his voice.

For a moment, Sandin's breath caught in his windpipe, threatening to suffocate him. This was far worse than the nyssavir he faced before. A winged creature loomed in the distance, flying ever closer to them. It was black as the night and large. It was too high in the air to make out much detail, but as it passed over them, Sandin made out clawed feet and a tail. The beast was flying in the same direction they were heading.

"So, we turn this boat around then, yes?" Arlith asked.

The king shook his head. "No. I don't know what that was, but we will press onward." It was subtle, but a shiver struck King Oliver then. The skiff became silent as all the men seemed to sense the same thing, that they were headed toward a wildly unknown danger.

Sandin knew there was no such creature in Abithia; none that was known of, at least. Why it flew toward his old home, he didn't know. The sun was getting low as the men took turns rowing. The skiff surged through the water and just as the sun casted its last light, the shore of Abithia came into view.

THE SKIFF WAS MOORED at the shoreline after navigating past patrol ships; Sandin and the others gathered themselves, shaking the weariness from their limbs. Sandin's knees felt stiff from sitting on the small boat for so long. The only light that shone was from the moon. It was a full moon, but the cliff angled in such a way that it blocked out most of the light. It would be a tough climb for them.

"Try to put your hands and feet where I put mine," Sandin told them. "With luck, none of us will fall."

"With luck," Drago mocked with a snigger.

"You are welcome to lead the way, my friend," Sandin shot back.

He saw a smirk on the man's face as he gestured an arm wide and said, "After you."

Sandin grabbed the rock face and began his ascent. He went slowly, allowing the others to stay with him. Hugging his body close to the cliff, Sandin climbed with ease. The rocks were rough, which made gripping them easy. The others were breathing hard, grunting more and more the higher they climbed. Sandin's fingertips grew increasingly raw, the cold of the night biting like teeth of ice at the exposed skin. Once he reached the top, Sandin clambered to his feet and wrapped his hands with the cloth of his cloak. He pulled his hood back over his head as it had fallen on the climb.

The rest of their group followed after him, Tiberius nearly falling to his death when the sword on his hip got snagged on a jagged rock.

When they all made it to the top, they each laughed—save for Sandin—in relief at not dying. They lay on their backs, chests heaving, lungs burning. "We must move on," Oliver said breathlessly as he rose to his feet. "Time is not on our side here."

With groans of protest, Drago and Arlith gathered themselves up; Tiberius did so silently. The trail leading to Kinesto was narrow; they had to walk one behind the other. They moved quickly, quietly. Walls of rock rose on either side of them. Once reaching the end, there was a wooden fence that had been erected to block access to the cliffs. Sandin moved out of the way so Drago could get by. They'd risk the chance of being heard as they broke through the barrier, but it was a chance they were all willing to take.

After many grunts and loud smacks of a human body upon wood, the fence gave way as Drago slammed his shoulder into it. Sandin was impressed by how strong the man was for someone of such short stature. After exiting the trail, Sandin led them away from Kinesto. There would be watchtowers there. The element of surprise was their best tool, so remaining hidden was crucial. They climbed around and over boulders, winding their way across the land where Abithians generally did not travel. It wasn't easy. Eventually, they had to veer down onto a more usable road; they kept their pace at a slow jog. The road wasn't busy at that time of night, but one could never be too careful.

To most of Abithia, there was but one way to enter Stoneforge Keep: across the drawbridge and through the courtyard. Unbeknownst to them, there was another way. Sandin would lead the king and his group of men over the top of the mountain that housed the Keep. They would venture into the tunnel at the peak and work their way through the perilous system of dark narrows. Sandin knew those tunnels better than anyone. Then, a horrible thought struck him.

What if Gadiel closed them off?

The queen knew of the passages, of course, but perhaps she hadn't considered an attack within her walls. As far into the plan as they already were, Sandin didn't see a point in bringing this up. As he thought about the plan, Drago interrupted his thoughts.

"When can we stop for a bite? I'm about to gnaw off my own hand." Before anyone could answer, however, another voice spoke from the dark rocks on the hill to their right.

"What have we here?" it asked.

Sandin turned to find something he dreaded, something he had hoped to avoid. In Abithia, not everyone was able to make enough coin to survive in a noble manner. Some resorted to violence, thievery, murder. By the light of the moon, Sandin counted twelve.

"Our business is ours, sir. I'd kindly ask you and your cohort to leave us be," King Oliver said confidently. The men snickered.

The first who'd spoken asked, "Do you know who we are, lad?"

Sandin knew *exactly* who they were and, he assumed, they'd know him if they got close enough to see his face. They were the scourge of Abithia; a disease Sandin hadn't been able to fully eradicate. He recognized them by the silver emblem shining upon their tunics. A crescent moon with a blade being stabbed into its center.

"Night Raiders," Sandin answered.

Chapter 39

ARA FELT HER WINGS becoming heavier, her breathing becoming shallow and labored. Flying a great distance was taking its toll on her; she would need to replenish her strength soon. Her hulking shape landed near the top of one of the many mountains she'd noticed when flying in. Ara didn't know where she was or where Cassandra had flown to; tracking her down would have to wait.

The sun was completely down, and Ara found herself abundantly grateful for the gift to see in the dark. The moon was shining brightly; however, her human eyes would have still struggled to see what was in front of her. As luck would have it, a family of mountain goats slept amongst the rocks. They weren't far from where Ara sat perched, and they were unaware of her presence.

Her shallow breath returned to normal, and with a small deal of effort, Ara lunged across a gap that would have been too wide for any other creature to leap. Jaws wide, Ara clamped down on the biggest of the goats, chewing once before swallowing. Such a delectable meal of meat, fat, blood, and fur. Ara caught the other two animals as they attempted to flee—a futile quest. They cried out and wriggled in her claws. She sat back on her hindquarters, tongue licking the blood of the first goat that had stuck to her teeth. Then she finished her meal off, feeling satisfied.

It wasn't until all three goats were in her belly that Ara realized what she'd done. It only seemed bizarre because she remembered what it was to be human. Not even a full day had passed since the cursed blood changed her, and she'd already turned away from her humanity. Or had the humanity left her before that? There would be no way of her ever knowing.

After eating and resting for a bit, Ara was feeling much better. She stretched her wings, noticing they didn't feel as heavy. With a bend of her strong legs, she jumped from the mountain. The air of the wind as she glided softly through the air was such a peaceful feeling. It was like she was made for it; this was her *true* destiny. Flying around the expansive land, Ara sniffed deeply every so often, hoping to catch Cassandra's scent again.

It was tedious work, but after a while, the faint smell of the mage's blood entered her nostrils. She turned in the direction she thought it was coming from but lost it. Turning her body, she listed to her left and found the scent again, then lowered closer to the ground. The scent trail amplified. There was a village beneath Ara. She saw no one on the streets; it was most likely that everyone was sound asleep at that time of night.

Dropping lower still, Ara made her way to the ground, landing noisily. *I'll need to practice landing more gently,* she thought.

The village was small, but the streets were wide enough for Ara to stalk through without stepping on things or brushing against the buildings. Her wings were folded tightly against her body; the only sound was the hot breath exiting her nostrils and the scrape of claws on stone. The scent of Cassandra was like a beacon shining brightly in the dark, just waiting for Ara to uncover the stone she'd slithered under. Ara began focusing on her hearing; horses neighing in the distance, the sound of grasshoppers singing their nightly songs. Finally, the hushed tones of a woman thanking someone for showing her hospitality. Bearing down on the sound, it increased as Ara encroached on a small hut of stone. There was but one window that she could find on the building.

Her great eye peered through the window. A pot of stew roasted above a hearth, small flames tickling the bottom of the cooking pot. Cassandra sat on the floor with a man and woman, conversing quietly. She could tell that her blood had turned cold—just like any other reptile's would be—but the sight of the witch made her hate burn hot like a furnace once more. Standing back up to full height, the beast gripped the wooden roof and ripped it away from the walls. All inside the hut screamed, save for Cassandra. She was on her feet, glaring up at Ara; the fear that she'd witnessed on the woman's face at the temple was gone.

Cassandra muttered something to herself in the ancient tongue then thrust her hand toward Ara. Her palm was alight, and blinding pain hit Ara's eyes. When her vision returned, Cassandra was flying away as the crow again. Ara had already grown tired of this game. Giving the people in the hut another look, seeing the horror on their faces, she considered devouring them just as she had the goats, but decided not to waste any more time. Ara took to the sky and the chase was on.

As the distance between the two creatures narrowed, a large mountainous city loomed in the direction in which they flew. Ara closed the gap between her and Cassandra. She thrashed a claw at her, missing as the bird careened away from the blow. Ara cursed as the witch gained more distance between them as they neared the city. A roar of desperation escaped her throat.

As Ara closed the distance again, Cassandra shifted her shape suddenly. She took on the form of an adult Eskasin eagle, a bird half the size of Ara's beastly form. The giant bird turned and flew at Ara, getting within range of her claws, but somehow avoiding them. Talons raked against the scales of Ara's neck, leaving shallow gashes. She screeched a cry of annoyance, twisting in the air to throw Cassandra off. The eagle dived down and Ara followed. As Cassandra landed, her form shifted back into that of a human, disturbing many people in the courtyard. Ara landed a short distance from her, feet slamming into stone and startling the men around them even more.

She glanced around the courtyard; men wore thin animal hides, and some carried shields and swords, others duel-wielding axes. There were a handful with spears in their fists. *Where have I gone?* she wondered.

Cassandra answered her question with arms spread wide, "Welcome to Stoneforge Keep, home of the queen of Abithia." She chuckled as if a joke had been made. Then she addressed the men, "Gentlemen, if you wish for your queen to live, then help me slay this beast! It wishes to kill her this very night!"

That was all the convincing those men needed, because they began charging at Ara with no regard for their lives. She was confused at first, but when a spear tore in between two of her neck scales, the confusion fled. Flooded with hatred, Ara swatted at the splinter with a roar, knocking it aside. A sword-wielding man charged; teeth tore him in two, the top half sliding down Ara's throat as intestines spilled onto the stone and his bottom half toppled over. Several of her attackers paused, frozen in shock or fear, but Ara did not relent. As they attacked, she swatted her massive paws at them; some were shredded by claws, and others cried out as their bones snapped from the impact.

Cassandra sat back, watching all of it with annoyance written on her visage. After a torrent of flame expelled from Ara's throat had burned down a few of the Abithians, Cassandra slapped her hands on her thighs. "How utterly useless these people are." She sighed as smoke plumed from Ara's nostrils. "I can fix you, Ara."

She felt her head cock sideways, the admission giving her pause.

Nothing happened between the two of them for a moment; there was silence, but Ara could hear more Abithians surging through corridors within the mountain, coming to see what the commotion was about.

"Look," Cassandra said. More men appeared behind her, staring at the beast with mouths agape, as the witch raised a hand. Ara didn't trust her in the slightest; trusting the sorceress is what led to all of this. However, she was curious. Cassandra walked over and placed a hand on Ara's giant leg. A tremor tore through Ara after the mage uttered *"Shaiel"*.

Ara felt her bones shifting as her body became smaller. She thought the woman may have killed her, but then she was on her two feet. She looked down, turning pale hands over, wondering if they were really hers. She'd been returned to her old body again, all that power simply vanished.

She was naked, noticing her exposed body—something that would have embarrassed her to death before. Looking back at Cassandra, the anger she felt just wouldn't quite simmer down. The smile that was on the woman's face only made the wrath burn hotter.

You killed Pa, she thought.

"No," she growled, taking a step back away from Cassandra's reach. "I don't want to be fixed. I *like* the curse!" With one final an-imal-like growl, Ara began turning back into the beast. The shifting magic was reversed again.

"Fine!" Cassandra bellowed. "You want to kill me? Then come and try! I am Lyreath Yoshikai, the last of my name, the greatest sorceress this world has ever seen!" Ara vaguely remembered the woman saying that Cassandra Morteum had been an alias.

The mage's body contorted, growing almost as large as Ara, gray feathers sprouting all over. Wings erupted from her back, claws growing from paws like a woodland bear. Her face shifted, turning into something akin to a wolf. It would have been terrifying if Ara wasn't a fierce beast herself.

In Ara's shocked stupor, the strange creature struck; jaws like a vice clamped down on her thigh.

Ara screeched, swiping at Cassandra, claws digging into flesh and meat. The searing pain in her leg lessened as the creature let go and backed away. With a beat of wings, Ara was out of the wolf creature's reach, if only for a moment. Cassandra followed. A pillar of flame poured from Ara's mouth, narrowly missing the witch as she changed direction, gliding down the mountain towards the sea. The flames danced throughout the courtyard, sending the screams of men to her ears.

Moonlight bounced off gray wings and fur as Cassandra appeared to be fleeing towards the nearby port. Ara was faster. She caught up, tackling the other creature from midair. They rolled across the ground in a tangle of claws, gnashing teeth, and blood. Ara attempted to incinerate her, but missed yet again, capturing small structures instead. Abithians ablaze with fire ran from homes, their cries a melody of anguish.

The terrain flattened out and Ara noticed that Cassandra was heading for the sea. She was going to try escaping through the water.

If she were to make it to the water and shift into a sea creature, Ara would probably never find her again and would never see her revenge fulfilled. She moved as if everything depended on it, beating her wings rapidly and then dropping down in front of Cassandra.

Cassandra struck at her, but Ara was quicker; she moved her head to the right of Cassandra's and bit down with force just behind her head. When she released her, the witch shifted back into human, blood leaking from her neck. Her sweaty hair was stuck to her forehead.

She crawled backward on all fours. "No," she begged, shaking her head frantically. Ara saw in her eyes—the finality of her life coming to an end. "Please, do not do this, Ara. I'm sorry. I—,"

Cassandra's words were abruptly cut off. Liquid flame encapsulated the woman's body. She was dead within seconds, and Ara sat there, watching the body melt, breathing in the scent of burning flesh. Never, Ara noticed, had she been more satisfied with herself. When all that remained was a pile of char and ash, Ara took flight once more, not knowing where she was going but feeling herself being pull away from Abithia.

Chapter 40

THE NIGHT RAIDERS MOVED around, trapping them, circular shields coming up defensively, swords poised on the rim of said shields. Oliver was surprised at their lack of axes like many of the Abithians carried. The bandits wore no armor or mail, only tunics and breeches and weapons. Their legs were bent at the knee, already taking a fighting stance. King Oliver's mind turned as his heart became like a drum; this snag wasn't part of the plan. He held up his hands innocently.

"Gentlemen, I believe we can all walk away from this unscathed if you would kindly just have a word with me," he said. He slowly pulled a pouch of coins from his belt. "Here, take this coin. It should be more than enough to urge you all to let us pass through."

The first man who'd spoken—evidently the leader—considered the pouch. King Oliver offered a warm smile as he bounced the pouch, allowing the money within to jingle. A smirk displayed on the man's face. "You see, that is where you are mistaken; we don't want *only* your coin. We want everything you have. The weapons you carry, the clothes on your backs; it all shall fetch a decent price at any of our markets."

Out of the corner of Oliver's eye, Sandin stepped forward with his head low. "Do you really want to find yourself in a quarrel with *me*, Jabez?" Jabez's eyes narrowed. Sandin lowered the hood of his cloak to reveal his face in the moonlight. Oliver saw the raiders hesitate, taking a small step back. All but Jabez.

Jabez sneered. "Sandin the traitor. You'll fetch the greatest price of all when we take your head to Queen Gadiel. Our transgressions will be forgiven, I think. Look around; you're sorely outnumbered." Oliver knew they had failed to talk their way out of a fight, so when Jabez turned to address his men, the king acted first.

Casting his coin pouch to the ground, he shouted, "Now!" The Sword of Gorenos flew from its scabbard as King Oliver and his crew launched into action. Sandin covered the distance between himself and Jabez, pulling the small blades free from behind his back. Two men rushed toward Oliver, and he backpedaled. Instead of attacking at the same time, however, one of the men jumped in front of the other.

The tip of steel cut through the cold air in a jab towards Oliver's eye. He turned his body as the sword missed its mark. Oliver swung his blade, cutting halfway through the wooden shield. The sounds in the air were nothing but the clang of steel and cries of pain. With a grunt, Oliver ripped the shield out of the man's hands, his blade still stuck in the wood. A well-placed kick to the Abithian's sternum sent him flying into his trailing comrade.

Oliver took that moment to place the shield on the ground, stepping on it, and ripping his blade free just as the men recovered and charged at him once more. In a desperate attempt to even the odds, Oliver gripped his sword in his fist as if it were a spear. He hurled it at the now unshielded man; there was a dull thud and a grunt as the sword buried itself into his chest, erupting out of his back with a spray of pink mist that caught on the moonbeams. The other raider surged forward after a moment of distraction. His eyes were wide, and his mouth set in a snarl. The king retrieved the shield at his feet.

As the raider swung at Oliver, he raised the shield; the blow caused what was left of it to splinter away, and the force reverberated up his arm, shaking his bones. The pieces fell to the dirt and the man's arm curled back, preparing to swing again. Before the blade could fall, Oliver lunged forward and gripped the sword-wielding arm with both hands. The raider slammed his shield into the king's face once, twice, before Oliver yanked on his arm and swept a foot out from under him, sending him falling to the ground. As the king stumbled to where his sword lay, still plunged deep into the first raider he fought, he saw bodies lying around; however, he couldn't see if any belonged to his crew as the strikes to his face had left his nose bloodied and eyes watery.

With blurry vision, the king retrieved his sword and turned as the other man scrambled to his feet. Oliver charged him, swinging with his teeth grinding together like a mad man. He knocked his foe's blade to the side, and then with a quick upward slice, separated the raider's shield-wielding arm from his body. Blood spurted vociferously as the man dropped his weapon and clutched his forearm where the crimson was pouring, screaming into the night. Oliver watched him for a moment, feeling nothing but derision and malice, reveling in the man's agony. He waited until the Night Raider began to fade, and then ended his suffering, plunging the tip of his blade through the man's heart.

When the raider was dead, King Oliver spun around and saw that Tiberius was on the ground, gripping a wound on his arm. There were few of the Night Raiders remaining; Oliver lumbered closer, his labored breaths sending plumes of white into the frosty air. Drago and Arlith were fighting back-to-back, wild looks on their faces as they expertly fought off multiple attackers. Sandin was fighting off three men simultaneously with nothing but his small, curved blades.

He continues to impress, Oliver thought.

Jumping in to help Sandin, the two of them dispatched the three raiders. King Oliver sliced into the belly of one man, sending his innards spilling into the dirt. He bled out and died shortly thereafter. The other two, Sandin brought down quickly, seeming to be invigorated to have the king aiding him. Both died by slashes to their throats. The last two of the Night Raiders were sent into the afterlife by Drago and Arlith—who were covered up to their elbows in blood. Nothing but red and carnage littered the ground around them.

One of their foes laid on his back, his breaths coming in and out rapidly. He grinned with bloody teeth as a wound to his stomach bled. Through a pained laugh, he said, "You'll never kill the Night Raiders; not completely. We will plague this world until its end."

Oliver placed the tip of his sword over the man's heart. "You may be right. But you'll never know for sure." And he plunged his blade until the tip struck soil.

"Tiberius," Oliver said as he approached the man. Arlith was already tending to his wound. There was a deep gash on his left arm. He winced, trying to take deep breaths as Arlith applied cloth and pressure to the wound. The king knelt at his side. "I feel we must send you back, my friend. This wound may prove fatal, and you may yet incur more. Arlith will accompany you."

He shook his head slightly. "This is but a flesh wound, Majesty. I would be remiss if you sent me back now. You need as many swords as possible this night. You have my word: once patched up, this will not slow me."

"Very well," the king said. "I'll hold you to that." The inquisitor gave a simple nod. Arlith began stitching the laceration closed, ignoring the curses and insults flying from Tiberius' mouth. Drago chuckled with each one. With the flow of blood staunched and the wound stitched, Arlith wrapped the wound in a clean bandage and helped Tiberius to his feet.

"Let's go," Sandin urged them. "We'll be lucky to make it there before the sun has risen."

The climb up the mountain was tedious; several times, Tiberius slipped on the rocks due to his injured arm. They didn't slow their speed for him, though, and he still kept up, though he was a bit behind. They climbed up the backside of Stoneforge Keep, and it wasn't as steep as the first cliff they'd had to ascend, but it wasn't effortless either. The smell of smoke hit Oliver's nostrils.

"Do you smell that?" he asked the group.

"Smoke," Drago verified.

"We've arrived," Sandin said to them as he paused. "This tunnel is very steep. Be mindful of where you place your feet; it will be dark, but if we go slowly, we won't fall." They all nodded, and the assassin led the way.

He wasn't kidding, Oliver thought.

They shuffled down the tunnel and after what seemed like forever, a small hint of light became visible as they neared the end. Slowly, the tunnel began to flatten out and the light grew brighter. When they reached the flattest part, the ceiling of the tunnel shrank, leaving them on their bellies to crawl.

"Quietly," Sandin said to them, looking back over his shoulder. He was nearly silent as he continued. Drago was probably the loudest of them, but Oliver found it difficult to stay quiet with the sword and pouches of various items on his belt.

There was a small grate of iron barring their path at the end of the tunnel. Sandin looked left and right before wiggling the bars. He'd obviously done this a time or two before. Feet rushed past where they lay, voices shouting frantically, the smell of smoke increasing.

With the grate pulled free, the men crawled out into a hallway dimly lit by flames flickering in sconces along the walls. "This way," Sandin said, waving them along. "That way is the courtyard," he told them, pointing down a corridor as the stone hallway split. "Through the courtyard is the drawbridge that leads out of the keep. This way to all the inner chambers."

They moved deeper into the keep carved in the stone, away from the clamorous shouts coming from the courtyard. "What is happening out there?" Drago asked, voicing the thoughts in Oliver's head.

"Don't know, but something is off," Sandin replied. "We can't worry about that now; press forward." And they did.

They found their way to what was a great hall and throne room; Oliver looked at the throne, admiring it for a second before they went through a door to the right. Sandin led them through stone corridors, showing them how to hide in shadows as footsteps would approach. Many times, weapon-clad men would charge by, not noticing them as they stilled their movement and crouched to make themselves smaller. Something was afoot within the keep.

I just don't know what it could be.

"This is the queen's sleeping chamber." Sandin gestured to the large, regal-looking door across from them. It appeared to be made of thick wood; ornately carved swirls and symbols were inlaid on its surface. "There should be no less than three men standing guard. Where are they?"

They stalked forward; Sandin swung the door open silently. "Empty," Oliver noted, looking past Sandin. "Where else would she be at this time of night?"

"Something is off here," Sandin answered. "We can try her war room next. She may be planning something, though at this time of night just doesn't make sense." Oliver gave a nod, and they shifted away from the chamber.

Sandin held up a finger as they closed around another wooden door. He pressed his ear up against it, then looked at Oliver and nodded. "Voices."

Oliver held up three fingers, counting down. They each drew a weapon, save for Sandin, preparing to fight. As his last finger closed, they burst through the door. Her war room was much larger than the one Oliver was accustomed to. His eyes narrowed as they landed on Gadiel. If there was shock on her face, it vanished before Oliver could see it. The queen jumped from her chair, running to the door behind it and left her advisors to deal with the intruders.

Sandin's hand was on the king's shoulder. "Go after her. Beware the Queen's Aegises. They have red paint on their shields and are *very* dangerous. I must go find Helfi now."

Oliver gave him a nod. "Be careful." Sandin offered him a slight smile and then left the way they'd come. The advisors slowly rose from their seats, shifting back as their eyes flashed with fear. There were ten of them. "Kill them." And as Oliver gave that order, his group of warriors flooded the Abithians in the chamber like a crashing wave; however, the only thing flowing there was blood.

Part 3

As One Ends, Another Begins

Chapter 41

SANDIN SNAKED THROUGH THE dark tunnels of Stoneforge Keep, nostalgia attacking him, recalling memories of when he lived there. He passed armored Abithians running by him several times, and finally asked one of them, "What's happening? Where's everyone going?"

The man looked at him as if it were obvious. "We've been attacked. We're going to set up defenses in case it comes back."

"In case what comes back?"

He shook his head. "We don't know what it is. Some colossal beast with wings, breath of fire." He closed his eyes and shuddered.

"That's impossible," Sandin replied, not wanting to believe it, but then...

The creature we saw from the boat, he thought.

The Abithian shrugged. "This is just what I've been told." And then he was off and Sandin continued his way towards the prison.

I haven't time to worry about that right now.

The entrance was an oak door with strips of iron inlaid in the surface, making it nearly impossible to break down without a battering ram. The guard entrusted to watch the prison entrance was asleep on a stool, so Sandin saw no sense in slaughtering him. With expert swift hands, he lifted the key ring and unlocked the door, sweeping inside quickly. Sconces were aglow with orange flame which casted a dim light over the cells. The prison cells were essentially pits in the floor of the cavern with iron bars latticing so that food and such could be dropped through easily.

Sandin's nose curled at the smell of prisoners who'd been wallowing in their filth for an inordinate amount of time.

"Helfi," Sandin called out as he walked alongside the cells. A deranged hand shot through the nearest cell bars, cracked fingernails clawing for Sandin's feet as he stepped out of reach. The people who were put here did not stay well-minded for long. The pitch and isolation made scholars go mad. "Helfi, it's Sandin. Where are you?"

There were groans issuing from other cells, but then Sandin heard a faint voice. "I'm here," as a hand waved in the air several cells away. Sandin shuffled through keys as he knelt next to Helfi's cell. There was a small lock on the latch of the cell bars, holding it shut. Finding the correct key, Sandin unlocked the cell and heaved it open, then reached down and helped pull Helfi free. When he was standing next to Sandin, they clasped forearms. The old man still looked as Sandin remembered. A bald head, long white beard, and piercing blue eyes. His bushy eyebrows were like elder caterpillars that never transformed. A prominent nose sat deformed from the many times it had been broken.

"What the devil are you doing here, boy?" Helfi asked, looking around as if to make sure everything was alright.

"Much has happened since I left Abithia," he said. "I will explain it all when given the chance, however, right now we need to go." He turned to walk away but Helfi grabbed his wrist.

"Thank you, Sandin. For coming, I mean. I didn't mean for you to come to my rescue when sending that missive, and I expected to die in that cell."

"How many times have you rescued me?" Sandin asked rhetorically, turning back toward the entrance to the prison.

Upon exiting the cell, he realized the guard was awake as sword on leather ricocheted off the walls. Metal glinted in the firelight. The tip of a blade was poised in Sandin's face. "I'd put that away if I were you," Sandin said.

In a mocking voice, the guard said, "And I suppose you'll do something about it, yeah? I'm the one with the sword here. What you're doing is forbidden."

He moved to thrust his sword into Sandin's belly, but the assassin was ready. He sidestepped the strike and grabbed the man's wrist, twisting around and wrenching the blade free. Sandin thrust the sword, plunging it into the man's sternum, feeling the blade bouncing off bone as it exited his back. Then he ripped it free, spattering the ground with crimson. With a grunt and a gurgle, the guard slumped to the ground and died.

"Let's go," Sandin said. "I fear my new friends need me." The word felt foreign on his tongue: 'friends'. He'd never used that term so liberally before, had scantily considered anyone to be a friend. Helfi was a friend, sure, but he was more of a father than anything. Ysra was a friend at one point, but that ship had long sailed.

RETRACING HIS STEPS, SANDIN led Helfi into the war room where he'd last seen King Oliver and the others. To say it was a massacre would be an understatement. *So much blood,* he thought.

Sandin had expected Oliver to let these men live, to let them escape with their lives. Every man had a dark side, that much Sandin knew, and it would appear that King Oliver had released his.

"What has happened here?" Helfi asked, a touch of fear in his voice. Sandin forgot that in his old age, Helfi had become far more caring about others than he used to be. When Sandin first met him, he was the kind of killer who would cut someone's throat just for looking at him crossly, and as the Royal Dagger that was his right. Many years had gone by since the man had taken a life. Years of murder weighed on anyone with a conscience. Sandin neglected to answer and simply pressed onward to the back of the chamber.

Pushing through the ajar door, Sandin was taken through a hall-way that led into an empty chamber smaller than the war room.

Shouting echoed from the direction Sandin and Helfi were head-ed. "Up there," Sandin whispered, increasing his speed. He burst through a door that led to a banquet hall. There was light provided by a hearth and copious sconces on the walls, sending shadows dancing across the Abithian flag hanging there.

"Stop running," King Oliver was shouting. "Turn and face me!"

"Come closer," hissed one of the Queen's Aegises, "and you will draw your final breath." Swords were poised to strike as Queen Gadiel cowered behind her guards, yet keeping a high chin and look-ing unafraid. Perhaps she did not fear death.

Sandin caught up to them and his eyes connected with Gadiel. Then her gaze darted back to Helfi. She sneered, "I knew you were in league with this *traitor*."

"Helfi had nothing to do with any of this," Sandin defended his mentor. "It was your actions, and yours alone, that led to my betray-al."

"I only did what was best for my queendom!"

Sandin put forth the rage, the pain of her initial distrust, into his words. "What you did was cowardice, and now you will die for it!"

At those words, the queen's protectors launched their attack, thinking they would catch the intruders off guard. Drago caught a poke through his thigh, sending him sprawling to the stone floor as Arlith fell the attacker. The other aegis tried for Oliver, but Tiberius fought him away as the king stalked closer to Gadiel. Their comrades made a clear path for him to approach, pushing the Abithian guards back. Sandin watched with a sense of indifference; he never would have thought he could feel such a way at watching her die. The smell of death was heavy in the air.

"I tried to broker peace," King Oliver said. "I tried to form a relationship between our nations." He stepped toward her slowly, raising his sword so that it was just inches from her throat. Tiberius killed an aegis with the edge of his blade smashing into the man's head, a sickening crunch and then a squelch as he pulled it free. "I wanted this Thousand Year War to end, but you just *had* to have your way, didn't you? You could have let us go on and have our beliefs, but you wanted to rip them away from us. And as the Sword of Gorenos steals your life, you will know that all of this was *your fault*; that all of it could have been prevented. If only you hadn't been so damn foolish."

Finally, her façade broke; Queen Gadiel's gaze dropped to her feet and her jaw trembled. "None of that really matters now. If it's not you that ends my life, it will be the monster."

Oliver's head turned quizzically. Sandin stepped closer as if that would wipe away his confusion. The other men looked at each other.

It must be true, he thought.

"Monster?" Oliver asked. "What is it you're lying about now, hm?"

Her voice shook. "This very night, a great winged beast descended from the skies with fire as its breath." She paused, her mouth opening and closing, looking for the right words. "If what my men say is true, this creature seemed to be chasing something else but found its way here. It devoured some, but the others..." she trailed off.

"The others what?" Sandin asked.

Her eyes darted to him, a flash of anger, and then turned back to Oliver. "There were but pieces of them lying about. Deep gashes from claws in the stone of the courtyard, soot and ash where the thing torched them. I was making defense plans when you all stormed in and *slaughtered* my advisors. Don't believe me? Let us take a walk to the courtyard and you will see the destruction yourself."

Arlith breathed a nervous laugh. "Clearly, she is lying. We can't trust a thing she says."

"Finish this and we can be rid of this *snake*, Majesty," Drago said through a grimace as Tiberius helped to bandage the wound on his leg.

"I am not lying," Gadiel argued. Sandin noticed a slight quiver to her hands. "My soldiers described to me a living nightmare. I wouldn't have been in that war room for nothing."

Oliver looked back at Sandin. "What do you think, Sandin? Is she lying?"

Sandin took a couple of steps closer. He finally shook his head slightly. "No, I believe she is telling the truth." After a scoff from both Drago and Arlith, he added, "I stopped one of the Abithians I saw running through the corridors when searching for Helfi. He told the same story; with that, you all saw the beast on our way here. Don't you remember?"

There was a collective realization that dawned on their faces. They'd all forgotten about what they saw whilst sailing to Abithia, caught up in the adrenaline, perhaps.

King Oliver nodded, inching his blade closer, nearly touching the exposed skin of her neck. "Aye, I remember now. However, whether or not you tell the truth matters little to me. You've betrayed my trust, stormed my land, murdered my people. You owe a blood debt to Gosatha, and I am the collector."

Sandin watched as if time had slowed, his breath bated. Queen Gadiel dropped to her knees. Oliver's blade followed her down; a quick swipe and she'd be gone. Her lips pressed into a hard line. She said, "Go on, then. Take your debt." Oliver looked at her as if confused. "Come on, young king. Send me to my death!"

He almost looks sad.

"No, Queen Gadiel," he said softly. "There are worse fates than losing one's life. The debt I must take will not be your head."

As KING OLIVER HAD commanded, Sandin—along with Grandmaster Helfi—had retrieved the queen's husband. Oliver and his entourage waited for them to return, and when they finally did, Sandin pushed King Consort Orion Lotus III forward. He stumbled, almost falling.

"Sandin," Oliver said. "Lead us to this courtyard."

Sandin nodded, taking the front position of their pack. The others followed behind with Arlith and Drago ushering Gadiel and Orion along. Several times Orion complained at their speed—it was far too quick for his fatigued legs to follow—and subsequently heard one of the Gosathan's smack him in the back of his head.

The stony corridors eventually ended, widening into the courtyard of Stoneforge. The frosty air of early winter crashed into Sandin; steam rolled off his body. Soldiers milled about, tending to the wounded, some retching. Sandin fought to keep his composure as he smelled burned flesh, saw the mangled corpses. He stole a glance back at Oliver and saw the same horror on his face.

Gadiel is no longer the greatest threat to this world, he thought.

They were in the middle of the courtyard when the soldiers finally took notice of their little group. Oliver gestured for their prisoners to step forward. "Kneel," he said loudly enough for their group to hear.

Many of the soldiers began subtly gripping spears and swords, shuffling into a circular formation around them, ripping axes from their belts. When it seemed as though all the Abithians held a weapon, one of the men shouted, "Engage!" The circle of soldiers slowly began closing in, their ranks ready to inflict death to protect their liege.

Chapter 42

THE BEAT OF ARA'S giant wings slowed, each one feeling as if they weighed the same as the collective waters of the Tamagau. She had no idea where she was flying, only followed the instinctive pull to another location. The cold of the night wore off as the rays of the sun shone down on her body, warming the cold blood in her veins. In the distance, a structure rose. Ara was tempted to use her improved vision to see further, but worried the effort would cause her to faint. Before long, Ara realized that what she was seeing was a mountain. She didn't know how or why but knew this was where she needed to go.

Ara realized where she was as the land became clearer. She'd only heard of this place once, briefly from Oliver. *Feral Ones.*

There was no beach that she could see, only cliffs that towered over the waters. If what Oliver had told her about this land proved true, no one—Gosathan or Abithian—had ever laid eyes on it except from down in the water below. As grass became trees, Ara saw animals scurrying through the forest below her. The sight of them left her mouth watering, however, the pull of this mountain was too strong, and she could not indulge on the succulence lying beneath just yet.

The mountain was incredibly steep, taller than the Gorgaw, and Ara felt warmth radiating from it. Near the top there was a cave large enough for three of her to fit. Ara landed on the rocks, the stone warming her feet as she stalked into the darkness of the cave. Her eyes adjusted to the absence of light almost instantly. There was nothing in the cavern, save for groups of bats clinging to the ceiling here and there. She explored the cavern until reaching an inner wall.

Good, she thought. *Nothing can sneak up on me here.*

Despite her fatigue, Ara knew she'd need to eat as much as possible before full winter set in. She had the strange feeling she'd be sleeping through the winter. Fire may be running through her, but the cold would still not be good for her body.

Rest at last, she thought, curling into a ball. She let the warm rock soothe her fatigued limbs. *Just a quick nap.*

ARA WOKE WITH A start.

Where am I, her voice shouted frantically in her mind. *Oh, right.*

It all came rushing back at once. Daylight lit the entrance to the cave she presumably would call home from that moment forth. The beast stood, stretching her legs and wings, feeling wonderfully energized. A deep rumble issued from her stomach.

So hungry.

The prospect of hunting was alluring, though she could go for another nap. Ultimately, Ara decided food was more important at the moment. Besides, she needed to maintain her strength and learn as much as she could about herself before unleashing death upon Oliver Jardanis. Her lip curled in a snarl.

Cassandra is dead; Oliver is next.

After leaving the cave, Ara launched herself into the air again. She found a wide-open plain where there were deer grazing. They saw her before she could snatch one up, and the pursuit began. Ara found it exhilarating, though tiring. Her predatory mouth salivated as she came dangerously close to catching one of the furry animals. It changed direction suddenly; it was difficult for Ara to keep up with sharp turns. She would need to practice her flying.

And practice she did.

While exploring, Ara took every chance she had to hunt for prey. Younger animals were far easier to catch, she noticed. The more she explored, the more Ara wondered if the Feral Ones were just a myth; thus far, she hadn't spotted any of them. Until, of course, she did. There was a village of sorts, but it looked like nothing Ara had ever seen. The huts were small, hardly noticeable, and made of nothing but sticks, grass, and mud. She flew over them, wondering if there were other villages around. The people saw her and ran from their homes across the rolling hills, coming to a stop in one large mass. She landed close to them with her head low.

Warily stalking up to the people—who she fully intended on making into meals—she became perplexed by their behavior, or lack thereof. They had weapons, primitive at best, but showed no aggression. Their eyes were wide, and the language she could hear coming from them made no sense; it wasn't anything she'd ever heard. It was a savage sort of guttural way of speaking.

The people were covered in animal pelts, but one man stuck out more than the rest. He came forward with hands spread wide, his eyes even wider. White markings covered his face. There was a wolf skin draped over his head and down his back. The upper fangs of the wolf sat atop his head. He was a rather large man, but Ara felt no fear toward any of them. A growl emanated from her throat as he approached. She wasn't sure why she allowed him to come near her, why she wasn't already tearing into them; however, she felt calm, at ease.

The man stopped just a stone's throw away, looked over his shoulder and shouted something to his people, and then fell to his knees. All the others followed suit, ignoring the mud darkening their animal-hide breeches. Then each of them dropped to their hands and placed their foreheads to the moist ground. If it was possible, Ara would have laughed.

They think me a goddess.

It was such a peculiar thing, to think that she was a human up until recently, and now these wild people bowed at her clawed feet. It was like there was an unspoken agreement made between them. Ara would not harm them, nor would they attempt to harm her.

With a growl and a roar, she launched from the ground, giving the people a start. As she flew over them, however, they jumped to their feet and began shouting, cheering. Even without knowing their language, Ara knew they were happy she was there. Everything she'd ever known seemed so silly then, even her vendetta against Oliver. This group of wild men knew nothing of the Thousand Year War or of anything else outside of their tiny haven. How peaceful that must be.

As she flew away, she looked for things that may help her get better at flying, to hone her skills. There was a hulking wooded area where the trees were like giants even to Ara. The trees were spread wide, and it was there that she would practice maneuvering while flying.

The trees provided an intense natural course of obstacles that would help improve her agility.

It's like I was meant to be here, she thought. *Like these trees were created for* me.

Contentedness spread through Ara as she found her way back to the cave, curling within herself. How long she would lie there... there was no way of knowing.

Chapter 43

"Order them to halt," Oliver commanded the queen.

Gadiel's face twitched. Oliver placed the edge of his sword against her neck, pressing in slightly. Finally, she shouted, "Halt!"

"Have them drop their weapons," he said.

"Drop your weapons." The soldiers hesitated, looking to one another. "Do it!" Metal and wood clashed on stone.

Oliver released a silent breath of relief. He smiled. "Thank you." His voice rose to address the soldiers. "If you've not yet guessed, I am King Oliver Jardanis of Gosatha." He waited, allowing the name to settle with them. "Your queen owes me a blood debt and I intend on taking payment now."

Nervous feet shuffled, waiting for him to behead her; however, Oliver thought himself of at least average intelligence. If he killed her in front of them they would bear down on him and his crew. Not only that, but he knew if this winged monster were to show again, their forces would be better combined.

Now, to apply the correct pressure, he thought.

"Unfortunately," he said, "Gadiel is *far* too integral to Abithia for me to kill her now. I've no interest in trying to rule both our nations; however, the debt must be settled. Any volunteers?"

He glanced at Sandin and found an unreadable expression as usual. Oliver walked in a circle around his group, eyeing each of the soldiers individually. He spread his arms wide. "None of you will fight for your queen? You all were so eager to take me as a group; can you not stand against me by yourself?"

Finally, a young man stepped forward. Oliver looked at him, wanting to shake his head in pity, but keeping a stoic look all the same. *He's just a boy,* he thought. The soldier had the boyish face that comes with youth.

Oliver nodded to him. "Choose a weapon, Abithian." The boy looked to the ground, retrieving a spear. None of his comrades tried to stop him, tried to sway his mind or take his place. "Know that you will die with honor."

The kid spat at his feet.

Oliver raised his sword, keeping it level, waiting for the boy to attack. With a cry, the Abithian charged, the point of his javelin aiming straight for Oliver's chest. Oliver stood still, and when the javelin got close enough, he flicked his wrist. The weapon bounced off the sword as the boy's momentum carried him forward. He landed directly on the sword. Oliver held him close with his opposite hand, twisted the sword, and laid him gently on the stone. His death was quick.

The king stood, looking over to Gadiel. He glared for a moment. *Her resolve remains,* he thought. Her husband, however, had wide eyes caused only by horror. *Orion isn't accustomed to the death which battle brings.*

Oliver turned back to the soldiers. "Who else? Which one of you will kill me for your queen? Step forward; pay Gadiel's debt." He paused. None challenged him. "Step forward!" Spittle flew from his mouth.

A man—seasoned by the look of him—stepped forward, grabbing a sword from the ground. Oliver pointed his sword at him. "You shall die with your honor as well." The man sprinted at Oliver, stopping just short of him.

The swing came swiftly, metal grinding on metal as Oliver blocked the strike. Their blades locked together, but Oliver could immediately sense the man was stronger. He twisted away, disengaging from their locked blades. The man charged again. His second strike came down harder than the first, knocking the king's sword toward the ground. In doing so, however, the Abithain's sword also plummeted to the stone. Oliver thrust his head forward, connecting with the man's nose. Bones crunched beneath his skull.

As the man stumbled back, Oliver launched his offensive. Two strong overhead strikes came down; the soldier blocked them easily.

However, this was what Oliver wanted, so when he feinted a third overhead strike, the man moved to block and left his belly exposed. Too quickly for the Abithian to respond, Oliver diverted his swing. The blade ran across the man's torso and made his arms drop. He grimaced, the shock rendering him defenseless against the next strike. His head rolled, stopping short of where Gadiel knelt.

There it is, he thought. For a moment, Gadiel appeared to waver. *A little more encouragement.*

Oliver breathed tiredly. He looked at Gadiel whose eyes were glued to her soldier's head. There was a silent scream stuck on his face. Oliver felt a knot working in his stomach, causing him to second-guess his choices.

I've come too far—done too much—to turn back now, he thought.

He spread his arms wide. "Is there anyone else? Anyone at all?"

Before another soldier can step forward, Gadiel said, "Stop." A voice hardly louder than a whisper.

Oliver turned. Her gaze was still downcast. "What was that?" he asked.

"Stop this," she said, raising her voice, standing to her feet. Oliver's group shifted, preparing for her to give the word of attack. "Kill me. Orion will take my place." She glanced at her husband. "Enough of my people have died, as have enough of yours. Take my head and let this war be done."

And so, we come to the end.

Her face fell, a tear streaking down the left side of her cheek. She shivered, either from the cold or the fear of dying she faced.

"I never wanted this, you know," Oliver said, his voice like stone. "I wanted peace. I wanted a partnership between our countries. And you spat in my face."

Her eyes lifted to his. "I know. The sins of the past can't be taken back." She paused, breathing deeply. "But they can be forgiven. You could kill me… it's what your father would do. It's what I would do if I were in your position." He tilted his head as the queen fell back to her knees. She looked at her soldiers until they did the same. "But… don't. If you say this blood debt is settled, if you give me your word to not spill any more Abithian blood, I will pledge fealty to you. Your gods, your beliefs; keep them all. Taking that part of your culture is worth no more spent life."

But how can I trust your word? he wondered. *I can't. Not* really.

"You know I can't believe you," he said quietly. "I placed trust in you once before and look where that landed me. I've no guarantee you won't stab me in the back again."

After shaking her head, Gadiel looked around, then her eyes snapped back to Oliver. Tears glinted on the lids. "I can't express my sorrow enough for my actions, King Oliver. I can only beg your forgiveness. Please, have mercy."

"You only wish to save your own head," Drago accused.

Oliver held his hand up to silence any other outbursts.

He smiled slightly. Peace between their nations was all he'd ever cared about. Oliver felt he'd become a better reader of people in such a short time as king.

"Arise," King Oliver commanded. "Let this night be the start of something new, something our world has never known. The Thousand Year War will forevermore be an afterthought." And as the queen stood again, Oliver marched forward and the two of them clasped forearms, and he felt a shaky breath escape her lips.

Oliver said, "You'll send word to your generals immediately—as will I—that battle is to be halted, and all military forces return home. You shall remember my mercy on this night; let it be all you remember of me." She opened her mouth to speak, but he held up his hand. His voice was low so only she and those close could hear. "To ensure our safe travel from Abithia, the King Consort will be coming with us aboard one of your ships. If you'd name Orion your successor he must be of value."

Her eyes glanced at her husband longingly. She nodded. "I should see you in one of our finest ships, Oliver." She turned her head and called out to one of the officers in her ilk. When he approached, she told him, "Send the birds to deliver messages to our ships and the forces on land. They're to return to Abithia at once."

The soldier saluted and scurried away.

"Excellent," Oliver said. He turned. "Sandin. Send the recall of our troops." Sandin nodded once and was off.

KING OLIVER SAT IN the war room in Stoneforge Keep, pinching the bridge of his nose with thumb and forefinger. A new threat was upon them all. A threat that Oliver had seen only momentarily.

There was a mix of advisors from Abithia and Gosatha, and as King Oliver glanced at them, he saw derision in their eyes; none of them were happy to be there together. Queen Gadiel was speaking, but he had a difficult time focusing on anything she said, his thoughts replaying that night.

Word was sent to the generals of each of their forces to halt battle and return home. There would be no more casualties caused by each other's hands. This wicked creature that had risen from the darkness was far more pressing. Since that night, Oliver had made Orion a temporary part of his entourage but not letting him in on any sensitive discussions. His trust in Abithia would have to be built, and that would take time.

He drank deeply of the mug in his right hand, the frothy ale sliding down, coaxing away his worry slowly.

"...I think it best if we each take some time to think of how we are to defend against this beast. What say you, King Oliver?" he heard Gadiel say.

He nodded his head, sighing tiredly. "Aye, I agree. Let's get through the winter, and then I will send for you to discuss our plans."

She nodded her agreement and the king rose. "Thank you all for your time," Oliver offered to the room, bowing to the queen slightly. Despite gaining her obedience, King Oliver wanted to show that he was not a thankless man. Though his memory of her betrayal would never fade, it could be mended if she kept her word this time around. Though, her husband would be the first to go if she crossed him again, and she knew as much.

"Sandin, a word, if you please," Gadiel said. Oliver looked between the two, nodding to Sandin before exiting the chamber. After getting another drink, Oliver sent the rest of his retinue to their ship, and waited with Tiberius.

After a minute, Sandin walked out, his expression unreadable as ever. "Well?" Oliver asked.

Sandin allowed a smirk. "She just wanted to tell me there would be no hard feelings harbored towards me. It was rather odd; I've never known her to apologize. I guess she technically *didn't* apologize, but I'll take it."

"Let's get out of here before she changes her mind," Tiberius whispered, a facetious grin on his lips.

BACK IN VALENDRA, KING Oliver delegated Tiberius to show Orion to his guest chambers where he'd have a guard at all times. Then, he was met by the warm arms of his mother, his sisters standing by patiently. "Oh, how I've missed you all." They'd spent several days in Abithia ironing out details of their peace agreement.

"Here, let me have a look at you," Amelda said as she grabbed his face with either hand, examining the shallow cuts on his face. His nose was still a bit swollen from the tussle with the Night Raiders, and there were green bruises under his eyes. One of the Abithian surgeons was far too keen on fixing the man's broken nose for him, no doubt reveling in the pain it brought. "My, what did they do to you?"

"I'd rather not relive that right now, Mother," he answered with a laugh. "I'm just happy to be home." Ruelle came running up to them; he wrapped his arms around her small frame, hugging her tightly as the two of them giggled. Camille and Layla wrapped their arms around him next.

"Are you staying for good this time?" Layla asked. She was nearly identical to their mother, having the same thin nose and curly hair. Camille, on the other hand, looked much like their father, and Ruelle looked like neither; she was her own little person, far too precious for a world so dark.

"At least until the winter has passed. That's all I can promise."

"Mother says the war is over. You really stopped it then?" Camille asked, eyes wide and hopeful.

He laughed. "It's true. I couldn't have done it alone, though. I had friends at my side all along. Remember, when times are hard and pressing, you don't have to go through things alone. Don't be afraid to ask for help." The three nodded. Amelda looked at him with an admiring smile.

"I'd like to throw a celebratory parade," Oliver said to the Queen Mother. "Now the war is behind us, a celebration is to be had. This battle for peace wasn't easy, and I don't wish to go back to fighting. Although, to be candid, our battles are only beginning."

His mother was practiced in hearing horrible news, and her visage remained intact. "What are you talking about, Oliver?"

He looked at his siblings. "Give us a moment." He offered a smile to help ease their troubled looks as they sulked away. Then he told

Amelda everything that happened in Abithia, from their fight with the Night Raiders, their infiltration of Stoneforge, and the strange creature they saw. A gasp escaped her lips at his rendition of the mangled corpses and char left behind.

"Where is it now?" she asked.

"No one knows. It vanished as if it had never been, though I don't believe we've seen the last of it. All we can do now is prepare for its return."

"You don't believe this could be the return of Bhishma?"

He shook his head. "No, I don't believe so. This one had wings and breathed fire. It sounds like something crafted from a nightmare. Perhaps it's one of the nyssavir come to finish its father's work. This I know: when I see it again, my blade *will* end its life."

His mother pulled him into an embrace. "You mustn't let any harm come to this kingdom, but more importantly, yourself. What good is a kingdom without a king?"

"I know, I know." He sighed, pushing her away so that he could look at her. He remembered when he didn't tower over her so easily. With a smile, he said, "So, can I count on you to plan the celebration?" He was no good at such things.

She laughed, "Of course. When shall it commence?"

"I'd hoped we could gather after winter has passed. Spring is always wonderful, and the cold doesn't offer much fun."

"Very well," she said. "I will see to it."

"Thank you. Now, I must find a drink." She took his arm as he turned to leave. "I'm mad with thirst." She said nothing but Oliver caught the glance she gave from the side of her eye.

Chapter 44

THE COLD DIDN'T BOTHER Sandin as much as it did the other people of Gosatha; he'd wandered the streets from time to time since the end of the war, learning as much about the kingdom as he could. Queen Gadiel may have sought to make amends, but he was no longer interested in living in Abithia. Valendra was a wealthy city, but on the outskirts, there were still those who lived without a home. The first time he saw the crumpled form of a child frozen in death, he was taken back to his childhood.

As a friendship blossomed with the Gilded Wolf—Drago—Sandin unleashed his concerns on the unassuming man.

He told him, "When I was a child, my bones were like kindling, my skin like sinewy rags hanging from them. My body was bruised from the boots of passersby, the older men in my village despised me based on my appearance. They thought me pathetic. Then Grandmaster Helfi found me."

Drago glanced sideways at him. "That's tragic and all, but what of it?"

"I've seen greater needs than what I suffered as a youth here in Valendra," Sandin explained. "A little boy, frozen to the cobble. I picked the child up in my arms, felt the pull of his skin as bare feet stuck to a wet spot on the stone."

I curse the gods for allowing this, he thought. Because of what he endured as a child, there was a rather soft spot in his heart for the orphans who died on the streets. What could he do to save them? Perhaps he could take in one or two, but he couldn't take them all in.

"It's horribly dreadful," Drago agreed, taking a draught from his tankard. "But what can be done?"

Sandin pondered, "Yes, what can be done, indeed?"

Sandin ventured the streets day after day when his primary duties were done. He'd gather up the little ones who'd frozen to death and bury their bodies where the birds could not peck away at their flesh.

"What weapons do we have that would penetrate the scales of this creature?" King Oliver asked the council in the war room. "I don't believe arrows to be strong enough; I fear they would only ricochet off the beast's armor."

No kidding, Sandin thought.

"I agree, Majesty," Lord Rionath said. "Swords will most likely be our best option."

Sandin had gleaned—of Rionath—that the man would agree with mostly anything the king said. He rolled his eyes at hearing the lord's voice, once again kissing up to Oliver.

"Swords are rather pointless if you can't get within range," Sandin argued. "Let's not forget this monster has wings and breathes fire."

"Spears then?" Rionath offered, receiving nods from the others around the room.

"This still presents an issue if we can't get close enough to kill the thing," Sandin continued to argue. "Hurling a spear may puncture it, but I highly doubt it would kill it."

"What would you have us do then?" he asked, looking at him sourly.

Sandin smirked. King Oliver must have caught it because he asked, "What's on your mind, Sandin?"

"I've prepared a drawing." Sandin reached into a pocket and pulled a piece of parchment out and unfolded it. He held it up for all to see. Their faces were a medley of confusion and awe. "It will use the same principles as the crossbow. Two able-bodied men will need to turn this crank until the string is set into place. There'll be wheels mounted on the front to adjust the aim, and there's a small trigger that will release the spear."

"I like this," Oliver said. "Well done, Sandin. Are there any arguments against the immediate production of this weapon?"

Looking around the room, Sandin could see several who might want to object, but held their tongues, thinking better of showing their opposition. This was most likely due to their animosity toward Sandin and the rest of Abithia. *These old coots will never let things go,* he thought.

"Rionath, get with the smiths and have this ready before the end of winter. I'd like an update once a fortnight."

"I will see to it, Majesty."

King Oliver dismissed them, and the men all left, grumbling as they went, but Sandin—and a couple of Gilded Wolves—stayed back. "I'd like a word, King Oliver," Sandin said softly. Oliver only just noticed that he had stayed; he'd been perusing the world map in front of him, paying close attention to the mead in his mug, and trying to figure out where the beast could have flown off to.

"Yes, what is it, Sandin?" He took a deep drought and burped.

Sandin glared at him for a moment, then said, "We're just halfway through the winter, and thus far I have buried the bodies of 28 children in Valendra alone." Sandin refused to sugarcoat it.

Oliver turned back to the guards, telling them to wait outside the chamber for the time being. He rubbed the back of his neck before saying, "What are you talking about, Sandin? Are you saying there's a child murderer on the loose in my kingdom?"

Shaking his head, he said, "No. There is a problem of homeless orphans in Gosatha. The children I've buried have all died from the cold or starvation, maybe both. I didn't think the disparity between Lowborn and Highborn would be so atrocious, but here we are."

King Oliver placed his hands on the table and his head hung down in front of him. He lifted his head and took another gulp, emptying his mug. "Thank you for telling me, Sandin. I don't take this lightly. Effective immediately, I'm placing you in charge of making sure things are fixed. For the time being, corral those without a home and bring them here. Have cots lined up in the great hall and clear the tables and chairs to make more room. After winter has passed, we'll figure out a more permanent solution." He hiccupped.

Sandin bowed. "Thank you. I doubt there are many who care enough to make a change." It's like a flood of relief washed over his skin.

Sandin turned, but as his hand grasped the door handle, Oliver said, "I was going to change it, you know." Sandin turned back slowly. "Before I became king, I dreamt of ridding the kingdom of the separation in Low and Highborn."

"Why haven't you?" It sounded like a good idea to Sandin, but what did he know about being a ruler?

Oliver sighed. "I just haven't had the time to figure out all the details. My reign as king has been nothing but fighting, trying to keep my people from dying. And now there's this; I just can't seem to stop losing my people." He shook his head. "No, I'm just making excuses for myself. Truth is I've failed, Sandin. This is why I need people like you around; those who will keep me accountable."

"You can't keep everyone alive, Oliver," Sandin replied as he pulled the door open. "Remember, you're not alone. You're surrounded by useful people—ones eager to help."

Oliver smirked. "I said something similar to my sisters."

"You're a wise man." Then he left the room, nodding to the two guards outside.

Sandin walked with a sense of purpose through the corridors of the palace. His mind was set on one goal: save as many children as possible. The first thing he did was grab one of the heralds, a young boy with curly, brown hair. "I need you and the other heralds to help spread a message."

"What authority do you have to demand our services, *Abithian*?" he spat.

Sandin grabbed the front of his tunic, curling his fist in and bringing the boy closer to his face. He pointed a finger at the clasp of his cloak. He hissed, "I am the Royal Dagger, *boy*. And it is by *that* authority with which I demand your services. Would you like to test me further?"

The herald's eyes grew wide, and he shook his head fervently, his brown curls bouncing around. "Good," Sandin growled. "Now go. Do as I have told you. Tell all the homeless to meet in the great hall." The boy nodded and sprinted away after being released.

After speaking with several other people, Sandin located an abundance of cots just waiting to be used. *These could have been put to good use long ago.* With the help of some of the royal aids milling about, Sandin was able to shove the tables and chairs up against the walls of the great hall. People began filing in before they'd finished laying out the cots.

"Are you th-the one in charge here, sir?" an older woman asked, shivering and stuttering through her words.

Sandin nodded as he wrapped a blanket around her shoulders with a gentleness unbecoming of the greatest assassin Abithia ever produced. "I am. Here, come sit down. I'll have a soup going around shortly."

"May the gods bless you," she whispered, patting his cheek with a cold, shriveled hand. He helped her sit down and then ran down to the kitchen.

"Hello, Fatilda," he said, startling the woman from writing down what he could only assume was more recipes. He held up his hands after she squawked. "Apologies. I didn't mean to startle you. I have a request, if you'd be so kind?"

"Of course. What can I do for you?" She took a deep breath, wiping her hands on the apron that never left her body.

He explained the entire situation, asking if she'd be able to whip up a soup or stew to be sent to the people upstairs in the great hall. "And this was all your idea?" she asked. He nodded and she beamed, wrapping her arms around him, pinning his arms to his sides. "Oh, I am so proud of you, Sandin. I just knew having you around here would be good for us. I used to plead with King Torril about getting the children out of the cold, but he didn't seem to care. I spoke until I was blue in the face, and nothing was ever done, and when Oliver took over, I just didn't expect anything to change."

Sandin croaked, "Well, I can relate to what these people are going through, so I'm glad to help."

"Oh, bless you," she said. "I'll get right to it."

"Thank you," he replied before dashing away. He went back upstairs, pausing in the tall doorway. There were many adults there and very few children. Though helping the little ones had been his primary goal, Sandin was glad to see adults in the hall as well. Just to be safe, Sandin rushed from the palace and grabbed a horse. Cold wind froze the condensation that built up on the stubble of his face as he clopped down a street away from the palace.

There he found several others attempting to sleep on the frozen ground. "Get up," he ordered. "Go to the great hall within the palace. Food and sleeping arrangements are being prepared. If you see any others like you, spread the message." He rode away before they could respond. As he made the rounds, Sandin collected three children and transported them to the palace. Each of them looked to be on the verge of freezing to death. He handed them off to a couple of handmaidens before returning to the cold and searching for more children.

Chapter 45

WINTER LEFT JUST AS quickly as it had set in, and the flowers of spring were beginning to burst forth from the frosty ground. Morning dew slickened the balcony as King Oliver stepped out on its ledge, breathing in the chilly air. There was a coldness that had settled over him, not by fault of the season. He poked at a droplet of water on the balcony railing, ponderous thoughts of the future in his mind.

For many months, Oliver had been the ruler of Gosatha, and in that time, he'd lost thousands of people. He'd been so distracted by his desire to end the Thousand Years War, that he'd almost gotten himself killed, and allowed several villages to be pillaged by the Abithians. Sure, he made them taste his steel, and in the end, they had peace anyway, but that wasn't the point. What good was a victory if it was being chased by a plethora of failures?

King Oliver turned away, heading for the newly crafted aviary. To better communicate with Abithia, he implemented the aviary and created another position within his Royal Body. The falconers oversaw the sending and receiving of messages using their freshly trained falcons. As winter had broken, it was time for Oliver to have Queen Gadiel visit his home. They were to discuss defensive plans they'd each enact in case the winged monster ever showed again. Thus far, there was naught but silence. Through months of cold, the beast had not attacked either of the empires, which Oliver found to be rather odd.

Perhaps it hibernates, he thought idly.

"Good morning, Majesty. What may I do for you?" The older man smiled, the whiskers of his wiry mustache flaring.

Oliver smiled back at him. "I need to send word to Queen Gadiel, Samuel. It's an invitation to the palace to discuss defense operations." Samuel began scribbling on a parchment. King Oliver added, "Oh, and tell her to bring something fancy. I wish to host a parade and subsequent feast to honor our new friendship."

"Very well," Samuel said as he finished up. "Will that be all, Majesty?"

"Aye. Do let me know if the queen responds."

"Of course." Samuel offered a quick bow before tying the note to a falcon's leg and whispering in its ear before it took flight.

"Fascinating," Oliver marveled.

"Aye, it is. How such a small creature could be so smart, I will never know. King Consort Orion has been very helpful in showing us how this all works, I should say."

Good to know he's made himself useful.

King Oliver chuckled softly, clapped the man on his shoulder, and said, "Thank you for keeping the aviary going, Samuel. I'll be sure to show Orion my thanks as well." The older man's eyes twinkled from the praise he received. King Torril hadn't often shown his subjects any gratitude, as subjects were expected to do as told without expecting thanks.

A few days later, King Oliver received a transmission back from Gadiel in response to his invitation. It read that she would be arriving in a fortnight. King Oliver went to the Queen Mother, telling her when to expect the Abithian queen. Whilst doing so, he got caught up in a game of hiders and seekers. Camille pretended like she was too old to be playing such a game, but after much prodding and poking from Oliver, decided to join in. They had a great deal of fun. More fun than he'd been privy to in a long time.

"Alright, ladies, I must be getting back to my kingly duties," Oliver said, blowing a raspberry in their direction for dramatic effect. They all giggled and then whined as he turned to walk away. "Don't fret, little ones; a party is among us! You will help Mother in preparing the festivities, won't you?" He arched an eyebrow at them as if he might scold them if they gave the wrong answer.

Each of them nodded their heads with smiles on their faces. Oliver thought about how little he knew of women. He knew they liked to dance, but that was about it. The last one he'd tried to woo would rather pierce his heart with a blade than honor him with a dance, though. A jolt of guilt struck him as his thoughts turned to Ara. He wondered if she was still living in Osta, if she still harbored any ill feelings toward him.

I can only assume she still hates me, he thought.

"I must go back to the aviary, Mother," Oliver said.

"Oh?"

"There was a woman I met," he continued. "Just before Father died. Her name was Ara; she was... fascinating."

"Sounds like you've found someone you fancy, then?" Her brows arched high.

Oliver could hear the hopefulness in her tone and hated having to tell her the truth. "I did fancy her. But Father was murdered and the investigation led me to her father—Gaius."

"I see," she said somberly.

Oliver said, "Though she undoubtedly still wishes me dead, I feel the need to check on her. Closure, you may call it?"

"Do as you must, Oliver," the Queen Mother said.

He left his family, heading back to his chamber to craft the note himself. With a mug in one hand, a quill in the other, Oliver poured out his regret on that paper. The sound of it scribbling furiously between his sips of ale filled his ears. Ara would know everything, every vulnerable thought in his head. Why he felt the need to do this, he didn't know.

Time passed as if twice its normal rate; Oliver downed two more mugs before he'd finished the letter and, once he had, he walked over to his chamber door and entered the corridor beyond. Well, he stumbled, rather than walked.

Up to the aviary he went, bumping into walls and reassuring the Gilded Wolves following him that he was perfectly fine.

"Ara," he told Samuel, handing him the letter. "Ara Lowborn of... er, Osta." He burped, swaying on his feet.

"I'll see it gets to her, Majesty," Samuel replied. "Say, are you alright?"

He smiled, but couldn't answer. It was at that moment the darkness took him.

Chapter 46

It was a new age in Valendra; one where homeless children would no longer freeze in the winter. Pride swelled within Sandin as he led the group to their new home. It wasn't much but would shield them from the elements. Oliver gave Sandin freedom to make decisions on behalf of the street dwellers. The taxpayers of Valendra didn't seem at all bothered by being asked to pay a bit more just to pay for this new home for the less fortunate.

Sandin had gotten to know many of those people over the last few months. Marlin—a man only thirty summers old—used to have a home. He had parents who loved him, a sister who adored him. A fire destroyed their home when he was younger, killing his family, and leaving him alone. Marlin had damaged his back as a baby, and though he could walk, he couldn't stand on his feet for long, rendering him useless to most of the work for Lowborn in Valendra.

There were many stories similar to Marlin's, and then there were others who were too sick to work, or their minds too far gone to hold a coherent thought. With King Oliver's approval, Sandin hired more hands to work in this group home to take care of the elders, the children, the ill-minded.

Pushing the heavy doors open, the atrium of the group home was filled with the hands that would be working there. They wore bright smiles, greeting the building's new inhabitants. For the first time in a while, Sandin felt his lips part with a smile of his own; a genuine smile, one not meant to manipulate. He perused around the edifice, finding sleeping chambers and a kitchen, a large, open area with wooden toys for the children to fill their time with.

Sandin looked back on the man he used to be—a killer with no remorse. How much he'd transformed, how far he'd come since then.

"It's truly amazing what you've done here," Marlin said, putting a hand on his shoulder. "I don't think any of us could ever repay you for this, my lord."

Sandin waved dismissively. "It was my pleasure, Marlin. No one deserves to live on the streets without a roof, or to die without food in their bellies." A few of the children gathered around, looking up at Sandin with happy eyes. He turned his attention to them, bending slightly at the waist. "No, every man deserves the chance to die with a sword in his hand like a warrior!" Sandin made stabbing motions toward the kids, receiving giggles from their small faces. A laugh escaped him as well.

SANDIN SCOFFED AT THE moniker of "spear thrower" given to his weapon conception. He hoped this was a tentative name. They were being brought to life at a rapid pace; carving out the wood to make the intended shape took the longest. A small wall was erected around Valendra with a portcullis not far from the palace.

"Looks like the wall is nearly finished," King Oliver commented. Sandin nodded. "And the spear throwers?"

"They should be operational any moment now," Sandin replied, motioning toward the large weapon to his left. The smiths were putting the final touches on the bow-shaped spear-hurler and then turned to the two men with grins.

"I believe it is ready, Majesty," the man with a thick mustache said.

King Oliver smiled brightly. "What say we test it out, eh?"

Sandin grabbed a spear that lay nearby. "Let's do it." The two smiths began turning the crank that pulled the rope taut until it locked in place to the rear with a *clink*. Sandin laid the spear into the narrow trench of the wood, carefully placing the butt of the shaft against the rope. Then he waited, looking over at Oliver.

"This was all your idea, Sandin," Oliver noted. "I would have you be the first to fire the weapon."

Sandin smiled, placing his hand on the large trigger. It took more force to pull than he expected, but when it finally released, the bolt launched with a *twang,* sailing through the air over a great distance. The two smiths jumped in the air with a jovial cheer; Sandin couldn't help but laugh along with Oliver.

"Well done," the king said with a clap of his hands. "Well done all of you. Now, I want a spear thrower placed on the outer perimeter of this entire wall. Leave no inch of it unarmed." Stone casters were already placed around the wall, leaving room for the spear throwers.

"Aye, Majesty," the mustached man said.

Sandin followed Oliver away, walking with his hands clasped behind his back. "The group home looks promising, just so you know," Sandin told the king.

"I'm glad to hear it." Oliver's eyes were downcast as they walked. *Something is bothering him.*

"What eats at you?" Sandin asked.

After a moment, Oliver answered, "How many people have died because of my actions? Too many... too many."

"I'm afraid I don't follow."

Oliver sighed deeply. "My southern villages were wiped out. Thousands of Abithians died by my soldiers. I killed men—boys even—in Stoneforge. The children of Valendra starve and freeze while I turn a blind eye. Their deaths... I'm to blame for them all." The king looked around, almost alarmedly, as if searching for something that wasn't there.

"You can't be blamed for what Queen Gadiel did," he argued. "That blood is not on your hands. And as for the homeless, you have righted that wrong; it's best not to dwell on the past, for if we do, our minds will delve into chaos at the hands of our guilt."

Oliver looked at him. "That was very wise. Who taught you that?"

"I must give credit to Grandmaster Helfi," Sandin said. "He's the most knowledgeable man I've ever known."

Oliver nodded. "How is he? I'm surprised he decided to stay in Abithia after what Gadiel did."

Sandin shrugged. "I haven't heard from him since. I hope he's doing okay." *Surely, someone would have told me if he'd fallen ill.*

"I will send for him," the king offered.

"Oh, you don't have to do that, Majesty."

Oliver waved his hand. "Consider it done. I'll have him join Gadiel on the trip here. I'm sure he'd be pleased to see you."

Sandin nodded, happy at the thought of seeing his old master once again.

"Do you see them?" the king asked.

"You've confounded me yet again, Majesty," Sandin replied.

Oliver looked into his eyes then. "The faces of the men you've killed. Do you see them?" He turned away, muttering about needing a drink.

So, that's why he's taken to the brown poison, Sandin thought.

"No, I don't see them," he answered honestly. "There is a bit of guilt I feel for how many I've killed, the ease with which I stole life from others. However, I don't let it consume me, because if I did, there would be nothing left but a shell of the man I once was."

W‌HEN THE QUEEN AND her entourage arrived, Sandin offered her a slight bow, and then clasped forearms with his former teacher. "Welcome to Valendra," he said, smiling slightly.

Helfi smiled back as he looked around. "Nice city they have here, I must say."

Sandin chuckled. Sweeping his arm wide so Helfi could see the lush terrain behind him, he said, "Wait until you see the palace." Helfi looked like a child who had been given their most desired prize.

"The parade will go around Valendra in a few days after we've had the chance to speak about our defense plans," Oliver said, "and then finish the night off with a celebratory feast. If that sounds good to you, of course." In reality, Gadiel didn't have much of a choice, but Oliver was ever the gentleman.

The queen nodded. "I must say, I'm surprised by your hospitality. Despite us having peace now, I never expected you to be such a kind man." Her face was ridden with guilt and Sandin assumed it was because of her betrayal and misplaced distrust in Oliver.

Oliver looked at her solemnly. "We have both shed blood that could have been avoided; however, I think it best if we look to the future."

"So wise in such a young body. How did you come to be this way, hm?"

Oliver passed a knowing look at Sandin.

Sandin enjoyed the dynamics of their new partnership. His heart felt like an intense pressure had been lifted. Despite it being a partnership out of dominance, he felt it was for the better. Gadiel may hold the grudge of her defeat for a time, but she'd eventually let it go... he hoped.

King Oliver chuckled. "Wisdom comes to each of us in its own time." He gestured to the wagons that had been waiting. "Shall we?" The queen smiled and nodded, climbing into the wagon.

Inside, King Consort Orion Lotus III smiled goofily as his wife sidled up next to him on the bench. Sandin could see Gadiel trying to remain stoic, but her eyes gave her away. The wagon lurched forward. Next stop: Valendra.

Chapter 47

ARA STRETCHED, UNFURLING HER scaled body; her joints cracked as if she were covered in ice. As her eyelids parted, the dim entrance to the cave appeared. Rising to her feet, Ara padded toward the light, feeling the warm stone beneath her feet. She'd only been out of her slumber for a minute, and already she could sense that something had changed within her.

My mind, she thought. *It feels... stronger.*

She didn't quite know how to express that but knew it was true all the same. Closing her eyes, Ara could sense the life force of the bats clinging to the ceiling of the cave.

What's this? she thought. *I feel each of them separately.*

With nothing but mental prowess, she sent a growl into the minds of the bats; their squeaks filled the cave as they fluttered around in a panic. Something like a chuckle sounded in Ara's throat. *Interesting.*

Walking on, a horrible pain shot through her stomach, coming from somewhere unknown. Ara stumbled, snarls escaping her throat as her teeth clacked together and saliva dribbled down her lips. She was hungry. There was no real way to tell how long she'd been asleep, but looking around in the valley beneath her mountain, she could tell that spring had begun. She would need to feed immediately.

Her wings didn't want to work properly, and Ara found that she could do little more than glide. Floating down into the valley, her first snack was that of a hare which did nothing to satisfy her ravenous appetite. The hunting was slow at first, but when her wings cooperated more, Ara was able to fly again as if she'd been doing it all her life. She startled a herd of deer from a cropping of woods, and as they ran through a field, the great beast swooped down, swatting at them with her claws. She'd killed a dozen of them before going back to enjoy her meals. Ara breathed deeply, invigorated by the sustenance, and headed back to her cave as the deluge of nightfall came.

THE FOLLOWING DAY, ARA practiced calling out to other creatures with her mind. At one point she hid behind the cover and concealment of a large boulder, prodding her consciousness into a nearby stag. The animal was unable to understand words, but she could tell that it was confused to have a voice coaxing it closer to the rock.

When the stag rounded the corner, Ara snatched it up and made quick with devouring it.

This is rather fun, she thought.

Her blood may be cursed, but it was also a gift; with the horrible hand she'd been dealt, she would be able to take all she wanted. Revenge was so close she could practically taste it. Finding Gosatha may prove tasking, but Ara was confident she'd be able to do it.

Another day passed, the sky transforming into night, and as Ara lay down in her cave, a vision came to her. She saw them, her enemies all gathered in one place, ripe for the taking. It was as if the cursed blood in her veins *wanted* Ara to get her revenge. They were trapsing about the royal city, celebrating for some reason. Perhaps—for them—there *was* something to celebrate, something to be happy about. The premonition ended and Ara growled. Something told her this opportunity wouldn't come again so easily; if she wanted justice for the crimes committed against her, she'd need to depart immediately.

This intuition must be part of the changes, she thought, glancing down at her reflection in the moonlit water

Ara found if she constantly reached out with her mind to sense other beings, her energy wasn't greatly affected. The more she practiced, the stronger she would become as well. Fish faded in and out of her area of influence as she glided swiftly over the Tamagau, not knowing exactly which direction to fly, but hoping her intuition would guide her. It *had* done a good job of that recently.

Finally, land came into view as the sun crawled up the sky, painting the black of night in orange and pink brushstrokes. Her lip curled into a beastly snarl of a smile. As she got closer, she could smell the people. She beat her wings fervently, rising higher into the air. Her wings took her so high that she was sure she would appear as nothing more than a black speck amongst the blue if anyone were to look up.

Ara circled around the city until the sun was a blinding ball of fire once more. Riding a strong current of wind, Ara splayed her wings out wide and then looked down, increasing the distance of her vision.

Befuddled, Ara snorted; she wasn't sure what she was looking at. She'd never been to—or even laid eyes upon—the great city of Valendra. However, she recognized the grandiose palace at its center. There were large devices scattered about in a wide circle around the city's outskirts. By the looks of the devices, Ara assumed it was some sort of new weaponry.

This is all for me. They fear me, and as they should, too. Oh, this is going to be a wonderful massacre.

The Gosathans had no idea what lurked above them, the death that was about to rain down on them like blood from thunderheads. The skin beneath her scales itched with anticipation; adrenaline was the catalyst to the burning fire in her body. Ara flew in wide arcs around the sky, waiting for the perfect moment, hungry for the warm blood of the meandering people far below.

Chapter 48

"THIS IS WHERE YOU'LL be sleeping," Sandin told the grandmaster as he showed him the chamber next to his. "I do hope you'll consider staying here after Gadiel returns to Abithia."

Helfi replied, "As you well know, my boy, I am still in charge of Shadowspire. I can't abandon it."

"I feel there's no need for the school anymore," he argued.

Helfi sighed. "You were always a good student, a good friend to me, Sandin, but there will *always* be a need for Shadowspire. You can't be so naïve as to think otherwise; we assassins aren't just needed for battles between kingdoms, but for those within as well. You should know that with as many lives you have taken in our home."

Sandin took a deep breath to calm the rising frustration. "I understand. I just wish things had been different. The war is over now; I thought you may wish to put all the killing behind you for good."

Helfi sat down in a wooden chair next to a table; an oil lamp was flickering and there was light coming in through windows. "It has been a long time since you've been to the school. I don't only teach how to kill anymore, but also how to survive. As you know, most of the boys I take in are troublesome, without direction in their lives. Shadowspire gives them direction, gives them control over their lives."

Sandin nodded. "I guess it's better if you stay there. Where would I be if not for you and your abounding wisdom?"

Helfi laughed deeply. "One does not reach this level of wisdom without a great deal of mistakes. Remember that."

"I will." There was a silence between them, then Sandin said, "The parade will be starting soon. Would you like to watch it from the balcony, perhaps?"

"That sounds wonderful. I may retire early, however; my knees aren't what they once were, and I'm afraid if I stand for too long you'll be carrying me back." That gained a chuckle from Sandin. Then there was a light knock, and the door cracked open, but the person did not come in.

"Yes?" Sandin asked.

"May I interest you gentlemen in a warm tea?" The voice was odd, raspy. It almost sounded like they were trying to disguise themselves.

"No," Sandin said. He turned to gather some things as he said, "We were just about to go observe the parade."

There was a shuffling of feet and a grunt from Helfi. Sandin whipped around. The grandmaster was standing with a man behind him, a knife to his throat. Sandin's heartbeat spiked with adrenaline. His hands were splayed wide to show he posed no threat—not until he had the chance, anyway. Sandin couldn't see the man's face as a hooded cloak was draped over him and his face was downcast.

Helfi's visage was like stone, but his hands were up in surrender. Already a bead of crimson dribbled from his neck where the tip of the knife was pressed. Sandin didn't miss the delicateness of the situation.

"Easy," Sandin said, taking a small, tentative step forward. "Put the knife down and we all walk away from this."

"Take one more step," the man said, though his voice sounded familiar that time. He had the accent of an Abithian. "And the old man will bleed out in this room." A hand reached up and pulled off the hood, revealing the face beneath. He was smirking with triumph in his eyes.

"Ysra," Sandin snarled. "I should have just ended you when I had the chance."

"Yes," he laughed, "you should have. I swam back through that nasty water, all the way to our homeland. I nearly drowned twice. It took days; I had to rest for months to get rid of the muscle spasms caused by what you did to me. I swore I'd finish the job Queen Gadiel gave to me, despite her recent... change of heart. *This* is just a happy accident. I always knew Helfi was *weak*."

"This is all your doing," Sandin admonished. "Surely you can see that."

"Gentlemen," Helfi cut in. "Why don't we all just take a step back and work this out calmly."

"Shut your mouth," Ysra growled in his ear, pressing the knife slightly harder. Sandin saw the faint twitch of pain on Helfi's face as more blood dribbled out. "I am in control here, not you, Grandmaster. Queen Gadiel gave me a mission, and since this dunce let me live, I *will* finish it. Even if I have to end your life too."

"Do not harm him, Ysra. I'm warning you." Sandin put forth all the venom he could muster into his words. "You've tried to kill me once already and we both know how that worked out. I was at a disadvantage, and you still couldn't take me out. There is only one way this can end."

A smile cracked his lips apart. "Then the gods will smile down on me in my death as I drag the two of you with me." Sandin tried sliding another foot forward, but Ysra clicked his tongue. "I said not another step. Now, take out those blades you love so much." Sandin did. "Down on your knees and slide them away." He did that too. "There, now was that so hard for you?"

Sandin's hand inched as slowly as possible toward the throwing knife that was concealed around his right ankle. Scarcely had he needed to use it. His eyes bore into Ysra. He felt the cold metal of the small blade, sliding it ever so slightly out.

Ysra kept smiling, his attention turning to Helfi. "You know, this is kind of ironic. You created me, Helfi, and for that I must thank you. However, that's not enough to keep you alive. Once you're dead, I'll kill that sludge over there, and Shadowspire will fall into my hands. And trust me, I have *big* plans for our old school. Perhaps my assassins will start this war back up again." He laughed then sighed. "Well then, that's enough chatter. I shall see you both in Icuzar."

Sandin sensed what was happening before it happened. In one fluid motion, he flicked the blade toward Ysra. It flipped end-over-end, heading straight for the assassin's eye. Sandin wasn't fast enough. His old friend plunged the knife he was holding into the neck of their grandmaster. Blood erupted over Ysra's hand, and he looked down at it, smiling. Just as Helfi fell to the floor, Sandin's knife impaled Ysra through the eye. He screamed, clutching his face as he stumbled, but kept his feet under him.

Sandin charged to his feet, running at Ysra who was still wailing. The sleek handle of the knife poking between the fingers of one hand while blood spilled out over them. A wooden chair laid on the floor between them on its side—knocked over in the commotion. Nimbly, Sandin stepped onto the chair and jumped. His foot shot out, the heel landing on the handle of the knife sending it further into the man's eye socket.

With a squelch, and one final grunt, the knife went through Ysra's brain, the tip of it sticking out the back of his head. He fell backward, dead before he hit the cold floor.

Sandin knelt at Helfi's side; the grandmaster was sputtering, trying to stop the flow of blood with his wrinkled hands. Sandin tried to help but he'd already lost too much, and the crimson ichor continued to gush. An artery had been severed. The old man faded too quickly to recover.

"Oh, Helfi," Sandin said, his voice a whisper, wishing in that moment that he could shed a tear. He felt Helfi deserved that much at least. He certainly didn't deserve a death like this. "I'm sorry I wasn't faster."

"Shh," Helfi raised a bloody finger up toward Sandin's lips, almost touching them. His hand went instead to Sandin's cheek, cupping it gently. "I am... proud of the... man you have... become." A bloody smile, a tear, and then Helfi's final breath exited his body.

"No. I do *not* accept this! Do not leave me alone! Not again!" Sandin yelled as loudly as he could, and then the words turned into groans of anguish, of tearless cries of horror as he found himself alone. First his parents, now Helfi.

Sandin closed the man's eyes with his shaking fingers then retrieved his curved blades from the floor. *You saved me when I was a child,* he thought, gazing down at Helfi's lifeless form. *Protected me from the death that life brings the less fortunate. Gave me a home when I had none. Showed me the way to a fruitful existence. And in the end, I couldn't even save you, couldn't let old age get to you before a blade.* Sandin knew he'd never forgive himself; if he hadn't invited him to Gosatha, he would still be alive. Just when Sandin didn't think things could get any worse, screams from outside erupted.

Chapter 49

AFTER OBSERVING THE PEOPLE and their processions of carriages and wagons far below, Ara finally grew tired of holding herself back. Pulling her wings tight, she dived down. The wind was a roaring waterfall in her ears, but despite that, she could still hear the screams and shouts of panic as people spotted her. She was a wolf, and they were nothing more than rabbits to be feasted upon.

Ara's wings spread out and the wind caught them, allowing her to level out. She wanted to revel in what she was about to do. She wanted to enjoy it. Flying around—low this time—Ara became aware of people bustling to reach the sinister-looking weapons. She let loose a roar, deafening to their human ears. They loaded the weapons with spears; finally, it was clear what they aimed to do. Ara found her curiosity piqued by them.

She didn't have to wait long to find out exactly what the weapons were capable of. There was a loud *twang* and a flash of movement from the nearest device. A spear came hurtling at Ara so fast that, even though she turned to dodge it, the spear still struck her wing. The sharp point made a tiny rip in the sinewy skin at the base of her left wing. She hardly felt it but would need to make certain she wasn't impaled by one of them.

A blow from one of these would be... devastating.

As she flew toward the first weapon, she could hear the wheels of the others turning towards her. Breathing deeply, the creature collected the flames in her throat and then spewed them as she flew by. Fire erupted onto the weapon and covered the two men standing next to it. The weapon became nothing but cinders and ashes in mere seconds; it took the screaming men a bit longer to cease their movement and die. More bolts fired at her, but Ara was better prepared then and was able to maneuver around them with little effort.

She was making her way back around to launch another volley of flames onto the soldiers, when a boulder came hurtling at her. The thing would have crushed her like a bug beneath a heel. Dust fell from the stone as it flew, poised to decimate her entirely. Flipping upside down, she watched—as if in slow motion—the stone sailing over her, nearly scraping along her belly. When she righted herself, she'd gone past the weapons and their operators. Ara sailed over a wall of stone.

Down on the streets, people were scrambling to get away from Ara, but there were so many gathered it made their escape slow, futile. A laugh filled her head. *They have made it far too easy for me.*

There was no mistaking the carriages belonging to members of royalty. They were regal, the gaudiest of them all. Large enough to fit a horse in them, gold and red paint adorning the surface, and being pulled by teams of four large horses. They would go first.

Sweeping low, Ara saw knights with spears poised to attack surrounding the carriages. She gained a bit of height as she flew over them, but at the last second, flicked her tail downward. The four horses of one carriage were smashed, their bones breaking and limbs ripping from sockets. Her powerful tail tore gaping holes in the animal's bellies. She could smell the delectable insides spewing out. *Such a waste.*

She came back, dodging meekly thrown spears, but took out the four horses pulling the second royal carriage. With each blow to the steeds, the carriages were yanked around the street, spilling the passengers inside. Finely dressed people she didn't recognize scrambled around the street. Ara already knew where her targets were before doing that, though. She could sense them, but after knocking them free, she could *see* them. She was so close to her revenge but also wondered if it would ever be enough. What would happen if she slaughtered this entire family? The Abithians would be next; they were directly responsible for Calder's death. None of them deserved the mercy of living.

Before taking the royal family, the Gilded Wolves guarding them would need to be dealt with. She spotted King Oliver pulling people to run in front of him back toward the palace. They thought they'd be safer there, it would seem. A dozen soldiers filed in behind Oliver, shouting, courage laced in their cries of determination. And yet, it was all for naught. With a quick spin, Ara's tail decimated all the guards; however, she could hear more of them running down the street behind her.

She glanced back to find more than a dozen charging her way. Ara ran forward, catching up to Oliver in only a few steps. He never had time to draw his weapon before she had him. She gripped him in her fist, not even feeling his weak, human punches along her armored scales. The woman was next. Ara lifted her, eyeing the Queen Mother curiously. She didn't have enough room to carry all of them, so Ara grabbed the next two girls. Leaving one behind, the beast took back to the sky, flying away from Valendra.

Several wingbeats later, Valendra was nothing more than a blight in the distance. The Jardanises in her clawed feet didn't stop screaming until she'd dropped them onto the ground. They all tumbled across rocks near a small stream. Ara landed on the opposite side, walking toward them slowly.

Finally, she thought. *Finally, Oliver will pay for what he's done. Vengeance. Is. Mine.*

He was on his feet first, jumping in between Ara and his family. The Sword of Gorenos ripped into the air; the point aimed at her shakily. "Do not come any closer, *monster*," Oliver threatened. "I will skewer you where you stand."

Ara had forgotten that no one knows her true identity.

"How do you know it can understand you?" The mother asked. She had the same eyes as Oliver.

"I don't." His voice was full of doubt and fear. It was a wonderful sight to behold, and Ara wished she could smile without it coming across as a snarl.

The two younger girls behind them were hugging each other, tears streaming down their faces. Cuts and bruises already decorated them from where they'd been dropped. Ara looked at them longer than she probably should have. Her heart began to soften for them. They were just two young girls who had nothing to do with any of it.

No. Every Jardanis must die, she thought, shaking her head.

Ara took a couple more steps; they were within range of her flames if that's what she chose to do. First, however, she needed them to know why. She needed them to know who she was.

Can you all hear me? she called out with her mind just like she'd practiced. By the panicked looks and the starts each of them had, Ara knew they could.

"Who—what are you?" Oliver stammered.

Do you not recognize me? No, I'd assume not. Come now, Oliver, think about it. Take a look at me, a good look; listen to my voice. She wanted him to put the pieces together himself.

Letting his sword fall by his side, the king looked at Ara for a long time, all of them silent. The two girls had stopped crying and were on their feet, sniffling and rubbing the tears away. Just as she began to think he'd never catch on, his eyes narrowed. "Ara?"

She laughed into their minds. *And here I thought you'd forgotten me.*

He looked stricken. "I don't understand. How is this possible?"

"Do you know this *beast*, Oliver?" his mother asked, her words a spiteful insult aimed to hurt her.

He nodded, but held a hand up to her so that she would stay quiet. Ara burned a gaze into the Queen Mother.

I'd rather not go into too much detail, but it turns out I come from a rather powerful bloodline. Everything we believed about the gods, about that sword of yours, about the great snake was a lie. I am the same as Bhishma: nothing more than the creation of a sorceress.

Oliver shook off the fear and smiled, the elegant politician façade returning to him. "If a mere human witch did this, then perhaps she can turn you back. You don't need to hurt anyone else, Ara!"

The creature shook her head, dipped a talon in the stream, and looked back up at him. *She was the last of her clan. I killed her for what she has done to me and my family. And you and yours shall meet the same fate.* She paused for a moment to see their looks of despair return. *You are correct about one thing though, Oliver. I don't* need *to hurt anyone; I* want *to.*

The older woman stepped in front of her son. Her arms were stretched in a protective gesture. "Please, Ara, was it? Do not hurt my son, nor my daughters; I'm sure you have your reasons for doing this, but I'm begging you to let them live. Take me. I will give my life willingly if it means they live."

"Mother, no," the two girls cried in unison. Their tears slowly returned, but Ara just found it to be insufferable the second time around.

Don't worry, Queen Mother. You will die, yes. All of you must die. Oliver took my family away from me. The Abithians took away the man I loved. They will see justice as well. The witch, Cassandra, construed all of this, but she has already paid for her sins. Now, Oliver must pay for his.

Ara stalked forward again. King Oliver held his blade level at Ara. He jumped back in front of his family. "I will not let you do this!"

With a flick of her tail, Ara knocked him several feet away where he landed hard in the stream. His breath was stolen from him as he leaned up, his mouth working to take in air. Ara looked back at him. *You misunderstand me, Oliver. You will all reunite in the afterlife, but you shall be last. There is nothing you can do to stop this.*

"No," he'd regained his voice, but it was still only a whisper. "Please, Ara. I'm begging you."

Don't worry. You will have another chance to kill me when I come for your other sister. The Queen Mother curled her body around the younger girls. It would do nothing to shield them from Ara's flame. She would make it quick. The fire in her throat was hotter than anything she'd ever released. Her mouth opened, tongue curled, and the black pitch of her throat glowed orange.

Chapter 50

THE STREAM SOAKED OLIVER'S breeches; his feet slipped over the rocks, providing little traction. Oliver scrambled to his feet, grasping the hilt of the gleaming blade. The inhale he heard was like a rattle of death; he could smell the fire before it left her throat. There was a scream that would not end as flames akin to liquid poured over his mother, over his sisters. The scream was ripping, tearing at his throat, he realized. His face was hot; however, he didn't know if it was from the burning bodies or from the rage that exploded within him and mingled with sorrow.

He sprinted forward before she finished spewing the flames. With a hard swipe, King Oliver cut through the scales of a hind leg. The armor of her scales was hard as stone, it seemed, but the sword still cut into Ara's leg. A roar of pain ripped through the air. She spun impossibly fast, clamping her teeth down on Oliver's sword arm. The sword dropped to the ground. There was pain unlike anything he'd ever felt in his life. It began at his hand and shot up to his shoulder. The crunch of bone was unmistakable, and then he was falling back. Ara gave one more growl, looked over her shoulder, and then launched into the sky. She faded from view quickly, but Oliver didn't know if it was because of the spots in his vision or because she was just that fast.

The sound of horse hooves filled his ears, and he tried to lift his head, but it didn't seem to want to cooperate. The pain in his arm felt weird; he tried to move his fingers, but it was like he couldn't feel them. And then Sandin was looking down at him, his mouth open and his brows knit tightly. For the first time, it seemed, Sandin wore a readable expression: horror.

"How bad?" was all Oliver could manage.

Sandin's voice came out low. "Don't speak. Save your strength. I'll get you out of here."

Something tight wrapped around the king's upper arm; he winced when it was cinched down. Oliver reached out, placing his other hand on Sandin's arm. "They're gone," he whispered as tears finally fell down his cheeks. There was so much rippling through him, he didn't know which one caused their descent. Sorrow. Anguish. Pain.

"What? Who?" Sandin looked around as Oliver glanced at the black pile of ash.

"Mother. Layla. Camille." Oliver weeped, unable to stop the heaves of his chest or staunch the flow of salty tears.

Sandin gripped the back of Oliver's head and pulled his face into his chest. He could feel himself drenching the assassin's black tunic with tears. It was a brotherly embrace if there ever was one, something that seemed odd coming from Sandin. However, with the present state of everything, Oliver was abundantly grateful for this unlikely friend.

"Everything will be alright," Sandin told him, laying his head gently down. "I have to get you to a surgeon, Oliver." He put his arms under the king, and then lifted with a grunt. Oliver grimaced; the pain of the movement was unbearable. He and Sandin made it atop the horse before darkness closed in around him.

The last thing he uttered before the pain swept away his consciousness was, "My sword..."

So, I'm not dead then, King Oliver thought. His eyes hadn't yet dared to flutter open, but he was aware that he was waking up. There was a soft bed beneath him, and he was covered in blankets. A heating pan lay beneath his feet. Hushed tones conversed in the room.

"Who...?" he asked. He had meant to ask who was there, but his tongue felt heavy. Slowly, his eyes opened as a hand was placed on his forehead.

"His fever seems to be dropping," a voice said. He knew that voice, but the man's face was still blurry.

When it cleared up, Oliver smiled. "Philip." Oliver hadn't spoken to him since the death of his father.

"Welcome back, Majesty," Philip said. "Take things easy, now. Don't want to go making the sutures rip away."

"Sutures?" he asked confusedly.

"Thank you, Philip, I'll fill him in," Sandin said, stepping closer so Oliver could see him. He smiled sadly. The king smiled back.

"How are you feeling?" Sandin asked.

Oliver thought for a moment. "I feel fuzzy."

Sandin chuckled. "Philip said you might feel that way. Said he gave you something strong to fight the pain. It will take a long time to recover, but you're one of the strongest men I've ever met. I know you'll get past this. I'll make sure you do."

"Sandin." Oliver curled a finger in, gesturing him to come closer. When he did, Oliver asked, "What happened?"

Sandin looked confused. "You don't remember?" Oliver shook his head. "The winged monster showed up to the parade. It took you, your mother, and two of your sisters. They were killed, and you... well, the creature took your arm with it."

King Oliver glanced down at his arm. Wrapped in red-stained bandages was half of his arm. The bottom half was no longer there. He remembered what happened. "Ara," he growled in a whisper. The pain of her bite came back to him.

"Who, Majesty?" Sandin tilted his head.

Oliver found the words just began spilling out without stopping, "There was a girl from Osta. Her name was Ara. She was one of the most beautiful girls I have ever met, and I tried to court her. Things were going well between us, but when I returned home, I found that my father had been poisoned. A strange woman came to me in the night, told me it was Gaius—Ara's father—who'd killed mine. So, I killed Gaius. Took his head. Now, through magic that I won't claim to understand, Ara has been turned into this *thing*. It's all my fault."

"Oliver, you can't think that way. There will be no good to come from it. Every man and woman are responsible for the choices they make."

Oliver gave a slight nod. "Yes, but my decisions have led to *this*." There was silence between them. King Oliver's eyes grew big. "Where is Ruelle?"

"I'm not certain. She visited you some time ago, but I think one of the handmaidens ushered her off to bed. It's late."

"I must see her. I need to know that she's okay. Ara said she would come for Ruelle next. She's going to kill her, and then me." He tried sitting up in his panic, but whatever Philip gave him made his head spin and he fell back onto the bed. The jarring motion sent a shockwave of pain through his arm. He gasped, clenching his teeth.

"Respectfully, stop this," Sandin said, putting a hand on the king's chest. "I will go check on your sister and you have my word I won't leave her side until you can stand again."

Oliver nodded, relaxing a bit more. Sleep was gnawing at him again. "You are a good man—good friend—Sandin. I'm glad I decided to trust you all those days ago."

Sandin sighed. "I regret that I haven't always lived up to that compliment in the past." The look in his eyes showed his mind was taken elsewhere.

"What's the matter? Something troubles you." Oliver asked.

Sandin smiled sadly again, shaking his head. "Even in the midst of your own tragedy you care for others." He paused. "Never mind. We can talk more later. Get some rest." Then he picked up the oil lamp that was flickering nearby and left.

Oliver laid back, closed his eyes, and said a silent prayer to the gods that they would give him good dreams. Somehow, he just knew he'd be stuck in an endless nightmare, being forced to watch his family burn again and again. He hoped he would be able to move on his own the following day, for what kind of king would he be if he didn't try to avenge his people?

Chapter 51

RUELLE'S CHAMBER DOOR WAS slightly ajar, casting a thin line of light from the hall into the darkness. Sandin stood outside the door for a moment, listening to see if there was any sound coming from inside. He heard nothing, so he poked his head in. The girl was sleeping soundly. Sandin walked in silently, placing the lamp down on a table, and then looked at the girl. Her face was puffy from crying.

Sandin wished he was capable of crying; perhaps it would help release some of the pain he was feeling. Oliver said his family's deaths were his fault, and he could relate to that. Helfi would still be alive if Sandin had done any number of things. He could have killed Ysra from the beginning, could have not invited Helfi to visit. He could have just been faster. Any of that would have saved the grandmaster's life.

Helfi and Ysra were probably being burned in the morgue as Sandin sat there thinking about them. He wondered what would become of Shadowspire. Who would take Helfi's place? Probably Tarshi. She was as noble as any assassin and highly skilled in her craft. Although, she preferred death by poison which wasn't something Sandin found enjoyable. Poison was often messy, or if one didn't get the amount just right, it could fail.

"Who are you?" a tiny voice squeaked out. Sandin's eyes shot over to the bed.

He'd been distracted by his thoughts and didn't notice her stirring. "Forgive me for startling you, Lady Ruelle. My name is Sandin. King Oliver has asked that I watch over you until he gets his feet back under him."

She sat up at that, looking a bit relieved. "He's okay then?"

Sandin nodded. "He'll be fine; however, it may take some time. I think he'll need his sister to be strong for him."

The girl smiled, jumped from her bed, and leapt onto Sandin. She flung her arms around his neck and buried her face into his chest. Sandin was taken aback at first, not familiar with children in such an affectionate way. After he realized she wasn't letting go anytime soon, however, he returned the hug and laughed. Ruelle climbed off, looking bashful, and muttered, "Sorry." She wiped a lone tear.

Sandin smiled. "Don't worry about it. You've been through a lot. We all have."

"Did your family die too?" The way she asked was so innocent that Sandin couldn't get mad. In fact, it made him chuckle.

He replied. "Something like that. I had an old friend die today. A man who saved my life on more than one occasion."

"That's horrible." She reached up and hugged him again, but he got the feeling it was for his benefit that time. Ruelle released his neck, hopping back onto the edge of her bed.

She sniffled, then said, "Mother always said that telling others about our troubles is the best way to heal. Want to tell me about your friend?" Her eyes shifted from sad and weary to wide and hopeful, probably wanting something to take her mind away from the day's events.

"How old are you, Ruelle?" he asked. "You're very... aware, for someone so small."

The girl grinned. "Ten years now; it's thanks to Mother I'm so smart."

Sandin smiled. "Well, the Queen Mother was very wise. And I'd be glad to share my story with you." He crossed his arms and looked around thoughtfully. "Now, where should I start? Oh, I know the perfect place." Ruelle wiped once more at a silent tear, then leaned forward. "Once, when I was only a couple of summers older than you, I was going through one of the trials at my school. We were all released into the wilderness where we were expected to survive on our own. The other boys and I were in a race back to the school, but the thing that made it so dangerous was the lack of rules. See, the other boys didn't care for me too much. They would make sure I knew that every chance they got, too."

"That's mean of them," she said, looking offended.

"It sure was. Well, there was one night when I was getting close to the school, where I made a fire. It was a cold night, and I wanted some warmth, despite knowing it could mean the death of me. Unsurprisingly, my smoke alerted the others to my location, and I didn't know this, but they'd formed an alliance with each other."

"An alliance?"

"It just means they were working together." Ruelle nodded and he continued. "The boys sneaked up on me, jumped from the bushes and attacked me." Ruelle gasped. "This went against no rules though. They beat me, stomped me, and left me to die. They didn't even leave my fire lit to keep my bones warm."

"What happened next?" She leaned ever closer, fingers crossed in her lap.

"My old friend, Helfi, appeared. Apparently, he'd been watching us the entire time. Helfi was a bit older when I was going through the school. His heart was a bit softer for kids like me. After he'd cleaned me up and fed me some bread, he disappeared back into the trees, vanishing like a spirit as if he'd never been there."

"Wow," she marveled. "He sounds like a good friend."

"He was," Sandin said, nodding. "Now, you need some rest. Lie down and get some sleep, okay?"

She nodded, yawned, and laid her head down. Soft snores came from her before long, and Sandin closed his eyes as well. He wouldn't sleep, but resting his eyes would help pass the night by.

The following day, Sandin and Ruelle ventured to the infirmary to visit the king. "You are to stay with Sandin or I at all times, Ruelle. Is that understood?"

She nodded. "I don't have to like it, though. You haven't even told me why you're being like this."

The king sighed. "The beast that took Mother and our sisters wants to take all of us, but we won't allow that. Don't be afraid; be strong. You must always be strong for our people. You are the future of Gosatha, Ruelle. You will be its next ruler."

"Surely, not," she scoffed. "You'll get married and have a son, brother. I just know it!"

He shook his head. "No. I've known for a while, Ruelle; it's not in the stars for me to be wed." Sandin saw her visage go steely, determined as the truth of the king's words settled.

He plans on dying right along with the creature, Sandin thought, but said nothing.

"It's time I began my sword training then." With that, the girl spun on her heel and marched away. She stopped in the doorway, turning to Sandin. "Aren't you coming?"

The two men chuckled. Sandin helped the king to his feet as the little girl continued on her way with them hot on her heels. "She's a handful," Sandin whispered to Oliver.

"Well, get used to it. You're part of this family now, although, I think you'll be safe from Ara." He said the last part facetiously.

Sandin's heart swelled with pride at Oliver's words. "Okay, sister, let's get you a blade," Oliver shouted to her. "I'd like for you to show her a few things if it isn't any trouble. I must go meet with Queen Gadiel."

Sandin considered his duties with the group home, but figured he could delegate some responsibility for a time. "Of course. Do you need me to take you to her?"

Though he appeared to be struggling, Oliver said, "I'll manage." Then he halted, breathing with slight difficulty. He said, "I sent a letter to her."

"Who, Majesty?"

"Ara," he said. "I sent a falcon with a letter. It returned a few days later with the missive I sent. I thought she was dead; I guess I know why the falcon couldn't reach her." Sandin merely nodded. Oliver pursed his lips, nodded to Sandin once, and departed.

Sandin left King Oliver and jogged to catch up to Ruelle. For someone so small, she could put a lot of distance between them with ease. The assassin didn't know what to think of Oliver's pseudo relationship with Ara; he only hoped it wouldn't get in the way of killing her, though he knew the king would do everything he could to protect his kingdom.

In the armory they retrieved two swords. Ruelle got one that was more like a toothpick. It was even made of wood. And Sandin got one only slightly larger. "This is all I get?" she asked, sounding dejected.

"You don't need anything real yet. You need to learn the basics with this training sword here, and then when you're bigger and stronger, you can have the real thing." She opened her mouth to argue, but Sandin held up a finger. "Ah, ah, ah. No complaining. Your first lesson has begun. Now, defend yourself."

In the corridor outside the armory, he assumed a fighting stance with his legs bent slightly. His spare arm tucked behind his back and his sword was up and ready to fight. Ruelle eyed him for a moment, then copied his stance. Sandin came at her first with a jab to see how she would react. She backed away, nearly tripping, although she did it quickly. He did it again but struck her in the belly before she could move away.

"Ow!" She scowled at him.

Sandin could only smile. "Now you've learned something. You can't always back away from your problems. You must face them, defeat them head on!" He jabbed at her again. This time, she swiped at his sword. It was sloppy and wouldn't be effective in a real duel, however, it was closer to what he was looking for. "Good," he said. "Now, you attack me with the same jab."

When she did, Sandin demonstrated a proper parry with a flick of his wrist. Her sword nearly tumbled from her hand. "Now you," he said. He jabbed again. She copied his movements, parrying his attack.

Sandin smiled. "You are a very quick learner, Ruelle. You'll make a fine swordsman yet."

Sandin smiled. "You are a very quick learner, Ruelle. You'll make a fine swordsman yet."

Chapter 52

THE PAIN OF THE gash in Ara's hind leg was searing, like white-hot fire melting away at her skin and muscle. Her blood dripped as she flew over the sea, trying desperately to make it back to her new home before it was too late. However, with each beat of her giant wings, Ara's strength diminished. The sense of victory she felt at sending those Jardanises to the afterlife was immense, but quickly fading as fear settled in.

She tried to calm her mind. *Only one more to go, and then Oliver can join them.* Ara then admonished herself for not trying to grab the last girl. Now that he knew of her intentions, the girl would be far more difficult to kill. She'd overestimated her own intellect, shouldn't have laid her plans out in full.

There it is. Finally.

The tall cliffs of the wild land came into her vision; Ara beat her wings harder to gain speed. As she made it over solid ground, a breath of relief swept through her, but then Ara realized she wasn't going to make it to the cave. She saw the people—Feral Ones—milling about their small village. They'd shed the furs due to the warmer weather and were wearing... well hardly anything. The women wore animal hide over their breasts; both men and women covered their genitals and wore thin sandals.

Ara's head swirled, making her laugh to herself—as if drunk—as she thought about how primitive these people were. She hoped they wouldn't cut her up and use her scales, her meat, her talons and horns for supplies. With very little control, Ara crash-landed into the dirt. Her body slid for several seconds, creating a deep trench from the impact and friction. She breathed out an exhausted breath which sent plumes of dust up in front of her eyes. The creature was at the mercy of the wild men who ran towards her as darkness closed in.

THERE WAS FAINT PRESSURE in small spots all around her. It was such a light touch that Ara hardly felt it, but when she reached out with her mind, she knew she was surrounded by the Feral Ones. Her eyes cracked open slowly. A fire crackled nearby with what looked like a hog roasting above it. Ara began to salivate even though she felt that cooked meat wouldn't taste the same to her as it did when she was human. Her head lifted and several of the people stirred.

Looking around her, Ara realized that many of the humans were resting against her scales. They hadn't tried harming her. As more of them noticed her awakening, they stood to their feet and stepped away. As they stared up at her hulking shape, their smiles reached their eyes. She craned her neck to look at her wound and found it wrapped in multiple long cloths. Sniffing it, Ara smelled some sort of poultice had been rubbed over the wound. There was also the faint scent of her blood.

The man who appeared to be the leader stepped forward, gesturing to the roasting hog. Was he offering their food to her? How could these people be so savage, so uncivilized, and yet be so kind to her? Maybe it was because they didn't know how many men she'd already killed. Ara shook her head, backing away as the people parted for her. She couldn't take their food. After she'd gained some space, Ara bowed to them, bringing her nose just above the ground. There were smiles all around when she looked back at them. They were all in her area of influence, and Ara wanted to try something that may help them communicate. She reached out and tried to push a single emotion upon them: gratitude. Ara knew it was successful when their smiles grew wider as they glanced around at each other.

Then, Ara limped away. The feeling of triumph returned to her, but not only because of her previous killings, but because she had found a way to communicate with the Feral Ones. They worshipped her as a goddess, loved her like one. They would protect her, fight for her, even die for her. She didn't know what she would use them for yet, but she knew they would prove useful in the future.

That night, Ara had to settle for eating meagerly before returning to her cave, as her wounded leg made it difficult to hunt at full speed. She looked forward to letting her mind drift away, knowing that with each sleep she would wake up a wiser creature.

After a full night of rest, Ara awoke to a rumbling belly, and left her cave to seek out sustenance. The thrill of the hunt: a feeling that was nearly indescribable. A rush of adrenaline and victory as prey slammed between razor-sharp teeth. Tongue slickened with the blood of another. Ara killed something she would have never considered herself capable of as a human. The brown woodland bear stood no chance, but then again, nothing did really. This bear would satiate Ara for the rest of the day.

Several days had passed by with Ara on the mend. She couldn't attempt to take the life of Oliver's last sibling with her leg still lacerated, but the longer she waited, the harder it would be to get to the girl. They will have hidden her, possibly increased defenses too, by time Ara was ready for another battle. Her leg was feeling better, but she wanted to give it another day or two just to make sure the wound was fully closed. It wouldn't bode well for the wound to reopen and have her bleed out.

After her meal, Ara lounged around with the savages. There was something about their way of life; it was so simple and without the hardships that she'd once known. Everything that was caught, hunted, grown, or made was shared amongst the people. There were not vast numbers of them, not nearly as many soldiers as the Gosathan or Abithian armies, but they had heart. They were strong too. Ara watched the men compete in games where they would lift stones so heavy she couldn't imagine any other men being able to heft them.

The Feral Ones cared about their home, cared for one another with more love than anything else. They didn't try to steal from each other, didn't try to kill their own or harm them in anyway. However, they would battle for fun as well, and it was exceedingly rough. They would end fights with bloodied noses, lips, and swollen eyes, the occasional stab wound or bloody gash. It was rather entertaining. The children would run up Ara's tail, climb her back using the pointy spine protruding through the scales. They would sit atop her head and look into her giant eyes.

Silly children, she'd think, but almost purred at the joy they found in climbing around her. *Perhaps, it isn't all mankind who will die by my flame.*

Trying to gain ground on the communication front, Ara would send messages to the leader with her mind. She even learned his name—Hono. He'd patted his chest with his hand, uttering the word. It only took a couple of times before Ara caught on, and she reciprocated.

"Ara," he said, but he couldn't say it without rolling the 'r'. Hono looked around, pointing at her and repeating her name until everyone around followed suit. It was like they were chanting, cheering for her. She lifted her head and spouted a flame toward the sky just for show, and that's when the name chanting really did become a cheer. They seemed to love seeing her abilities in action and, Ara being a gracious goddess, couldn't help but indulge them.

One night they were all singing a native song as Ara laid on her belly. Hono sat a short distance away on a stump, his shoulders and head bobbing and swaying to the melodious symphony of voices. Ara was stricken with a thought—nothing of great import, however, she wanted to know what their land was called.

Hono. The man looked at her with a smile. She pointed at the ground with one huge talon; Hono looked down to where she pointed but looked back up in confusion. She wasn't being clear enough. She pointed at herself. *Ara.* Then pointed at him. *Hono.* Then pointed at the ground again. Realization dawned on his face.

"Draconia," he told her. She repeated the word back to him and he nodded happily.

Draconia. She said the word to herself a few times. In a world where she'd entered as a Lowborn, where she wanted to be anything but herself, Ara finally found a place where she felt she belonged: Draconia.

Chapter 53

"We must kill this creature," King Oliver said. The people in his war room were being ridiculous. "Slaying it is our *only* option."

"You only say that because she wants to kill the rest of you Jardanises," Gadiel said cooly. "Which I understand your point; however, if we can capture it, we can study it. There may be weapons we could develop if given enough time."

"No. This is something I *will not* risk. You are welcome to salvage what you can from her body." There was finality in his tone; the argument was done.

She sighed. "Very well, King Oliver. It is as you wish. Like I've already told you, I believe the catapulting net we've developed will be instrumental. If we can use that and your bolt thrower in succession, we may just have a chance at killing the thing."

He nodded. "Thank you, Gadiel. I agree. We will have your invention built and placed near the spear throwers. I'll leave it up to you as to where weapons will be built in Abithia."

"My home will be just fine, I think. There is ample space in the mountains to house my entire queendom if need be." She smiled, which Oliver thought looked odd as she didn't do so often.

"You were right, you know," he said, eyes glancing around at his silent councilmen. He'd briefed them beforehand as to what he'd speak of, so they already knew what his admission would be.

"Hm? What are you referring to, Majesty?"

"The gods. The serpent. My people's history and beliefs. You were right about it all. Ara told me so, confirmed everything you said. So, I want to apologize for my stubbornness before. If I could go back and change my decision, I would." He looked back up at her to find an unreadable expression.

The councilmen remained silent, though a few fidgeted in their seats nervously.

Gadiel sighed. "I would think it prudent that we move past these errors in our judgement; both of us chose poorly. Still, I must beg forgiveness for my betrayal. I don't think I've done so properly."

He waved his hand dismissively, feeling truth in the words he was about to speak before they came out. "I harbor no ill feelings toward you. The past is behind us and should stay there." The king rose from his seat, ending the meeting, and walked out of the room with Sandin and Tiberius trailing him. A goblet of wine sloshed in his hand as he brought it to his lips.

Tiberius said, "I still can't believe it's that little redheaded girl from Osta. You're sure you didn't imagine that, Majesty?"

Without faltering, he said, "Yes, I am sure. I wouldn't imagine hearing her voice in my head. It's all I can hear now, save for the screams of my mother and sisters." None of them said anything after that.

The king handed his goblet to Sandin, and swung open a heavy door that led to a small room; heat smacked him in the face. He heard Tiberius curse behind him and stifled a chuckle. The smith chamber was always toasty, the ovens where swords were forged making it hard to breathe.

Walking up to one of the smiths—Ensio—he said, "Is it ready?"

"I'm just now finishing up the final touches," Ensio replied. He was curled over a table with a monocle on his face, tinkering with something. "And here we are." He turned, holding up the project he'd been working on for the last few days.

"Wow," Oliver said, marveling at the contraption.

"So, that's what you've been excited for," Sandin said with a laugh.

"How does it work?" Tiberius asked.

"Allow me." Ensio grabbed Oliver's injured arm. "Don't worry, I'll be gentle." He began strapping it onto the nub where he'd lost his arm. Ensio's grip reminded Oliver of Ara's teeth tearing into him. "Now, you won't be able to use this until your arm is completely healed. If you do, I can't promise that it won't hurt something crazy."

King Oliver nodded, already feeling a throbbing pain pulsating in his arm where the new hand was attached. His mouth went dry, desiring some ale or wine to wet it. The device looked like a metal glove that a knight might wear. The forearm of the attachment had intricate lines etched into it, flowing down the wrist. The hand and fingers were adjustable and were capable of being locked into place. He would hold the Sword of Gorenos again. Oliver's smile stretched to his ears.

Ensio took the gauntlet back, looking over his work proudly. The king clapped him on the shoulder. "Thank you, Ensio. This will serve me well in battle, I think." The smith nodded, smiling back at him.

"Just don't lose your other one," he joked. Oliver laughed, although he didn't find the joke funny; he just didn't want to make the moment awkward for Ensio.

"Well, I best be going. I need to see Queen Gadiel off." Ensio offered a quick bow as King Oliver and his entourage left the sweltering room.

Cool air rushed up to meet Oliver as he stepped across the threshold. He breathed deeply, finding that his neck was slick with sweat as the air touched it. A shiver ran up his spine.

After finding the queen, the two of them traded plans for their weaponry, and Gadiel left in a carriage. The design of the catapulting net was brilliant. It was similar to the concept for their spear thrower, but the net would be stuffed inside of a square-shaped device. The edges of the net will have iron weights attached all around to help propel the net and weigh down the beast. With luck, they'd be able to capture Ara in a net and then finish her off.

I must pierce her heart, he thought. *If it's the last thing I do.*

Oliver thought to pray to the gods that they'd guide his way in the future, but what would be the point in that? There was no way of knowing if they were real. His faith in them had vanished with the enlightenment Ara provided. Maybe the gods did exist and just didn't care about any of the mere mortals. The not knowing—to Oliver—was worse than if he knew for sure they were not real.

One thing Oliver knew, though, was that he was thirsty. That's what he kept telling himself, anyway, ignoring the true reason behind this new hobby he'd acquired.

With one last look at the plans for the net weapon, King Oliver steeled himself for the coming days. Ara would stop at nothing to get to Ruelle, and he'd be damned if he let that happen. The monster must die; there was no other option. Even if Oliver had to die too, he'd jump down her throat if only to shred her from the inside.

Chapter 54

Daily lessons with Ruelle made Sandin realize how much he enjoyed teaching. Imparting the knowledge he had gained over the years made him proud. The girl made him laugh constantly, and when she failed to complete a task, he didn't admonish or berate her. Unlike when he'd learned to fight, Sandin didn't slap her hands with watered reeds as she performed knuckled pushups. He wouldn't be a harsh teacher. He showed her the proper way; told her it was okay to make mistakes as long as she learned from them. Then, he would have her try again and again until she got it right. And when she did, he'd give her praise.

She always showed up to their lessons looking dejected, no doubt because she missed her mother and siblings. But by the end, she would be laughing and smiling as if nothing was wrong. It made Sandin feel good to be able to bring some joy to her. Ten days it had been since the beast last attacked. The people of Valendra were on edge, not knowing when the next onslaught would come, but knowing that it *would*. Even if Oliver never told them what she wanted, they would be anxious until the creature was slain.

The other thing eating away at Sandin, was the newfound love for drinking King Oliver had become partial to. Sandin knew it was because of the lives he'd taken, could see that it haunted him. The shadows beneath Oliver's eyes would have been enough for any killer to understand what was wrong. He just didn't know how to help him. So, he did what he'd promised: trained the man's sister in combat.

"What if she gets me?" Ruelle asked one day. Oliver told his sister Ara's goals; he said he wanted her to be fully prepared to fight for her life if it came to it. Sandin was impressed by how well she took it, being a girl of only ten summers and all.

"I won't allow that," Sandin said. "It's now my life's work to ensure you stay alive. It is my oath to you. My blades will taste the blood of that creature before you die."

She giggled and shook her head. "Why do you care so much about me?"

"I care about you because your brother does. Oliver has become a great friend to me, and though I was raised a killer, my heart has softened to the two of you. I never had much of a family when I was a boy. My parents died when I was very young, and I went to

Shadowspire not long after. My brothers were the boys I competed against, nearly died at the hands of. My father was a man who taught me how to kill." He took a deep breath. "Oliver is my brother now, and you... well, you are the sister I never had." Sandin smiled at her and pinched her cheek, laughing when Ruelle swatted his hand. "Now, I must go see to some other matters. I'll see you later; stay out of trouble."

Sandin left the girl to continue practicing her sword flourishing on her own. He peeked over his shoulder at her. *She'll be ready for a steel blade soon.*

Luckily, Ara hadn't damaged many of their monster-killing weapons. What had been destroyed was being replaced, and the net weapons were almost finished as well. They would be well-fortified before long; he just hoped—as did everyone—they'd be finished in time for when she strikes again. As Sandin walked around the outer wall, his hands behind his back, a falcon flew in and landed on his shoulder.

"Hello there, little one," he said to it, untying the note from its ankle. Something had happened to Sandin since living in Gosatha. His heart and soul, black as the night from years of being an assassin, were becoming brighter. He felt a change within himself that was difficult to describe. It was like all the pain, the rage that he felt inside was melting away—ice under summer rays.

Sandin found that he didn't have to be known as *just* an assassin but could be known for kindness as well. It was unbecoming of a trained killer but that's not who he wanted to be, or so he thought. Unfurling the letter, Sandin began to read.

Dearest Sandin,

I hope this letter finds you well. I know much has happened between you and I, but I hope and wish that you would consider taking over Shadowspire. I was saddened to hear about Helfi. He was a great man and teacher, as you well know. I can't fathom replacing him with anyone but you, Sandin. You will be welcomed back to Abithia with open arms, whether you decide to take this position or not. Please, do let me know what you decide.

-Regards,

Gadiel

He stood there, just staring at the note. He read it and reread it several times before folding it up. Then, he sent the falcon away; he was unable to give her an answer presently. He would need to confer with Oliver. Just when Sandin thought he was out, they tried to pull him back in. No, he wouldn't do it. He was done with that life, done with the murder. How could he turn his back on that and still be the man who teaches others how to take life? Did it even have to be the same, though? Could he not take the job and change the school's ways? He didn't know how that would go over with the queen, but those were the thoughts plaguing him. And knowing himself, it would eat away at him until he made a final decision.

"WHAT SHOULD I DO?" Sandin asked.

King Oliver was looking over the world map in his war room by himself. He took a deep drink of wine. "Why are you asking me? It's your life, Sandin."

"That's not what I wanted to hear. You're supposed to help me make this decision." He said it jokingly, although he was serious.

Oliver laughed, then asked, "Want to know what I really think?"

"Please."

"I think you should take the job." He paused for a moment as Sandin looked down, not understanding why he was feeling disappointed. "But only after Ara has been killed. I need you here. I need you to look after Ruelle."

Sandin's gaze shot back up. "And then?"

"After she is slain and Ruelle is safe, return to Abithia. Teach at Shadowspire. I've seen you with my sister; you have a great passion for teaching others in the way of the sword."

Sandin nodded. "I guess it's settled then. You want to know why I ask your opinion; even a mule has a good idea every now and then." Oliver moved to kick his rear as if the two really were brothers. He nearly fell over, his head no doubt swirling from the drink.

Putting a hand on his shoulder, Oliver shrugged him off, an annoyed look crossing his face. "I'm fine," he muttered, taking another drink.

Sandin's jaw clenched. He took a calming breath. "Permission to speak freely, Majesty?"

"Aye."

"I think this habit of yours has become too much," he said quietly, grabbing the goblet swiftly.

"Put it back," Oliver said. When Sandin disobeyed, Oliver slumped into a chair with his chin tucked and his eyes closed. "What has become of me?" A lonely tear trickled down his cheek. "I can't get them to stop—the dead faces from showing themselves to me—unless my mind is soaked with a drink."

"It's not easy," Sandin said. "Perhaps, it's because you care so much about others. But you must let this go, Oliver. Your kingdom needs you sober-minded, needs you alive. Ruelle needs you... I need you."

Oliver's eyes met Sandin's. "Keep me accountable, Sandin. If you see a drink in my hand, take it from me."

"As you command, Majesty," he replied. "And as for the faces, I shall pray to the gods—if they listen—to spare your mind of its guilt." Sandin saw Oliver's chest rise and fall with a deep breath.

Oliver nodded, then stood, his hand outstretched. "Thank you, my friend." They clasped hands, both men with tight-lipped grins on their faces.

Sandin turned with goblet in hand, making his way to the falconry chamber to write back to Gadiel. The proposal Oliver suggested was better than choosing one or the other. He could have both—for a short time anyway—but only if everything went according to plan.

It struck him then; how often did things in his life go according to plan without a hitch?

Chapter 55

ARA STRETCHED HER LEG; it was still slightly sore, but she could hold herself back no longer. The time to finish what she'd started had come. With the Draconians gathered around her, she sent mental images to each of them, showing her flying away. They looked around, confounded by her sudden need to leave, so she transmitted more. Images of her attacking Valendra hit their minds, and she was curious to see if this would make them turn on her.

They looked around excitedly at each other, and then Hono approached. He patted his chest. "Hono," he said, then pointed to Ara's back. He did this a couple of times.

He wants to come with me, she thought.

She shook her head with a light snort. It was not time for that, but Ara knew the day would come when she'd need him and his people. She just wasn't sure when. She wasn't even sure how she knew that, just figured it was due to the intuition she'd developed. With no other words or images sent to them, Ara bent her powerful legs and sprang from the ground. She let her wings catch the air, gained altitude, and turned toward Gosatha.

THE BEAST FLEW HIGH over the land, excitement rippling through her. As great as her mind had become, her increased intuition, she couldn't feel if her vengeance would be obtained that day. That was part of the exhilaration: not knowing what would happen. It fed the flames of determination. The sun warmed Ara's back which was a welcome sensation since the altitude caused her blood to run even colder than usual.

The city of Valendra grew closer, the palace looming like a giant. Her body undulated with laughter, a chuffing sound. They couldn't stop her with their new weaponry the first time. Why would it be any different now? Despite that, Ara would be loathe to face the Sword of Gorenos again. It's blade had done a number to her, ignoring her scaled armor.

As Ara flew closer, she dropped down on the city. A bell began to ring. *They have learned.* It was a warning for all to hear, letting everyone know that death was coming for them.

With ease, Ara dropped over and behind the low wall. She craned her neck over her shoulder to see what the soldiers there were doing. There were more weapons than before, and some looked a bit different. The wheels grinded on stone as the weapons turned in her direction, but that was all, so she turned back to focus on the palace.

The bell continued to chime and was beginning to annoy her. It was loud enough to irritate her ears. Growling, Ara changed course and flew toward the bell's location. There was a tower that looked like a temple with a bell atop it. A man stood there turning a crank that caused the hull of the bell to sway from side to side.

Enough of this.

Ara released a torrent of flame onto the bell and its ringing mechanism. A scream escaped the man as he caught fire, tumbling from the roof of the temple. The bell followed him, clamoring as it rolled to the ground. Ara changed course again, glad to be rid of the raucous device.

Landing on one of the palace's many spires, her claws dug into the stone and wood. She took a few moments to catch her breath, closing her eyes and listening to the shouts coming from within the edifice. There was much to sift through before she found anything she recognized.

"...to the morgue, Ruelle. I will not hear any arguing. Go. Now!" It was the unmistakable voice of King Oliver.

Ruelle. So that's her name.

"I want to fight! I'm strong now. I can take care of myself. Tell him, Sandin!" The girl's voice was very young. Ara shook that thought away, fearful she would change her mind about killing the girl if she learned too much about her. She didn't need to find mutuality between them.

"I must agree with your brother, Ruelle," another man's voice said. Must have been this Sandin, a man she'd yet heard of. She pondered who he could be to them. A friend, or perhaps a cousin? If so, his name would be on her list as well.

"Sandin will stay by your side, Ruelle. I will not have you argue with me again."

How sweet, she thought sarcastically as the conversation faded with their descent into the morgue.

There was an aerial bridge connecting two spires of the palace. Several men ran out with determined looks on their faces, bows and arrows aimed at her. She glided toward them. As they sent a volley at her, she tucked her wings, diving beneath the arrows. With a crash of Ara's tail, she decimated the bridge, sending the men shouting and falling to their deaths. They were far too high to survive such a fall.

Soldiers flooded the streets, looking up to keep eyes on her. She still hadn't spotted Oliver or the girl.

That's right. They were hiding her in the morgue which will most likely be beneath the palace.

This only caused them to evoke her ire even more. In the distance, the familiar twang of their new spear-launching weapons rang out. Ara dived down without looking, and a moment later, heard the clash of a spear striking stone. She snarled, sweeping low to the ground and sending a blaze through a group of ten spear-wielding men. Armor and flesh oozed off their bodies. The faint smell of burning hair and metal wafted into her nose.

Ara landed for a moment to concentrate. She searched for Oliver's mind—then after finding it—realized he was exiting the front of the palace. She turned to face him with her fangs bared. He didn't look worried; his face was like a stone.

Bring me the girl, she shouted into his mind. He clutched the side of his head with a hand. More softly, *Bring her now.*

"You will never get to her, Ara," he said with confidence. "You should have never told me your plans. There are myriad places to hide within the palace; so many that you couldn't fathom."

I know she's in the morgue, she transmitted with an arrogant tone.

He looked taken aback. "Well, I see your hearing is rather impeccable now, though, that doesn't change anything. I'll do anything to protect my sister. Her life is more important than mine. So, be my guest and take me, rip me to shreds, burn my body if you want. Just know this: you will *never* get to her."

Oh, don't say that, Oliver. Her voice was almost singing in his head as she developed ideas that would get to him. *You care for more than just her. I know how much you care about your people, the lengths you would go through to keep them safe.* Her flames warmed her back as the soldiers continued to burn on the cobblestone street.

His eyes narrowed. "What are you getting at?"

Beginning now, I will destroy *one village for every day you make me wait.* She paused, elation running through her as the color drained from his face. He hadn't thought this through very well. *The burning*

*men behind me is a mercy compared to what I will do to your villages.
I wouldn't make me wait too long, Oliver; for what is a king if he has
no subjects to rule?*

Without any warning, Oliver looked past Ara and shouted,
"Now!"

She whipped around too slowly. While she'd been enjoying toy-
ing with the handsome king, others were flanking her. Oliver kept
her talking so they could move into position. They were too far
away for her flames to reach; her only option was to fly. Before her
wings could stroke the air though, one of the foreign weapons fired.
A blob of black sailed through the air, wrapping around her head.

A net?

Ara began thrashing around wildly as one of the spears was
launched as well. The sharp tine pierced a wing. The pain was
subtle. Another bolt was fired and landed in a much more delicate
spot. The spear embedded into her chest. Ara roared into the air,
louder than ever; the men on the ground covered their ears as they
too cried out in pain. She gripped the shaft of the spear in her
teeth through a hole in the net and ripped it free. Searing pain shot
through her core as she began ripping at the net with teeth and
claws.

Soldiers ran at her, throwing spears with all they had. She
pumped her wings once which sent them tumbling along the slick
stone of the street. Her wingbeats were too powerful for them to
fight. The spears they'd thrown dropped instantly to the ground,
and then she was too high for them to reach.

She spoke to King Oliver once more but allowed her voice to flutter into the minds of those within her area of influence, *You have made a grave mistake, Oliver. I will be at the River Ilshath every day when the sun is highest, waiting for your surrender. Nigh is the fall of Gosatha.*

Chapter 56

"WHAT HAPPENED? ARE YOU alright?" Sandin asked Oliver.

He'd made his way to the morgue to tell them they could come up for the time being. Ara gave him an impossible ultimatum and he didn't know how he would stop everyone from being killed. Tiberius offered the king a waterskin, which he took gratefully.

"I'm fine," he said. "There were a few casualties, though. She left Valendra, but we are *far* from being rid of her. The net worked for a moment, and we were able to stick her like a pig, but it wasn't fatal."

"You need to let me help, brother," Ruelle cut in. Her arms were crossed over her chest. Oliver was becoming impatient with her constant need to put herself in harm's way, the impudent attitude she carried. *Does she not see how silly she's being?*

"Enough," he snapped. "You'll stop this insufferable whining now. You're too young to stand in battle." His voice was calm. "Do you understand me?"

She looked as if he'd struck her, only nodding as her answer. Her face became red. Then she asked, "May I go to my chambers?"

"Go," he said softly. She skittered up the stairs. The men waited a moment, giving her space, and then proceeded up the steps as well.

"She has given me an ultimatum," Oliver said quietly. There was a silence and then he continued, "She said she's going to raze one Gosathan village a day until I give her Ruelle. I can't just hand my sister over to her. But I can't just allow her to kill everyone either."

Sandin sighed. "We need to take the fight to her somehow."

"Well, I do know where she'll be. She told me she'd be waiting at the River Ilshath at midday. However, an approaching army won't fool her."

Tiberius said, "I think I have an idea. You may call me insane, but it may just work."

Oliver shrugged. "A little insanity is just what I need."

"You're sure?" Oliver asked. "I don't want you to feel like you're obligated to do this. There may be no coming back from this fight."

Tiberius nodded, looking around at Sandin and the Royal Council. "It would be my pleasure to lay down my life for the king and his family. Besides, I've lived far longer than I would have ever thought.

These old bones are tired, Majesty. If I am to die whilst bringing that beast down, then eternal slumber it will be." He smiled.

"But, Majesty," Rionath argued. "If you die in this gamble, the kingdom will be left without a leader."

"Leaving Gosatha without a ruler is the last thing that'll happen. You have my word on that," Oliver said. "Any other objections?" King Oliver looked around the room. "Then it's settled. We will leave tomorrow before midday. Get your affairs in order, Tiberius; I shall do the same." To the councilmen, he said, "You bring my army shortly after the sun is at its apex; with luck, our timing will catch her off guard." He turned to Sandin. "Join me, if you would."

They departed the war room, and just as they did, a messenger came to a screeching halt in front of them. "My King," he said through labored breaths.

"Speak, boy."

He took a deep inhale. "Silvesca... has fallen."

Oliver shook his head, sighing, then wiped sweat from his lip. "Thank you for the information." He stared down at his feet for a moment, then motioned for Sandin to follow.

He knocked on Ruelle's door, pushing his way in when she gave the word 'enter'. "Well?" she asked before he had the chance to say anything.

Oliver sat down on the foot of her bed. "A plan is in place, Ruelle. Please try to understand that what I'm about to tell you isn't easy for me to say." He looked at her. Her eyes flashed with worry, but she nodded.

He smiled happily. This was his baby sister, growing like a weed. She was beautiful like their mother, strong like their father. And yet, he didn't want to have this conversation. He didn't want to tell her that he may not come back, and that she would have to assume a role she was not yet ready for. But it had to be done.

"What we're about to do is dangerous," he began. "I'm going to do everything in my power to put this monster in the ground. Silvesca has been destroyed; it can't continue. The reality of the situation is that I may not come back." He winced at her sharp inhale. "I know. I know this isn't what you wanted to hear." Her eyes began to fill with tears.

"Not what I wanted to hear?" she cried, standing abruptly from her bed. Her hands were balled into fists. "Of course this isn't something I'd want to hear! You're my big brother, the last of my family. You can't leave me." She was sobbing. Oliver felt tears rise to his eyes as well.

Oliver swallowed the knot in his throat. "I need you to understand, Ruelle. Please, tell me that you do. Our people must be protected. I'd be a coward if I don't face her."

"But you'd be alive," she whispered. "You would be here with me."

"This is what it means to be king." She wasn't going to get it, not until it was her turn to sacrifice for their people. Oliver stood. "Sandin will watch over you. Won't you?" he turned to the assassin who was standing near the door silently.

"Of course," Sandin said. "Ruelle, I have given you my word that I'll protect you until the creature is dead. My oath still stands whether

King Oliver is here or not." Oliver thought he saw a slight hesitation, a faint tremble to the man's bottom lip.

She cried harder, throwing herself facedown onto her bed. Oliver placed a hand on her back, feeling it rise and fall with her sobs. His tears fell onto the back of her gown. "I love you, Ruelle." He waited a moment, realized she wasn't in the mind to say it back, and then turned away. "Let's go," he told Sandin.

"She needs you," Sandin said in the hall. "I wish you would reconsider this."

"What would you have me do?" Oliver turned to face him. "What better answer is there, Sandin? Would you have me do nothing? Maybe I should hide behind these walls, send a few hundred men to die in my place. No, that is what a coward would do. We've known each other long enough for you to know that I'm no coward. Tell me if I'm wrong." He waited with bated breath.

Sandin deflated. "Just promise me that you'll fight tooth and nail to come back."

"I promise." He said the words, though he knew deep down that he would break it if it would stop Ara from hurting anyone else. "Stay with her, please. If I'm not back by the morning, it's probably safe to assume that I won't be returning."

Sandin nodded, reaching his arm out. Oliver grasped it with his steel prosthetic. "It has been a pleasure to serve you." They let go of each other. Then the assassin dropped down to a knee.

King Oliver laughed, "Oh, get up. Enough of that. You aren't one of my subjects, but rather a friend, a brother if I can be so bold." The two of them smiled, laughed, and then hugged as brothers might. Oliver clapped him on the back before turning away.

Back in the royal chambers, Oliver sat before a desk beneath a window as the sun melted into the horizon. A mug of ale sat on his desk from the previous day when he'd passed out before finishing it. Lifting the mug, he emptied its contents, but not into his gullet this time. No, he'd had enough. He pulled out a piece of parchment, an inkwell, and a quill. Dipping the quill in the ink, he began to write, hoping the action would be for naught. The king almost laughed then, wondering what his father would think of it all. *Even now,* he thought. *I find myself pursuing your approval, Father.* He wondered how the great King Torril would have handled Ara.

None of that mattered, though; it was Oliver who would be remembered for his actions. It was he who would go down in history as a failure to be mocked, or a hero to be praised.

Chapter 57

ARA SAT ON A hill, taking in the beauty, the masterpiece she'd created. Flames reached toward the sky like claws, scraping up from Icuzar, creatures thirsty for a rain that would never come. The wound in her chest had finally stopped leaking. It itched something fierce. She'd cauterized it herself after setting Silvesca aflame. She'd taken several of the citizens there as food to bolster her energy.

She thought, *Strange how it seems I can taste the despair running through their veins.*

Night was about to settle in; she would need to find a place to rest. After gliding a bit, Ara found a place near a river that looked like it would do well enough. She wasn't worried about anyone finding her there and lay down to close her eyes.

That night she dreamt of a battle so devastating it left a landscape riddled with dead, both Gosathans and others. Some of them were creatures like her. She felt a pang of longing for something she didn't have. A family, children to call her own. The dream had awoken her, and she wondered if this was a premonition of the future. She shivered as the sun began to awaken across the horizon.

Flames still licked the air; Ara smelled the smoke even from a league away. She turned, putting the ashes of Silvesca to her back. The meeting point wasn't far away. The beast would stay there and wait until midday. If the king showed without the girl, the next village would not be as lucky as the last. It would bleed much, much slower.

I hear them. Their scent is carried in the wind. But something is... off, Ara thought.

The hooves of two horses approached. Ara sat by the stream with her head resting on her front legs. She stirred as they approached. Oliver, she could see clearly, but the girl was covered in a thick coat, a decorative scarf adorning her head and face. Ara couldn't see her properly. Something about her scent smelled peculiar.

"We're here," Oliver called out, seeming careful not to get too close. "Just as you demanded."

As he climbed from his horse, Ara lifted into the air, sending the horse into a frenzy. Oliver tried regaining his beast's composure as Ara flew in a wide circle. With a deep breath, she loosed a deluge of flame upon the ground. A ring of fire surrounded them, ensuring no one would be able to aid the king, and Ara landed in front of them again.

The girl stayed on her horse which seemed to be handling Ara's presence better. *Come to me, girl.* She didn't move. Oliver was taking slow, tentative steps toward Ara. There was something odd about him. It took until he was pulling the gleaming sword free for Ara to notice what it was.

She remembered ripping part of his arm from his body. The flavor of his royal blood was so enticing that she'd wanted to finish him off, but the desire to have him watch his last sibling die was greater. The same arm she'd destroyed had been mended; it gleamed almost as brightly as the sword. He fiddled with the metal fingers with his good hand, making them cinch down onto the hilt of his weapon.

"This ends now, Ara," he said. "This is where you die."

She let her laughter fill his head. *Don't make promises you can't keep, Oliver. Your human body pales in comparison to the one I've been cursed with. Your blade will not be that which fells me.*

Oliver bent at the knees and raised the sword in an offensive posture. Something on his face almost made Ara shiver. He looked... determined beyond reason. With a glance over his shoulder, he shouted, "Now, Tiberius!"

What? What is this? Her voice was shouting inside her head. What she'd thought to be his sister was the High Inquisitor—Tiberius Theron. Her eyes narrowed, recognition dawning on her.

That's why the smell had been off, she thought. The mind of the man felt different from what Ara was expecting of the little girl. *I should have probed his head sooner.*

Speaking inside both of the men's heads, she growled, *You stood witness at my father's murder. You are the one who held me back. For that, you will die as well.*

Tiberius had jumped from the horse's back, thrown the extra garments off him, and strolled next to the king with a sword of his own. Together, they began to circle. Ara waited patiently. She could melt them with her flames, but where was the fun in that? No, Tiberius would die slowly while Oliver watched.

He really thinks he can defeat me? She laughed at the notion.

Finally, they were close enough; Oliver was to her right, Tiberius to her left. She spun, whipping her tail toward Tiberius. She had fully expected to send him flying, but the man jumped over it. She swatted at Oliver just after, but he ducked, rolled, and popped back up to his feet. A piercing pain shot through her tail and, looking behind her, Ara saw that Tiberius had plunged his blade into her thick hide. It didn't go through as easily as Oliver's blade had.

Using the distraction to his advantage, Oliver charged at her. His sword was a breath from impaling her heart when she recovered. With a beat of her wings, she jumped, floating back to a safe distance. The force of her wingbeat sent Oliver crashing to the ground. She flicked her tail just before landing, sending the Inquisitor's sword far enough away that it would no longer be a problem. She heard the man curse.

"Forgive me, Majesty. I'm afraid I won't be of much use without my sword," Tiberius said. Still, he pulled a knife from his belt.

The king recovered but didn't answer. He stalked forward as if he were not the prey in the situation. His eyes never left her. *Give up, Oliver. Surrender me the girl and this will all be over. I'll grant you the mercy of a quick death.*

With a primal scream, King Oliver surged forward again. Ara was expecting him, though, and lunged forward at the same time. His arm was pulled back, and he was too slow. She thrust a clawed paw toward him, gripping him tightly, and tossed him aside as if he were nothing more than a feathery piece of debris in her path.

Without missing a beat, Ara went for Tiberius. He stood there, gaping, as she crashed down on him. Her growl was so fierce that it knocked the man to the ground. Drivel dripped from her bared teeth onto his lap. Ara looked back to see if Oliver had recovered yet. He was on his feet, hand clutching at his chest like the wind had been driven from his lungs. She growled, moving her feet so she could face Oliver when she killed his friend, and noticed her circle of fire waned.

With a talon placed gently on his sternum she increased the pressure. Tiberius groaned, kicking his legs and trying to shove her claw away. He stabbed three times with the knife, though Ara ignored it. She pressed down more, the tip of her claw burrowing into his skin, tearing through muscle and bone. He wailed.

Ara never tore her gaze away from the king as he dragged a leg forward. Blood trickled from a wound on the side of his head. When the talon had punctured completely through Tiberius, she stepped away. She watched as Oliver dropped to his friend's side.

A chortle escaped her as she sauntered around them, their pain feeding into her joy. Their trickery hadn't worked, and because of the effort they made her expend, Ara planned to make their suffering last. She would leave them, see how many villages she could decimate in a single day. But first, the king would watch her devour his friend, one agonizing bite at a time.

Chapter 58

Blood. The damned blood. It pooled beneath Tiberius, turned the dirt under him into thick mud. The hole was large enough for Oliver to shove his fist into, and he would have done so if he thought it would save the man. The king's ankle had been twisted, maybe even broken; a strong throb was ebbing through his whole leg. It didn't compare to the stab of sorrow in his very being.

I'm losing another, he thought.

The blood covered his hands, moistened his breeches. Oliver's armor felt heavy; he ripped it free, allowing it to clatter to the ground. He looked at the monster. Ara wanted this, wanted him to watch his friend die. That was the meaning behind it all. She wanted to watch as Oliver lost everything. Wanted to watch his heart break at the suffering his family and friends would endure.

Turning his gaze back to the Inquisitor, the man's breathing was shallow and fast. His eyes were wide. "You didn't deserve this death, old friend," Oliver said. His voice brought his eyes to Oliver's. Tiberius' hand slowly reached up, shaking, covered in blood and small bits of rock and dirt.

"You were better," he whispered. Oliver cocked his head sideways, not understanding what he meant. "You were better than your father. I want you to know that." Blood dribbled from the edges of his mouth.

Oliver smiled and took the man's outstretched hand. "Thank you, Tiberius." His breathing became more laborious. He grimaced with each painful gasp. "You can go now, my friend. Don't worry about things here; I've got it sorted. I'll see you in Volharis."

Tiberius nodded, smiled with red teeth, and then died. His breathing stopped, his eyes went blank, and his arm slipped from Oliver's hand limply. The king sat on his knees for a moment more, the crown on his head feeling heavy. He closed his friend's eyes and stood, turning to face Ara again.

Shame, her voice entered his mind. *I prefer my meals to still be breathing.*

With his sword pointed at her, he said, "For every life you have taken, I will make sure that you suffer. You shall die this day, and your soul will be taken to the pitch of Icuzar. By my blood, I will see that your quest fails."

Strong words, her voice entered his head again, dark and melodious. *For someone who can hardly stand. How long must this game continue, Oliver? How long will you let me devour your subjects? Already, one of your largest cities has fallen, and you don't care. Perhaps I will destroy the whole of Gosatha before I scratch that sister of yours from the palace. And you call yourself a king; you're undeserving of that crown.*

Oliver narrowed his eyes. "I don't care, you say. No, I care more than you could fathom. This crown atop my head sat on a table in my chambers for months, but not today. Today, I *finally* feel as though I've earned the right to wear it, and you can't take that from me. I will carve through your belly before another Gosathan dies!" Laughter in his head. He couldn't take it anymore.

Ignoring the pain in his leg—and all through his body—Oliver rushed forward. She had thought he was too injured to move so quickly, and that he used to his advantage. Ara lifted a clawed foot to strike out, but he sliced through the air in a quick arc of his blade. He felt the faint resistance as the two collided; however, his sword was sharper than the pad of her foot was tough. It cut through like a hot knife through butter. She reared on her hindlegs, a terrible screech ripping at Oliver's ears.

Not letting up, Oliver swung the blade again. The edge of his sword struck the side of a claw; vibrations danced up his arm as Ara took a step back, roaring in his face. The smell of dead flesh wafted into his nostrils and nearly knocked him off his feet. It would have smelled better to be shoved inside a cow's rear.

Suddenly, fangs were closing in on Oliver. He dove to the side, inhaling sharply as pain tore through his ribs; he'd landed on jagged rocks. When he climbed to his feet, Ara's next attack was already on its way. Her tail came flying toward him. In the time it took to release a breath Oliver had made a decision. There was enough room under her tail, and he was in no shape to attempt jumping over it. That left only one avenue for him. He went flat. The tail rushed over him; wind from the missed attack fluffed his hair around, and then he was back up, running at the beast again, albeit slower.

Her side was wide open for an attack. The sword screamed through armor and flesh, coating Oliver's hands in blood almost dark as night. The sound of her pained cries would have been like music to his ears if it weren't painful, sending his brain cracking against bone. The back of Ara's front paw came streaking toward him. A loud thud and pain like being smashed by a war hammer, and then darkness enclosed around him.

Chapter 59

WHERE HAD SHE GONE? One moment Ruelle was there and the next she'd disappeared. Sandin asked her if she was okay, but the boasting silence had given him pause. He would have expected a grunt at the least, but there was nothing. The girl's room was empty. Dread filled Sandin, panic made his heart thunder.

"No," he muttered to himself as a horrible thought struck him. "She wouldn't." He ran from Ruelle's room. His feet smacked the smooth stone of the palace corridors, and his cloak trailed in the wind behind him. People looked at him sideways as he passed, probably wondering what had gotten into him.

"Ruelle," he shouted, breath eluding him as he made it into the stables. "No, no, no." One of the horses was gone. It very well could have been taken out by someone else. A messenger, perhaps, but with everything that was happening, Sandin believed the worst. Snatching a steed of his own, he pulled the animal from the stables and leapt onto its back. There was no time to worry about a saddle. He gripped the horse's mane with his fists and squeezed his legs together to keep himself balanced. He kicked with his heels, shouting, "Hyah," to elicit more speed.

As Sandin approached the portcullis to leave the city, he noticed it was unmanned, and the guards who should have been standing sentry were dealing with a small brush fire not far away. The portcullis stood open. *That clever girl,* he thought, impressed by her skill of distraction. Nothing but the sounds of hooves on stone, the rush of wind, and the pounding of his heart made it to Sandin's ears. The Gosathan army was mere moments from storming through the gate, so she'd gotten through in the nick of time.

I swear, he thought. *If she gets herself killed...*

He remembered where the river was; a place near where the other Jardanises were killed. He still remembered the stink that was in the air left behind by their scorched bones. There were shapes moving in the distance; he just knew one of them had to be Ruelle. Beyond, there was faint smoke.

Oliver will never forgive me if something happens to his little sister under my watch.

Sandin would never forgive himself, either. All the progress he'd made in turning from the enjoyment of killing would be reversed if he let harm befall the little girl.

Harder, faster; Sandin pushed the horse to go past its limits. He could see her hair billowing behind her. "Ruelle!" She looked over her shoulder, knew he was there, but didn't stop. The monster was close. He could see her fighting someone—probably Oliver. "Stop!" The girl didn't stop; she was upon them, finally halting her steed and jumping from its back. The horse reared, whinnied, and trotted to a safer distance. Sandin caught up just as Oliver was sent flying through the air, landing hard on his back. A black ring encapsulated them all.

The assassin jumped from the horse as it slowed.

The creature licked at blood coming from her side, not noticing the two of them. Sandin grabbed Ruelle by the shoulders, but she shrugged him off, that look of determination on her face making the resemblance between her and Oliver uncanny. "Let's go. Now." He whispered, slow and deliberate.

"Hey!" Ruelle blurted, making Sandin start. Ara's attention snapped over to them. The slits of her pupils—and the violet that surrounded them—narrowed even more; she growled as she stalked forward, limping slightly. "Leave my brother alone and get out of Gosatha! Crawl back to the shadows where you belong!"

Such a strong voice in such a small body, came Ara's mental voice.

Sandin heard laughter inside his head, and assumed the same was happening to Ruelle based on the look on her face and her nervous glances around them. *You* insolent *girl. You should have stayed hidden, but no, you Jardanises must always be so* valiant.

"I'm not going to let you hurt him further," Ruelle growled. She had more confidence than Sandin, it would seem. He began walking slowly to the side, trying to get an angle on the monster. If Ruelle could stall long enough, maybe he could flank her. It seemed to be working. Her focus was straight as an arrow, unwavering from anything but Ruelle. She may as well have been salivating. "I'm not afraid of you."

Then you are a fool, Ara snarled.

"Run!" Sandin shouted. He was close enough. *I'm faster than any man she's faced,* he thought.

He had to believe that. Dashing up her tail, he found the scales to not be slick like he'd expected, not like a snake's would be. The bony spikes decorating her spine made for excellent footholds, and he traversed her like a forest cat. Stealing a glance at Ruelle, Sandin growled to himself. She wasn't running but was standing in front of Oliver's body like a naïve sentry. She was going to get herself killed.

He was on her upper back when Ara decided she'd had enough. He felt her back expand with the inhale, heard the flame in her throat crackling. Up her neck, her head, leaping over twisted horns. As he jumped, he pulled both curved blades from behind his back, spinning them as he ascended, pinky fingers through the holes. He twisted, staring directly into her maw, the shining sun in all its glory. It scorched his cheeks, his lips.

His father's silver ring glinted, catching his eye. *Strength through adversity.* Much adversity he'd gone through in his life. Then, as he began to fall, he drove his blades as hard as he could into the beast's snout. The force and his weight dragged her face toward the ground, closing her jaws with a *snap.*

Sandin ripped his blades from her face, dodging a bite immediately after. Blackish blood dribbled from the wounds; Ara shook her head, licking at the blood and growling at them. *Who are you?* she snarled in his head. *Why do you interfere? This could have been over. Their deaths were meant to be the last.*

"I am the Dagger of Gosatha," he returned with as much venom as he could muster. "And I will not allow you to harm my family any longer!" Ara cocked her head sideways, seemingly confused by his words. "Nor do I believe you would stop with them," he said.

Suddenly, Ruelle burst in front of Sandin with the Sword of Gorenos raised above her head. Ara must have been just as shocked because she took a hesitant step away from them, then recovered her wits.

Enough of this! Ara shouted at them. Her mouth opened; Ruelle was about to be shredded by the teeth of this monster. Sandin was frozen, powerless; the fear kept him rooted to the spot. His training at Shadowspire taught him how to deal with high-stress situations, but nothing could have prepared him for this. It was too much, the threat too great.

Teeth clacked together as the girl somehow dodged the attack. She'd just narrowly avoided being eaten; her face was contorted with anger. She heaved the heavy sword which looked foreign in her small hands. Crying aloud from the effort, Ruelle swung the blade. It sliced through Ara's bottom lip. A blood-curdling screech rang out. The monster's head bashed left and right, cracking into Ruelle like a whip, sending her screaming through the air.

"Ruelle!" Sandin shouted, already running to her. There was a small laceration to her head, but as long as there wasn't internal bleeding, she would be okay, but there would be no way for him to know for sure at that moment. Miraculously though, her eyes fluttered, staying open; however, she looked dazed. Sitting up and coughing, a groan escaped her lips.

"Why did you do this, Ruelle?" he admonished.

"I just wanted to save him," she cried. Her eyes became wide as she looked over Sandin's shoulder. He turned; Oliver was on his feet, limping his way to the sword. The battlefield went still, silent, save for the scraping sound of his footsteps and the haggard breaths coming from him.

It was then Sandin noticed the blade's position after being thrown from Ruelle's hand; the hilt had been lodged between two large stones. The tip pointed at the sky and angled slightly. King Oliver looked between the beast and the other two, his face tired. Ara was still huffing and growling, rubbing at the copious amount of blood issuing from her mouth. Sandin helped Ruelle to her feet, keeping his hand on her wrist.

He's going to go for the sword in that state? Sandin wondered as the king stood just before the blade.

"My beautiful sister," Oliver began. "I won't be able to go back to the palace with you after all. I hope you'll understand." Her eyes were frozen in shock. Oliver pointed at the black creature. He growled her name, getting her attention. "You said you wanted me to watch my entire family die, and then you'd kill me too. I must say that your mission will not end as you wished." He smiled at her, a defiant gleam in his eyes.

She hissed vehemently at the king. Her shoulders hunched as her legs bent. It struck Sandin that she looked ever more horrifying with all the bloody wounds on her face.

"You hate me, Ara," Oliver said, his voice not bitter or angry, but resolved. "I never imagined I would leave here alive." He laughed, not sounding amused. "I just thought I would drag you to the afterlife with me. I can see now that I was mistaken."

Sandin took a tentative step forward. "My King," he muttered, not knowing what to say. He didn't know what Oliver was thinking. The young king looked at the lifeless body of the High Inquisitor for a breath. Sandin said, "My friend." He didn't know if Oliver heard him.

His eyes snapped to Sandin. "You made me a promise. Do you remember it?" Ara was close to him, her gaze unwavering on the man. Sandin nodded his head, readying himself to fight the creature once more. "Surely you'll forgive me for my selfishness... won't you?" A single tear tumbled from Oliver's left eye, rolling down his cheek, and cutting a trail through the grime.

"Aye, Majesty." *What does he mean?*

Sandin shook his head, pleading for the man to run. "Oliver, step away from her before it's too late. We'll take her down together." A low rumble came from Ara's throat.

To Icuzar with you all, Ara growled in their minds.

Oliver smiled before looking back over to Ara. "I wish things had been different. Truly, I do. Unfortunately, Ara, I can't allow you to have victory; you shall not feel my life end beneath your flame." With no other words, King Oliver fell. The Sword of Gorenos plunged into his chest, erupting through his back. The blade shimmered crimson as his body slid down its length. The crown tumbled from his head, settling at the base of the sword.

Sandin rushed forward, the threat of the monster be damned.

He pulled Oliver off the blade, turning him over. Call him crazy, but Sandin swore that just as the light faded from Oliver's eyes, so did a little light fade from the world itself. Ruelle's screams pierced his ears, shaking him out of his stupor. Sandin found the beast to have wide eyes, filled with as much shock as Sandin felt. He was deflated, defeated. Sandin wanted to give up, to let the monster devour him and the girl. But he'd made a promise; Sandin steeled himself, turning and capturing Ruelle as she aimed to barrel past him.

No, I must not betray my oath so quickly.

Chapter 60

ARA WAS SURPRISED MORE than anything. Out of all the scenarios Ara had contemplated before this, Oliver sacrificing himself just to foil her plan was not one of them. Then anger struck her, but then again, her anger was always but a breath away. Her growls intensified, drowning the girl's screams as the other man tried to pull her back. She heard him whistle and a brown stallion came trotting up. Ara looked back down at Oliver's lifeless body. The gleam of the crown caught her eye, and she noticed that half of it was covered in his blood.

He won, she realized. In falling on the blade, Oliver had taken away the chance for her to see his face when the last of his kin was killed.

His sacrifice stole the ability for Ara to take his life from him. In his death, he'd won the battle.

However, she would not lose the war. To the child alone, she said, *This isn't over girl. We shall meet again.*

The man stopped struggling to wrangle the girl away as Ara turned to leave. Something was telling her to go, that the time to fight would come again. She didn't want to ignore her intuition. A greater, more glorious, battle awaited them all.

Ruelle took Ara by surprise, standing tall, defiant in the face of death. "Why did you do this?" Her voice began to rise with each syllable. "You're a curse upon my family, and for that, I will see you dead. You coward, monster; you do not deserve to live."

Ara would have smirked if not for the pain throbbing through her entire face, the burning cut on her foot. *Coward? Monster? No, little one, I am* much *more. I am hunger, pain, suffering. To you I am death.* She spoke slowly then, annunciating each word separately. Not knowing where it came from, she said, *I. Am. Dragon.*

Ara left without allowing any other words to pass between them, flying back toward Draconia. Her bottom lip was split in half, the wind rippling through the gash and sending stabs of hot pain through her mouth with every second that passed. The stab wounds near her nose paled in comparison, although they hurt as well. The strength of her wings was quickly fading. Spots danced on her vision; she shook her head, willing them away, if but for a moment.

Ara found the Draconians, the Feral Ones, collapsing amongst them as they looked over her wounds concerningly. She laid on her side, letting them smear that same poultice from before all over her. The pain in her foot only returned when they touched it, wrenching a growl from her throat; however, it was not malice, but agony. The blade had nearly cut her to the bone.

And I would be dead without these people, she thought idly.

Hono stood in front of her, smiling sadly. She closed her eyes, focusing enough energy to send him a mental image of the cave she called home. There was much she needed to do, preparations that needed to be made before she went back to Gosatha.

After some time, a bit of strength returned to her limbs, and the pain had subsided enough for her to move. The victory she so desperately desired was but a thought in the wind.

And why should I feel victorious? Oliver took away the delicious victory I so wanted.

The defeated feeling didn't last though, because Ara knew what the next step would be. Her instincts told her what she needed to do.

The dragon had been wrong. She thought her vendetta was against Oliver, against the Abithians who took Calder from her. Even as powerful as her mind had become, Ara was still a fool. She knew what it was then. That humanity was the disease, and she the cure. It had always been this way; the abhorrence she'd always felt for the Lords and Ladies who would march passed starving children. The men who would execute Lowborn for stealing bread from the market. *They* were the true enemy.

Not the Draconians, however. Ara had watched them hunt, witnessed the way they killed their prey. They were as much beast as they were human. The world referred to them as 'Feral Ones'; that was because they didn't understand them. Not like Ara did. They only wanted to live their lives. They didn't wish to rule over mankind, did not want wars or to line their pockets with riches. Still... They were malleable.

She'd been daft to think she could embark on such a quest by herself. As much as it pained her to admit—even to herself—Ara would need help. Already, the magic in her blood and the power of her mind were brewing something deep inside her.

Flying up to the cave expound much effort. The battle left her body weary. From the cave, she opened her jaws wide, using all mental fortitude to lure the bats into her maw. As energy spread through her limbs, Ara felt something else forming within her belly. Something to be used as a weapon in the years ahead. She curled up, resting her torn chin gently across her front legs, closing her eyes to dream away the pain. The Draconians would be her subjects, she, their queen. They would fight this war for her, give their lives for her noble cause. However, they would need a way to get across the Tamagau. They would need *steeds*, and she—being a benevolent queen—would provide.

Chapter 61

THE FUNERAL WAS NEARLY unbearable. From what Sandin was told, the pyre was built higher than any king in Gosathan history. Ruelle had been inconsolable, latching onto Sandin with her face buried into his stomach. As the fire was laid upon the logs, Sandin had to force his eyes away in fear he would tear down the structure before the flames could ruin Oliver's body.

My liege is gone, he thought. *Now what do we do?*

"This can't be real," Sandin said, reading the words to himself again. A missive had been brought to him moments after the funeral. The Royal Council stood around him, watching him take in the late king's final words. "Are you sure this is authentic?" He'd read them three times and still wasn't certain.

"We've all looked over the letter carefully, my Liege," Lord Tindar said, his voice spewing eloquence. "And we have all agreed that it was written by the late king's hand. You are to step into this role immediately, unless of course you have qualms with it. Should you choose to ignore the request, you may appoint someone else, with the council's approval, of course."

Sandin thought of the Gosathan forces. They'd arrived too late to stop Ara, to stop Oliver from falling on his sword. But then, Sandin was there, and his presence did nothing. Could he—an assassin—handle such a responsibility?

Sandin looked down at the note once more. He shook his head, sighing deeply. "Why would he do this?" He looked over at Tobias. "I know you have an opinion, Lord Tobias. Speak freely."

The lord took a deep breath, glancing around at his fellow councilmen as if Sandin still made him nervous. *Good,* Sandin thought.

"For the first time in possibly my entire life," Tobias said. "I find myself agreeing with King Oliver. I hadn't wished the man dead, though he and I rarely saw eye to eye, as you know. However, your leadership capabilities speak for themselves, I think. It would be a tedious task finding someone better suited for this role."

Lord Tindar added, "It would seem King Oliver trusted you beyond all else, sir. As someone who watched him grow into the man he was, I would mention that he was never terribly trusting of those outside his family. Take it as a compliment, if you please."

Sandin thought back to the day he'd asked Oliver why he trusted him so. And though he remembered the answer, he also remembered not quite believing him. How could he—now that Oliver was gone—deny the blessing of trust Oliver bestowed upon him? He wouldn't do such. Taking the compliment was the smallest gesture of gratitude he could give in that moment, and it was the greatest of compliments Sandin could ever hope to receive. Oliver trusted him to the bitter end.

He placed the note on the table before him. "I'll do it. I shall act as High Regent until lady Ruelle's sixteenth birthday, at which time she will assume the throne as Queen of Gosatha." He made eye contact with each of the councilmen. "You all have my word that I will lead and protect your people to the best of my ability."

"Very well," Tindar said. "We will hold a ceremony this time tomorrow for your inauguration. An aid will help you prepare." He paused, then turned back and said, "This goes without saying, but I shall say it anyway; our confidence is in you, Lord Sandin. Don't take that lightly."

The lot of them bowed out of the room, leaving Sandin behind. He walked slowly, making his way for Ruelle's chamber; she hadn't left since the day Oliver died. He couldn't blame her. He too had found it difficult to find direction in his life, and it dawned on him how he'd always been at the behest of others. Grandmaster Helfi taught him how to kill. Queen Gadiel told him *who* to kill. Because of Oliver, he'd grown into more than just a mere assassin; he was a man people could rely on, a man who was worthy of trust. Oliver had given him his heart back.

Sandin knocked on the chamber door. "Ruelle, it's me. May I enter?" There was no reply, nor had he expected there to be. He pushed into the room anyway. Darkness swallowed the light from the corridor. "There's a letter from Oliver. He has addressed both of us. I think you should read it."

There was a ruffling sound. The girl's voice came out raspy, like her throat was still torn from screaming. "I don't think I can bear it." An oil lamp ignited beside her bed. Even in the dim light, Sandin could see how puffy her eyes were, the shadowed rings beneath them.

"Have you slept at all?" he asked.

She knuckled her eyes. "Hardly." Her lip quivered.

"Allow me to read it, then," he said softly. "You must hear what he had to say."

Ruelle nodded, staring at her hands in her lap.

After a couple of slow breaths, he read, "Ruelle, if you're reading this letter, then it's because I'm dead. I've realized that I must stop Ara no matter what. I'm sorry for leaving you alone, truly I am, but this must be done. I hope you understand and forgive me." He paused, allowing the words to sink in for a moment, then continued. "This may seem selfish to you, and believe me, I've considered that. However, all that's happened is because of me, and I must fix it. It's only now that I feel I know what it means to wear this crown. I know you will make a great queen one day, but for now, Sandin will look over our people as High Regent. Keep him in line for me." She laughed, a sort of tired, sad sound.

Sandin went on, "Remember, if ever you are missing me, Father and Mother, our sisters, we are but a thought away. Look inside your heart, and there we shall be. Forever your brother, Oliver." She sobbed tearlessly.

Sandin moved forward, draping his arm over her shoulders. "Your brother gave his life so that we may live to fight another day. We mustn't squander that."

Ruelle looked up, bleary-eyed. "Thank you, Sandin. I understand why Oliver would have you as High Regent. You're my brother just as much as he was."

Pride swarmed in his chest. He chuckled, "Stop, before I shed a tear."

She laughed through tears. "And here I thought you couldn't cry." Then, "So, when will my lessons resume?" She wiped the sad look from her eyes, replacing it with a terrifying determination.

Sandin rose to his full height, stretching an arm out with his hand invitingly. His other arm was behind his back, a parody of a gentleman. "Why, my lady, I thought you'd never ask."

Epilogue

The peace between Gosatha and Abithia flourished; trade between the two nations was greater than ever. Queen Gadiel had since passed on the crown to a daughter that only she and her husband knew existed. Her Highness, Queen Silvala Lotus, now sat on the throne. Likewise, Queen Ruelle Jardanis had taken her place beneath the crown of Gosatha. She'd been ruling for nearly four years.

In that time, through the prospering of their queendoms, fear still clung to most like a leech. The dragon, first of her kind, had left scars in the minds of all who'd been close enough to feel her might. No one knew when Ara would strike again. Weapons were forged, defenses bolstered—all in preparation for when the creature returned.

Sandin had resumed his post as Dagger of Gosatha. Ruelle told him he could return to Abithia and teach at Shadowspire like she knew he wanted, but he refused. He'd made a promise to Oliver that he wouldn't return until Ara was slain.

"I can take care of myself; you've made sure of that," Ruelle had told him, feeling like she was holding him back from the life he really wanted.

"If a man doesn't honor his oath, then what sort of man is he?" he'd shot back at her. She just rolled her eyes at him.

Sandin swore he was happy being the Dagger. Only when someone threatened the weak, those who couldn't defend themselves, did Sandin need to deal with them expeditiously. He felt his place was at Ruelle's side, giving her advice when the time called for it, and working to keep orphans under a roof. That was perhaps his greatest work.

Ten years since Oliver forfeited his life; ten years of silence, and then the warning bell began to ring. Ruelle and Sandin had been in a meeting with the council. Defensive plans had long been set in stone. "Rally our soldiers," Ruelle ordered, a gleam of excitement in her eyes. "We have only minutes before she arrives."

"Queen Ruelle," one of her body protested. "You mustn't rush into battle!"

She smiled, glanced at Sandin, and ignored the councilman altogether. The shouts of, "You're just like your brother" only widened her smile.

They sprinted from the palace, grabbing horses from the stables. They rode out to meet Ara before she could make it all the way to their city.

The pyres had been lit. A trail of warning flames burned brazenly for leagues across Gosatha. Then, in the distance came the dragon. No, *dragons*; a horde of winged beasts. Queen Ruelle's army had formed behind her and Sandin. She'd been just a girl the last time they'd met; a girl who hadn't been old enough to even have her first bleeding. All of that was different now. Ruelle was a woman, fierce in her own right, trained to fight by the best. She trotted her horse ahead as Ara's ilk landed in the distance.

Her silver ring sat proudly on her thumb as it wouldn't fit anywhere else. It was a gift from Sandin on the day of her coronation. He told her where it came from, what it meant to him. It was one of her most prized possessions.

Besides, Ruelle thought. *There's only one ring he cares about these days.*

Sandin got married a few years after Oliver's passing. She was one of the handmaidens that assisted with the group home. Ruelle had been their flower girl, and she smiled, thinking of the beauty the ceremony beheld. Then, shaking her head, she refocused on the dragons and the men who stood with them.

So that's where she's been, Ruelle thought, taking note of all the Feral Ones in the dragon's ranks. Their crude weapons, unkempt appearances, and garbled shouts were unmistakable.

Ara stalked towards Ruelle with a man on her back. Ara's lip was pulled back with her fangs gleaming. Scars riddled her face. The queen smiled at the sight of them, remembering the one she created.

"I see you've brought an army," Ruelle called out to her, a tone of welcoming, like greeting an old friend.

The voice echoed in her head, a feeling she didn't miss. *You have grown much, my dear. Let us finally settle this.*

Ruelle trotted back to join her troops, her heart hammering in her chest. She ripped the Sword of Gorenos from its scabbard, lifting high for all to see. "Take heart, men! For today is a day of reckoning! Today is a day of victory! Today is when *they die*!" The throng of soldiers echoed her cries of rage. A unified wrathful roar thundered through the battlefield as they surged from the frontline.

The mother of dragons roared into the air as the army surged forward. The work she'd done over the years was evident, and Ruelle had no idea how Ara created more dragons without a mate.

The Mother Dragon turned to her children—a thousand dragons, a Draconian rider for nearly all of them, but allowed her voice to float into Ruelle's mind. Her area of influence had grown exponentially in the past ten years. She called out, *Fight, my children! Do not lament, for today you* die *for me. Today you shall feast upon man flesh! Show these humans their place.* She paused, smoke curling from her mouth as a flame built. Her eyes met with Ruelle's as the queen galloped onward. *It's been too long since my flame has bathed over the flesh of men. The age of man is over; the time of the dragon has come.*

Acknowledgements

Sure, the book was written by me; however, it wouldn't be nearly as great without the ones who helped me along the way. To the few who read my book before it was ready, helped me fix all its issues. To my friends who listened to my nonsensical ideas, who let me spout different plots and scenes to you.

I thank you all.